'The joy of a Grisham novel is turning the
pages as the plot propels you forward . . .
Suffice it to say *Sooley* follows the familiar
Grisham playbook – short chapters, plenty
of foreshadowing, and a rapid-fire prose
that's easy to read and hard to put down'
Independent

Praise for Seely

'Read it, you'll want to cry too'
Bill Clinton for The Guardian

Also by John Grisham

A Time to Kill
The Firm
The Pelican Brief
The Client
The Chamber
The Rainmaker
The Runaway Jury
The Partner
The Street Lawyer
The Testament
The Brethren
A Painted House
Skipping Christmas
The Summons
The King of Torts
Bleachers
The Last Juror
The Broker
Playing for Pizza
The Appeal
The Associate
Ford County
The Confession
The Litigators
Calico Joe
The Racketeer
Sycamore Row
Gray Mountain
Rogue Lawyer
The Whistler
Camino Island
The Rooster Bar
The Reckoning
The Guardians
Camino Winds
Theodore Boone
Theodore Boone: The Abduction
Theodore Boone: The Accused
Theodore Boone: The Activist
Theodore Boone: The Fugitive
Theodore Boone: The Scandal
Theodore Boone: The Accomplice

NON-FICTION

The Innocent Man

John Grisham

SOOLEY

HODDER

First published in Great Britain in 2021 by Hodder & Stoughton
An Hachette UK company

This paperback edition published in 2022

3

A CIP catalogue record for this title is available from the British Library

Paperback ISBN 978 1 529 36804 8

Printed and bound in Great Britain by Clays Ltd, Elcograf S.p.A.

Hodder & Stoughton policy is to use papers that are natural, renewable
and recyclable products and made from wood grown in sustainable
forests. The logging and manufacturing processes are expected to
conform to the environmental regulations of the country of origin.

Hodder & Stoughton Ltd
Carmelite House
50 Victoria Embankment
London EC4Y 0DZ

www.hodder.co.uk

To the memory of
MICHAEL RUDELL
(1943–2021)
Not only the finest lawyer I've ever known,
but a perfect gentleman and a loyal friend

Sooley

Part One

CHAPTER 1

In April, when Samuel Sooleymon was invited to try out for the national team, he was seventeen years old, stood six feet two inches tall, and was considered to be a promising point guard, known for his quickness and vertical leap, but also for his erratic passing and mediocre shooting.

In July, when the team left Juba, the capital of South Sudan, for the trip to America, he was six feet four inches tall, just as quick but even more erratic handling the ball and no more accurate from the arc. He was hardly aware of his growth, which was not unusual for a teenager, but he did realize that his well-worn basketball shoes were tighter and his only pair of pants now fell well above his ankles.

But back in April when the invitation arrived, his neighborhood erupted in celebration. He lived in Lotta, a remote village on the outskirts of Rumbek, a city of 30,000. He had spent his entire life in Lotta doing little more than playing basketball and soccer. His mother, Beatrice, was a homemaker, with little education, like all the women in the village. His father, Ayak, taught school in a two-room open-air hut built by some missionaries decades earlier. When Samuel wasn't pounding the basketball on the dirt courts throughout the village, he tended to the family's garden with his younger siblings and sold vegetables beside the road.

For the moment, life in the village was good and fairly stable. Another brutal civil war was in its second year with no end in sight, and though daily life was always precarious, the people managed to make it through the day and hope for better things tomorrow. The children lived in the streets, always bouncing or kicking a ball, and the games offered a welcome diversion.

Since the age of thirteen, Samuel had been the best basketball player in the village. His dream, like every other kid's, was to play college ball in America and, of course, make it to the NBA. There were several South Sudanese players in the NBA and they were god-like figures back home.

When the news of his invitation spread through the village, neighbors began gathering in front of the Sooleymons' thatched-roof hut. Everyone wanted to celebrate Samuel's breathtaking news. Ladies brought pitchers of cinnamon tea spiced with ginger and jugs of tamarind juice. Others brought platters of sugar-coated cookies and peanut macaroons. It was the greatest moment in the village's recent history, and Samuel was hugged and admired by his neighbors. The little ones just wanted to touch him, certain that they were in the presence of a new national hero.

He savored the moment but tried to caution everyone that he had only been invited for tryouts. Making the Under 18 team would be difficult because there were so many good players, especially in Juba, where the leagues were well established and the games were played on tile or even wood floors. In Lotta, like other remote villages and rural areas, the organized games were often played outdoors on concrete or dirt. He explained that only ten players would be chosen for the trip to America, and there they would be joined by five more players, all from South Sudan. Once combined, the team would play in showcase tournaments in places like Orlando and Las Vegas, and there would be hundreds of college scouts. Perhaps a few from the NBA as well.

Talk of playing in America added more excitement to the occasion, and Samuel's cautions were ignored. He was on his way. They had watched him grow up on the village courts and knew he was special enough to make any team, and to take their dreams with him. The celebration lasted well into the night, and when Beatrice finally ended it, Samuel reluctantly went to bed. But sleep was impossible. For an hour, he sat on his cot in his tiny bedroom, one that he shared with his two younger brothers, Chol and James, and whispered excitedly with them. Above their cots was a large poster of Niollo, the greatest of all South Sudanese players, soaring high above the rim and slamming a dunk in his Boston Celtics uniform, one which Samuel often fantasized wearing.

He rose early the next morning and collected eggs from the family's flock of chickens, his first chore of the day. After a quick breakfast, he left for school with his backpack and his basketball. James and Chol followed him to their neighborhood court where he shot for an hour as they retrieved the ball and fed it back to him. Other boys joined them, and the familiar noise of bouncing balls and friendly banter echoed through the sleepy morning.

At eight o'clock, the games reluctantly broke up as Samuel and his brothers left for classes. He was in his last year of secondary school and would graduate in a month. He considered himself fortunate. Less than half of his peers—boys only—would finish secondary, and only a fraction even dreamed of university. There were no classes for the girls.

As Samuel dribbled off to school, his dreams were now drifting to colleges far away.

CHAPTER 2

Two weeks later, early on a Friday morning, the entire family made the long walk to the bus station in Rumbek and watched him leave for Juba and a long weekend of vigorous competition. They waved him off, with his mother and sister in tears. He would return the following Monday.

The departure was an hour late, which for South Sudan was quite prompt. Because of bad roads and crowded buses, the schedules were flexible. Often there was no bus at all and breakdowns were common. It was not unusual for a bus to quit in the middle of the road and its passengers be sent off on foot to the nearest village.

Samuel sat on a crowded bench in the front of the bus, wedged between two men who said they had been riding for three hours. They were headed to Juba to look for work, or something like that. Samuel wasn't certain because their English was broken and mixed with Nuer, their tribal tongue. Samuel was Dinka, the largest ethnic class in the country, and that was his first language. English was his second. His mother spoke four.

Across the narrow aisle was a woman with three children, all of them wide-eyed and silent. Samuel spoke to them in English but they did not respond. The mother said something to the oldest child and Samuel understood none of it.

The bus had no air-conditioning and dust from the gravel road blew through the open windows and settled onto everything—clothing, bags, benches, the floor. It rocked and bumped along the main gravel road to Juba, occasionally stopping to pick up a hitch-hiker or let off a passenger.

Once it was known that Samuel was a basketball player who just might be headed to games in America, he became the focus of attention. Basketball was the new pride of South Sudan, a bright promise that sometimes allowed the people to set aside their violent history of ethnic conflict. Generally, the players were lean and tall and they played with a fierceness that often surprised American coaches.

So they talked basketball, with Samuel holding forth. They stopped in every village and took on more passengers. Full capacity was a moving target and before long the younger men, including Samuel, were ordered by the driver to crawl on top of the bus for the ride and to make sure none of the bags and boxes fell off. As they approached Juba, the gravel turned to asphalt and the constant bumping eased somewhat. The passengers grew quiet as they passed miles of shantytowns, then blocks of sturdier homes. Six hours after he left Lotta, Samuel got off the bus at the central station where swarms of people were coming and going. He asked directions and walked for an hour to the University of Juba.

He had been to Juba once before and was again struck by its modern facilities, paved streets, frantic traffic, tall buildings, vibrancy, and well-dressed people. If he failed to make the team, he planned to continue his studies in the city. If at all possible, he wanted to live there and pursue a profession.

He found the campus and then the gym and stepped nervously inside. It was new, cavernous, with three full-length courts and few bleachers. There were no intercollegiate sports in the country, no college teams with schedules and logos, no fans to watch the excitement. The gym was used for intramural sports of all varieties, and for assemblies and rallies.

At the far end he saw a man with a clipboard and a whistle tied around his neck, watching a four-on-four scrimmage. Samuel walked around the court and approached him.

.   .   .

Ecko Lam was forty and had spent his first five years in southern Sudan. His family narrowly escaped a guerrilla attack on their village and fled to Kenya. They eventually settled in Ohio and assimilated into an American lifestyle. He discovered basketball as a teenager and played four years at Kent State. He married an American of Sudanese descent and pursued his dream of coaching at the Division I level. He bounced from job to job, rising to the level of an assistant at Texas Tech, before being hired by a nonprofit to scout for talent in Africa. Two years earlier he had been selected to establish leagues and coach summer all-star teams in South Sudan. He loved his work and was still driven by the belief that basketball could make a difference in the lives of South Sudanese players, male and female. Taking his Under 18 team to the U.S. for the showcase tournaments was by far the best part of his job.

He had never seen Samuel play in person but had watched some tape of the kid. A coach from the country had passed along a glowing recommendation, saying that he had the quickest hands and feet he had ever seen, not to mention an astonishing vertical leap. His mother, Beatrice, stood six feet tall, and the scouting report predicted that Samuel was still growing. At 6'2", he was the shortest invitee.

On film, a video from a cell phone, Samuel dominated on defense but struggled with the ball. Because he lived in a village, his experience was limited, and Ecko suspected he would have difficulty competing against kids from the cities.

Twenty players from around the country had been invited to try out, and they were trickling into the gym as the afternoon went on. Ecko noticed Samuel as he slinked around the edge of a court, obviously a kid from the country intimidated by the surroundings. He finally approached and timidly asked, "Excuse me, but are you Coach Lam?"

Ecko offered a wide smile and replied, "Yes sir, and you must be Mr. Sooleymon."

"Yes sir," he said and thrust forward a hand.

They shook vigorously and touched each other on the shoulder, the standard Sudanese greeting. "A pleasure to meet you," Ecko said. "How was your trip in?"

Samuel shrugged and said, "Okay. If you like the bus."

"I don't. Have you ever flown on an airplane?"

"No sir," he said without the slightest embarrassment.

Of the twenty invitees, Ecko was almost certain that none had ever seen the inside of an airplane. "Well, if you make my team, we'll fly halfway around the world. How does that sound?"

Samuel couldn't stop smiling. "Sounds wonderful."

"It will be great, son. The locker room is over there. Get changed in a hurry and start shooting."

Samuel entered a long room lined with small wire cages. He picked an empty one and changed quickly into gym shorts, a tee shirt, and his well-worn shoes. Five minutes later he was back on the court. Ecko tossed him a ball, pointed to an empty basket at the far end of the gym, and said, "Stretch and warm up, then start shooting from the arc."

"Yes sir." He dribbled away, using only his right hand, went through a quick series of rather lackadaisical stretches, and began shooting. Ecko smiled at the fact that yet another seventeen-year-old was bored with the notion of stretching.

Ecko monitored the scrimmage while watching every move Samuel made. His shot needed work. On the plus side, he delivered it from the top on an impressive, fluid jump. But he cocked low, at his forehead, and his right elbow strayed. Not uncommon for a kid with little coaching.

He missed his first ten shots. Nerves, thought Ecko.

By late afternoon, all twenty players had arrived. Ecko gathered them in a corner of the bleachers and asked each one to stand, give his name, and describe where he was from. Half were from Juba. Two were from Malakal, a war-ravaged city three hundred miles away. A few others were from the country, the bush.

Ecko's next order of business was the most problematic. He said, "We are all South Sudanese. Our country is torn by civil strife, where warlords fight for power and our people suffer, but this team will be united as one. You will be followed closely by our country. You will be its newest heroes. The quickest way to get cut from this squad is not by a lack of talent or hustle, but by any show of ethnic rivalry. Understood?"

All nodded in agreement. Ecko Lam was a legend in their circles and they were desperate to impress him. He and he alone held the key to a trip to America. They envied his coolness, his perfect English, and, most especially, the latest Air Jordans on his feet.

He picked up a uniform and continued, "This is what we will wear." He held up a jersey. "As you can see, it is plain, simple, reversible, something you might see in a gym class here in Juba. Gray, no color, no fancy logo. We wear this to remind ourselves of where we come from and of our humble roots. I wish I could give this uniform to all twenty of you, but I cannot. Only half will make the team and I do not look forward to giving the other half the bad news. But ten's enough, and will be joined by five more South Sudanese now living in the U.S. My assistant coach, Frankie Moka, is holding a similar tryout in Chicago. We will meet his players in Orlando for a few days of practice before the games begin. There will be sixteen teams in all, four from the U.S., the others from places like Brazil, the U.K., Spain, Croatia, Senegal, Italy, Russia, and I can't name them all. There will be eight teams in Orlando and we will play each one. The other eight will compete in a similar tournament in Las Vegas. The top four from each tournament will meet in St. Louis for the national showcase. Any questions?"

There were none. The boys were too shy to ask and none wanted to appear too eager.

"And just so you'll know, this trip is sponsored by the big shoe companies. You know their names and they're being very generous. Some of the money is also coming from the Manute Bol Foundation, and some has been donated by other NBA players from our country. At some point, when we're over there, we'll write thank-you notes and do photographs. There is a chance that we'll meet Niollo, but no promises."

They were too stunned to respond.

He split them into four teams, assigned their positions and matchups, warned them against excessive fouling, and started the two scrimmages. With no refs to interfere the play was extremely physical, and that was okay with Ecko. He whistled a few of the more brutal fouls, but for the most part let them play. After twenty minutes of nonstop action, he called for a break and offered them water. As they sat sprawled in the bleachers, dripping with sweat and catching their breath, he paced with his clipboard and said, "Nice work, men. Lots of good hustle out there. I expect that to continue because we are South Sudanese and we play from the heart. Nobody quits, nobody loafs, nobody goofs off on the court. Now, in about an hour we will walk around the corner to a dormitory where you'll stay. We'll have dinner there, then watch a movie, then go to bed. Get a good night's sleep because tomorrow will be a long day."

CHAPTER 3

On Saturday morning, Ecko marched them back to the gym, half of which had now been taken over by a city youth league. Confusion reigned for the first half hour as Ecko argued with a recreation official and threatened to call someone with clout. An uneasy truce was ironed out and the Under 18 practice was given two of the three courts. Once the youth league coaches realized who Ecko was, they grew quite cooperative. Their younger players watched Samuel and the others in awe.

Two assistant coaches arrived to help Ecko with his day. They organized the first event, a series of suicide sprints from mid-court to the baseline, about fifty feet. Racing in three groups of guards, forwards, and centers, the winners faced off for a two-out-of-three contest. All of the players were quick and fast, but none could touch Samuel. He won every sprint going away.

One coach then took the four centers under a basket for a rough session on rebounding and blocking out. Ecko took the guards and forwards and, using two cameras, filmed their jump shots. Samuel had never had a coach break down his shot, and it was not a pleasant experience. "A mess," was how Ecko described it, but with a smile. They started at the beginning and with the basics. "Think of all the shots you've ever taken, Samuel. Probably a million, right?"

"At least."

"And they've all been wrong. Time and time again all you've done is reinforce bad habits. If you want to play at a higher level, start over and start now."

They watched the film again and again. Ecko had averaged 15 points a game his senior year at Kent State and knew what a perfect jump shot looked like. "No two are the same," he explained to Samuel, "but the great ones have the same basic parts. Three things. Start just above the head, aim the elbow at the basket, and take the pressure off your left hand."

Samuel was eager to be coached and tried to unwind his bad habits, but it would take time. Ecko sent him to the free throw line to do nothing but shoot for ten minutes with both feet on the floor. Before each shot he was to say out loud, "Aim the elbow at the rim."

The drills continued throughout the morning and by noon the boys were bored. Ecko finally split them into four teams and unleashed the scrimmages. He again warned them about rough fouls and for good measure assigned an assistant coach to referee. He took a seat in the bleachers and studied every player.

By far the best point guard was Alek Garang, a well-known player from Juba who had starred on every tournament team since he was twelve years old. A scout had passed along his name to some American coaches and he was getting letters. The trip to the U.S. was crucial for his future.

The dreams and best-laid plans were to play well enough to be noticed by an American coach, who would then pull strings and "place" the recruit in a boarding school for a year of elevated competition and more stringent classroom work. Ecko knew every college coach, every boarding school, every high school basketball factory, and every rule in the NCAA handbook. He knew the cheaters, their bagmen, the schools to avoid, and the facilitators who should be indicted. He also knew that every kid on the floor right then in Juba needed an extra year of coaching and polishing before entering the rough world of American intercollegiate basketball.

. . .

After showers and pizza for dinner, the tired players stuffed themselves into two vans and rode through central Juba to a modern shopping mall near the capitol. Ecko let them go with instructions to meet at the cinema on the first level promptly at eight for a movie.

The boys stayed together as they drifted from store to store, gazing into windows, shaking their heads at price tags, trying on caps and shoes they could not afford. Samuel had a few coins and wanted to buy souvenirs for his younger sister and brothers, gifts they were certainly not expecting.

The movie was *Focus* starring Will Smith, the most popular American actor in Africa. Though he didn't say so, watching it was Samuel's first experience in a real cinema. It was a thrill and only reinforced his desire to live in the city, but he also kept thinking of his brothers, James and Chol, and his sister, Angelina, and how proud they would be to see him in such modern surroundings.

Watching Will Smith race through the streets in a sports car with a slinky woman on his arm was certainly entertaining. And Samuel, along with the other nineteen players, believed in his soul that it was not just a dream. The Miami Heat were currently paying Niollo $15 million a year to play basketball, money they could not comprehend. And Niollo was one of them, a poor kid from the bush of South Sudan, a Dinka, now starring in the NBA and most likely driving fancy cars and living the big life.

Back in the dorm, Ecko gathered the players in a television room and ordered more pizzas. Growing boys who were tall and skinny and burning thousands of calories each day could not be fed enough, and they devoured the pizzas. They were curious about his life, his upbringing and education, and how he discovered basketball. Why had he not made it as a pro? Why had he chosen to become a coach? Now that he had seen them play, could he say they were good enough for a college scholarship? Could he tell who might just make it to the NBA?

No, he could not. They were still growing and their skills were developing and in need of competition. Some had plenty of natural talent but all were rough around the edges and inexperienced. At least four of them would be sent home at noon the next day.

At the moment, Samuel was on the bubble. Alek Garang was the number one point guard, with Samuel a distant second.

Ecko talked to them, listened to them, and watched them carefully. For young men who had seen plenty of war, poverty, and violence, they, at least for the moment, preferred to talk about basketball in America, and movies and pizza and girls. Ecko was always listening and waiting for words or comments about the conflict. Each of them had been touched by it. Each knew someone who had died or disappeared.

But on that Saturday night, in the safety of a modern dormitory on a campus, the boys were safe. Their future was nothing but basketball.

CHAPTER 4

At only six feet two inches, Samuel still had trouble folding his legs onto his bunk for a night's rest. Above him, his bunkmate, Peter Nyamal, was five inches taller and somehow slept with his feet dangling in the air. Early Sunday morning, Samuel eased from the room without making a sound and left the dorm. He strolled through the campus and enjoyed the solitude and again vowed to study there, if, of course, things didn't work out in the NBA. He sat on a bench and watched the sunrise and smiled as he thought of his family back in Lotta. He had never left them before and they seemed so far away. At that moment, James and Chol were gathering eggs for breakfast while Angelina stood at the kitchen table with an iron heated by a fire and pressed her dress and their white shirts, their Sunday best. They would walk as a family to the village church for nine o'clock Mass.

Samuel roamed some more and found the student center, the only building open at such an hour on a Sunday morning. He paid five cents for a carton of mango juice and smiled at a pretty girl all alone at a table. She was pecking on a laptop and ignored him. About a year earlier, he had actually seen and touched a laptop. There had been only one in his school, and for a brief period of time there had been internet service in Lotta. That, along with cell phone coverage, had been knocked out by the guerrillas. Roads, bridges, cell towers, and utility lines were favorite targets. They were destroyed so often that the government stopped building them.

His mother, Beatrice, had no education. His sister, Angelina, was being taught at home by their father. How, then, was it possible for some young women in South Sudan to make it to college? He rather liked the idea. He had watched several college games on television and had always been surprised at the number of female students screaming in the stands. Another reason to play basketball in America.

In a reading area, he flipped through the *Juba Monitor,* one of two dailies in the country, neither of which made it to Lotta. He found a copy of the other one, *The Citizen,* and reread the same news. As he was finishing his juice, three college boys came in and looked him over, then ignored him. They chatted away in their big-city English. Their clothes were nicer; their shirts had real collars. Samuel knew it was time to leave.

He found the gym and the front doors were locked. As he walked away, he saw a janitor exit from a side door. He waited a moment until the janitor was gone, then tried the door. It opened and he walked into the same locker room the team had been using. The courts were dark but the early sun was flooding one end of the building. Samuel found a bag of balls and, without even a hint of stretching, began shooting.

An hour later, Ecko Lam entered through the same side door, and as he walked through the locker room he heard the familiar sound of a bouncing ball. He eased into the shadows and peeked around the bleachers. Samuel was glistening with sweat as he fired away from twenty feet. He missed, sprinted after the ball, dribbled between his legs, behind his back, feinted right then left all the way to mid-court where he turned around, took a few quick steps, and fired again. Another miss. And another. The form was better and he was trying mightily to break old habits, but the elbow was still straying too far. And, for the moment Ecko really didn't care. The gorgeous part of his jump shot was the point of delivery. Off the dribble, Samuel pulled up and in a split second rocketed upward and flicked the ball away at a height few other guards could match.

If only he could hit.

After a few minutes, Ecko strode onto the court and said good morning.

"Hello, Coach," Samuel said, flinging sweat from his forehead. It was not yet 8 a.m. and the gym was thick with humidity.

"You have trouble sleeping?" Ecko asked.

"No sir. Well, yes, I guess. I wanted to walk around and see the campus, and I found a door back there that was unlocked."

"I watched your last fifteen shots, Samuel. You missed twelve of them. And you were as wide open as you'll ever get."

"Yes sir. It will take some work, Coach."

Ecko smiled and said, "The scouting report says your mother is six feet tall. Is that right?"

"Yes sir. All my people are tall."

"When do you turn eighteen?"

"August eleven."

"You could try out next year, Samuel."

"Thank you, Coach. Does this mean I'm done for this year?"

"No. You want to shoot some more?"

"Yes sir."

"Okay. Go to the free throw line. Keep both feet on the floor. We know you can jump. Take the ball higher. Aim your elbow directly at the rim and deliver it slowly. When you make ten in a row, come find me."

"Yes sir."

. . .

The first drill was a shooting contest, held on two courts. Every player took 20 shots from the free throw line, and the hits and misses were recorded. The top four were then put in a shootout, complete with banter, catcalls, cheap shots, laughter at misses, all manner of verbal abuse. "This pressure is nothing," Ecko kept saying as he offered up his pointed observations. "Imagine you're in the Final Four with the game on the line and a hundred million people watching, including everyone here in South Sudan. This pressure is nothing."

Alek Garang shot 90 percent and won going away. Samuel struggled to hit half of his shots.

They moved back five feet to the college arc—20 feet, nine inches—and started with the guards. Each took 20 open shots in a row. Garang hit 11; Samuel only 4. The forwards went next and Ecko was not pleased with their percentages. The best hit only a third of his shots. Because every big man fancies himself a long-range gunner, Ecko humored the centers with 10 shots each. Few found the bottom of the net.

He broke them down into teams of three for half-court scrimmages. His tone changed dramatically as he stopped smiling, yelled more, whistled more, found far more deficiencies to point out. The gym became tense as Ecko went on the warpath. A bad shot got a whistle and harsh rebuke.

Samuel rested and watched from the bleachers. It had been a terrible morning and things were not improving. His shooting was pathetic, so bad that in the scrimmages he hesitated to take a shot. Hard to score when you don't shoot. He had guarded Alek Garang for 15 minutes and the slick one had scored almost at will. Ecko yelled and whistled and seemed irritated by Samuel's presence on the court. By noon, Samuel knew he was finished.

After a break and some cold pizza, Ecko divided them into groups of four for half an hour of incredibly dull drills—ball screens, pick-and-rolls, and such. One of the assistant coaches led four players to the locker room where a chalkboard was wiped clean and apparently ready for Xs and Os. Instead, Ecko appeared and addressed them by saying, "Look, men, there's no easy way to do this. It's by far the worst part of coaching, but I have no choice. You are great players with great futures, but I cannot include you on this trip."

They slumped in their chairs and looked at the floor.

Ecko continued, "We have some money for the bus rides. I wish you the best. Be careful out there." Though he had done it before, it was still heartbreaking. The boys would travel by bus and on foot back to their homes with their magnificent dreams broken. They would continue to play, and to grow, but he knew that none of the four would play in America. And without that chance, their futures were bleak.

They were too stunned to speak.

Ecko said, "Look me in the eyes." All four eventually did.

He said, "I wish I could take all twenty, but I can't. I'm sorry."

Peter Nyamal slowly stood and wiped his cheeks with the back of a hand. He said, "Thank you, Coach, for the opportunity."

They shook hands and embraced. Ecko said, "I wish you the best, I really do, and I hope to see you again."

The other three stood, proudly, and embraced their coach. An assistant led them through the side door and walked them back to the dorm. They quickly gathered their things and headed for the bus station.

Two hours later, the same scene was repeated as Ecko said good-bye to four more. He hated this part of his job but had learned that it was best to get it over with.

As the team enjoyed a long break back at the dorm, Ecko and his two assistants debated the last two cuts. He wanted to break camp with four guards, four forwards, and two centers, but the two bigs were lacking. The team would find help in the U.S. where a high school All-American named Dak Marial would join the team. Dak was a rising senior at a fancy California prep school and had already committed to UCLA. Most rating experts put him in the top three prospects in the country. He had fled South Sudan with relatives when he was a boy.

Ecko did not want to take either of his two centers, but finally settled on one. Neither assistant wanted to include Samuel, who, so far that weekend, had looked terrible on offense and mediocre on defense. Both rated him as the third best guard. One referred to him as a "nonshooting guard." But Ecko loved his speed, quickness, and leap, and he was convinced that the kid would put in the hours necessary to become a marksman.

They finally agreed to cut one center and one forward. Samuel Sooleymon was the last player chosen, though he would never know it.

. . .

The players did know that some serious roster trimming was under way. Eight of their friends had vanished, their lockers and rooms cleared. Who would be Ecko's last two victims? As they played foosball, shot pool, and looked at girls in the student center, they laughed and joked about who might be next. But it was a nervous laughter.

. . .

Coach Lam's favorite restaurant in Juba was Da Vinci's, a place known for good food and even better views. It sat practically on the Nile River, on the eastern edge of town, and most of its tables were outside on a deck beside the water. He arrived first with a van loaded with five players and they followed him to a secluded corner of the deck where he congratulated them on making the team. Moments later, the two assistants arrived with the other five, and when the boys realized that they had been chosen they wanted to celebrate. Their frayed nerves were finally put at ease.

Samuel had convinced himself that his long ride back to Rumbek would be a dreadful one. He had tried to imagine the pain of telling his family and friends that he didn't make the cut. They would be crushed and he would never get over the disappointment.

Now, however, the future was glorious again. He was headed to the U.S. to play basketball against the world while a hundred head coaches watched intently and their assistants filmed every move. He would proudly carry the dreams of his people on his broad shoulders and soar, just like the great Niollo.

The players and coaches sat around a long table and ordered soft drinks and juice. The mood was joyous and every conversation was about the trip, from the airports and jets, to the long flights, to the hotels and amusement parks, to the games and the arenas and all those scouts. Were they really going to Disney World?

It was Ecko's third Under 18 team to take to the U.S., and he reveled in their excitement.

CHAPTER 5

At seven Monday morning, a van left the dorm again as Ecko took four of his new players to the bus station. He parked in a gravel lot outside the bustling terminal and took the boys to the rear door of the van. He handed each a handsome vinyl gym bag with the South Sudanese flag brightly embroidered on both sides. "Inside you'll find a new basketball, some practice tee shirts and shorts, along with some caps and other goodies. Before we leave in July, you'll be fitted for new shoes, but that comes later."

He walked them inside and said goodbye to each with a warm embrace. They thanked him again and again, and they hugged each other, said goodbye again, and got lost in the crowds.

Samuel's bus to Rumbek left at 8:30, only half an hour late. It was not crowded and he had an entire seat to himself, for the moment. Beside him was his old duffel and his shiny new gym bag, which he continually checked on. It was already hot and the bus inched along in city traffic. Once again, Samuel marveled at the city noise—the relentless horn-blowing, the angry shouts, the friendly greetings, the rattle and roar of old engines, the sirens. Finally, the bus picked up speed as the traffic thinned and they left the central city. The road was still asphalt as they passed through the shanty-towns but soon became gravel.

Suddenly, the bus stopped, its passenger door jerked open, and three smartly dressed and armed government soldiers hopped on board. They wore identical khaki uniforms, maroon berets, shiny black boots, and all three had the same cocky smirk that was expected. Each carried a Kalashnikov rifle, or a Kallie as they were called in many parts of Africa. Samuel immediately recognized the weapon because there were so many of them in his country.

The soldiers glared at the passengers—the usual collection of harmless peasants, students, commuting workers—and didn't like what they saw. They ordered the first two rows cleared and sat down. One barked at the driver to proceed, and the bus was off again.

It was not at all uncommon for government soldiers to hop a ride on the buses. They were given priority and no one objected. They expected to be accommodated and had the weaponry to get what they wanted. But their presence could mean something far more ominous than simply catching a ride from here to there. It was not uncommon for the military to accompany buses into the rural areas where bandits thrived and guerrillas waited to attack.

After half an hour it was obvious, at least to Samuel, that the soldiers were not just along for the ride. They were on high alert, watching the road, the traffic, the settlements, the trails. They whispered among themselves. One talked on a satellite phone. Cellular service outside of Juba was scarce and unreliable.

The bus stopped in a village and four passengers got on as one got off. Minutes later they were back in the bush, the gravel road dry and dusty, the sun baking the fields and woods.

The ambush happened so fast it must have been carried out by experienced thieves. An open cargo truck suddenly appeared from a dirt trail in a bend and blocked the road.

The bus driver said, "This is it!" He hit the brakes and the bus rocked to a halt.

The soldiers lowered their heads, clutched their Kallies, and prepared to attack. One yelled at the passengers, "Heads down!

Everyone!" Two crouched by the driver. The third moved to the rear and put his hand on the door latch.

Then, the sickening sound that was all too familiar. The *Tak-Tak-Tak-Tak* of an assault rifle. Samuel ducked even lower but was still watching. The leader of the gang was in the middle of the road firing at the sky. Beside him were two others, just boys, probably Samuel's age or younger, dressed in their best imitation of real soldiers, a hodgepodge of leather ammo belts and guns on both hips, along with their rifles. One wore a white cowboy hat. One had on basketball shoes. They swaggered toward the bus, all three yelling threats, as two others hustled to the rear of the bus.

A soldier squatting inside the front door said, "Go," and all hell broke loose. The driver opened the door and two soldiers rolled out and landed on their knees with Kallies blazing. The thieves were stunned and their hesitation cost them their lives as the better-trained government soldiers wiped them out. At the same moment, the third soldier kicked open the rear door and shot the two thugs at near point-blank range.

The gunfire lasted only seconds, but it was horrifying nonetheless. One of the bandits managed to spray the front of the bus and shatter the windshield before going down, and the sounds of exploding glass and ricocheting bullets hung in the air long after the shooting stopped. Samuel, head still low, quickly checked on the other passengers. "No one's hurt," he yelled to the driver. He walked to the front, looked through the pockmarked windshield, and saw a sickening scene that he would never forget.

A boy of no more than twelve was walking from the cargo truck toward the soldiers. He held a rifle with both hands, high above his head, as if to surrender. He was frightened and may have been crying. A soldier ordered him to lay down the weapon and he did so. He fell to his knees, touched his fingertips to his chin, and begged for his life. The two soldiers stood over him. One kicked him in the face and knocked him flat, facedown. The other raised his Kallie and fired away, strafing the boy's back and head. *Tak! Tak! Tak! Tak!*

When all was quiet, the passengers cautiously lifted their heads and watched as the soldiers cleared the road, then dragged the six dead bodies to the cargo truck and piled them together near the fuel tank under the driver's seat. In no hurry, they searched through all pockets and kept the money and valuables. They confiscated their weapons and found two sat phones in the cab. They turned a valve, drained the diesel from the tank, and let it run over the dead bodies. One soldier ripped off a tee shirt from a corpse, soaked it with lighter fluid, and wrapped it around a large rock. They backed away, lit the tee shirt, and tossed it at the cargo truck. *Whoosh!* The noise startled even the soldiers and they stepped back again. The fire roared and engulfed the truck and sent thick, black exhaust boiling upward. Flames shot from the dead bodies as the clothing caught fire, then the flesh began sizzling.

The soldiers laughed and admired their work.

The bus driver swept glass from his dashboard and resettled into his seat. Along with his passengers, he watched the fire and waited for the soldiers. On the bench in front of Samuel, a mother with a small child was crying. Samuel looked at a man across the aisle, but both were too stunned to speak.

Eventually, the soldiers retreated to the bus and got on. No one made eye contact with them. The driver waited until he was told to proceed. As they drove away, Samuel looked through his window at the awful scene. His lasting image was the burning bodies.

The road ran straight for a mile or so, and when it swept to the right he turned and saw a tall, thick cloud of grayish smoke drifting high into the air. What would the next bus see as it approached? Who would clean up the mess? Take away the bodies? Report the incident to the authorities?

In South Sudan, many obvious questions went unanswered, and survivors knew to stay quiet.

The soldiers were laughing among themselves and ignoring the passengers. The driver pointed to holes in his windshield, said something funny, and the soldiers laughed at it too. After half an hour, one of them stood and walked down the aisle, looking at the passengers and their bags and sacks of goods. Samuel's new gym bag caught his attention and he asked, "What's in it?"

Samuel smiled and replied, "Basketball stuff."

"Open it."

The soldier was Dinka—all three were—as was Samuel, and with the endless ethnic conflict raging through the country he felt somewhat comfortable being among his own. Certainly they wouldn't steal from him? He unzipped the bag and showed it to the soldier, who asked, "Basketball?"

"Yes sir. I'm on the national team. We're going to play in the United States in July."

The soldier grabbed the bag and took it up front and showed it to his buddies. They removed the new ball, two practice tee shirts, two pairs of gym shorts, two pairs of white socks, and three caps with a South Sudan Under 18 logo on the front. They examined them, then removed their maroon berets and put on the caps.

One of them turned and looked at Samuel and said, "Up here."

Samuel walked to the front and took a seat behind them. They asked questions about the team, the tournaments, the trip to the U.S. One claimed to be a fan of Niollo and said he loved the Miami Heat. They asked if Samuel would play for an American college. What about the NBA?

The bus stopped at another village and two passengers joined the ride. Back on the road and still sitting with the soldiers, Samuel asked, "Got time for a question?"

"Sure," said the biggest talker, undoubtedly the leader of the gang. All three were still wearing the U18 caps.

"Who were those men back there?"

"A band of thieves, some nasty boys who've been causing trouble around here."

"But no more," said another with a laugh.

Samuel said, "How did you know they would stop the bus?"

One picked up a sat phone and smiled at it. "They use these too and we like to listen. They're not really that smart."

"So, they're not guerrillas?"

"No, just a gang of raiders looking for someone to rob, rape, and kill."

"They would have killed us?"

"You never know with these thugs. Last week they stopped a bus on the main highway west of Juba. At night. Got everybody off the bus and they lined them up along its side. Made the driver get on his knees and beg, then they shot him. They robbed everyone, took their bags and luggage. There were two young ladies, one with a child. They took them back on the bus and raped them for an hour or so while the other passengers listened. Two boys sneaked off in the dark and escaped."

Samuel glanced to his left and looked at a peasant woman of about forty. Her teenage daughter sat next to her. How close had they come to a disaster?

The leader continued, "You? A fine young man of, how old?"

"Seventeen."

"I joined the army at seventeen. Three years ago. You, they probably would not have killed you, but there's a good chance they would've taken you and forced you to join the gang. If you resisted, then they would've shot you." He lowered his voice and looked at the girl. "She wouldn't have stood a chance. And the driver? Well, they always kill the driver."

"Standard procedure," added another.

"I guess we owe you a big thanks," Samuel said.

"It's our job."

They removed the caps and put them back in the gym bag, along with the ball, shirts, shorts, and socks.

The leader said, "So, when you make a million dollars in the NBA, you'll come back here and buy us a beer, right?"

"All the beer you can drink."

"We're going to remember that."

They handed back his gym bag and Samuel returned to his seat. He was four hours from home.

CHAPTER 6

There was no welcoming party at the terminal in Rumbek. Samuel saw no one he knew. The bus was hours late and he was not expecting anyone to wait on him. He flagged a moto-taxi and hopped on the back, clutching his two bags. The driver, a kid of no more than fifteen, handled the bike like all the rest, reckless and daring and determined to terrify his passenger. Samuel hung on for his life and managed to follow the custom of not complaining about the daredevil antics. The walk to Lotta was three miles and would have taken an hour under a blazing sun. The taxi ride was twenty cents, so Samuel splurged and laughed to himself about spending big money now that he was a star.

Beatrice was behind the house watering her vegetables when she heard Angelina squeal with excitement. She ran inside and saw Samuel standing in the kitchen, wearing a South Sudan practice tee shirt, modeling it like he owned the world. "I made the team, Mom!" he yelled as he grabbed his mother and lifted her into the air. Beatrice hugged him back and began crying as Angelina bounced around the house, looking for someone else to tell. Finding no one, she ran into the street with the unbelievable news and within seconds the neighbors knew that their dream had come true. Samuel Sooleymon was going to play basketball in America!

A second celebration materialized within the hour as the village gathered on the street in front of the house. As Ayak came home from school with James and Chol, a loud cheer went up when Samuel ran to greet them. The neighbors brought boiled peanuts, sesame snacks, cinnamon tea, and mandazi, a popular fried pastry.

Samuel proudly showed off his new weapon, a Spalding NBA Street Ball, and explained that it was made of a durable rubber and designed for outdoor play. He tossed it to James who passed to a friend and before long the shiny new ball was crisscrossing through the crowd as the older boys passed it, held it long enough to admire, then zipped it to the next one. A radio began playing music as the day grew long and the shadows crept in.

As the sun set, the most glorious day in Lotta's history was coming to an end, and there was so much hope for even more excitement. Their native son was on his way.

. . .

The family sat in the dark house until late in the night, talking and laughing and dreaming of what might happen in America. Back on the bus, Samuel had decided not to tell his family about the bandits, the soldiers, the ambush, the smoldering corpses. He would be on the bus again in early July as he headed back to Juba for the trip and he did not want them to worry.

Later in bed, though, he could not shake the image of the young boy being killed for no reason. He was about the same size and age of Chol, who was twelve. Who was he? Where was he from? Did he have family? How did he end up raiding highways with a gang of thieves? Would anyone grieve over his death? Would anyone even know about it?

And though the soldiers had done their duty and probably saved a few lives with their ambush, Samuel was still bothered by the ease with which they killed and the complete lack of remorse over any of it. They had laughed as they watched the fire. They had reboarded the bus as if nothing had happened. Was it possible to kill so many and do it so often that they had become numb to any feelings? But they were young, like Samuel. Their fathers and grandfathers had probably fought the North in civil wars that lasted for fifty years. They had grown up with violence and killing. It didn't bother them. Now, with yet another civil war raging through South Sudan, the bloodshed and atrocities were only getting worse.

Beatrice had a cousin who'd been murdered in a village slaughter only an hour away. Everyone in South Sudan had a story.

From burning bodies to basketball glories, Samuel's mind raced back and forth when he should have been sleeping.

He woke up at dawn and felt tired, but life had a new meaning and there were important matters at hand. He dressed, gathered his eggs, swallowed breakfast in three bites, kissed his mother goodbye, and took off down the road, backpack over his shoulder and his new street ball bouncing away. All alone on the dirt court where he had spent half his childhood, Samuel vowed to perfect his jump shot with endless hours of practice. He would see Coach Ecko Lam and his new teammates in just over two months when they reunited in Juba for a week of practice, and he was determined to handle the ball like Steph Curry, shoot like Kobe, and play both ends like LeBron. No one would work harder. No one would spend more time on the courts than Samuel.

At seven, James and Chol appeared with their old basketball. Three more boys arrived with theirs. The five became rebounders and feeders as they retrieved Samuel's shots and fed the ball back to him.

Ball high, elbow aimed, shoulders squared, an easy jump. Samuel repeated Coach Lam's instructions before each shot. And for some reason he counted. After 200 he began to tire. At 300, it was time for school.

He'd read that Kobe took 500 shots a day when he was a teenager. He'd also read that Steph Curry once hit 77-straight three-point shots in practice. He liked those numbers.

.   .   .

At the end of May, Samuel finished his final year of secondary studies and was given a certificate in an outdoor graduation ceremony. There were ten others in his class, all boys, and their principal reminded them of how lucky they were to complete their studies. Across their young and troubled nation, only a third of all boys got a certificate. One in ten for the girls, and those graduates were found only in the cities.

Samuel had applied to the University of Juba and been accepted. He planned to enroll there in the fall, though he did not have enough money for the meager tuition and expenses. If things didn't work out in the U.S., he would return home, move to Juba, find part-time work, hustle for student aid, and somehow get by as another starving college boy. He had seen the bright lights, was about to see even brighter ones, and vowed to seek a better life away from the poverty and violence of the bush.

Those thoughts, though, were rather remote as he proudly held his certificate and listened to the principal go on and on about the country's need for younger leadership. He tried to listen but his thoughts were on July and the trip of a lifetime, the incredible opportunity to play in front of college scouts. He did not want to spend the next year studying economics or medicine at the University of Juba.

.   .   .

The send-off was not what the neighbors wanted. They fancied another block party with music and dancing late into the night. Beatrice and Ayak were grateful but felt otherwise. They wanted their son to go to bed early, get plenty of sleep, and make a quick getaway.

The family breakfast was quiet. They ate eggs and pastries and drank tamarind fruit juice, coffee for the adults. Angelina, James, and Chol were torn between the excitement of their brother's big adventure, and the sadness, even fear, of him leaving home. The family had always been together, and the thought of Samuel going away, now or next month for university, was unsettling.

He joked with his siblings and promised to send postcards, though mail service in rural South Sudan was virtually nonexistent. He promised to call whenever he could. Coach Lam, of course, had a cell phone and had promised to devise a method of calling home, though it seemed unlikely the family would get a call so far from Juba.

When it was time to go he grabbed his carefully packed gym bag and stepped outside where a dozen neighbors loitered in the front yard to say goodbye. He thanked them, hugged a few, then hugged his siblings. Angelina was wiping tears. Beatrice gave him a small cardboard box filled with food for the bus ride, and he hugged his mother for a long time.

For the occasion, a cousin who owned one of the few pickup trucks in the village had washed the dirt and mud off and parked it in front of the house. The tailgate was down. He took Samuel's gym bag, tossed it in, and patted a cushion on the tailgate. A throne for the guest of honor. As the crowd inched closer, Ayak pulled a small envelope out of his pocket and gave it to his son.

"What is it?" Samuel asked.

"It's money, cash. From all of your friends. They collected a few coins from everyone and the bank converted them to pounds. About ten."

"Ten pounds?" Samuel asked in disbelief.

"Yes."

"That's far too much money, Father."

"I know. But you can't give it back, can you?"

Samuel wiped his eyes and stuffed the envelope into a front pocket of his only pair of pants. He looked into the faces of his friends and neighbors and softly said, "Thank you, thank you."

His cousin said, "We're going to miss the bus." He got behind the wheel, slammed the door, and started the engine.

Ayak stepped forward and embraced Samuel. "Make us proud," he said.

"I will. I promise." Samuel took his place on the cushioned tailgate, his long legs dangling almost to the dirt street. He waved at Beatrice and his siblings, nodded again at his father as the truck moved away.

Ayak stood there, waving goodbye as only a proud father can do.

Samuel returned the wave and wiped his cheek.

He would never see his father again.

CHAPTER 7

Ecko Lam was lounging in the bleachers with three of his players and waiting for the others to arrive. The gym, the same one they had used in April, was busy with a summer basketball league on one end and a volleyball tournament at the other. Things would clear out somewhat tomorrow, and Ecko had been promised one full court for practice. He was desperate to get his team to Orlando and to a real gym for more intense workouts. He knew that for the next three days his players would practice hard but would also be distracted by thoughts of the trip.

He saw Samuel enter the gym with his team bag and look around. Ecko realized immediately that he was taller than in April. He called him over and they went through the standard handshakes and embraces.

"How much have you grown?" Ecko asked.

"I don't know," Samuel said.

"Come on, Samuel, you've grown several inches."

"No way," Samuel said.

Ecko looked at the other three and asked, "Right? He's taller?"

"Maybe an inch or so," said Riak Kuol, a forward.

"You were six feet two the last time you were here, right?"

"Yes."

"Come here."

They walked into the locker room where a narrow board eight feet tall was attached to the wall next to a chalkboard. Ecko nodded and Samuel pressed his back to the yardstick.

Ecko smiled and said, "Six feet four. You've grown two inches in the past two and a half months. What are you eating?"

"Everything."

"Keep it up. Taller is always better."

.   .   .

By dinner, all ten players had reported. Ecko gave them the night off and instead of a hard practice they ate pizza in the dorm and talked about life. The coach said little and wanted the boys to get comfortable with each other. They would live together for the next month, sleeping three and four to a room, eating every meal together, sweating buckets in practice, winning and losing and pushing each other to whatever limits were in their way. They would laugh and probably cry, and along the way they would discover a small slice of America.

Ecko saw basketball as one of the few bright spots in his native land, and he dreamed of returning with his players and helping to build a new nation. He asked if any of the boys had encountered violence. Riak Kuol, a Murle from Upper Nile state, said that a relative had been murdered in a village burning only two weeks earlier. The man's family had fled and disappeared and were probably hiding in a refugee camp.

Samuel told the story of his bus ride home back in April and his close call with the bandits. Quinton Majok, a Nuer from Wau, the fourth largest city, had relatives in a refugee camp in Uganda.

They talked late into the night, and Ecko became convinced that he had chosen well. They were kids, just boys about to leave on a journey they could hardly imagine. They spoke the same English, though some better than others. Abraham Bol, an Azande from

Upper Nile, won the award for the most languages. He spoke five—two tribal, English, Arabic, and some pretty good French he picked up from a missionary. His dream, after basketball of course, was to speak ten languages and work as an interpreter for the United Nations.

At midnight, Ecko shut down the party and ordered them to bed. He promised tomorrow would be brutal.

.   .   .

However, the next day began not with a half hour of painful stretching, nor with a round of Coach Lam's much dreaded suicide sprints, but with a most exciting order of business. It was Shoe Day! In the locker room, Ecko stood in front of a stack of identical bright boxes with the Reebok logo on all sides. He explained that the major apparel companies—Nike, Reebok, Adidas, Under Armour, Puma—were not only sponsoring the tournaments in the U.S. but also providing plenty of gear. In a random drawing, Reebok had picked the team from South Sudan. Some of the players may have preferred other brands, but in an instant they were forgotten. Reebok was now the favorite as they happily ditched their old shoes and began trying on the new.

Ecko looked at the pile of battered, torn, and slick-soled old shoes and shook his head. How many hours had they pounded away on dirt and mud courts? All of them should have been discarded months ago. Every decent high school player in America had a collection of basketball shoes, some of which they actually wore on the court. For his players it was Christmas morning as they opened boxes, held up the pristine Reebok Revenge models, and slowly, gingerly, tried them on. They passed them around and helped each other get the right size as all ten seemed to chatter at once.

Samuel's old pair were size elevens and had been too tight for a month or so. The 12.5 fit perfectly. At the rate he was growing, he wondered how long they would last.

When they were all fitted and admiring their new shoes, Ecko called them to order and began a mini-lecture on proper attire. They should notice that everyone now had the same shoe. All were identical, all were equal. In practice, everyone would wear the same shorts, socks, and shirts. Nothing else. No bandanas, no sweat bands, nothing to draw attention to the individual. They were a team of equals, with no stars and no scrubs. As a coach he would strive to keep the playing time equal, at least in the early games. However, as they proceeded, it might become obvious that a player deserved more time on the court, and perhaps another player deserved less. He would make those decisions later. For now everything was equal.

He picked up a game jersey, the same one he had shown the team back in April. "You've seen this before. It's a plain gray jersey with matching shorts. No fancy logo. No name on the back. Nothing that says 'Look at me.' We will wear these unremarkable uniforms to remind ourselves of the simple and humble origins of our people. These uniforms will constantly remind us of where we come from. And when we distinguish ourselves on the court, and we are asked why we wear such simple clothes, we will proudly say that we are South Sudanese. Our country is young and poor, but we will make it a better place."

. . .

Two days later, the team met for an early breakfast in the dorm cafeteria. Most had been awake for hours. The excitement was palpable as they chattered away and ate cereal and toast. Ecko encouraged them to eat heartily because it would be a long day.

They wore identical yellow tee shirts with the South Sudan flag brightly printed on both the front and back. Coach Lam explained that such shirts were necessary because they would be passing through crowded airports and it was often easy to get separated.

The words "crowded airports" only added to the excitement.

Two vans unloaded them at the Juba International Airport.

They were limited to one item of luggage, the vinyl gym bag they had been given back in April. Twenty pounds max because Coach Lam wasn't about to pay extra for baggage. With the flashy black, red, green, and blue national flag also printed on their bags, the South Sudanese Under 18 team was a veritable wave of color as it filed through the airport's lobby and began getting second and third looks.

Ecko had not embarrassed all of them by asking who had or had not been on an airplane. However, he knew for a fact that none of them had passports or visas. Given the nature of the trip, getting them from the government had been relatively easy.

As they stood at a large window and watched an airplane taxi away from the terminal, Samuel reached into his pocket, removed his passport, and stared at it, almost in disbelief. A passport!

Their airline was Ethiopian Air, a major carrier on the continent and one with an exemplary safety record. Ecko had assured them that the flight would be safe, even fun. No one had doubted this. Not a single player seemed even remotely reticent about flying.

When the Boeing 737 pushed back, Samuel closed his eyes and savored the moment. He thought of his parents and his siblings and already missed them. Would they ever have an opportunity like this?

He got lucky and had a seat by the window, and when the plane lifted off, his stomach floated a bit, much like a good case of the butterflies before a game. At altitude, the flight attendants served peanuts and sodas, and Samuel fell in love with at least three of them.

The flight to Addis Ababa, Ethiopia's capital, took two hours. They disembarked and killed three hours roaming the terminal, soaking in all the sights and sounds, and especially keeping an eye out for more pretty flight attendants. They boarded a 777 and flew eight and a half hours to Dublin, Ireland, where they stayed on the plane for an hour before taking off for Washington Dulles. When they touched down they had been traveling for twenty-six hours.

And they weren't finished. Because of delays, they had to hurry from one terminal to another and sprint to catch a Delta flight to Orlando, by way of Atlanta.

The thrill of aviation dissipated somewhere over the Atlantic, and when they stumbled out of the Orlando airport and into the sweltering Florida heat they had been traveling for almost thirty hours.

They folded themselves into three taxis for the ride to their hotel somewhere in the sprawl of central Florida. It was an inexpensive hotel just off an interstate, and Ecko, always budget-minded, put three and four to a room and cautioned them against complaining. They did not; they were too tired.

CHAPTER 8

Francis Moka was thirty-five years old and worked as a scout for the Denver Nuggets. He was born in London after his parents fled Sudan in the early 1990s. At the age of twelve he was six feet tall and caught the attention of a youth league coach who signed him up and taught him the game. At seventeen, he was recruited by a private academy in Florida to play basketball and, of course, become a student-athlete. He accepted a full scholarship to Stanford but was hounded by knee injuries and played little. He excelled in the classroom and graduated with honors. Like his close friend Ecko, Frankie, as he was known to everyone, aspired to coach Division I college basketball.

Frankie and his five all-stars strode into the spacious high school gym and were introduced to Coach Lam and his gang from the mother country. Of the fifteen, all but one had been born in South Sudan. For a moment there was the typical awkwardness as the players looked each other over, sized up one another, wondered if this or that one could really play, while Ecko and Frankie tried to keep it light. The team would have no rivalries, no squabbles, no grudges. They would compete for positions but each would get an equal chance, and the coaches demanded allegiance to the team.

Not surprisingly, Dak Marial got more attention than the others. According to several recruiting sites, he was either the third- or fourth-rated high school prospect in the nation and had already committed to UCLA. In other words, Dak was already riding the rocket his teammates were dreaming of. But his story was even sadder than most. When he was seven years old, he watched as both parents were burned alive in the family's hut during a raid. An aunt fled with him into the bush and they almost died of starvation before stumbling into a refugee camp. Remarkably, the camp had a dirt basketball court with two backboards and plenty of balls, courtesy of the foundation established by Manute Bol. Dak started playing and grew up with the game. After six years in the camp, Dak and his aunt arrived in the U.S. where relatives were waiting.

After an hour of conversation, during which every player was required to say something, Ecko split them into five teams of three for half-court scrimmages.

. . .

It was Ecko's third South Sudanese team to compete in the showcase. The sites were moved each year to encourage participation by scouts, but the venues didn't really matter. The games attracted hundreds of college coaches and their assistants, but the stands were usually empty. Few American basketball fans were curious about eighteen-year-old players from Croatia or Brazil, especially in the middle of the summer. Two years earlier, Ecko brought his team to Orlando for the first time and learned the valuable lesson that the theme parks were too strong a distraction. Sure, the players were eager to strut their stuff and impress the scouts, but they were just as eager to see Disney World.

Therefore, on the second full day in Orlando, Coaches Lam and Moka loaded the team into two long white vans and took them to the Magic Kingdom. They drove to the front gate, laid down a few rules, gave them passes and cash allowances, and said so long. See ya at six.

Ecko had been there twice and loathed the place. A long hot day in the sun, fighting crowds, waiting in lines, and the players should be ready to forget about Mickey and concentrate on basketball.

The two coaches drove back to Orlando, to the campus of the University of Central Florida. They parked near the CFE Arena, went inside, and made their way to the floor where the team from Brazil was practicing. The coach was unhappy and had a deep voice, one that boomed with what was certainly some very colorful language, in Portuguese.

Ecko and Frankie weren't there to watch a practice, though their team would play the Brazilians in a few days. They were there to pick up their packets, team guides, schedules, etc., stuff that was all available online, but the real reason was to see their buddies. Several dozen of them were sitting courtside, in the expensive seats, ostensibly watching the action on the court but in reality just checking to see who showed up next.

The world of college coaching is small and insular and everybody knows everybody else. Gossip roars through its ranks: who's got a new contract and who's headed for the chopping block; who's looking for an assistant and who wants to get rid of one; which school wants to up its game and which one is short on money; which school is planning a new arena and which school desperately needs one. And the deadliest rumor: Who's being investigated by the NCAA?

And that was the light gossip. When the chatter turned to recruiting, everyone talked at once, but little was actually said. Secrets were jealously guarded.

Ecko's team was getting more and more attention. The year before, the South Sudanese had placed third in the tournament, but his boys had stolen the show with their rim-rattling dunks and gravity-defying blocked shots. What the scouts and the media loved was their enthusiasm for the game, their endless hustle, their selfless play, their support for one another, and their smiles. They came from a troubled land, but they were proud of their country and wanted the world to know it.

"Got any five-stars?" asked an assistant from Missouri.

"They're all five-stars," Ecko said. "I don't fool with four-stars."

"So you're going all the way?"

"We got it won, fellas. My boys are already at Disney World celebrating."

"Seriously, who's your best?"

"That would be Mr. Marial."

"Okay, okay. I think he's spoken for. Who's number two?"

"A guard named Alek Garang."

"From where?"

"Juba, but he may go to Ridgewood this season."

The coach shrugged it off and feigned disinterest. It was well accepted that the South Sudanese who were playing high school ball in the U.S. were a year or two ahead of their friends back home. The competition and coaching were simply stronger in the U.S. The great ones would catch up and compete at a higher level. The good ones would likely not make it.

"Who you watching?" Ecko asked another coach.

"Americans?"

"No, we know them already. The foreign kids."

"Well, everybody's buzzing about that Koosh Koosh kid?"

"Beg your pardon."

"You know, that big guy from Latvia with the last name that sounds like Koosh Koosh. Only he can pronounce it. No one can spell it."

"Latvia?"

"Yeah, he plays for the Croatians?"

"Makes perfect sense."

"One of those Eastern European teams. Kid's six ten and can shoot from mid-court."

"We got three of those," Frankie said with a straight face.

"Gimme their names."

"Not now. You gotta watch 'em."

"Yeah, yeah," his friend said, waving him off.

Other coaches, almost all of them assistants, came and went. There was a hospitality room in one of the luxury suites, and Ecko and Frankie parked themselves there for lunch and enjoyed the camaraderie of old and new friends.

.   .   .

After dinner at the hotel, the team gathered in a small conference room on the second level. Frankie passed out schedules and practice plans to each player. Ecko called the team to order and demanded attention. He said, "Okay, here's our schedule for tomorrow, so listen carefully. At seven a.m. sharp we meet here in this room for the first call home. Tomorrow is July the fourteenth and your families are waiting to hear from you around two p.m. East Africa is seven hours ahead of Orlando. Breakfast is here at the hotel at seven-thirty. I know you're still jet-lagged, so go to bed early tonight. Very early. At eight-fifteen, the vans leave for practice back at a high school. We practice from nine to noon, three hours and it will be intense. Memorize the practice plans before you go to sleep tonight and memorize them again before breakfast. At noon we return here to shower and eat lunch. At one-thirty we leave for UCF where we'll stay for an hour, watch part of a practice, then leave at three and go to Rollins College to check out the venue and watch part of another practice. At five we leave Rollins, come back here, change, leave here at six-thirty, go back to the high school for a one-hour shootaround. Back here for dinner at eight, bed at ten."

As he spoke his tone became sharper, and by the time he finished he sounded like a drill sergeant. "Got it?" he barked.

The responses were the usual, casual acknowledgments that the coach had said something.

Ecko looked at Quinton Majok and asked, "Quinton, who, in your opinion, is the dumbest player on this team?"

Majok, already established as one of the team clowns, pointed without hesitation to his roommate, Awino Leyano. "Him," he said.

Ecko said, "Stand up, Awino."

He slowly unwound all eighty inches and smiled at his coach. Ecko said, "Okay, Awino, give me back tomorrow's schedule, in perfect order."

Awino stopped smiling and said, "Well, first of all, Coach, I'm much smarter than Quinton."

"We'll see. The schedule, please."

"Okay, here at seven to call home, then breakfast at seven-thirty, then take the van to practice, from nine to noon, three whole hours which is a lot more than I need, then back here for lunch. Leave here at one-thirty for UCF, stay there until three, then go to Rollins, stay there until five, then back here to change and go to a shootaround, then come back here and eat."

Ecko stared at him as if he had just stabbed someone. Finally, he asked, "What time do we leave here for the shootaround?"

"Uh, six."

"No! Wrong! Sit down."

Awino folded himself back into his chair. Ecko glared at the others and growled, "Samuel, what time do we leave here for the shootaround?"

"Six-thirty."

"And what time is dinner tomorrow night?"

"Eight."

"Thank you." As Ecko paced a bit his team seemed stunned by his harshness. Then he continued, "If you're late for, or miss, a meal, a meeting, a van ride, or anything scheduled, it's an automatic one-game suspension. No questions asked. Listen to me and to Coach Moka and hear what we say. Each night I will give you the schedule for the next day and I will ask one of you to recite it back to me perfectly. Understood? Pay attention."

CHAPTER 9

There was no cellular service in Lotta and very little in Rumbek, but Ayak Sooleymon had arranged a favor from a local military leader, a lieutenant in the regular army. At exactly 2 p.m. on July 14, he was sitting under a shade tree near the Sooleymon home holding a satellite phone and chatting with Ayak, Beatrice, Angelina, James, Chol, and about a dozen curious neighbors. The call came from an American number at ten minutes after two.

Samuel was on the line, using Ecko's cell phone.

The lieutenant said, "Greetings, Samuel, how are you?"

"Very fine, sir. I'm in Orlando and we are preparing for the games."

"Excellent, Samuel."

"How are things in Lotta?" Always a dangerous question.

"We are good, Samuel, and we are very proud of you. I will now hand the sat phone to your father. Good luck over there, son."

Ayak took the bulky sat phone, said "Hello, Samuel," then listened as his son asked about each family member. All were doing well. How was the flight? Samuel said it was long and tiring but also exciting. Beatrice took the phone and asked what he was eating. A lot of pizza and tacos, delicious stuff. Angelina was next and Samuel described their day at Disney World. Epcot was next, after a lot of basketball. James and Chol got only a few seconds of air time, but they were thrilled nonetheless to hear Samuel's voice. Ringing off, he promised his father he would call back in five days as scheduled, and he would have much more to talk about. He thanked the lieutenant, who promised to make his sat phone available for all calls.

Samuel handed the cell phone to Ecko, thanked him, then raced to breakfast. Quinton Majok was on Frankie's phone. Other players were waiting. The five living in America had cell phones. None of the South Sudanese owned one.

Game One: South Sudan versus Croatia

In the handsome locker room of the Alfond Sports Center at Rollins College, the boys from South Sudan dressed quietly in their humble uniforms and new Reeboks and listened to their coach. Ecko was saying, "For the tournament here in Orlando, the games are a bit different. There will be three periods of ten minutes each with five minutes in between, no half-time. The games will last about an hour instead of two. You've seen the schedule and you know the games are stacked up. You'll play seven in eight days, so someone here is worried about your legs. Not me. Not Coach Moka. If we make it to St. Louis, the format will revert to two twenty-minute halves with a fifteen-minute break. Right now I'm not thinking about St. Louis. They've placed us in the bracket with the toughest competition. Any questions?"

Nothing from the team. "Now, C Squad will play the first period, B the second, A the third. There is no first string or second. Frankie and I will rejuggle the squads before the next game. Each of you will play ten minutes and we expect ten minutes of all-out, balls-to-the-wall hustle."

Quinton Majok shot up a hand and said, "Coach. Balls-to-the-wall? I'm sorry."

Ecko laughed and said, "Yeah, right, my bad. It's American slang for throw everything you've got at your target, your opponent, whatever you happen to be doing or facing."

Quinton said, "I like it."

"Good. Anyway, nonstop hustle. Aggressive man-to-man D. Crash the glass. Block out everybody. Take only good shots. Let's start out rough, lots of hacking and holding and see how the refs will call it. These are Division I refs and they're used to a physical game. Any questions?"

"Yeah, Coach, where did balls-to-the-wall come from?" asked Quinton.

"I think it was Michael Jordan. That good enough?"

They took the floor in their simple uniforms, no fancy warm-up outfits, no customized jackets or tear-away pants. As they jogged through the standard layup line, they shot glances at the other end. In a stark contrast, the Croatians were all white, and very well turned out in red-and-white warm-ups with the pants boldly striped, obviously copied from Indiana.

Samuel bounced on his toes, fidgeted nervously, fist-pumped his teammates, waited for the ball, and couldn't help but take in the surroundings: the beautiful and modern gym of a wealthy small college, the scouts lounging in the seats at midcourt, the three cocky refs, the atmosphere of big-time basketball in America. But where were all those cute cheerleaders they always showed on television?

He was the point guard for C Squad, up first and raring to go. Ecko huddled the entire team for a few fiery words. He said he wanted mayhem on the court and nonstop racket from the bench.

Koosh Koosh was six feet ten, two inches taller than Awino Leyano, but he came nowhere near the tip-off. Awino slammed it back to Samuel who sprinted past everyone, drove hard to the rim, and missed an easy layup. On offense, the Croatians took their time and screened hard. With four seconds on the shot clock, Koosh Koosh got the ball behind the arc and nailed a beautiful 30-footer.

A 2-3 zone awaited Samuel when he crossed mid-court. Ecko had predicted this. His players were known for their soaring dunks, alley-oops, and easy put-backs, but not for their long-range bombing. They could expect tight zones that dared them to shoot long.

Samuel missed his first, and badly. Koosh Koosh hit his second three. Evidently, he was immune from the jitters.

Three minutes in, the first foul was called, a shooting violation on a Croatian forward, and Riak Kuol went to the line. The pause was needed, and Samuel stopped near the bench and looked at Ecko who said, "You gotta relax, man. Run the offense, take your time. These guys are a bunch of douchebags."

Samuel, breathing heavily, repeated, "Douchebags, Coach?"

"Sorry. Cocky, overrated. Just settle down."

Riak missed the first, made the second, and they were on the board, but behind 12–1. At five minutes, Croatia sent in three subs, but Ecko had no plans to substitute. At six minutes, and trailing 16–1, he called his only time-out of the period. He sat down the five starters, smiled at them though they did not return the smiles, and said, "I assume you guys plan to snag a field goal or two here in the first period."

All five looked at their Reeboks.

.   .   .

The tournament was about winning and losing, and national pride, and bragging rights, and all that. It was about the folks back home, watching, when able, the games on a large-screen television hung outside a town hall and yelling at the sight of a player they knew. It would be a notch in Ecko's belt, were he to win or place, something to add to his résumé as he dreamed of a head coaching job. But it wasn't called a showcase for nothing. It was more about the players and the scouts there to watch them, and boys' dreams of playing in America.

Ecko wanted to win as badly as any coach, but beyond that he wanted his kids to have more opportunities. So, he encouraged them to take chances, to shine. He loathed selfish players and promised to bench anyone for taking a terrible shot, but he wanted every kid to look good.

· · ·

Awino Leyano put back a miss, stuffed it hard, and there was the first field goal. Riak Kuol blocked a shot at the stripe, swatted the ball to Samuel, who sprinted downcourt but pulled up. When the defense relaxed he was wide open and nailed a 25-foot jumper. It was gorgeous, and Ecko glanced at Frankie. From way behind the arc, Samuel jumped high, though unguarded, and released the ball with near perfect form.

After ten minutes of frantic play, the buzzer sounded—the first period was over. Croatia led 21-15. C Squad was drained, drenched, ready to sit for a few minutes. They watched B Squad struggle with the same jitters and fall behind by 12.

Samuel enjoyed the break, the cold water, the role of a temporary spectator. He had scored two buckets, had a steal and only one turnover. Not a bad first outing. He caught his breath and looked at the scouts sitting across the way behind the scorer's table. Half were white, half were black, most were young, under forty, all dressed casually, not a single necktie or suit anywhere. Most wore polo shirts with school colors and logos, and from across the court Samuel could spot assistant coaches from UNC, Syracuse, Kansas, and Oregon. They laughed and talked and had only a casual interest in the game. They all seemed to know each other. Behind them was a row of video cameras, and Ecko had explained that all games are filmed and any coach can get all the tape he wanted.

What would it take to make an impression? That was the question every player was asking himself. For Samuel, it was speed, quickness, his extraordinary vertical leap, and the fact that he was growing like a wild weed.

After the second period, Croatia was up 40-30. Samuel and C Squad were rested and ready to go, but they were done for the day. In the last period, Mr. Dak Marial established himself as a true All-American and took charge of the game. When Alek Garang hit two straight threes, the Croatians ventured out from their suffocating zone and Dak went to work underneath.

Samuel watched the game and cheered for his team, but he also kept an eye on the scouts. With Dak in the game, along with Koosh Koosh and Alek Garang, the scouts were showing more interest. All had cell phones and worked them constantly.

With a minute to go, Alek tied the game at 52 with another three-pointer, and the South Sudan bench went wild. Both teams missed bad shots, and with 18 seconds to go Riak was called for a shooting foul. With an exuberant wide grin he asked the referee, "What?" The ref wanted to tee him up but relaxed and warned him. The Croatian guard hit both free throws, and Alek missed a last-second shot.

Game over. Croatia 54, South Sudan 52.

. . .

No team was expected to go undefeated. The year before, Ecko had taken a 5–2 team to the finals and almost won it all. In the locker room, he reminded the team of this and told them to shake it off. They had six more games and shouldn't worry about the first one.

They showered, changed, and went back to the court to watch one of the American teams play the Italians.

CHAPTER 10

Game Two: South Sudan versus Italy

As promised, Ecko and Frankie retooled the squads and started C against the Italians, who had lost by 20 to a hotshot American team. The game was at CFE Arena, on the UCF campus, and it was by far the finest basketball court any of the South Sudanese had ever seen. There were almost 10,000 seats, and though most of them were empty they still made for an impressive sight.

Dak Marial was on C, along with a 6'6" shooting forward named Jimmie Abaloy, a Sudanese American who had lived seventeen of his eighteen years in Trenton, New Jersey. He started the game nicely with three consecutive long-range jumpers, and the Italians never caught up.

Samuel played the second period with B Squad and missed all three of his shots. After two games, it was clear to him that he was the third-best point guard, after Alek Garang and Abraham Bol. But, at 6'4" and growing, he wasn't sure how long he would be considered a point guard or even a shooting guard. Ecko wasn't sure either.

After a 13-point win over Italy, the players showered and watched the next game. Each took up at least two seats and they enjoyed popcorn and sodas, just like real fans. Four players from the U.K.

stopped by and said hello, and soon they were making friends. Two of the Italians saw the crowd and came over. One had signed with Texas Tech, the other committed to Central Michigan, and their English was quite good.

An assistant coach in an Auburn shirt appeared and said hello to Jimmie Abaloy. They stepped away, walked to an upper level and sat in a section all alone. They talked and laughed for a while. Samuel watched them with great envy.

So, that's how it happens.

Game Three: South Sudan versus Ukraine

It was Thursday, July 16, the day the players would remember because all eight teams would play in four straight games at the Amway Center, the NBA palace that was home to the Magic. Ecko and his team arrived early and were given a tour of the cavernous arena. They walked around the empty court and soaked in the incredible atmosphere of basketball heaven. Samuel tried hard to convince himself that he was standing on the same wood where LeBron had played, and Kobe, Shaq, Niollo, and Steph Curry. Their guide led them off the court, through a tunnel, and they stopped at a wide door with the words "Magic Locker Room" painted in the team's colors. She opened the door and they stepped inside for the highlight of every tour. The locker room was hard to grasp—wide and round, wood-paneled with thick, luxurious blue and silver carpet. There were fifteen lockers in a semicircle, each wide and deep enough to hold a small vehicle. There were luxury recliners, large television screens, anything a player could really want. Down the hall was a team room, a television room, a cafeteria, a training room, a weight room, a media room, and a shower with enough private stalls to accommodate several teams of sweaty players. And there were other rooms that they didn't have enough time to explore.

After the locker room, they rode an escalator to the second level and strolled along an empty concourse that looped around the entire court. They stopped at the luxury suites, one with an open door, and were invited to take a look from the corporate view. A hostess fixed them sodas and offered snacks and they were enjoying the fine seating when a vice president popped in and said hello. He welcomed them to the home of the Magic, and to Orlando, and to America, and said he was looking forward to the afternoon's games. It was almost noon and he asked if they'd had lunch. Ecko said they had not, and the VP spoke to his assistant and arranged lunch back in the locker room, in the players' cafeteria. He told them to finish their tour and he'd meet them down there in half an hour.

All fifteen players dreamed of the NBA, but at that moment each one knew that this was his future.

The guide took them to the top level, to the cheap seats, and from way up there the court did indeed look far away. There were 20,000 seats in the arena and Samuel knew that the Magic had been averaging about 17,000 per home game, so he figured many of these seats had not been used that much. However, he did not ask the guide for any figures. That might have been perceived as unkind.

Ecko insisted on perfect manners and behavior off the court. They were representing their people and others were quick to judge. Nothing but politeness, lots of smiles, and humility. They were lucky to be there and should show their gratitude at every chance.

They were excited to return to the locker room. The dining table was prepared for them with box lunches and soft drinks, and they were eating and chatting excitedly when, suddenly, everything went silent.

The great Niollo walked into the room. The boys froze. All food and drink were forgotten. Wide-eyed, slack-jawed, stunned, they gawked at him and tried to decide if he was really there. Ecko, an old friend, embraced him and introduced Frankie, then said to the team, "Gentlemen, Niollo has driven up from Miami to watch you play."

Niollo smiled and said warmly, "Welcome to Florida, my brethren, and greetings from Miami. I'm sure you feel right at home here because it's almost as hot as South Sudan." They laughed nervously. Niollo! The greatest of all players from their country.

He continued, "As you know, I was born in Wau, but left the country when I was a kid and went to the U.K. with my family."

They had his bio memorized. As he talked, reality slowly settled in. They knew he had just finished another losing season with the Heat, his fourth team, after spending his first eight seasons with Boston. Things were not going well in Miami and he was expected to move on. He was now thirty years old and at his peak, still great and always a legend back home.

Ecko thanked him for dropping by and said, "What Niollo would never brag about is that he has won both the NBA Sportsmanship Award and the Citizenship Award. He supports many charities and youth sports programs in our country, and he is responsible for you being here. Thank you, Niollo."

Niollo smiled and tried to deflect any more attention. Instead, he said, "Thanks. Can I have a sandwich?" He sat at the table, surrounded by the starstruck kids, and between bites talked to them for half an hour. When it was time to go, a photographer with the Magic took a hundred photos and promised to deliver them later in the day.

Niollo walked with them out of the locker room, onto the court, and into the prime seats where they watched the U.K. beat Brazil in the first game. In the second one, with Niollo cheering them on, they played their brand of inspired basketball and easily manhandled a bunch of Ukrainians, 73–43, with half the team getting double figures. Samuel did not, but was happy he hit three of six from long range.

Game Four: South Sudan versus Brazil

On the front page of its sports section, the *Orlando Sentinel* ran a large photo of Niollo sitting in the seats surrounded by his boys from South Sudan. That, plus the 30-point thrashing of a good

Ukrainian team, brought more attention to Ecko and his players. When they tipped off against the Brazilians, there were a few more spectators in the stands at UCF. And, more important, more scouts, or at least that's what Samuel thought he saw during pregame warm-ups.

He realized he preferred the college court over the NBA arena. The seats, though empty, were closer, and the rims and backboards didn't look as far away. Then he laughed at himself and remembered the dirt and mud courts where he came from.

He didn't start against Brazil. His squad for the game was B and Ecko planned for them to play the third period. However, bad luck struck just seconds after the opening tip when Alek Garang went down with a pulled hamstring and limped off the court. Trainers from UCF took him to the dressing room and sent for the team doctor. Ecko yelled for Samuel to get in the game at the two—shooting guard. Abraham Bol had the point, Samuel's usual spot, and the offense was disoriented and sputtered badly. South Sudan trailed by 10 after the first period. Squad C, with Dak Marial hammering inside, cut the deficit in half, and after two the score was 41–36.

In the third period, Samuel returned to the court at the point and the offense found its rhythm, especially when Jimmie Abaloy got hot from the arc. He loosened up the defense and Samuel began feeding the ball inside to Quinton Majok. After a 14–2 run the Brazilians used their only time-out in an attempt to regroup and cool things off. It didn't work. Samuel hit two consecutive threes and South Sudan was up by 13. Brazil had more inside height and heft than any team in the tournament and kept going low for easier buckets. That didn't work either. Time and again, their shots were blocked, swatted away, and slapped into the stands by the kids who could seemingly spring over the backboard.

With two minutes to go, Ecko noticed their big man, Daniel Abdul-Gaber, trailing a play. He was winded and needed a break. Ecko used his only time-out and asked Daniel if he wanted to come out. On this team, the answer was always no.

"Good," Ecko said. "Look at me. We're up by fourteen and we got the game. Let's win by twenty. These guys are cocky and think they're good. Right now we're handing them their asses, but I want more. Two minutes to play and I want nonstop balls to the wall, okay? Can you do it?"

All five smiled, grabbed hands, and yelled, "Let's go."

Showing no mercy while still playing with their usual exuberance—high fives, chest bumps, low fives, shouts of encouragement, even laughter—they ran the Brazilians out of the gym and won by 24.

CHAPTER 11

After four straight games it was time for a break. On Saturday, July 18, Ecko and Frankie filled the two vans and took the players back to La-La Land, this time to Epcot. They deposited them at the gate with the same instructions and warnings, gave them enough cash to enjoy themselves, said they would be back promptly at six, and said goodbye. The boys were almost as excited as they were before a game.

Ecko and Frankie returned to UCF and went to the coaches' suite for a long day of private, unscheduled meetings with scouts. It was the networking game, the match-making, the convincing, evaluating, and promising routines that were part of their job. Because South Sudan was so far away and so far off the radar, and because its competitive leagues were still primitive compared to most of the world's, especially those of the U.S., U.K., and Europe, its coaches felt compelled to lobby harder for their players.

An assistant from Ohio State asked about Alek Garang's hamstring. As expected, Alek was getting his share of interest, and his injury was generating plenty of gossip. Ecko repeated what the doctor had said: It wasn't a severe pull but he would need to sit out a few games. An assistant from Memphis wanted to talk about Riak Kuol and worried that he needed another year of high school play, in the U.S. The head coach from Lehigh was impressed with Quinton Majok. Ecko thought the kid could play at a higher level and said so. The head coach from Overland, a well-known New Jersey prep school that was nothing but a basketball factory, wanted to talk about Abraham Bol, and Ecko gave him plenty of time. However, he would never advise one of his players to enroll there. An assistant from Eastern Illinois was a former teammate at Kent State and wanted Ecko's inside scoop on Awino Leyano. Ecko thought it was a good match, but he knew that his old pal had one more year on a contract that would not be renewed.

And so the day went. Greetings from an old friend or a new acquaintance, followed by a private chat as they stepped outside the suite and walked around the arena. All conversations were private, all scouts careful not to say something that might be heard by another. Ecko played it straight and was honest about each of his players and their potential. It was counterproductive to exaggerate someone's talent, or brag about his work ethic, or pass along inside information about the kid and his family. The proof was on the court for everyone to see. Three of his players were drawing no interest, and he understood why. They would never play in the U.S.

After four games, the players had been watched by hundreds of college and high school scouts, and as the tournament progressed the interest in the best ones intensified.

After lunch, in the suite, the head coach at North Carolina Central appeared and got a bear hug from Ecko. His name was Lonnie Britt and he had played four years at Toledo. He had also played against Ecko, and they had been friends ever since. For three years, they had been assistants together at Northern Iowa and had spent many pleasant hours together with their wives and young children. Ecko thought Lonnie had the potential to head coach at the highest level, but so far his four years at NC Central had not attracted much attention.

He took a seat between Ecko and Frankie and asked loudly, "Okay, who do you have for me?"

"Who do you want?"

"Give me Alek Garang, Quinton Majok, and Jimmie Abaloy, for starters."

"Is that all?" Those three were likely headed to bigger programs. NC Central was a historically black school in Durham and played in the Mid-Eastern Athletic Conference against similar colleges. It was often referred to as "that other school in Durham."

"How about Abraham Bol?"

They were watching a loaded American team, Houston Gold, pick apart the team from Croatia. Frankie was called aside by an assistant from Southern Mississippi, and they soon drifted away.

Ecko said, "Bol says he's too good for college, gonna declare for the draft."

They laughed and joked some more. When the suite was practically empty, Ecko said, "Let's take a hike."

They walked to the upper deck and found seats. Ecko said, "I got a kid that I really like. Samuel Sooleymon, still only seventeen and growing."

Lonnie said, "I saw him Thursday against Ukraine. Didn't show too well."

"He's a little rough around the edges, needs another year of high school here, but so far no luck."

It was often harder to match up players with private high schools than colleges because so few of their coaches were at the tournaments. And virtually no public high school coaches bothered with the events. Getting a foreign kid assimilated into a new town meant moving the family, and finding a host, and then there was the always troublesome issue of being accused of recruiting. The public high school coaches had plenty of homegrown talent and the foreign kids were usually headaches. The prep schools and basketball academies were more aggressive in their recruiting, but they too had plenty of players.

"I didn't see much," Britt said.

"Give him another look. We play this Gold team tomorrow at Rollins and he'll see more action with Garang on the sideline."

"He's not a point guard."

"No, he's not. At the rate he's growing he'll be playing the three by the fall."

"I didn't like his shot."

"He's a work in progress, Lonnie. Trust me."

"That's just what I need in my program right now. Kids who can't play but just may have some potential."

"I know, I know, but right now your program needs some help."

Lonnie managed to laugh. "Who else is looking at him?"

The great question. College coaches were cocky in their belief that they could spot talent, but they were always insecure enough to want validation. Thus, the standard question: "Who else is looking at him?"

"Everybody," Ecko said with a laugh.

"Gee, I've never heard that before."

.   .   .

Other than the three open-air schools, the only building with any official status in Lotta was Our Lady's Chapel, a small hand-some stone-and-brick sanctuary built by the Rumbek diocese ten years earlier. A priest from there arrived each Saturday afternoon for Mass and the entire village turned out. The front pews were reserved for the village elders and their wives, some with multiple spouses, and the younger families who arrived early found seats inside. The crowd always spilled out and covered the small courtyard.

Long before the service began, the priest sought out Ayak and Beatrice. He had a small gift for them, a copy of Thursday's edition of the *Juba Monitor*. On the front page of Section B was the photo of Niollo sitting in the seats at the Amway Center, surrounded by the smiling faces of the team from South Sudan. Above his left shoulder and leaning into the picture was Samuel. His parents were thrilled and gawked at the photo before sharing it with everyone else. Beatrice was so excited she could hardly breathe.

Later, from the altar, the priest waved the newspaper and informed the congregation that after four games their team had won three and lost one. According to the newspaper, the boys were playing well and getting lots of attention.

And he had even better news. Tomorrow, Sunday, a wide-screen television would be hung above the front steps of the church, and at 8 p.m. sharp the game would be televised for the entire village to watch. The Sooleymon family would be given front row seats.

Nothing else he said during Mass would be remembered.

CHAPTER 12

Game Five: South Sudan versus Houston Gold

Gold was a nationally known AAU program financed by a wealthy Texas businessman who loved the game, had played in college, and wanted his three sons to excel and become stars. It was his pet project and he spared no expense. The teams, and there were at least a dozen of them for ages twelve through eighteen, held tryout camps throughout Texas and recruited the best players. Making the team meant a year-round commitment to playing in the top showcase tournaments, being taught by coaches who were well paid, traveling by luxury bus or even by air, and being inundated with gear and equipment most colleges would envy. The boss cut a sponsorship deal with Nike and the players were rumored to have at least five different uniforms. Not surprisingly, the program had produced dozens of college players and two alumni were in the NBA.

Playing for Houston Gold meant scouts were always watching. The players were gifted and special and they were constantly reminded of this. Their swagger was legendary, to the point that some college coaches shied away from the program, but not many.

For the early game at Rollins, they took the floor in their snazzy NBA-style warm-ups and refused to look at the other end of the court. There, the boys from South Sudan were hamming it up in their simple, phys-ed-style uniforms, unimpressed with Gold's greatness, unbowed by their four easy wins.

Gold had played the day before. Ecko's team had not, and he decided to go with tempo and try to run them into the ground. He pressed full-court and wanted shots early in the clock. It worked beautifully in the first period as Samuel and Abraham Bol forced three turnovers and Riak Kuol blocked two shots down low.

All five Gold starters were rising high school seniors. Four had committed to big schools. Though they were well coached, they were, of course, individual stars, and this often led to some low-percentage circus shots. Feeling the pressure, their guards missed four straight from downtown, and their fiery coach used his only time-out for a tongue-lashing.

.   .   .

On the other side of the world, the village of Lotta was packed around the television hanging below the cross of Our Lady's Chapel and roared with every good play.

When Samuel hit his first, and only, three-pointer, his people screamed, yelled, gave glory to God, jumped up and down, and pounded Ayak on the shoulders. There were some chairs scattered about but no one could sit.

.   .   .

South Sudan led by 11 at the end of the first period. Ecko put in C Squad, his best in his opinion, with Dak Marial and Quinton Majok at the forwards. Gold went with a smaller lineup and fresher legs, and the coach slowed down the game. The highlight reel shooting stopped and its offense began to click. After the second period South Sudan was up by 9.

The third period belonged to Benjie Boone, a 6'5" shooting

guard who had committed to play at Kentucky but was rumored to be reconsidering and thinking about the NBA draft. He hit three straight bombs and tied the score. There were six lead changes down the stretch as both teams fought and clawed. Gold kept substituting. Ecko did not. He had promised his players equal time on the court and would stick to his word regardless of the score. He rotated Samuel and Bol at the point, but only because he had to. Alek Garang was suited up but couldn't play.

And he was greatly missed. Neither Samuel nor Bol could buy a basket late in the game, and with no threat outside, the defense smothered Dak Marial and Quinton Majok in the paint. Gold pulled away and won by six.

In the locker room, Ecko took responsibility for the loss, said he'd been outcoached and had decided to try something different. After five games his goal of equal playing time wasn't working and he and Frankie would start substituting more. More hustle, scoring, and defense would mean more playing time.

The boys were crushed and understood what Ecko was saying. He reminded them that last year's team lost two games but qualified for the national showcase, then almost won it. They were still alive with two games to go but they could not afford another loss.

Samuel stood and said, "Say, Coach. We got the rest of the day. How about we find a high school gym and have a good practice?"

Ecko replied, "I don't know. You play tomorrow."

"Come on, Coach," said Dak Marial, the unofficial captain. Others chimed in and the request quickly became unanimous.

.   .   .

In Lotta, the villagers were much quieter as they drifted away from the church and returned home. The loss stung but the thrill of seeing Samuel playing in America had not dissipated. Tomorrow's game would not begin until 10 p.m. their time, and everyone would be back at the church to watch their hero.

· · ·

Late Sunday night, after the players were in their rooms and all lights were off, Ecko went down to the hotel bar and met Lonnie Britt for a beer. They had shared many in their younger days when coaching at Northern Iowa and they treasured these little reunions. In a dark corner they replayed the day's game, with Lonnie full of wisdom about what his friend did wrong.

Ecko listened and agreed with most of the criticism. He would have done the same if Lonnie had lost.

Lonnie said, "But you're not supposed to beat those guys, Ecko. They're cherry-picked and treated like pros. They dressed out twelve today. Twelve seventeen-year-old kids who are still in high school and who'll sign with big schools. It's a pretty amazing program. A lot of talent."

"We should've beat them," Ecko said, sipping his beer. "I'm worried about advancing. My guys are not ready to go home."

"You'll win the next two."

"Don't say that."

"You know the greatest play I saw today?" Lonnie asked with a smile.

"The block?"

"The block. That kid came out of nowhere and looked eight feet tall."

"I told you."

With four minutes to go and South Sudan up by one, Benjie Boone bounced off a screen at the top of the key and pulled up wide open from 25 feet. Samuel, who was guarding him, was nowhere to be seen, until the last possible second. Boone, smooth as silk, lifted high with his perfect and uncontested jump shot. Samuel launched himself from the free throw line and slapped the ball hard just as it left Boone's right hand. The ball landed in the third row of seats.

The All-American was so rattled he did not make another shot.

Lonnie shook his head and said, "He looked ten feet off the ground."

"Well, his standing vertical leap is thirty-four inches. Forty-five when he's moving. Give him a running start and he can jump over the backboard."

"But he can't shoot and he can't dribble."

"He's coming around, okay? He works incredibly hard and he's still growing."

"Who else is looking at him?"

Ecko smiled and shook his head. "Truthfully, no one right now. If I were you I'd take a chance."

A waitress brought a bowl of pretzels and inquired about another round. No thanks. Maybe later.

Lonnie frowned and glanced around. "I got a problem, Ecko. A new one."

"What is it?"

"Two of my players were arrested last night in Durham."

"For what?"

"Armed robbery."

"Oh, come on, Lonnie. You serious?"

"As a heart attack. A couple of real blockheads. They're in summer school, most of my kids are, and they went out on Saturday night and found some serious trouble."

"What happened?"

"I don't know all the facts but I've been on the phone all day. My AD. The President. The police. But they ain't saying much. Looks like the boys went to a party, smoked some pot, and got in the car with the wrong guy. They had plenty of pot but ran out of beer. The driver stopped at a convenience store, and for some reason decided it would be smart to pull a gun and rob the cashier. Fortunately he didn't pull the trigger. All three are charged with armed robbery. AD says they gotta go. Now."

"Good kids?"

Lonnie took a sip of beer and kept frowning. "Good guys, I love 'em, but both come from bad homes. One, Clancy, has a brother in prison. He was my number seven last season, played 15 minutes a game. A junior with little time for classwork. The other, Fonzo we call him, will be a sophomore and is pretty lazy. I have great kids, Ecko, for the most part."

"But the kids are not armed robbers. Sounds like little more than a dumb mistake."

"Yeah, but they're facing serious charges."

"You gotta replace them?"

"Yep, for this season anyway. I have to meet the AD and the lawyers tomorrow and they'll try to work a deal. But the kids are out of the program for at least a year."

"Sooleymon?"

"I'm thinking, okay? Be honest with me, Ecko."

"When have I ever been dishonest?"

"Never. But you do love your players."

"Same as you."

"Sure, most of the time."

"Lonnie, Samuel could be the steal of the tournament. He's not getting looks because he's not scoring. But he will. When I first saw him back in April he had the worst jump shot in Africa. He's come a long way and he's still working hard. And growing."

"He'll never be a point guard."

"No. Forget the point. He'll be at least six six by Christmas."

"What about classwork?"

"He's from the bush, okay? He just finished secondary school in his village so you gotta figure he'll need some help. Surely you can get him in."

"Probably so. Central is not exactly like the other school in Durham."

"Oh, so you think Duke worries about SAT scores?"

They shared a laugh and ordered another beer. Ecko was excited by the possibility and pushed even harder. At midnight, Lonnie glanced at his watch and said, "I need to go. I can't stick around for the game tomorrow. I have an early flight to Durham and meet with the AD at noon. Then, I have the pleasure of going to the jail."

"Sorry man. Gotta be tough."

"You got it. Imagine telling two twenty-year-olds that they're kicked out of school for at least a year."

"Sounds like they have bigger problems."

"Can you believe that my entire career hinges on the decisions made by a bunch of immature kids?"

"Didn't we have this conversation twenty years ago?"

"We did. And nothing has changed."

"Sign Sooleymon. He'll make you a genius."

CHAPTER 13

In 1979, Chevron discovered oil in the southern region of Sudan and soon realized that the country had the third largest reserves on the continent. After a few years, the Sudanese ruling party in Khartoum nationalized its oil fields, kicked out the Americans, and signed a lucrative deal to sell all its crude to China. By the mid-1980s, $12 billion a year was flowing into Sudan. With various civil wars raging throughout the country—North versus South, Islamic versus Catholic, tribe versus tribe—the oil riches only intensified the conflicts. In 2011, South Sudan was given the right to choose independence, and it did so overwhelmingly. Supported by billions in foreign aid from the U.S. and Europe, and propped up by oil revenues, South Sudan became the world's newest country and its future seemed bright. Most of the money, though, remained in Juba as the ruling elites siphoned off billions and feasted on the unlimited cash. While they stashed it in Swiss banks, and bought apartments in London and mansions in Melbourne, and sent their kids to the Ivies, and armed their soldiers with an astonishing arsenal of guns, tanks, and helicopters, the people suffered even more. The money was not used for schools, hospitals, roads, or infrastructure.

The peace was fragile and temporary. Ethnic rivalries grew more bitter as half a dozen warlords and strongmen jockeyed for more of the money and a seat at the table. In 2013, yet another civil war erupted and the new country spiraled into violent chaos. Tribal lines were fortified as heavily armed militias attacked and burned villages, then waited for retaliation. The atrocities shocked the world. At least 400,000 people were murdered. At least four million, mostly women and children, were displaced and forced to scramble to safety in sprawling refugee camps.

Peace agreements came and went. The best way for a guerrilla commander to get the attention of Juba, and a bigger slice of the pie, was to burn some villages, commit some atrocities, and leave the rotting corpses in the mud for the benefit of Western cameras. After some of this mischief, Juba might offer another peace deal, with cash and arms to boot.

. . .

Among the proud villagers who watched Samuel and his team on the big screen were some spies, sent in to take the measure of the town.

Just after midnight, the gunfire erupted. Beatrice heard it first, woke Ayak from a deep sleep, and yelled for the children to put on their shoes. The sickening *Tak-Tak-Tak-Tak* of the Kalashnikovs was a sound they had heard before. The family ran outside and joined their neighbors who were trying to determine where the gunfire was. It seemed to be coming from everywhere, and plenty of it. People were yelling, pointing, and running in different directions.

Suddenly, lights appeared and a military truck rumbled down the dirt street. Soldiers jumped out, brandishing their Kallies. One look and the people knew they were rebel soldiers, not regular army. They fired at random into the air and began yelling for the men to form a single line. A fourteen-year-old boy, a neighborhood kid well-known to all, broke and ran toward an alley, and was gunned down like a stray dog. His mother screamed and his father started toward him when a soldier knocked him down with the butt of his rifle.

"Hands up! Hands up!" the commander barked at the other men. *Tak-Tak-Tak-Tak*. The gunfire was horrifying and more soldiers swarmed through the village, grabbing men and older teenage boys.

Ayak managed to say to Beatrice, "Run! Take them and run to the bush."

Other women and children were scurrying about, not sure which direction was safe. Was anywhere safe? A gasoline bomb was tossed into the hut across the street from the Sooleymons' and it was quickly engulfed in flames. Then there were fires everywhere, up and down the street.

The men were marched in a group toward the center of town, passing other burning homes. A fifteen-year-old girl was wrestled away from her mother, stripped naked, and shoved to the rear of a troop truck. Near the church, men from throughout the village were streaming in, all with their hands up.

"We're just having a meeting," a commander kept yelling through the mayhem. "Hurry up! Hurry up!"

When the men were out of sight, some of the soldiers remained and went about their business of torching the homes, laughing as they did. Beatrice managed to ease into the darkness with Angelina, James, and Chol, who tripped over a dead body and shrieked. "Hush!" his mother warned. Other women and children were looking for places to hide and somewhere to run. For a moment they stopped and listened to the horror of popping fires, Kallies, and the screams of their neighbors.

At the church, the men were ordered inside, and when it was full the rebels kept packing in more men and boys until they were pressed together so tightly they had trouble breathing. More kept coming and when they could no longer fit inside, the commander ordered them to lie down, outside, in the dirt around the church.

Two soldiers opened fire on the wide-screen television and destroyed it. The gunfire rattled the men inside and they cried for help. On cue, incendiary bombs were tossed through the four windows and the front door and three hundred prisoners screamed in blazing agony. One man, his clothing on fire, jumped through a window and was met with a hail of bullets. Other men jumped too and were easily gunned down in target practice. Ayak made it to the front door and was killed on the steps under the remnants of the television.

Outside, some of the men lying facedown in the dirt broke and ran, only to be slaughtered. The killing was for sport and thoroughly indiscriminate. Flames and thick black smoke poured from the windows as the dying prisoners continued to scream, their voices fading.

Beatrice and her children crept in the black darkness and found a pig trail that led out of town. Hundreds of other women were moving and whispering. The lights of a troop truck washed over them and they hid in a patch of thorns. Suddenly there was gunfire nearby and the voices of angry guerrillas. A woman screamed as she was shot. The women saw the silhouettes of more soldiers on foot behind them, coming, looking for them. The children followed Beatrice through a thicket away from the road and were soon lost in the blackness. In a small opening they stopped and looked down at their village. Dozens of fires were raging and the guns were still rattling away. James and Chol were crying and Angelina hushed them into silence. They eased on, always aware that others were nearby, moving as quietly as possible, going somewhere. They stumbled into an opening and came face-to-face with a squad of guerrillas guarding a group of women and children. They barked at Beatrice and her children to sit down and they did.

"Where are you going?" the leader demanded.

She was too traumatized to respond and had nothing to say anyway. A teenager with a gun walked over and told Angelina to stand up. Another joined him and they stripped off her clothing.

"Please, no, please!" Beatrice begged, and one of them kicked her in the face.

Another teenage girl was stripped, and she and Angelina were led away, naked. Minutes passed as Beatrice tried to breathe and fight back the tears as she wiped blood off her forehead. Without a word, the guerrillas disappeared into the darkness, and the women scrambled away with their children.

. . .

At noon, Monday, July 20, the players met in the hotel conference room for their scheduled calls home. Using Ecko's cell phone, Samuel punched in the number of the lieutenant's satellite phone. There was no answer. He tried again, and half an hour later tried once more. This was troubling but not terribly disturbing. All communications in South Sudan were unreliable.

CHAPTER 14

Game Six: South Sudan versus Newton Academy

The Nukes, as they were known, had become one of the more noted basketball factories in the country. Nestled in the Smoky Mountains north of Knoxville, the school had only a hundred students, half boys, half girls, all serious and talented basketball players. Tuition was low, scholarships abundant, academics touted but not stressed, and admission was impossible unless a player had the skills to play in college. Virtually every student signed a scholarship at some level. Few public schools would play them, and so they feasted on other like-minded sports schools and travel programs, like Houston Gold, a team their U18 boys had beaten a month earlier in another showcase.

With redemption on their minds, not to mention a painful trip home that would be far earlier than expected, Ecko's players took the floor with determination and resolve. In the first period, Dak Marial lived up to his hype and dominated the inside on both ends. He scored 12, blocked three shots, and led his team to a 10-point lead. Samuel played the second period, and though he didn't score, he blocked two shots, stole the ball twice, and had two perfect assists to Abraham Bol deep in the corner. Ecko got every player in the game, but with five minutes to go, and their lead down to 7, he reinserted Dak, who, along with Quinton Majok, shut down the Nukes' inside game. Samuel reentered with three minutes to go and promptly drained a long three that put them up by 15.

The thumping did wonders for the team's morale and they hung around UCF to watch Houston Gold eke out a two-point win over Croatia. Gold was still undefeated and clinched the first seed. Croatia and Brazil were both 4–2, as was South Sudan. The U.K., their last opponent, was also 4–2. The winner of that game would likely advance to the national tournament in St. Louis.

.   .   .

During the game, as Ecko and Frankie lounged in the coaches' suite and worked the scouts, a call came from a sat phone in Rumbek. It was the lieutenant, and he had some dreadful news. Ecko stepped outside the suite and walked to the upper deck.

The city of Rumbek was under siege by rebel forces and many of the surrounding villages, especially Lotta, had been destroyed. The lieutenant called it a massacre. An army helicopter had flown over Lotta and reported that the destruction was thorough, devastating, and the fires were still smoldering. Hundreds of dead bodies, mostly men and boys, were lying in the streets and on the roads. Government forces had been unable to retake the area and were fighting for their lives. The situation was dire and reinforcements were on the way. It was impossible to identify bodies at the time, but the casualties were staggering. Indeed, identification might never be possible. Lotta was deserted but for the guerrillas, who were mopping up. The helicopter was hit by fire and barely escaped.

After the call, Ecko sat for a long time far up in the cheap seats and watched his players in the reserved seats. They were laughing, bantering, savoring their win and itching for one last victory to send them on. He watched Samuel, and his heart ached. Almost twenty years as a coach, and Ecko had never been faced with such an awful task. He reluctantly returned to the suite, pulled out Frankie, and delivered the news. They discussed what to do next, but neither had a clue. No one was equipped for such a nightmare.

They walked back to the suite and Frankie opened his laptop and began searching for headline news from South Sudan, but there was nothing. Evidently, massacres were so common that another one was not newsworthy. He found a site from Juba but the reports were only of a rebel attack on the city of Rumbek.

. . .

They waited until after dinner at the hotel, and when the team retired to a large conference room to watch soccer reruns on ESPN, Ecko pulled Samuel aside and said, "Follow me." The kid seemed to be expecting bad news and had worried since his attempts to call home. He sat on the edge of a bed and faced his two coaches.

"What's happened?" he asked, bracing himself.

There was no way to soft-pedal it, so Ecko relayed the conversation with the lieutenant and spared no details. He ended with, "It looks like all the homes have been burned and everyone has fled the village, and there are many, many casualties."

Samuel leaned back, lay on the bed, and covered his face with both hands. He cried for a long time and was unable to speak. His coaches cried with him, unable to say anything that would help.

Frankie whispered, "I'll go tell the team," and left the room. He walked downstairs to the conference room, turned off the television, and told them what had happened.

. . .

"I have to go find my family," Samuel said.

Ecko shook his head and replied, "You can't do that, Samuel, not now anyway. It's a war zone and you can't get near it."

"I have to go."

"I'm sorry. It's not going to happen, at least not now. Maybe later."

Samuel sat up on the edge of the bed and wiped his face with a sleeve. "I should've been there."

"You can't blame yourself, Samuel. For now, until we know more, let's pray for a miracle."

"I have to go."

"No, Samuel."

He wiped his face again and took a bottle of water from Ecko. "I just knew something bad was going to happen. When I left home, I just had this feeling down deep that something bad would happen. I shouldn't have left."

"You couldn't have stopped it, Samuel."

"I just knew it. I just knew it. My father, my mother, Angelina, James and Chol. Why wasn't I there with them?"

"Because you were here and they were so proud of you for being here, Samuel."

He wept again, deep painful sobs that shuddered through his body.

The door opened and Frankie walked in, followed by all fourteen players. They huddled around their friend, hugged him, said they were so sorry, and wept with him.

CHAPTER 15

They stopped at the edge of a dry creek and rested on some boulders. There were twenty of them, six women who were now widows, and their children, and they huddled together in the predawn darkness and whispered now and then. Beatrice knew two of the other women; all were from her village. All believed that their husbands and sons were dead, though they could not yet dwell on the massacre. It felt as though it was still happening.

They were desperately thirsty and hungry and had nothing but the clothes they were wearing. The smallest children whimpered and clutched their mothers, who were dazed, exhausted, and stricken with fear. They did not know where they were, nor where they were going. They weren't sure they were fleeing the carnage in one general direction, or whether they had been moving in circles. The narrow footpaths they had tried to follow forked and twisted and led them nowhere. Several times during the night they were aware of others moving silently in the pitch blackness of the woods.

The sky to the east began to lighten, so they at least had a sense of direction. East over there, north to its left. But what did it matter when they had no destination? All that mattered was food and water. And safety. There were no sounds; no gunfire, no trucks. Nothing. Did the silence mean they were safe?

Emmanuel, a teenage boy from Lotta, appeared and asked if he could join them. Of course he could, but they had nothing to offer. He said he had passed a small farm an hour earlier and thought they should try to find it. Maybe the farmer would give them food and water and tell them where to go.

Beatrice asked him if he had seen Angelina but knew the question was useless. He did not know her. His own family had been slaughtered by the rebels—mother, father, three older brothers. If he had a gun he would go back and kill the rebels. Going back might be suicide but they still wanted to see their homes. Maybe there were survivors. Maybe Angelina had somehow been spared. And maybe Ayak had escaped and was looking for them. Beatrice desperately wanted to go search for her daughter and husband.

Emmanuel said that he had escaped into the woods and climbed high into a tree on a hill, and from there he had watched the village burn. There was nothing left. The gunfire had continued as the rebels executed the men.

Weak and bone-weary, they followed Emmanuel along the creek bed, hoping to find a pool of water or even a puddle, but it was the dry season and the ground was parched and cracked. The sun was up and getting hotter, but mercifully the creek ran beside the woods and there was shade. Emmanuel turned onto a dirt path made by livestock and they walked half a mile and stopped. He told them to sit and wait while he approached the farmer and asked for help. They waited in the shade and listened for sounds of other people, possibly soldiers. They prayed for food and water.

Emmanuel came back with nothing. The farmer had little food for his own family and he was out of water. He said they were about six miles south of Lotta and that other villagers had stopped by in the night, begging for help. He felt sorry for them but had nothing to share. There was a camp further south and he had heard the rumor that there was water and shelter there. That sliver of hope lifted their spirits somewhat, and they began walking.

And walking.

. . .

The coaches were up early. They ignored the free breakfast in the lobby and took their coffee to the conference room where they opened their laptops and began searching. There was nothing on the U.S. sites, nothing out of Johannesburg. The BBC was reporting a fierce conflict in and around the city of Rumbek, but the story was not significant. After decades of conflict and massacres, and broken peace accords, and countless dead civilians, more bad news from South Sudan was not worthy of coverage.

On the fourth try, Ecko got the lieutenant on his sat phone. According to him, the battle had shifted and their army was gaining on the rebels. They hoped to reclaim the villages in a day or so. Lotta was still controlled by the rebels and it was in the hardest hit area.

The lieutenant asked about Samuel, and Ecko said things were awful. No, he did not know if Samuel had relatives in other parts of the country.

Ecko called a coach in Juba but the guy knew almost nothing. They were fighting in and around Rumbek, but there was plenty of bad news across the entire region. The coach promised to work the phones and call back if he found something.

After an hour, they had learned little. Evidently, Samuel was the only player touched by the fighting. The other nine from the country had all spoken to their families the day before.

Frankie said, "I sort of hate to bring this up, but we have a game at two o'clock."

"Oh yeah. That. Any ideas? Our team is not exactly in a competitive mood right now."

"But we have to play. Right?"

"The boys will want to play, I'm sure of it."

"And Samuel?"

"Let's talk to him."

Game Seven: South Sudan versus the United Kingdom

There was no chatter in the vans as Ecko and Frankie drove the team to Rollins College for the seventh and final game. None of the usual banter and joking, no singing. The players had convinced Samuel to dress out and sit with them on the bench, so they could stay close to him. He had no desire to play and just wanted to leave and go find his family.

It was Frankie's idea to start the five from the States, including Dak Marial and Jimmie Abaloy. Perhaps they might not be as affected as their teammates from home. Besides, it was their strongest lineup and a rousing start might inspire the others. The U.K. team had won three straight and its two losses had been by a combined six points.

Watching his team warm up, though, Ecko knew they were in trouble. They were listless. The smiles were gone. He tried to fire them up with his usual pre-tip-off pep talk and warned them of what they already knew. A loss would send them packing.

Fortunately, the U.K. came out cold and missed its first four shots. Dak hit his first two short jumpers and yelled at his teammates on defense. When Jimmie Abaloy took a low-percentage shot from too far away, Ecko yanked him out of the game and chewed on him. Anything to get their attention.

Samuel sat between his coaches and tried to encourage his friends, but the bench was flat. After the first 10 minutes the game was tied at 14, and Ecko sent in his B squad. Midway through the second period, the U.K.'s star forward took charge of the game and couldn't be stopped. His name was Abol Pach, and, to rub salt in the wounds, he was one of them. He had been born in London to Sudanese parents from Juba, and he had verbally committed to

Michigan State. Pach hit from everywhere—behind the arc, the top of the key, inside, outside. When pressed he streaked to the basket and slammed down impressive dunks. Pach scored 14 points in the second period alone and his team led by 10.

The sky was falling and there was no way to stop it. Ecko put in his best players and they chipped away at the lead, but Pach was on fire and wanted the ball. When he hit back-to-back bombs, the air left the building for the boys from South Sudan.

There were tears in the locker room and little was said. Ecko and Frankie talked to them, told them how proud they were, what an honor it was to coach such great people. Samuel sat in a corner, blaming himself for everything. But his thoughts were back in Lotta and he just wanted to go home.

CHAPTER 16

They walked for an hour and stopped when they found shade. Emmanuel went ahead to look for water and came back with nothing. But he found a gravel road and saw other people from the village moving south and east. They decided to follow it.

Beatrice tried not to think of what was behind them. She tried not to think of Samuel. James and Chol complained of headaches and hunger, and she kept promising them that they would find water soon. Their crying had stopped and they, along with the others, moved in silence, their gazes fixed on the path in front of them, dazed, traumatized, and frightened.

The group followed Emmanuel to the gravel road and saw a dozen or so mothers and their children. The sight of more people was not comforting. They, too, were desperate for water, food, and shelter. There must be hundreds if not thousands searching for help, and even if they got lucky there would not be enough for everyone.

They rested again and Emmanuel disappeared. He returned, smiling with the news that a camp was not far away. He was told there was water.

On the gravel road, they heard a truck and quickly ducked into the bush. Peeking through weeds, they watched and listened as it approached. There was gunfire, the familiar sound of Kallies, and the children began crying. It rolled past them with dust boiling in its wake. A troop truck full of soldiers. Rebels. For fun, one of them aimed his rifle in the air and fired a few shots. They were laughing as they disappeared in the dust.

. . .

Ecko was tired of Orlando and ready to leave. As the players hung out by the pool, he and Frankie put together a plan. There was some expense money left and they decided to spend a couple of days sightseeing in Washington. Frankie called their travel agent, who booked rooms and changed their flights.

The following day, they packed and went to the airport where they said goodbye to the Americans. Jimmie Abaloy and Dak Marial boarded a flight to Newark. Nelson Wek was headed to Omaha, by way of Chicago. Nyal Roman boarded the same flight and would go on to Akron. Ajah Nyabang had the longest flight, to San Francisco. Before breaking up, the players huddled around their coaches and Ecko offered a short, emotional prayer. There were long hugs and sad farewells and promises to keep in touch.

He sat next to Samuel on the flight to Washington and talked about the future. Ecko was of the firm opinion that Samuel should stay in America and apply for citizenship, but that plan raised more questions than he could answer. He would seek advice from their embassy in Washington.

Samuel was overwhelmed by thoughts of staying.

Ecko repeatedly reminded him that he could not go home because there was no home. Ecko had friends in Juba but they were in no position to adopt an eighteen-year-old kid. Samuel could not think of a single relative who could take him. All of his extended family lived in Lotta. And that was where he was going, to find them.

Ecko showed him a list of a dozen NGOs and relief organizations working in the refugee camps, both inside South Sudan and in neighboring countries. He promised to contact all of them, and to hound them until he found someone who knew the Sooleymon family. If they survived, they would eventually make it to a camp, he was certain of that. Once they were found, he would try to arrange a trip for Samuel to go see them. But it would take time. Going back now would be dangerous and unproductive.

At Reagan National, Ecko rented two white vans that were remarkably similar to the two they had used in Orlando. Their hotel was in McLean, near an interstate. They checked in and the players went to the pool.

.   .   .

Lonnie Britt had resisted the suggestion that he make the four-hour drive from Durham to Washington, but Ecko had insisted. The two old friends talked for an hour as Lonnie fought the traffic on Interstate 95. By the time he arrived in McLean, he knew he had just landed another basketball player, one that no one else was looking at.

Lonnie had dinner with the team and tried to cheer them up. They were tough kids, resilient and still hopeful, but they were crushed by their elimination. They knew they were as good as any team they had played, and to be going home with nothing was so disheartening. Of the nine who would make the long flight to Juba, only three—Alek Garang, Quinton Majok, and Riak Kuol—had a chance of playing in college. Had the team advanced to the national showcase, perhaps two or three others could have been noticed.

Afterward, Ecko asked Samuel to stop by his room. Lonnie was waiting and offered his sincere condolences. Samuel thanked him but said little. However, his demeanor changed when Lonnie said, "Samuel, I want you to come play for me at North Carolina Central. I'm offering you a full scholarship to come play for the Eagles."

Samuel was speechless and looked at Ecko in disbelief.

Lonnie said, "I've seen you play and I'm impressed with your game. Ecko says great things about you and he's convinced me to take a chance. What do you say?"

"I don't know. I can't think of anything right now. Thanks, I guess."

Ecko moved in for the kill. "Here's the deal, Samuel. We're going to the embassy tomorrow to talk about immigration. Lonnie's going with us and we'll explain that you'll be staying here and headed down to Durham. We'll ask the embassy to pull strings and help expedite a student visa."

Samuel shook his head and said, "Thanks, Coach, but I need to go home and find my family. They're alive and they need me."

Ecko said, "Listen to me, Samuel."

"Maybe not all of them, but I just know that my mother is alive and she needs me right now."

"We'll find them, Samuel, but you can't do it by yourself. Right now we have no idea where they are. The village is gone and Rumbek is not safe. What good will it do your family if you get killed too?"

Lonnie said, "We'll do everything we can to help you find them, Samuel, I promise, but for now, play it safe. Come to Durham with me. You can stay in my house, with my family, until classes start. Then you'll move into a nice dormitory and meet all your new friends. They're a great bunch of guys, Samuel, and they'll be glad to meet you."

"But I don't have a dime. How am I supposed to go to college?"

Ecko said, "Let me worry about that. Your scholarship covers tuition, room, board, and books. Coach Britt can find you a job. We'll make it happen."

He buried his face in his hands and managed to say, "Thank you."

CHAPTER 17

The camp was between two small hills that cradled a narrow creek. Bunched along its banks were dozens of makeshift tents and lean-tos made of stripped branches and dried scrub. Smoke from two fires drifted upward and at first gave them hope that food was being prepared. The creek bed was dry but there were pools of muddy water. Women and children shuffled about with little to do.

Emmanuel told them to wait under the shade of some trees as he left to scope out the camp. He disappeared down a trail and as he approached the settlement he was stopped by two men blocking the trail. "What do you want?" one of them asked. Both were armed, one with a club, the other with a machete.

Emmanuel said, "I have women and children with me. We're from the village of Lotta and we were attacked."

"You can't stay here," said the man with the club.

"Please. We are starving and need water. We've been walking for two days and nights."

"You can't stay here. There's no food and the water is almost gone."

"Please. We're dying. There are children."

"We're all dying. And the farmers have told us to leave. We're using their water and they are not happy about it. They have threatened to call soldiers to clear the camp."

"But we can't keep going. Please help us."

"There is no room for you here and it's too dangerous."

"You have no choice," said the man with the machete.

"Please. Just some water and something to eat."

The men looked at each other. The one with the club tossed it aside and disappeared. The other one said, "Just wait."

"How long have you been here?" Emmanuel asked.

"About a month. Most of us are from the village of Ranya. Where are you from?"

"Lotta. It was burned Sunday night by the rebels."

"They burned our village too. We've been here but now we have to go. The farmers are very angry and do not want us on their land."

"When will you leave?"

"Tomorrow."

"Where will you go?"

He shook his head as if he had no idea.

The other man returned with a bucket of water and a cloth bag filled with something. They followed Emmanuel up the trail to the trees where Beatrice and her group waited. One of the men said, "I'm sorry but you cannot stay here. It's too dangerous." He put down the bucket and held a small wooden ladle. "The water is dirty but we've been drinking it. We have no choice." As he gave each person a few ounces of the brownish liquid, the other one opened the bag and began handing out fistfuls of raw peanuts.

The water was wretched but it quenched their thirst. The peanuts tasted like chocolate candy. "Eat slow," Beatrice whispered to James and Chol. "Make it last."

But they couldn't eat slow.

. . .

The two vans stopped near the Lincoln Memorial and the team got out. Frankie gave them instructions and left to find a place to park. The boys were soon lost in a throng of tourists visiting Abe and milling around the Reflecting Pool.

Ecko drove Samuel and Lonnie to the embassy of the Republic of South Sudan on 31st Street near the Naval Observatory. Their ten o'clock appointment was with a Ms. Maria Manabol, a pleasant young lady Ecko had spoken to three times already. She met them in a small conference room and offered them coffee. After a round of chitchat, during which she expressed her condolences to Samuel for the tragedy, and managed to get in a word or two about the basketball team, she asked Ecko and Lonnie to step into the hallway. They left Samuel at the table and followed her to an office. She closed the door and motioned for them to have a seat. She began with, "My father was a government soldier who was killed in the war when I was a little girl, so I know what he's going through. Luckily, I had an uncle here in the States and he sent for me and my brother. I'm very sorry."

They nodded gravely and waited.

"Yesterday, government troops pushed the rebels away from Rumbek and secured the area. They went into the villages and found what they expected. In Lotta, the rebels herded several hundred men into the parish church and set it on fire, so we'll never know the exact number of casualties. Most of the victims were badly burned. So far they've found over two hundred bodies scattered around the village, mostly men and teenage boys. Sad to say, but this is not uncommon in this war. The atrocities are beyond description. The cleanup is dreadful work. About a hundred men have been identified, primarily by the voter registration cards in their wallets. The female casualties are more difficult because the cards were left at home when they fled. All the homes were burned."

She picked up a remote and aimed at a television on the wall. "This is difficult to watch and I didn't want Samuel to see it."

The video was shot with a handheld camera by someone walking with the soldiers. The corpses were grossly swollen and stained with dark blood. Soldiers with masks and gloves were tossing them into the rear of a troop truck. After thirty seconds, Ecko looked away.

She punched a button and the screen went blank. "Does Samuel have a laptop or cell phone?"

"No," Ecko replied.

"Good, then maybe he won't see this. It's out there, on the internet."

"We're planning to get him a phone and a laptop this morning. He'll need them."

"Okay, well, maybe he won't look for this. They found his father, Ayak Sooleymon, and identified him with his registration card. Evidently, he was in the church and managed to get outside before he was shot. So, his death is confirmed."

"Any idea about his mother and siblings?"

"No, nothing. As you know, over four million of our people have been displaced by the wars and are living in refugee camps. Let's hope she finds one. It is extremely difficult to locate people, but we try every day and sometimes we get lucky. Most of them, though, are in camps in neighboring countries. Some have been there for years."

"I can't imagine," Lonnie said.

"As I understand the plan, he will be going with you to Durham."

"Yes, to play basketball."

"Well, thanks to you, Coach, he's a very lucky young man."

"He doesn't feel so lucky," Ecko said.

"I'm sure that's true. We'll expedite a student visa and Samuel will be free to enjoy college. I'll need a few signatures today and we'll contact Immigration."

Ecko and Lonnie said "Thank you" at the same time.

She said, "I'll wait here for a moment while you tell him about his father."

"I think he knows."

"I'm sure he does."

Ecko and Lonnie stood, and as they opened the door, Lonnie said, "We play Howard here on December the nineteenth. I expect Samuel to be in uniform. We would love to have you as our guest."

"Why, thank you. My husband and I enjoy college basketball, and we'll be there."

.   .   .

Samuel and Coach Britt were in the hotel lobby, fiddling with his new cell phone and laptop, when the players returned. They had been briefed and knew that their friend would not be returning to Juba. His bag was packed, with some new items from J.Crew, all courtesy of Ecko and his dwindling expense account.

After a round of long, emotional farewells, they watched him walk out the door with Ecko and Lonnie. As wounded and hurt as he was, Samuel was living their dream. He would stay in America, and study on a scholarship, and play in nice gyms and fine arenas. And they were so happy for him.

At the car, he hugged Ecko and thanked him for everything. Looking into Samuel's sad eyes, Ecko was certain he had grown another inch.

Part Two

CHAPTER 18

The days didn't matter anymore. They were all the same. They walked for three days, then another three. They walked early in the morning to beat the sun and rested during the hottest hours, then walked again at night. They slept on the ground, close together for protection. They were starving and beyond thirst, and when the fatigue was so numbing they could not go on, Emmanuel found rotten fruit from a cape fig tree and they devoured it. He cajoled a bag of peanuts from a Dinka farmer, along with a gourd of water. Another farmer, one of the Nuer tribe, cursed and threatened them with a machete. They slowly walked on, listening always for the sounds of trucks and soldiers. Ten or twelve days after the massacre they joined another group of refugees and word filtered back that they were going to Uganda. Beatrice did not want to leave her country—she had never left it before—but Emmanuel had heard more than once that the camps were more dangerous in South Sudan. Rebels raided the settlements, killing and raping, and taking what little food there was. He became convinced that Uganda was where they should go, and the more he talked to the other men the more he was certain that they were going in the right direction. Uganda was keeping its borders open and trying to help the flood of refugees, but its camps were being overrun. So many were fleeing

South Sudan, desperate to get away from the violence. Ethiopia and Kenya were also rumored to be safer, but they were much further away.

They walked on, weary and hungry, hoping to see the border just around the next turn. There were over a hundred of them, almost all women and children, one long sad parade of misery. Most were barefoot. Few carried belongings. None had food or water. Near the border a large crowd had stalled where the road was blocked by a row of tents. They rested beside the road as Emmanuel went to gather information. People kept coming by the hundreds.

Beatrice pulled James and Chol close to her on the ground and looked behind them at the endless line of refugees. There had to be food and water in the camp. Why else would so many be drawn to this place?

They spent the night there on the ground, and early the next morning moved forward. When they passed through a checkpoint they learned that they had now left their homeland. A sign in English read: "Welcome to Uganda—Rhino Camp Refugee Settlement." A man in a uniform directed them to a tent where they joined a line to be processed. As they waited, Beatrice asked the man if there was any food and water. Her children were starving.

He smiled and nodded and said there was food and water, just beyond the tents. At a table, she gave another officer their names and said they were from the village of Lotta. She asked if anyone had seen Angelina, but the officer shook his head and said, "No, we're taking in a thousand a day and we can't keep up."

"Please look for Angelina Sooleymon, please."

He nodded as if he'd heard this before and entered their names in a registry. He asked if she had any documentation. No, she did not. She explained that everything had been lost when their house burned. She had no money, nothing but the filthy and ragged clothes they were wearing. From the tents they shuffled on and were directed to a long line of starving people waiting behind a large truck. Beatrice could smell something in the air. At the truck, workers were dipping ladles into large vats and filling tin bowls with hot porridge. Others were handing out plastic bottles of clear water. The refugees waited patiently, dazed and in disbelief that they were finally getting food and water. Beatrice thanked the workers and sat with her boys beside the truck to eat and drink.

. . .

After a week in Coach Britt's basement, with warm family meals cooked by his wife, and hours of video games with his children, Samuel moved into his dorm room on the NC Central campus in south Durham. It was modern, more like an apartment than a dorm room, and not far from the athletic complex. He would share it with another basketball player who was expected in a few days. Lonnie moved him in, then walked with him to the football field and locker room, and introduced him to his new boss, T. Ray. For the unheard-of wage of $7.25 an hour, the state minimum wage, whatever that meant, Samuel landed his first job—assistant equipment manager of the football team.

"Football players are a bunch of pigs," T. Ray growled as he walked Samuel around the expansive locker room. "Right now you're the lowest man on the pole so you get to help clean the locker room after every practice. Then you'll help with the laundry, then you'll spend every afternoon on the practice field doing whatever else I tell you to do. Got it?"

"Yes sir."

"Report here at eight each morning and we'll get to work. Coach Britt says you need all the hours you can get until classes start, right?"

"Right."

"Okay. Welcome aboard. I'll introduce you to some of the assistant coaches. The players will start arriving in an hour or so. They're pretty rough on equipment managers, at least at first, so don't take it personally."

Samuel nodded but had no idea what to expect.

"Here's Rodney, your new best friend and head student manager."

Rodney welcomed him on board, gave him a proper team polo and shorts and told him to change clothes. Rodney was impressed with his state-of-the-art Reeboks. From there they went to one of the many storage rooms, and together loaded a cart with freshly cleaned practice tee shirts, jerseys, pants, and socks. Each article had a uniform number marked on it. Using the team roster attached to a bulletin board, Samuel began placing the practice uniforms into each individual locker. Rodney showed him the right way to arrange things just so. The work was light and easy and Samuel was thrilled to be so close to a team. His practices would not start for another month and he had no friends on campus, other than Rodney.

He was also thrilled to be earning $7.25 an hour and grateful to his coach for securing the job. He had no money and needed the income. All of his meals would be in the student cafeteria, but he had to purchase a service contract for his new cell phone, plus a few other incidentals. As soon as possible, he planned to start calling the two dozen aid organizations he had researched online.

After practice, he found the library, then the Wi-Fi, and he figured out the printer in a copy room. He began printing color maps of his country and those around it, and piecing together a large collage of an area roughly three hundred square miles. He pinpointed the known refugee camps and settlements within the grid. And he read, article after article, newspaper and magazine stories, and reports filed by the United Nations and an impressive group of NGOs.

With no internet service in his village, he had limited skills with his laptop, but he was learning quickly. If finding his family depended on his technical skills, he would not rest until he mastered the internet. It was a gargantuan, uphill struggle, and he had only the slightest clue of the challenge. But that didn't matter. What mattered was that he believed he would find them, somehow, some way.

At night, he covered one wall of his room with maps and made notes on them. He read online for hours. For his entire life he had heard stories of the diaspora of the South Sudanese but had never grasped the enormity of the crisis. Four million people, one third of the country's population, had been displaced by decades of wars, with half living in camps and settlements inside the country. The surrounding countries were absorbing the other half of a massive and unmanageable overflow. There were 900,000 in Uganda, 200,000 in both Ethiopia and Sudan, another 100,000 in Kenya. Other South Sudanese had scattered even further from home, all in search of safety and food. Bidi Bidi, the largest settlement in Uganda, now held over 200,000 refugees and was beyond the breaking point. The governments of these countries were doing all they could do, and appealing for international help. It was arriving, but there was too little of it.

Eighty percent of the refugees were women and children. The men were either dead or off somewhere fighting. Only Syria and Afghanistan had more refugees. One United Nations study predicted that without a meaningful peace agreement, South Sudan would soon displace more of its people than any other country.

Working late into the night, Samuel marked the location of each refugee camp, and there were dozens of them.

In some of the older settlements in Uganda and Kenya, the refugees were given small tracts of land to grow vegetables and construct shanties. Some residents had been there for years and had lost hope of returning home. Makeshift schools were being run by aid workers. In the camps, which seemed to be newer and less organized, the conditions were often far worse. Cholera outbreaks were common. There was little or no health care. The refugees lived in tents and huts and began each day with the quest for food and water.

When he was exhausted, Samuel said his prayers and asked God to save his family, whatever was left of it.

CHAPTER 19

Beatrice and two other women from their village had managed to stick together and vowed to continue to do so. Three women with eight children, ages four to thirteen. They slept the first night at Rhino Camp in a field on the edge of the sprawling settlement. At dawn they began walking toward the center and soon found a food distribution point, a place where trucks rolled in with vats of warm porridge and rice. The line was long and slow-moving. The women, desperate for information, talked to other women as they waited. They learned there was an area on the far side of the settlement where aid workers from many countries operated under large tents and handed out clothing and medicine. There were a few doctors but getting to see one was difficult. James was having fevers and needed to see a doctor.

The women wanted to bathe and find better clothing. They were wearing rags, and their shoes had been abandoned days ago. After breakfast, they drifted with the crowd, past rows of flimsy dwellings, ramshackle lean-tos, and dirty tents. They noticed small fires where women were cooking and saw hundreds of teenage girls hauling water in pots on their heads. They stepped over a narrow creek choked with sewage and waste, then saw another long line and joined it. There was a food truck far ahead, and food was their priority. Their first days in Rhino Camp were spent waiting in long, slow lines for food, and sleeping on the ground with their children pulled close.

. . .

On August 11, Samuel woke up early and wished himself a happy birthday. He was now eighteen, but he was not in a mood to celebrate. He knew that he would go through the entire day and keep his secret to himself. He said his morning prayers and ached for his mother and family.

After he showered, his phone rang and he grabbed it. Ecko Lam was calling to wish him a happy one, and they talked for half an hour. Ecko was still in South Sudan and would be returning home soon. Samuel was thrilled to learn that his coach was in Rumbek, meeting with the military, looking for Beatrice and her children. But the news was not good. According to survivors in Lotta, the people had fled in all directions. Some had been hunted down and killed by the rebels. The nearest camp was the Yusuf Batil settlement in the state of Upper Nile, a hundred miles from Lotta. There were many camps, some run by the government with basic services, others created by hungry people desperate for protection. In the government camps the refugees were registered and received better care, but it was still the old "needle in a haystack" scenario. Ecko planned to use his time gathering information and making contact with aid groups and military leaders and would report back when he returned to the States.

He wanted to know every detail of Samuel's first days on campus, and was delighted to hear he was working and loved his job. Classes would start in two weeks and he was eager to make friends. The football players were nice enough but it wasn't his sport. He longed to get in the gym and start practice.

When the call ended, Samuel sat on his bed and had another good cry. And he thanked God for people like Ecko Lam.

. . .

The unquestioned leader in the clubhouse was Devon Dayton, a burly middle linebacker from Charlotte. He was loud, funny, cocky, and always carrying on some nonsense with his teammates. He was also intimidating, as were most of the large young men. Samuel had never seen so much bulk in one place.

As the locker room bustled with early morning preparations, Samuel walked through with a stack of clean towels and Devon called out, "Hey you." He was sitting on a bench with two other heavy linemen and seemed irritated. Almost a thousand pounds of muscle and beef.

Samuel set down the towels and walked over.

"What's your name?" Devon demanded.

"Samuel Sooleymon."

"That's a mouthful. Too many syllables. Where you from? You talk funny."

"South Sudan," Samuel said timidly. Others had gathered around to enjoy the moment.

"Where's that?"

"I think it's in Georgia," said another.

"Africa," Samuel said, waiting.

Devon said, "Well, my gym shorts were still a bit damp when I put them on this morning. You know what it's like running around out there in wet gym shorts?"

Samuel had watched practice for two days and knew that all gym shorts would be soaked with sweat within the hour. "Sorry," he said.

"Samuel Sooleymon," Devon repeated loudly. "Can you spell it?"

"I can."

"Okay. Walk over to that chalkboard and write your name."

Samuel did as he was told. Devon and the others studied the name with disapproval. One of them said, "That's pretty weird."

Weird? The roster was loaded with some first names that Samuel had never seen before and wasn't sure how to pronounce.

Devon said, "We need to shorten it. How about Sam? Just plain ol' Sam?"

Samuel shook his head and said, "My father didn't like Sam."

"I got it," another one said. "Let's go with Sooley."

"I like that," Devon said. "Sooley it is, and Sooley, from now on, I prefer dry gym shorts in the morning."

A coach barreled through the door, screaming, and the team suddenly lost interest in changing names. They scrambled out of the locker room and when they were gone, Samuel erased his name from the board, picked up the towels, and put them on a rack. T. Ray told him to hustle up and get the bottles of cold water to the field.

Football was a strange game. Its practices were organized mayhem as a hundred players covered the practice field and did drills while half a dozen coaches yelled and blew whistles. The morning sessions were noncontact and primarily conditioning, brutal calisthenics as the sun grew hotter, and enough wind sprints to cause the heavier guys to collapse. After two hours, the players returned to the locker room, stripped, showered, and left their dirty clothes in a pile for Samuel and the other equipment managers to wash, dry, fold, and place neatly in the lockers. After a long break for lunch and rest, the players were back for an hour with their coaches—offensive linemen in one room, wide receivers in another, and so on. At three, they suited up in full gear and walked back into the sun.

Samuel and two other equipment managers tidied up the locker room, then hurried to the field to resupply the water and sports drinks.

At first, the full-contact drills were frightening, as three-hundred-pound brutes tried their best to kill one another as their coaches yelled at them to hit even harder. Indeed, the hardest hits, the bone-jarring collisions and vicious tackles, excited the coaches the most and drew the wildest cheers from the other players. Samuel was thrilled that he played basketball.

After three hours of violence, and as the players melted in the heat and humidity, the head coach finally relented and blew the last whistle. Samuel hurried to the locker room to clean up. The mood was much quieter as the players dragged themselves in, stripped, and headed for the showers. They took their time getting dressed. They would break for dinner and return for more meetings that night. Samuel was working ten-hour days and counting his money.

As he scooped up a pile of filthy practice jerseys, Devon yelled, "Hey, Sooley, over here."

Samuel stepped over, anticipating a gag of some variety. The team quickly bunched around Devon, who said, "Say, look, Sooley, we know it's been a rough summer for you, and we know today is special. Since you can't be home to celebrate, we figured we'd do it here."

A wall of bodies opened and Coach Lonnie Britt stepped forward with a large birthday cake, complete with candles and the words "Happy Birthday Sooley" scrawled in maroon and gray, the team colors. Like an amateur choir director, Devon waved his hands and the team sang a boisterous rendition of "Happy Birthday," most of them deliberately bellowing off-key.

Samuel was stunned and speechless. Devon said, "We're glad you're here, Sooley. We know you're playing the wrong sport, but we love our basketball players. Most of them anyway."

Coach Britt handed the cake to Devon and hugged Samuel, the kid with the big smile and very sad eyes.

. . .

Beatrice and her little gang spent the third night on the ground but under a large military-style tent with a hundred others. After two meals that day, the hunger pangs were subsiding and the children were coming to life. The future was bleak and the past too painful to dwell on, but maybe the worst was behind them.

As she huddled with James and Chol and waited for them to drift away, she knew it was the middle of August. Samuel was turning eighteen, somewhere, and she prayed for his safety.

CHAPTER 20

The following Saturday, the team had a light practice in the morning and was released for the rest of the day. Samuel and the three other equipment managers finished the laundry and cleaned the locker room. He left the field house and returned to his dorm to find someone else moving in. It was Murray Walker, his new best friend. They said hello and shook hands and sat on their beds.

Coach Britt had given Samuel the name of his roommate and said he would call. Samuel, living online when he wasn't working, had checked out the kid and knew he was a rising sophomore who had averaged only five minutes a game during his freshman season. Five minutes, two points, one rebound—the slimmest production of all thirteen players. He was six feet tall, had walked on, survived the cuts, and made the team.

"What's all this?" Murray asked, nodding at the wall covered with maps and notes.

"It's a mess, isn't it? I'll be happy to take it down."

"No, that's okay. Coach told me that you're from South Sudan, in Africa."

"What else did Coach tell you about me?"

Murray smiled and shrugged. "Well, he said you've been through a lot lately, I guess. I'm real sorry."

Samuel rose and stepped to the wall. "I'm from a village near the city of Rumbek, in central South Sudan. The village is gone now, and my mother is somewhere there." He pointed at the wall as if he had no idea where she was. "I'm hoping my brothers and sister are with her."

"Refugees?"

"Something like that. My father was murdered by rebel troops last month."

"Oh man, I'm real sorry."

"Thanks. It's been pretty bad."

"I can't even imagine."

"The website says you're from here, Durham."

"That's right. Born here."

"Why'd you pick Central?"

"Because nobody else wanted me. I wasn't exactly heavily recruited. Coach Britt invited me to walk on and I made the cut. My parents went to school here so I've always pulled for Central."

"Your family's here?"

"Yep. Ten minutes away. My Mom's a lawyer and my Dad runs a food bank."

"What's a food bank?"

"It's a nonprofit charity that collects food and gives it away to folks who're hungry."

Samuel sat down on his bed and looked oddly at Murray. "Hungry people around here?"

"Lots of them."

"You're not kidding?"

"I'm dead serious, man. I know it's hard for you to believe, but here in the land of plenty there are a lot of poor people. You want to go see some? I need to make a delivery."

"Not really. I saw enough back home."

"Let's get a burger and I'll show you around. My truck is loaded with food for a pantry."

"You have a truck?"

"It's a hand-me-down but it works."

"What's a pantry?"

"Come on, I'll show you. My Dad asked me to make a delivery."

"Well, I'm kind of low on cash right now."

"Okay, I'll buy you a burger. You can buy next time."

They parked in a McDonald's and got out. Samuel noticed the stack of boxes in the bed and asked, "So, where does the food come from?"

"We buy some, a lot is donated. We have a warehouse full, actually three warehouses, and we're feeding ten thousand people a week. My Dad's the boss and he runs a tight ship. I work there part-time."

They sat in the window, ate, and talked basketball. Murray wanted to know everything about the tournament in Orlando, the wins and losses and all the scouts watching. Two years earlier, his summer team played Houston Gold in Atlanta and got crushed. They talked about Coach Britt. Murray loved the guy and Samuel said he had probably saved his life. They talked about the two former players arrested for armed robbery. Murray described them as a couple of good guys known to make bad decisions, said the rest of the team was worried about them. They had lawyers and there was a good chance they would take pleas to lesser charges and avoid jail, but they would miss a year of school and basketball. He said Coach Britt was careful who he signed, but when it came to recruiting nothing was for certain. They talked about the conference, the other schools, the road games, and life on campus.

"Plenty of girls?" Samuel asked.

"Oh yes, lots. And they like athletes. With your strange accent they'll be all over you."

"Sounds awful. Wait till I speak to them in Dinka."

Which led to a long discussion of life in South Sudan.

They talked nonstop and left the restaurant friends for life.

CHAPTER 21

Now Chol had the fevers and his seemed to be worse than his brother's. After breakfast, Beatrice made both boys follow her through the dirty and hectic streets of the settlement as she asked directions to the clinic. There were three, she was told, or maybe four, and the largest one was a mile away. She led the boys in that general direction. With each step she looked at each face, hoping to see Angelina. She had dreamed she would find her here, along with Ayak, and they would be together.

Beatrice eventually found the clinic and was not surprised to see a long line of mothers and their sick children waiting in the blazing sun. The morning passed before they made it inside the sprawling and packed tent. They missed lunch and needed water.

The clinic was run by a Lutheran ministry out of Hamburg, and the doctors and nurses were German and spoke with accents. James and Chol were fascinated to see white people, a rarity in that part of the world. A nurse examined the boys and determined they had malaria, a common affliction in South Sudan. And they were probably malnourished, but otherwise healthy. She gave Beatrice a bottle of pills with instructions.

"How long have you been here?" the nurse asked.

"I don't know. Maybe a week."

"Are you getting enough to eat?"

"No, there's never enough, but we're not starving anymore."

"Where are you staying?"

Beatrice shrugged and could think of no response.

"Okay, where are you sleeping?"

"On the ground."

"You have no roof?"

"No."

The nurse opened a drawer and pulled out two cards with numbers stamped on them. She handed one over and said, "There is a distribution center around the corner. Take this and go there and get clothing and water."

Beatrice thanked her and grabbed the card.

The nurse handed over the second one, light blue in color. "There is a new section of the settlement that is opening up. At the distribution center, you will see a sign that says 'Housing.' Hand this to them and they will assign you a new tent, one large enough for your family."

Beatrice wanted to cry but immediately thought of her friends from Lotta. "But I am with others," she said. "And they have children."

"How many?"

"Two families."

The nurse handed her two more blue cards, smiled, and said, "You will sleep in your own tents tonight. Bring the boys back in a week."

Beatrice forgot about the missed lunch and hurried to the distribution center where she found yet another long line of people waiting to get inside. She heard a loud voice and looked across the street. Under a canopy, a priest with a bullhorn was conducting Sunday Mass and thousands were sitting on the ground around him.

For the first time in forever, Beatrice knew the day of the week.

. . .

Sleep was difficult and Samuel wasn't getting much of it. He awoke in the dark Sunday morning and remembered that Murray had not made it back. He had a girlfriend in town and said he might stay at home.

Samuel showered, put on his best clothes, ate breakfast in the cafeteria, then walked two miles to the Sacred Heart Catholic Church. He enjoyed the service, thanked God for his goodness, and prayed fervently for his family.

There were few black people seated around him. Murray, a Methodist, said there were not many black Catholics in the South. Evidently, he was right.

Sunday's practice would be a three-hour scrimmage, at night, when supposedly things would be cooler. But in the middle of August nothing was cool, and by the time Samuel returned to his dorm his shirt was soaked. He changed into gym shorts and walked ten minutes to Central's gym, officially the McDougald-McLendon Arena, but a title that unwieldy begged for a nickname. For decades the gym had been known simply as The Nest. Samuel had his own key, thanks to T. Ray. He found a rack of balls and began shooting for the first time in days. It felt good to be bouncing the ball, taking shots, retrieving at a leisurely pace, dribbling, then pulling up for another shot. The air in the building was only a few degrees cooler than the outside heat, but for the moment it was the perfect temperature. His shots were hitting home with a remarkable frequency. He backed further away and found his range.

How many shots could he take alone in one hour with a reasonable amount of hustle? There was a clock on the wall and he timed himself. He talked to himself before each shot and mentally went through the basics. From behind the arc, he hit the first two, then missed three. Two-for-five. Three-for-six. Four-for-ten. Six-for-fifteen. Twelve-for-thirty.

Sixty minutes later, he had taken 200 shots and made a third of them.

That wasn't good enough.

. . .

The tent was six meters by six with a thick plastic floor, a door that zipped open and closed, and three windows that opened for ventilation. Beatrice, a tall woman, could almost stand upright without ducking her head. It was too large for a hiking tent and too small for the army, and must have been designed for refugees. Beatrice didn't care how or why it was designed. It gave her and the boys their first moment of privacy and sense of place in many days. After they moved in, with nothing to move, she zipped the door and windows closed and huddled with James and Chol in the complete isolation. But as the air grew thick and hot, she quickly unzipped it all and stepped outside. Her friends from Lotta were on either side, and both were convinced she had managed a miracle to get the tents.

Their journey was over. They had survived the massacre and the nightmare of fleeing, and they had arrived in a place that promised safety, food, water, and now a roof.

The children at first hung around the tents, too timid to venture far, but by dark they were playing down the street with a group of kids. The tents, and there were thousands of them, all identical, were staked in a perfect grid, block after block. Each tent was exactly two meters from the one next door, so that through the vinyl fabric walls a family spat four tents down was shared by many. Once inside, the women and children soon learned to whisper about everything.

The small plots provided for two meters of ground in front of the tent and next to the street, and two meters behind for cooking and urinating. A few outhouses were scattered through the community, but not enough. Long lines of people waited while others relieved themselves wherever they could. The stench of shit and urine permeated the air. The acrid smoke from cooking fires hung like a fog over the area.

Beatrice longed for the day she would have something to cook.

CHAPTER 22

Monday, August 17, the first day of classes. Samuel woke up early, turned on lights, slammed drawers, showered making as much noise as possible, but was completely unable to rouse his roommate from his nightly comalike hibernation. Samuel dressed, left the dorm, and hustled over to the student union to drink coffee and watch the coeds. He had roamed the campus for hours and knew every building. At nine he had Sociology; at ten, African Studies; at noon, General Math. The most exciting part of the day would begin at three in The Nest when the team met with the coaches for the first practice. Under the current NCAA rules, they could be on the floor for exactly one hour four days a week until late September when the real work began. The first game was in early November.

He had been in the U.S. now for almost six weeks, and on campus for the last two, and the culture shock was fading. He marveled at the students and their affluence. Every single one had a cell phone and laptop, and most of them, especially the girls, did little but stare at their screens. And the clothes. Most wore cut-offs, tee shirts, and sandals, but there seemed to be an endless supply. Murray's small closet was filled with more shirts than any ten men had in Lotta. Samuel realized immediately that no student could function without just the right backpack. He purchased one with his first paycheck, and with Murray's help. He was startled at the number of students who owned cars and brought them to school. Parking on campus was difficult and highly regulated, but the traffic was still a mess.

In spite of his burdens, he was thrilled to be on an American campus and starting classes. When he walked into Sociology, there were a hundred students in a large hall, and at first glance he didn't know a soul. Then, near the back, he saw the smiling face of a freshman football player. He sat beside him as the professor called things to order. All laptops opened.

Samuel took a second and closed his eyes and thought of his mother.

. . . .

At 2:55, Coach Britt blew his whistle and all warm-ups stopped. He herded the players to a section of the bleachers and said hello.

There were sixteen of them: ten returning, two transfers, two freshmen, and two invited walk-ons. Of the ten returning, three were seniors, five were juniors, two, including Murray, were sophomores.

Coach Britt began by introducing the Director of Athletics and invited him to say a word or two, which he seemed delighted to do. He welcomed the team, talked about what a great season it would be, and so on. His real purpose, though, was to talk about their two teammates, both now out of jail but facing serious charges. He took responsibility for their dismissals and said the university had no choice. If they were eventually cleared, then he and the President would consider reinstatement. He did not want the incident to distract the team.

The AD left, and Coach Britt took over. He introduced the five student managers, all volunteers, and went on about how important they were to the program. He introduced his associate head coach, Jason Grinnell, and his two assistant coaches, Jackie Garver and Ron McCoy. The four had been together throughout Lonnie's four-year tenure at Central. He introduced the director of basketball operations, the director of player development, the assistant director of operations, the team doctor, and the two trainers.

In Lotta, Samuel had two friends whose families owned small televisions with satellite reception, and generators, and he had watched plenty of college and professional games from the U.S. He was mesmerized by the spectacle of the game and motivated by its excitement, popularity, and pageantry. He understood most of it, but there were always lingering questions. The most puzzling was: Why do college teams have so many men in dark suits on the bench? Who are these people? Does a team with only five players on the court really need half a dozen coaches? Often, there were more men in dark suits than players in uniform.

He had posed these important questions to Murray, whose response was something like "That's what everybody else does. Why does the football team need a hundred players?"

Coach Britt said there were six new faces in the crowd. He introduced the two walk-ons, then he introduced the two transfers, the first being Sherman Batts, who played the previous season at a community college in Florida. The second was Trevor Young, a high school all-American who hadn't played much at Virginia Tech and would sit a year.

Then the two freshmen. Samuel Sooleymon, from the African republic of South Sudan, and Michal Rayburn from Wilmington. He bragged on each for a moment, then glanced at his watch and said, "All right, the NCAA says that we have only forty-five more minutes today. Let's move to the dressing room and pick lockers. Seniors first, as always. Then we'll hand out practice uniforms, new shoes, anything else you might need. Tomorrow you'll get your first physical exams so be here a few minutes early."

CHAPTER 23

Each day began the same. There was nothing to vary the routine, nothing to change schedules that did not exist. For the displaced and war-scarred, waking in safety with the promise of food and water was a gift from God. They knew so many who had not survived.

Beatrice woke first and gently shifted her weight on the hard ground, careful not to wake her boys. The first rays of sunlight peeked through the mesh-covered window above her. She heard a few soft whispers from the nearby tents as mothers moved about. As always, her first thoughts were of her children. James and Chol were with her and they would soon be awake and asking about food. Angelina was gone and finding her would be a miracle. And where was Samuel? The team was scheduled to return by the first of August at the latest. Return to what? Surely Samuel by now knew of the massacre. There was no home, no village. Where would he go? In her dreams he finds Ayak and together they find Angelina, and the three of them are here, somewhere in the settlement, looking for Beatrice and the boys.

She had her morning prayer, followed by her morning cry. It was best to cry alone while the boys slept. For a long time she softly rubbed their legs as things came to life around her. More voices from the tents, more people moving in the mud street in front of the tents.

Soon, they would embark on the daily adventure of finding breakfast. The food drop-offs were well-known. The sounds of straining truck engines usually meant aid workers were arriving. Everyone in the long lines knew how to wait patiently for hours. There was plenty of food, and once those who had been starving realized this they were content to wait. They waited an hour for a breakfast of porridge and water, an hour for a lunch of beans, rice, and a small loaf of bread, an hour for a dinner of whatever was left over from the earlier meals. No meat, no fruit, nothing with a hint of sugar, but there were no complaints. The people had known the fear and physical pain of hunger and were relieved it had ended.

Beatrice and the boys moved around the sprawling and growing settlement. They waited in numerous lines at food points. They waited in lines for secondhand clothing and shoes. They roamed the dirt and mud streets with no destination in mind. They found a small market area and wondered how anyone had money to buy anything. They heard Dinka, their language, and Nuer, that of their biggest rivals, and Azande, Bari, Murle, English, and other unknown tongues. Like many of the mothers, she was searching. She had taught the boys to watch carefully, to quickly examine the faces of all teenage girls. It was possible that Angelina was in the camp and they might find her.

Beatrice saw an aid worker, a white woman, in a smart shirt with the words "Doctors Without Borders" monogrammed over the pocket. She was talking on a mobile phone and standing outside a large military tent being used as a hospital. She lowered her phone, took a deep breath, and noticed Beatrice staring at her from five feet away. Beatrice assumed she spoke English and said, "May I ask you a question?"

"Of course," the lady replied with a warm smile.

"Is there any way to use a phone around here?"

"There is some cellular service but not much. Here at the hospital we have our own antenna and generator. There are a few others in the settlement." She had one of those European accents.

"I'm looking for my children. My son went to America this summer to play basketball. I don't know where he is and he doesn't know where we are."

"Does he have a mobile phone?"

"No. All I have is the name of his coach."

"Where does the coach live?"

"Somewhere in America, but he's South Sudanese."

"Somewhere in America," the lady repeated, amused. "Okay, give me his name and tell me what he does and I'll try."

"His name is Ecko Lam and he coaches the basketball teams from South Sudan. All the paperwork was in my house."

"I see. Okay, here's what I suggest. Meet me back here around noon the day after tomorrow. Maybe we'll get lucky."

"Thank you so much."

. . .

The first football game was at Bethune-Cookman in Daytona Beach. For budgetary reasons, only half the team and four of the managers made the flight. To which Murray observed, "Surely they can play the game with fifty players."

Samuel had a free weekend, his first since arriving. Late Saturday morning, after he had managed to get Murray out of bed, they walked to the gym, flipped on some light switches, and loosened up. It was an unwritten policy that any player on the team could shoot baskets during the off-hours, as long as no coaches were present. Every player was handed a key to the outside door, shown the light switches, and given the code to the locker room.

After four practices, it was obvious to the rest of the team that Sooley was blessed with lightning speed and quickness. He had easily won the suicide sprints. His running vertical leap was measured at 45 inches, higher than any of the coaches had ever seen. He weighed in at 190 pounds and measured six feet four and a half and was still growing. He loved the game, loved being on the floor, and regardless of how grueling the conditioning, he kept a smile on his face.

But he couldn't shoot and he couldn't dribble, a couple of the basics for a point guard. On defense, he could spring like a gazelle and slap away shots, but his quickness was often a liability. A simple pump fake would send him soaring.

After shooting for half an hour, Murray walked him through some ball handling drills and showed him the secrets of protecting the ball while watching everything on the floor. On the depth chart he was the number three point guard, behind Murray and Mitch Rocker, a senior and three-year starter. Another inch of growth, and another bad scrimmage kicking the ball out of bounds, and Sooley would become a small forward. Clearly, he was about to be redshirted. He had just turned eighteen and had little to add to a team with plenty of experience. Coach Britt was expecting to start three seniors and two juniors.

. . .

The Walker family lived in Durham's Trinity Park neighborhood, ten minutes from Central's campus. Their house was on a shaded street of two-story homes built before the war.

Murray's mother, Ida, was born and raised in Durham and had never ventured far from home. Her father had been an executive with one of the largest black-owned life insurance companies in the country and her family had enjoyed a comfortable upbringing. Her husband, Ernie, was raised dirt poor in the tobacco fields north of Raleigh and had vowed to never forget the pain of hunger. He was the executive director of the Durham County Food Bank and took great pride in feeding 11,000 people a day.

Ernie had certainly not missed many meals recently. He was grilling chicken breasts on the back patio when Murray and Samuel arrived late Saturday afternoon. The heat index was close to a hundred and Ernie was soaked with sweat as he labored over dinner with a set of steel tongs and listened to the Central football game on the radio. He welcomed Murray's new roommate, said he'd heard nice things about him and so on, and talked football. After a few minutes in the heat, the boys went inside to the kitchen where Mrs. Walker was grating cabbage for slaw and boiling ears of corn.

Miss Ida, as she would be called from then on, was the executive director of Durham Legal Aid, where she oversaw a staff of twenty attorneys serving an endless supply of poor clients. She hugged Samuel as though she had known him forever and told him to sit at the table while she sliced him a wedge of banana nut bread. Murray fancied himself a chef and commenced poking through her slaw and this drew a rebuke.

Samuel was instantly enthralled by Miss Ida. He had never been in the presence of a woman who was the unquestioned boss of everything around her. She quizzed Samuel about his classes and his adjustment to life in America, and she was careful not to mention his family. Murray had briefed them on the tragedies and the ongoing uncertainties, and they were already prepared to support Samuel in every way possible. As she buzzed around the kitchen, she asked Murray about his professors and which ones he preferred. After only two weeks there was little to report. They talked about Jordan, Murray's older sister. She was in law school at Vanderbilt and Samuel was in love with her, though they had yet to meet. He was following her on social media. They talked about Brady, an older brother who had dropped out of Yale and was disrupting the family. But that conversation was cut short.

Ernie entered the much cooler kitchen with a platter of barbe-cued chicken and Miss Ida told him exactly where to put it. As he listened to the family chatter on, Samuel could not help but think of his own poor mother. He had no idea where she was, or even if she was alive. Where was she living? Who was she with? Please, God, let her have Angelina, James, and Chol with her. Let them be safe.

Beatrice was as warm and personable and intelligent as Ida Walker, but she had never been given the chance to enter a school. In Lotta, as in much of his country, the luckiest young girls were given only a few years of basic instruction before being sent home to wash and cook. Most received no education. Beatrice could read and write, nothing more.

Samuel longed for his mother and said a quick prayer for her well-being.

Even as Ida cooked and talked and bossed around her husband and youngest son, she kept one eye on Samuel. He was a deeply wounded boy who needed all the love and support they could give.

CHAPTER 24

Near the end of practice, as the players were winding down and finishing the obligatory 50 free throws in a row, Samuel heard Coach Britt say the magical name, "Ecko." Samuel turned and saw his old coach stride onto the court, and he ran over for a hug. Ecko said he was passing through and wanted to say hello. Samuel thought it was odd that he had not bothered to call. Coach Britt blew his whistle and told the team to go shower.

Later, in Coach Britt's office, Samuel sat and they talked about the team from South Sudan and caught up with all the gossip. Murray joined them, and when Lonnie closed his door, Ecko stopped smiling. He said, "Look, Samuel, I have good news and bad."

Samuel closed his eyes as his shoulders slumped.

Ecko said, "Two days ago, I received a call from a French lady, a nurse working for a nonprofit called Doctors Without Borders. She's in Uganda at the Rhino Camp Refugee Settlement."

"I know where it is, Coach. I have it on a map. There are over one hundred thousand of my people living there."

"Including your mother. Yesterday I spoke to Beatrice. She is safe and doing okay."

Samuel placed his palms over his eyes and fought back tears. "Thank God, thank God," he whispered. They watched him for a moment, then Ecko said, "I told her where you are, what you're doing, and so on. She was excited to know that you're here, in college."

"You spoke to my mother?"

"I did, and she'll call back in the morning, around seven. She's using a nurse's phone. They will call your cell."

Samuel breathed deeply and wiped his cheeks. A long minute passed before he said, "Okay, and the bad news."

"Your brothers are with her and everyone appears to be healthy. However, Angelina didn't make it."

"Didn't make it? What happened to her?"

"She was taken away by rebel soldiers when they burned the village."

"No!" Samuel bent over, rested his elbows on his knees, and covered his face again. The emotions came in waves as his body shook and he kept whispering, "No, no, no."

Murray, Ecko, and Lonnie glanced at each other then studied the floor as the long minutes passed. There was nothing to say, nothing to do but sit and be there for support. They could not begin to imagine the horror of what Samuel and his family were going through. In a file, Ecko had some paperwork for each of his players and he knew that Angelina's sixteenth birthday had been September 2.

Whether she lived to see it could not be known. Ecko had doubts, as did Samuel. The killing was so casual, the atrocities so unspeakable, it was difficult to believe that the enemy would have much use for the girl after a while.

"I should've been there," he finally whispered.

Coach Britt stepped out of his office to make sure the locker room was empty. When he returned, he said, "Let's go to my house. Agnes is cooking dinner and my kids would like to see you, Samuel."

.   .   .

His phone rang with an international call at 7:04 the following morning. Samuel was staring at it, waiting. He'd been awake for an hour, though he had slept little. Murray was dressed and sitting on his bed, waiting too.

A pleasant lady with a slight accent identified herself as Christine, and when Samuel said hello she handed the phone to Beatrice Sooleymon.

When Samuel said, "Mother, is it really you?" Murray eased by him, patted his shoulder, and left their dorm room.

They talked for twenty minutes. As difficult as it was, Samuel wanted to know what happened that night in Lotta, and Beatrice, through many tears, told the whole story. She wasn't sure what had happened to Ayak but she feared the worst. Samuel confirmed that his body had been identified by government troops. Beatrice took it as well as could have been expected. She'd been almost certain of it anyway. She described how they took Angelina, then their flight away from the village, the days and days of travel with no food and water. But they were in a better place now, safe and surrounded by good people who wanted to help each other. She wanted to know all about his new college and life in America, and, well, everything he was doing. They cried a lot but also managed a laugh or two. Samuel wanted to go home, to reunite with his family, to somehow rescue them, but it was not possible. He asked what he could send them, but Beatrice said she wasn't sure. Maybe later. Maybe if and when they were given a more permanent residence he could send packages.

From his research, Samuel knew there were people who had fled his country with nothing and had been living in the settlements for many years. Most lived in harsh, unsanitary conditions with barely enough food to survive. Violence was rare, but disease was common and spread by raw sewage, dirty water, and contaminated food. Efforts to provide education were hamstrung by a lack of facilities and teachers. Dozens of aid groups from around the world labored heroically in the camps and settlements.

The more Samuel had read, the more discouraged he became. They had lost their home, many of their friends and family, and their way of life.

As he talked to his mother, he could almost feel the strain of hopelessness in her voice. In two months her world had been rocked and violated, and there was no going back. He realized that he was her bright spot, and it would be his challenge to lift her spirits. When it was time to go, he chatted with the French woman, Christine, and was told he could call her number once a week. They agreed that every Wednesday at 7 a.m. eastern time would be the chosen hour. Beatrice and her boys would appear outside the tent hospital and Samuel would call from America. Christine warned that the cellular service was not always reliable.

.   .   .

He stuck his phone in his pocket and left the dorm. He had no desire to talk to Murray or anyone else. He needed time alone to think about Angelina and grieve. He took a long walk around the campus and sat for an hour on a park bench as the university came to life. Classes were not important. Basketball could wait. He would call T. Ray and get excused from work.

His day would belong to Angelina. He thanked God for the safety of his mother and brothers, and vowed to one day extricate them from the camp and bring them to America.

For the moment, though, he just wanted to be alone. He tried not to think about her final hours, but chose instead to dwell on childhood memories of his little sister picking fruit in their rear yard, eating too many berries and getting sick, and tagging along behind her big brother to the basketball courts.

He should have been there for her.

.   .   .

Ecko and Lonnie Britt were shown to a corner table in an elegant downtown restaurant. Once seated, Ecko picked up his sparkling white and perfectly ironed cloth napkin and said, "Wow. You did say you're treating, right?"

"I got it. No problem. They're afraid I might leave so they jacked up my expense account."

"And salary?"

"They want to talk but I'm not so sure."

"Is that why we're having lunch in a swanky place? The privacy?"

"Yes. We probably won't see anyone from Central in here for lunch."

A hostess handed them menus and asked about drinks. They were fine with water.

"All right, let's hear it," Ecko said.

"You know it, Ecko. I'm forty-one and I've been here for four years. Won almost seventy percent of my games and I don't want to get stuck here. I want to move up. The question is: Who'll be in the market come next April?"

"Who's on the hot seat?"

"Yep. Who's on the hot seat? I figure Dulaney at Iowa is toast. Lost twenty games the last two years."

"I can't believe they kept him." Ecko was scanning the menu and shaking his head. "Thirty bucks for smoked salmon?"

"It's worth it. I'm buying, okay?"

"Forgive me, Lonnie. I'll always be an immigrant."

"Yes, and you instinctively order the cheapest thing on the menu. Relax. This is on Central."

"Dulaney's buy-out was too big so they kept him for one more year. Should be a disaster. They'll fire the AD too. Talbott at Miami is retiring."

Lonnie smiled at the news and asked, "Has he announced it?"

"Not yet."

"Where do you get your gossip?"

A waiter approached and described the specials. Both ordered tomato salads and grilled trout. As soon as he left, they jumped back into the gossip mill that all coaches found irresistible. Lonnie was ready for a move up and Ecko believed his friend could handle a bigger program, though perhaps not in a Power Five conference. The guy at Richmond was on the ropes, but Lonnie had something bigger in mind. Ecko knew the AD at Creighton and knew he wasn't happy with their program. The coach at Texas wanted a new contract but the school was balking. And so it went, around the country in half an hour as they ate their salads and schemed of ways to find bigger jobs.

When their entrees arrived, Ecko changed the subject with "What are you going to do with Samuel?"

"I don't know. I didn't exactly want the kid, as you might remember."

"Thank you, again, Coach. Together we probably saved his life."

"How's that?"

"Well, if I had not chosen the kid back in April, he would have been at home with his family when their village was raided. Knowing him the way we do, he would have tried to save everyone. He'd probably be dead now."

Lonnie shook his head and mumbled, "What is wrong with those people?"

"We, those people, are cursed, and we're not happy unless there are at least two civil wars raging. You gave the kid a scholarship, a dorm room, a team, an education, a chance to play here, his dream. If he had gone home with the team, who knows what would have happened. His village was burned to the ground."

"What a nightmare. I can't imagine."

"I'll hang around and see him tonight. Why don't you give him a week off, let him mourn in private."

"Sure. Whatever. I'll probably redshirt him anyway, though that's the last thing I need."

"So, he's not lighting it up in practice?"

"Let's just say his game has not changed in the past two months.

He's a great kid. He fits in. Always a big smile. Plays hard and all that. Can jump out of the gym. There's just no place to put him right now."

"Be patient with him. He might surprise you."

"That's what you keep saying. And I admit there are moments when he springs up, lifts the ball high, lets it go when he's forty-five inches off the court, all smooth and fluid and he just sort of hangs there like Michael Jordan, but the damned ball never goes in."

"That could be a problem."

"His ball handling has improved a little but he'll never play at guard."

"Give him some time. He's just a kid."

"They're all kids, Ecko."

"They are indeed, but this one is special."

CHAPTER 25

Murray and Samuel finished unloading a truckload of canned vegetables at a pantry and stopped by the offices of the International Rescue Committee in central Durham. Miss Ida was familiar with its work and mentioned it to Sooley, who researched it online. A Ms. Keyser was expecting the two basketball players from Central.

She gave a quick overview of the IRC's history and work: It was founded by Albert Einstein in 1933 to help European Jews resettle in the U.S., and had grown into one of the world's largest humanitarian organizations. It worked in the regions hit hardest by war, persecution, genocide, and natural disasters, and provided shelter, food, and health care for the most vulnerable. In many instances it relocated them in Western countries. In the past forty years, the IRC office in Durham County had helped over eight hundred refugees from twenty-five countries resettle in the area, including eighteen from South Sudan.

"Do you know anyone here from your country?" she asked.

"No."

"No relatives here in the States?"

"No."

"The relocation process can be long and difficult. Demand is great, supply is not. U.S. Immigration is currently allowing only five thousand a year into the country from South Sudan. The need is much greater. Not surprisingly, many of the world's refugees would like to come here. I believe Ida Walker said that you plan to seek citizenship."

"Yes I do."

"That's good. The fact that you're already here is crucial. Please, don't even think about going back."

"He's not," Murray said and got a laugh.

She continued, "There is no easy way to get your family here, but your best chance is after you have become a U.S. citizen and can sponsor them. Without a sponsor, it's almost hopeless."

"How long will it take?"

She smiled and glanced at her notes. "A long time, Samuel, a very long time. First, you need to finish college. That's four years."

Murray interrupted with "Probably five, the way he's playing."

"I'm sorry."

"He'll probably redshirt this season, so he might get another year of college."

"Right. Okay, whatever, but staying in school and graduating are important. Then get a job and start a career. The more success you have here the better your chances of sponsoring your family."

"That's not really what I wanted to hear," Samuel said.

"I know. It's a long process, even when it works. Sometimes it doesn't."

"But they're in a camp, barely getting enough food and water."

"Along with many others. Look, I'm happy to open a file and you can call me anytime. You can stop by. You can even volunteer if you'd like. We have a college internship program and we love our students. Ida said you've made contact through Doctors Without Borders."

"I spoke to my mother two days ago through them. Is it possible to send her money?"

"I don't know but I'll find out. We have an office in Uganda, in

Kampala I believe. Rhino is an established camp and I'm sure we have someone there."

"I've read everything about the camp that's online. There's a small market where you can buy food and basics. They have nothing, only one change of clothes from a distribution center in the camp. They sleep on the ground, no blankets. I'd really like to get some money to them."

She smiled warmly and said, "I'll figure it out. Call me tomorrow."

. . .

The food trucks were delayed and delayed again, and then they stopped coming. But the lines held firm and continued to grow as desperate people waited in the sun.

Beatrice and the boys left one line and went to another, then another. Rumors were flying that there was food on the west side of the settlement and when they arrived there was a swarm around a United Nations truck. Workers frantically dipped small portions of rice into whatever bowls the people brought. Those with none were simply given two handfuls.

The hunger terrified the refugees because it brought back painful memories from the recent past. They had all been hungry and their primary prayer each day was for enough food to sustain life.

Ninety-seven percent of the water in Rhino Camp was trucked in, and when those trucks too failed to show there was an uneasiness in the streets. Hungry children bawled as their mothers went door-to-door and begged for food. The tent hospitals, all run by foreign NGOs, were inundated with thousands of desperate people pleading for something to eat.

It rained for a week, nonstop, and the gravel highways used by the trucks flooded and washed out, cutting off food, water, and supplies. The dirt streets turned to mud and the rainwater pooled in puddles and began running down the hills. The narrow creeks rose with raw sewage and spilled out of their banks. The tents leaked around the windows and tore along the roofs and before long the deluge sent filthy water running under the floors of tents. The bore-holes used for pumping water collapsed under the weight of the softening soil. The outhouses and crude privies filled and flooded and human waste ran free. It rained until everything—every person, every tent, every shanty, every jeep and truck, every field hospital—was soaked and caked with mud.

When the rain stopped and the skies cleared, the sun bore down on Rhino Camp and before long the mud returned to dirt. The doctors and aid workers braced for another wave of malaria.

. . .

Bright and early on Wednesday morning, September 30, Samuel eased quietly out of his dorm room, leaving Murray dead to the world, and went outside where he found a park bench. He punched in the number for Christine, the French nurse. He could almost see her and wondered what kind of person leaves behind safety, security, a much easier life, to volunteer in one of the worst humanitarian crises in the world? Samuel considered himself to be a compassionate soul, but his sympathy had its limits. He was awed by aid workers willing to risk their health, even their lives. Perhaps it was because he had just escaped the harshness of the developing world that he had such a dim view of going back. Perhaps some privileged people carried a bit of guilt and wanted to get their hands dirty. Or, perhaps they did indeed value every life.

He had a list of things to discuss with his mother, the most important of which was how to send her money. With Murray's help, he had opened a checking account and applied for a credit card. He was saving his money and proud of the fact that he could handle it himself, just like every other student.

Ms. Keyser at the IRC had come through and referred him to yet another NGO, one that specialized in routing money back to Africa. Each year immigrants scattered around the world remitted home over $2 billion, money desperately needed by their families. Though South Sudan was a small, poor country with a limited number of expats abroad, its immigrants were sending back $300 million a year. Coordinating these payments and making certain the money arrived at its intended destination was a challenge, but Samuel had found a way and couldn't wait to explain it to his mother.

There was no answer on Christine's end.

CHAPTER 26

He went to the gym, turned on only one row of lights so he would attract no attention, stretched for all of five minutes, and began shooting. When he thought about his family, he missed. When he concentrated on his form, he hit. An hour passed and he realized how much he enjoyed the solitude of a deserted, semidark gym, with 3,000 empty seats, and not another person around. At 8:30, when the count was at 420 shots, a janitor walked under the backboard and said good morning. Samuel said good morning, said he was on the basketball team and had a key. The janitor didn't care and disappeared.

Samuel stopped for water at ten o'clock and realized he would miss his first class. He decided he was taking a break from classes, if only for a day, and would do nothing but shoot. He skipped them all and stayed in the gym until noon when a group of alumni appeared for a meeting. He hustled back to his dorm and took a shower.

Coach Britt was old-school and believed that basketball players should be lean, limber, flexible, and quick. He preferred finesse over bulk and muscle. Therefore, he did not stress weight training. As an assistant at DePaul, he'd witnessed an entire team decimated with torn muscles and spasms a year after the program hired a drill sergeant who loved barbells and bench presses. Coach wanted speed over strength.

But Samuel had been mightily impressed with the play, not to mention the physique, of Abol Pach, the U.K. shooting forward who had almost single-handedly sent South Sudan packing in their last game in Orlando. Pach was one of them, a Dinka from Juba, lean and fluid but thicker in the arms and chest than most young African players. The program listed him at 6'7" and 220 pounds.

Though Samuel had watched the final game from the bench and in a dizzying fog of uncertainty over events back home, he vividly recalled Pach's strength and intimidation around the rim. There was a rumor that he spent an hour a day pumping iron. Samuel also had an indelible memory of the vast and modern weight room where the Magic players lifted when off the court. If the game's best players wanted strength, then that was good enough for him.

An assistant football coach named Willis, one of two white guys on the staff, was in charge of bulking up the team. At first he told Sooley that the weight room was a waste of time for basketball players, but Sooley persisted. By then the African kid with the big smile was one of the more popular fixtures in the locker room.

Willis found a workout plan for basketball players, one designed to strengthen the core and add a few inches to the chest and biceps without restricting flexibility. He showed Samuel the proper and safe way to use the weight machines, weighted bars, bands, and dumbbells. He measured him at 6'5" and weighed him at 195. And he gave him a key to the weight room.

After six weeks on campus, Samuel had fallen into the rather enjoyable routine of beginning each day with an hour or so alone shooting baskets, then an hour or so working as an equipment manager, then at least two hard hours on the court in practice, and a final hour in the weight room. His studies were not motivating and he was cutting more classes than permitted. He had trouble concentrating and was bored with the notion of homework. Besides, he was on the slow track to diddle for a year as a redshirt. That meant five years of college. Surely that was enough. He could always catch up later.

. . .

Ernie Walker put the finishing touches on a pork shoulder that would be roasted for two hours in the same deep dish with potatoes, beets, and carrots. He admired his work, checked the oven, and slid in the pan. He and Ida both enjoyed cooking, and they had decided that Wednesday nights would be the family dinner with Murray and Samuel.

Though the Central campus was only ten minutes away, they had seen little of their youngest son during his first semester. He wanted to cut the cord and they did not resist. But during the spring of freshman year, word spread among his teammates that his family had a nice house in town and there was always something good to eat. Ida and Ernie had found themselves cooking more and more. Now that they had quietly decided to unofficially adopt Samuel, they were enticing the boys with Wednesday dinners, Saturday cookouts, and Sunday brunches after church.

Ida called and said she was running late. Ernie assured her that their dinner was in good hands. She called him at least four times a day with updates on her hectic schedule, and around five every afternoon she called to inform him she was running late again. He always listened patiently and reminded her to slow down. She was the boss and could come and go as she pleased, but with a staff of younger attorneys she believed in setting the right example. She worked harder than any of them and often needed the calm, steady voice of her husband to settle her nerves.

Ernie checked the oven, set the table, poured himself a glass of ice tea, no sugar, and went to the den to read for a few minutes. He had a stack of newspaper and magazine articles he'd found on the internet at his office and began reading a long piece from *The Guardian*. The journalist had visited four of the refugee settlements in Uganda and described the daily lives of the people, almost all of whom were from South Sudan.

The disconnect seemed too far-fetched. It was difficult to believe that the nice young man rooming with their son had a mother and two brothers living in a dismal place known as the Rhino Camp Refugee Settlement. Ernie and Ida were talking to Ms. Keyser at the IRC and brainstorming ways to extract Beatrice and the boys, to get them into the immigration pipeline to America. But the sad truth was that there were at least half a million South Sudanese ahead of them, most with sponsors and paperwork properly on file. Ms. Keyser was too professional to use the word "hopeless," but after several conversations it was apparent that the chances of a family reunion were slim.

Ida arrived after six and immediately went to the oven for a quick inspection. "Who's coming? Do we know?" she asked Ernie.

"Of course not. That would require some forethought."

The table was set for five but the number was always a moving target. Murray was often not bothered with notions of planning and was known to invite anyone he passed in the dormitory hallway. He might call home with the number of guests, or he might not. His invitations were usually limited, though, by the number of friends he could stuff into the cab of his Toyota pickup. Four long-legged basketball players seemed to be the max.

When he walked in with just Samuel, his parents were relieved. Murray immediately went to the oven and as his mother said, "Don't open that!" he yanked it open and took a whiff. "Smells delicious."

"I'm glad you approve," Ernie said.

"Close the oven!" Ida growled as she stepped toward him. He grabbed her and lifted her and spun her around as she tried to free herself. Ernie laughed as Ida squealed, and once again Samuel was astonished at the horseplay.

The men sat around the table as Ida sliced tomatoes for the salad. "Any luck this morning?" Ernie asked. It was Wednesday, and all of them knew the importance of the phone call.

Samuel smiled and said, "Yes, I spoke to my mother this morning."

"Hallelujah," Ernie said, rubbing his hands together.

"How is she?" Ida asked.

"She is safe, as are James and Chol." He said the rains had stopped and the food trucks were running on time. The U.N. had completed a water pumping station and each person was getting almost twelve kilos of water a day, but the lines were long. The money Samuel had wired the week before had arrived and Beatrice said she almost felt wealthy. She was very careful with it because the neighbors watched each other closely and money could cause trouble. She had been able to buy some canned foods and personal items, and she had shared these with her two friends from Lotta. They were still living in the tents and had no idea how long they would be there, or where they would move to next. They had been told, though, that the tents were only temporary.

When dinner was served, the conversation shifted from Africa to the basketball team. They were practicing two hours a day and Coach Britt was trying to kill them. As a sophomore, Murray was worried about playing time and moving up the bench. As a redshirt, Sooley was just happy to be on the court. His four-year career was well ahead of him.

As always, he quietly enjoyed the meal. The meat and vegetables were delicious, the sauce rich and tasty. But he had seen too many photographs and videos of the long lines of hungry refugees waiting for a bowl of gruel. The internet brought life in the camps to his laptop in living color, and he could never again savor a fine meal without thinking of his family.

CHAPTER 27

Lonnie Britt was not an early riser and for about half the year he managed to sleep at least until seven. But from late September when the real practices began until March when the season was over, he was usually awake before six and worrying about something. The day's practice plan; the first game only five weeks away; a recruit who had committed then changed his mind; the starting five; and the next five; who wasn't going to class; should he cut a walk-on who could add nothing but locker room humor; and recruiting. Always recruiting.

And if he didn't have enough on his mind, add the drama of a kid whose father and sister had been murdered and the rest of the family was living in a refugee camp in Uganda. Plus, two former players had lawyers who were haggling with a prosecutor over the terms of a plea agreement.

He was wide awake at five and at 5:30 his wife kicked him out of bed so she could sleep another hour. He showered quietly, checked on the kids, and left in the dark for his favorite coffee shop near the campus. There, as he ate scrambled eggs and sipped black coffee, he scanned the Raleigh newspaper and noticed that the preseason collegiate rankings had been announced. Not surprisingly, Duke was the consensus number one pick, primarily because it was likely to start four eighteen-year-old freshmen who would be gone by next June. Like all coaches, Lonnie loathed the idea of freshmen entering the NBA draft, the infamous one-and-done game, but it was not something he worried about. It was rare that a player in the Mid-Eastern Athletic Conference was drafted after only one year. It had never happened at Central. Lonnie knew his freshmen were safe. And, like all coaches, he was openly envious of the remarkable talent that the one-and-done programs attracted.

Not surprisingly, Central was not in the top 25. It had never made the list—pre, during, or post season. According to the online buzz, the Eagles were expected to finish fourth in the MEAC, behind Delaware State, Florida A&M, and Norfolk State, but those predictions were proven wrong every season.

Two years earlier, they had won 23 games, took the conference tournament, and made it to March Madness before getting bounced in the first round. A year ago, they had won 20 games but didn't qualify. Another 20-win season and Lonnie would be in a position to move to a bigger school.

He drove to The Nest and parked in his reserved space. The small lot was empty. It was 7:30. He unlocked the door that led to the locker room, flipped on some lights, and was headed to his office when he heard a bouncing ball. He made his way to the bleachers and peeked around a corner. Sooley was all alone at the far end, in the dim light, launching bombs from deep, and rarely hitting. His shirt was off and his dark skin was glistening with sweat. After each shot, he ran for the rebound, dribbled this way and that way, took it behind the back, between the legs, then squared up and shot again. The leap was always extraordinary, even if the ball kept bouncing off the rim.

The most impressive image at the moment was the kid in the gym at 7:30, and he had been there for a while.

One of the problems with his game, and perhaps his biggest one, was where to play? He was not going to be a guard and not ready to play forward. Lonnie had already decided to delay those worries and watch the kid develop. He would sit the upcoming season as a redshirt.

He watched him for a long time and tried to imagine the fear and confusion in his world. On the court, he was all smiles and energy, even when he was screwing up. Off the court, though, he often gazed away, his smile gone, his thoughts drifting to another continent. Lonnie had coached plenty of players from broken homes and rough neighborhoods, but none with problems as complicated as Samuel Sooleymon's.

He eased onto the court and said, "Good morning, Sooley." The nickname had become permanent. Samuel resisted at first, at least with his team, but he soon realized that nicknames were common in the U.S., and usually endearing.

He was surprised and dribbled over to mid-court. "Hey Coach."

"Getting an early start."

"I'm here every morning, Coach."

"How many shots so far?"

"One forty-two. Just got started."

"How many have you made?"

"Forty-nine."

Lonnie rattled the numbers for a second and said, "That's about thirty-five percent. And there's no one guarding you. Not too impressive."

Samuel shrugged and said, "Well, that's why I'm here, Coach."

Lonnie smiled at the perfect answer. "I guess so. Look, Coach Grinnell got a call yesterday from an assistant dean who said you're missing classes. What's going on?"

His shoulders sagged as he glanced around and looked thoroughly guilty. "I don't know, Coach. No excuses."

"I know you have a lot on your mind. I can't imagine, and you know we're concerned about you and your family."

"Yes sir. Thank you."

"But, you're here on a full scholarship, Sooley. Do you know what this means?"

"I think so."

"It means that someone else is paying for your college education. It means that the taxpayers of North Carolina are on the hook. The janitors who work here. The bus drivers. Your professors. Murray's parents. Me. The other coaches. All of us are paying taxes, and some of that money trickles down to Central. It allows you to study here for free and to earn a degree. The least you can do is go to class and make the grades."

"Yes sir. I'm sorry. I'll do better."

"From now on, Coach Grinnell will check every day. When you miss, I'll know it."

"I won't miss anymore, Coach."

Lonnie clapped his hands and Samuel bounced the ball to him. "Top of the key." Lonnie got in the lane and began rebounding as Sooley shot from 20 feet. After a few misses, Lonnie said, "Slow it down. You're working too fast. Concentrate on making each shot perfect." A moment later, "Square up, shoulders at the basket." A moment later, "Keep the elbow in. Visualize each shot. Watch the ball go in before you shoot."

After 50 shots, 18 of which went in, Lonnie kept the ball and walked to the top of the key. "You need some water?"

"No thanks."

The managers had noticed that Sooley consumed far less water than the other players.

Lonnie said, "Murray is passing the hat around the locker room to raise some money for your family. I'm sure you know this."

Samuel looked surprised and said, "No sir. He hasn't told me."

"Well, maybe I shouldn't have said anything. Point is, the coaches can't help out. If we donated we would violate NCAA rules against financial assistance to a player, or some such nonsense."

"Thanks, Coach, but I would never ask for that kind of help."

"I know. I'm sure you've met his mother, Miss Ida."

"Several times, yes."

"Ida Walker is a force and she wants to organize an effort to help your family. She called last night to check on NCAA rules and regs. I have to talk to the school's lawyer today."

"But she's a lawyer."

"Different kind. Not many lawyers understand the NCAA. Coaches either."

"She didn't tell me about this."

"Sounds like she's just getting started. Maybe I shouldn't have said anything, but I want you to know that your coaches and the school are behind you a hundred percent."

"Thanks, Coach. But I don't want the other players donating money. I would never expect that."

"Sooley, they don't have any money, okay? They're a bunch of broke college kids, same as anywhere else, but they want to help. They know what you've been through and they know about your family. They care, and we care."

Samuel bit his lip and nodded.

Lonnie said, "I'm keeping the ball. You get to class."

.   .   .

In response to the ongoing and worsening crisis in South Sudan, the United Nations, in 2015, budgeted $800 million in aid to the region, with the money to be divided primarily among the neighboring countries. Aid aimed directly for Juba had become suspect. Reports from the field repeatedly said that the desperately needed cash was bottled up and diverted by the government. Uganda was to get half of the money. Over 700,000 South Sudanese were living in twenty refugee camps and settlements, and by midsummer around a thousand were arriving each day. The situation was dire. The demand for food, water, medicine, and shelter became overwhelming.

For several reasons—lack of funds, bureaucracy, regional feuds, corruption—less than one third of the U.N. commitment arrived. Uganda did its best with the money as NGOs scrambled to plug the gaps. Camps hurriedly designed for 5,000 refugees were over-run with five times that. Children died of starvation, malnutrition, malaria, and other diseases.

The current crisis attracted the world's attention again and was well covered by the Western press. Late each night, Sooley read the stories and reports online. After lights were out and the dorm was quiet, he sat on his bed and scrolled through the internet. Occasionally he found photos of the Rhino camp—Beatrice had said they were in Rhino South—and he studied the faces of hundreds of his people, hoping desperately for a glimpse of his mother, or James or Chol. He still clung to the prayer that Angelina was there, somewhere, searching for her family.

When he was certain Murray was sound asleep, he turned off his laptop, pulled the sheets over his head and said his prayers. Often, he allowed himself a good cry.

CHAPTER 28

Beatrice kept her coins hidden in a small plastic pouch that never left her body. She hid it in a cotton scarf tied tightly around her waist. She had shared some of the money with her two friends from Lotta, and had sworn them to secrecy. No one had money in the camps, and any rumor of it would be dangerous.

The new arrivals were being housed in tent cities, or at least the lucky ones. Thousands more were outside the gates, waiting to be admitted, registered, and hopefully fed. Once inside they slept on the ground until a tent was available.

In the older sections of the settlement, where many of the refugees had lived for years, the homes were made of wood, baked bricks, and thick straw, and built to last for years. The Ugandan government had given some of the homeowners a small plot of land to grow vegetables and raise chickens and pigs. This created commerce, and there was a busy market area in the center of Rhino Camp South. Refugees with a little money could buy better food, medicine, clothing, and other necessities. There was a lot of bartering and trading.

With the $100 Samuel had sent her, Beatrice bought a few items that would not attract attention. He said he had a job, in addition to being a student, and that he would send more. "Don't send too much," she had said. He always promised to come rescue them, but cautioned that it would take a long time.

Knowing her oldest child was safe and prospering was enough to lift her spirits, but the monotony of life in the camp was taking a toll. There was so little to do to pass the time. No home to clean; no food to cook; almost no laundry and no creek to wash it in; no school for the children. The weekly outdoor Mass attracted thousands and gave them a hint of normalcy.

On a Wednesday, she was up early with the boys and chatting with her neighbor about the daily search for food. There should be three food trucks within a half hour's walk and they debated which might have the shortest breakfast line. This was a favorite topic of conversation for people with little else to do, and since food and water dominated their lives they talked about them nonstop.

When the children, all eight of them, were awake, the three women began the trek toward the chosen food distribution point. They chose badly and waited two hours for a bowl of rice and small loaf of bread. When they finished eating, Beatrice sent James and Chol with her two friends and began the sixty-minute walk through the crowded streets to the Doctors Without Borders hospital.

Each week more people packed into the camps. She passed tent cities, streets lined with shanties that looked flimsier than tents, and other streets with sturdier homes. In some sections the people were packed tightly together, and in others the sprawl went on for miles. All were displaced, all driven from their homeland by men with guns. Her parents had talked of the old days when famine forced people to leave their homes in search of food. Now they were driven out by warlords and their heavily armed militias.

Christine appeared at the hospital's entrance a few minutes before two, on cue, and as they waited for the call the nurse asked about James and Chol and about their health. As usual, the hospital was crawling with patients and long lines branched out in every entrance.

Her phone buzzed. She smiled, said "Bonjour," and handed it to

Beatrice. Christine left them to their private moments and went to check on patients.

. . .

On Wednesday, November 11, Samuel finished the call with his mother with the usual mix of emotions, but couldn't dwell on his family right then. It was an important day because the first game was that night, and though he wouldn't play, he would wear the Eagles game uniform for the first time and yell from the bench. He returned to his room, woke up the deadhead Murray, and took off for the gym. He shot for an hour, went to all his classes—he hadn't missed a single one now that he knew that someone was watching—and washed dirty football jerseys for an hour. The team had lost four straight and a bad season was finally coming to an end. At 5:30, he was in the basketball locker room playing video games and listening to rap as his teammates drifted in.

Four of the starting five had been set since before the first practice. Mitch Rocker was a senior point guard who had started the past two seasons and was captain of the team. Two more seniors, Dmitri Robbins and Roy Tice, started last year at forward and had not been challenged. A junior, Duffy Sunday, played 20 minutes a game the prior season and was much improved as the shooting guard. None of the three big men had dominated in practice, but Melvin Montgomery, another junior, had more experience and would get the start at center.

It was a veteran team and the players had high expectations. They certainly expected to rout their first opponent, a small private college from Charlotte that no one had ever heard of. It was one of those ridiculous preseason sleepers, anything but a real game, and few fans showed any interest. When the Eagles took the floor, The Nest was not even half filled, but that made no difference to Samuel Sooleymon. He smiled at his teammates in their handsome maroon-and-gray uniforms, just like the one he was wearing. Number 22, one of the few remaining numbers but Samuel didn't care. He would have taken any jersey. He smiled at his coaches, the ball boys, the team managers, the referees. No one in the building was as happy as Sooley. He savored the pregame warm-up, but missed every shot from long range. He laughed on the bench, yelled at his teammates on the floor, and glanced occasionally at the student section. No benchwarmer ever enjoyed a game more.

There were thirteen players in uniform, including Sooley and one of the walk-ons. The other had not made the cut. The two transfers were not allowed to dress out but sat at the far end of the bench and were expected to make noise. Of the thirteen, everyone saw action but him. Even the walk-on, Rontae Hammer, played five minutes and hit a three. In the second half, the Eagles played down to their opponent's level and the game turned sloppy. Afterward, Coach Britt yelled in the locker room and seemed unhappy, but a 30-point win against a bunch of short, slow white boys was what it was.

Four nights later, while the football team was on the road, the Eagles hosted another mystery school that started five players who would have struggled against Central's women's team. In an embarrassing blowout, nine players scored in double figures, a team record. Murray hit three bombs and had 12 points. He was firmly entrenched as the number two point guard behind Mitch Rocker, and it looked as though he would see limited playing time. In Samuel's muted opinion, his roommate was simply not quick enough. After three months on the practice court, Samuel could easily dominate Murray in one-on-one drills.

After two pushovers, it was time for the NC Central Eagles to go from bully to patsy, though that was certainly not their plan. They rode the bus ninety minutes to Winston-Salem and took the floor against Wake Forest in Joel Coliseum in front of 9,000 rowdy fans. For Samuel, it was a breathtaking moment to trot out for warm-ups in front of a packed house. Though he would not get near the court after the whistle, his stomach was flipping nonetheless. Evidently, the entire team had the nerves and nothing fell for the first five minutes. Down 14–0, Lonnie called time-out and asked his starters if any of them had plans to score that night. They wanted to and tried mightily, but their rim had shrunk. Wake was up by 20 at half-time, and Samuel, unsmiling, rather enjoyed Lonnie's half-time histrionics.

They were not effective. After clawing to within 15 early in the second half, Central withered under the pressure of a full-court press and fell to pieces. Lonnie yanked his starters but the second team was even more confused. With the offense out of sync, the defense lost focus and Wake got red hot. The 30-point loss made for a long bus ride back to Durham.

On Saturday, November 21, the Eagles flew on a charter to Knoxville for another game they would have preferred to avoid. Playing in front of 20,000 fans, none of whom were rooting for them, the Eagles fought respectably but still lost by 20. Afterward, back in the dorm, Murray would explain that the big schools need a few easy wins early in the season and were happy to pay a weaker program up to $100,000 to drive over for a butt-whipping.

"So Tennessee paid us to come into their place and get slaughtered?"

"Sure. They're called 'guarantee' games. They're guaranteed a win and we're guaranteed a check. Everybody does it. Just part of a typical season. Plus they cover our travel expenses."

"What do we pay our victims?" Sooley asked.

"A lot less. I've heard ten thousand. Plus they buy their own bus tickets."

"Only in America." At least once a day Sooley was stopped cold and shook his head in amazement at the excesses of American culture, especially college athletics. He still had trouble grasping the idea that his full scholarship, valued at about $22,000 a year, was free, and that Central was paying him $7.25 an hour to fold towels and clean up after the football team.

On November 24, the last day of classes before the Thanksgiving break, Central hosted Campbell in another sleeper. With only a few hundred fans watching—the students had already fled—the Eagles proved that twenty-year-olds can easily lose focus. They were going home tomorrow, for four days of Mom's cooking and no practice and no classes to worry about, and they didn't bring their game. But Campbell did. According to the Vegas odds, another American oddity that Murray was still trying to explain to his roommate, Central was going to win by a dozen points. Instead, the Eagles lost by 10, at home, and Coach Britt was furious. He told his players to get out of his sight—he didn't want to see them until Sunday afternoon, at which time they had better show up ready for a grueling practice.

CHAPTER 29

For the past fifteen years, Christine Moran had tended to the dire medical needs of the poorest people on the planet. She was from the lovely town of Besançon in eastern France, near the Swiss border, but had not been back there in a decade. She had studied nursing in Paris and wanted to see the world. Médecins Sans Frontières, Doctors Without Borders, signed her up and sent her to Bangladesh for two years. From there she went to Tanzania and spent three years caring for people from Burundi who were fleeing genocide. After five years with refugees, she returned to France and worked in a hospital in Lille, but quit after four months when she realized her patients were hardly ill compared to those in the developing world. She returned to Africa and was assigned to the Kakuma Refugee Camp in Kenya, home to 200,000 displaced souls, most from Sudan and Somalia, though they came from twenty other countries as well. Many of them were children with no parents, and it was those faces that haunted her when she tried to live in France. The sad hopeless faces of malnourished children, some dying, others hanging on and slowly improving. She had held hundreds of them as they drifted away forever.

Three years ago, she had been assigned to Rhino Camp South and found it to be a better settlement than most. They were all overcrowded and depressing, all packed with displaced people who had lost everything, but the Rhino camps were somewhat organized and the food and water usually arrived on time. DWB ran two large tent hospitals, and the staff, a mix of European, American, and African doctors and nurses, worked nonstop for at least twelve hours a day. It was an arduous schedule, a challenging way of life, but they were driven by a deep humanitarian desire to make a difference, one patient at a time. Most burned out after a few years and retreated to the safety of the civilized world, but even then they never forgot their work in the camps and took quiet pride in the lives they saved.

Christine kept her cell phone close but not on display. Their coverage was limited and air time was cherished. She enjoyed sharing it with a few of her patients, those with relatives in the U.S. or Europe. She had spoken to Samuel on two occasions and asked him to call relatives of other people in the camp, and he happily agreed to do so.

Each Wednesday at precisely 2 p.m., she walked to a certain corner of the hospital tent, made eye contact with Beatrice, and led her to a small room where supplies were stored. They waited until 2:05. The phone rang. Christine said, "Bonjour, Samuel." She handed the phone to his mother for a brief chat and went outside.

. . .

Lonnie's wife kicked him out of bed at six because he was fidgety and kept waking her up. It was obvious, at least to her, that he couldn't sleep. But she could if he would just leave.

At his favorite diner he flipped through the newspaper, but only to have something to do as he ate. The only news he cared about was basketball and he monitored the sport ten hours a day online. Duke was 6–0 and its closest game had been an impressive 18-point win on the road over Villanova. Kentucky and Kansas were numbers two and three, both undefeated.

Lonnie put the paper down, worked on his breakfast, and

began fuming again about the previous night's loss to Campbell. As always, he expected to split the pre-conference games and he was realistic about the early losses. But he and his staff had pegged Campbell as a win.

He drove through the empty campus and parked by the gym. He walked through the locker room, approached his office door, and stopped when he heard a bouncing ball. It was 7:20, the day before Thanksgiving, and the only students on campus were foreign and all were still sound asleep. Except Sooley. Lonnie peeked around the bleachers and watched the kid dribble and shoot. He shook his head, went to his office, and watched the edited version of last night's fiasco. He called Jason Grinnell, his associate head coach and closest friend, and replayed the game again. He called two recruits to wish them Happy Thanksgiving.

At 10:30 his wife called with a short grocery list. He asked if it was okay for him to return home. She said yes, but only if he could forget basketball for the next forty-eight hours. He said he could but both knew it was a lie. He locked his office door and had taken a few steps toward the locker room when he realized the basketball was still bouncing.

Sooley was soaked and broke into his customary grin when he saw his coach walking toward him. "How long you been shooting, Sooley?"

"I don't know, Coach. Two or three hours."

"How many shots?"

"Six ninety."

"And how many have gone in?"

"Three forty-three."

"That's almost fifty percent."

"Yes, but, as you say, there's no one guarding me."

"And all from the arc?"

"Ninety percent."

"Do you know what our team is shooting from the arc?"

"Twenty-eight percent."

"Twenty-eight percent. That's pretty lousy. What do you think of our team, Sooley, after five games? You have a different perspective from your end of the bench. I'd like to know what you think."

Sooley smiled, dribbled a couple of times, said, "We're good, Coach. It's early. We have a lot of experience. Once we get into conference we'll be okay."

Lonnie smiled and asked, "Where's Murray?"

"Sleeping when I left the room."

"He needs to spend more time in the gym, don't you think?"

Sooley wasn't about to pass judgment on his roommate or any other member of the team. Murray's problem was that he'd rather spend time with Robin, his latest girlfriend. Evidently, they couldn't get enough of each other and the dorm room was their favorite love nest. Sooley was spending at least an hour in either the library or the commons each night, waiting for the text that all was clear.

"He's good," Sooley said. "Just needs some more playing time."

"Gee. I've never heard that before. If you were me, would you give him more playing time?"

"Sure, Coach, I'd give everybody more playing time."

Lonnie laughed and glanced at the backboard. "So how many shots today?"

"A thousand."

"Atta boy. I'm picking you up at six for dinner at our place, right?"

"Yes sir. And thanks, Coach."

"And Murray is joining us?"

"Yes, he said so."

"Have you ever eaten turkey?"

"No sir, don't think so."

"It's overrated. Agnes is roasting a duck instead."

"Never had that either."

"And you're staying with the Walkers?"

"Yes sir. They've invited me for the break."

"Good. I imagine the dorm can be a lonely place."

Not for Murray. "Yes sir, but I'm fine."

"Did you talk to your mother this morning?"

"Yes sir. They're doing okay, I guess. Life in the camps is not easy but at least they're safe."

"And no word on your sister?"

"No sir. Really, Coach, we're not expecting to hear anything. She's gone and we know it. We still say our prayers but it would take a miracle."

"We're saying our prayers too, Sooley, all of your coaches."

"Thanks."

"I'll see you at six."

.   .   .

Samuel had spent many nights at the Walkers'. His spot was on a long sofa in the basement, between a ping-pong table and a sixty-four-inch flat screen where he and Murray watched ESPN on Friday and Saturday nights. Robin was usually there, though Miss Ida would not allow her to sleep over. In Samuel's quiet and humble opinion, Miss Ida wasn't too keen on her youngest child getting so serious with a girl at the age of twenty. But it was also evident that Murray was somewhat spoiled and usually did what he wanted.

This visit was different, though, because Jordan was home from law school. Samuel had followed her on social media, and was thoroughly smitten long before she walked through the door and hugged everyone. She was twenty-four, gorgeous, sexy, smart, and unattached. Samuel was scheming of ways to propose marriage, something he would have done without hesitation back home. There, though, the rules were different. Marriage proposals were often made to fathers of young teenage girls. A man could have more than one wife. A father could give his daughter as a gift. And so on. A rather different world.

Late Wednesday night, the family watched a movie in the den, a tradition, and Samuel couldn't keep his eyes off Jordan. Miss Ida caught him a couple of times but he couldn't help himself. She missed nothing.

He slept late on Thanksgiving Day, and, following the aromas, went upstairs to the kitchen where the entire family was buzzing around, all talking and laughing. Brady, the wayward son, had arrived after midnight, and was eager to meet Sooley. He'd heard so much about him. Each Walker seemed to be preparing a dish of some sort and everyone had opinions about the others' technique, knowledge, and ingredients. Samuel found a seat at the table and stayed out of the way. Pecan waffles, another tradition, were served and everyone sat down for a long breakfast. A massive turkey stood ready in a pan on the stove, waiting to be roasted for at least six hours. Five, in Ernie's opinion. At least seven, in Murray's.

As they ate, the family went through the menu for the afternoon's feast. In addition to the turkey, there would be oyster dressing with cranberry sauce. Candied yams. Collard greens in ham hocks. Corn fritters. Giblet gravy. Jalapeño cornbread. Pumpkin and pecan pies. At first, as he stuffed another pecan waffle in his mouth, he thought they were joking about so much food for one meal. Then he realized they were quite serious.

He enjoyed the rowdy bantering and warmhearted fun, but there were flashes when he couldn't help but think of his mother and brothers, and his neighbors and friends from Lotta. Some dead. Some missing. The lucky ones barely surviving in makeshift huts, shanties, and tents, patiently waiting in line for hours for another bowl of rice.

CHAPTER 30

Late Sunday, the team gathered at The Nest for a much-dreaded practice. Their coach, though, was in a better mood. In the film room, he made them watch the Campbell game and replayed some of the worst of it. Then they took the floor for two nonstop hours of drills, with all four coaches yelling at even the slightest mistake.

Two days later they rode the bus ninety minutes to Greenville to play East Carolina, a 10-point favorite, and lost by three in overtime. It was their fourth straight loss and led to another quiet bus ride back to campus. Other than the loss, the most disturbing event of the night was a bad injury to Evan Tucker, a second-string forward. Midway through the second half he went up for a rebound and landed on his elbow, shattering it. He was still at the hospital in Greenville with Coach Jackie Garver. The X-rays were not promising and he would not be returning anytime soon.

The football season was over and the team won six and lost that many. Samuel had made many friends in the locker room and hated to see it end. Lonnie pulled some strings and kept him on the payroll, a couple of hours a day tidying up the weight room and doing whatever T. Ray wanted. The $7.25 an hour was important and Samuel spent little of it. His goal was to send as much as possible to his mother.

Murray and Mitch Rocker, the captain, had organized a small relief fund for refugees in Uganda. They had a website and were soliciting donations from the student body. Without naming Samuel, the website painted a grim picture of life in the camps and settlements and pleaded with the students for humanitarian relief. By December 1, they had raised almost a thousand dollars, and Sooley was grateful beyond words. The challenge was getting the money into the right hands. Beatrice had warned him that refugees with a little cash were often targets.

:   .   .

Beatrice had managed to discreetly buy shoes and clothing for the eight children, James and Chol and the six others from Lotta. This had not gone unnoticed in their neighborhood, and it was well known that her son was studying and playing basketball at an American college, but so far there had been no trouble.

Their dismal existence improved dramatically with the news that a new school was opening at the far edge of Rhino South. Early one morning, she and her two friends and their eight children walked an hour, following the crowd to see if the rumors were true. They were stunned to find a spanking-new modern building that workers were still finishing. A sign announced the opening of a U.N. school for all children and the excitement was palpable. They waited in line for hours, filled out the paperwork, and left to find lunch. The following day they returned to the school and handed over their children. Well-dressed administrators and teachers, all Ugandan, all men, welcomed them and handed out pencils, pads, and workbooks. The women left their kids and drifted back to their tent village, childless for the first time in months. A long school day meant everything—education and a nice lunch.

And uniforms. When the children were released late in the afternoon, they were given identical outfits—white shirts and navy shorts for the boys, white shirts and navy skirts for the girls. They were excited to be dressed alike. All were suddenly equal now, all accepted members of a real school.

. . .

A four-game losing streak will breed discontent in any locker room, and Central's was no exception. Jabari Nix was a sophomore forward who had averaged five minutes a game the year before and got about the same in the early games. His best friend was DeRell Compton, a 5'10" guard who couldn't shoot. They were dissatisfied with their playing time and it was obvious they were unhappy.

Samuel stayed away from them. He wasn't playing at all but was still delighted just to be on the team. He watched as Mitch Rocker and Roy Tice, two of the seniors, tried to offer them encouragement. Murray was playing ten minutes a game and not happy about it, but he was still optimistic things would improve. He had said several times that Jabari and DeRell could cause trouble.

After Friday's practice, Sooley and Murray showered and returned to their dorm room. Robin had gone home for the weekend and Murray was lost without her. He suggested they eat out and they drove to a pizza place. There was a home game tomorrow and Coach Britt had imposed a strict 10 p.m. curfew. Coach Garver had threatened to check their rooms.

While they were eating, Murray's phone rang and he talked to Harry Greenwood, a junior forward who lived off campus. Harry's father was a lawyer in Charlotte and the family was more affluent than most. After the pizza, they drove to Harry's apartment where a party had materialized. The whole team was there, along with some nonathletes and a bunch of girls. The music was loud, the beer flowing, and the girls were friendly and flirting. Sooley had quickly learned that on campus the athletes were special and admired by the other students. Murray, single for the evening, soon zeroed in on a couple of coeds and introduced his roommate.

Samuel declined a beer. Where he came from, kids, as well as their parents, couldn't afford alcohol or drugs, and he had not been exposed to the temptations. He was chatting with a pretty coed named Nicole, who seemed curious about where he was from. A friend handed her a joint, and, quite casually, she took a hit and offered it to Sooley, who declined. He was suddenly aware of the aroma in the apartment and realized that pot was everywhere. He was not that familiar with the smell but it was obvious. Several students, nonplayers, were crowded over a small table in the kitchen doing something that they preferred to keep out of view. He found a bathroom, locked himself inside, collected his thoughts, then, without a word to anyone, left the party. Central was at least an hour's walk away.

Without the benefit of an automobile, he had not seen much of the area and was not sure where he was. The sky to his right was illuminated by the brighter lights of downtown Durham, but they were far away. He zigzagged for a while in that general direction but was soon lost. He turned along a narrow street with fancy modern condos on both sides, no doubt a white section of town. There were no sidewalks, and as he walked at the edge of the street he was aware that he was being followed by a car. It was the Durham police, inching along behind him.

It was Friday, December 4, and the air was cold. Sooley kept both hands stuffed deep in the pockets of his Central pullover.

He had been in America long enough to understand the rules of engagement for young black men walking through white neighborhoods at night, and he was suddenly stricken with fear.

The car pulled beside him and a gruff voice said, "Stop right there." Sooley stopped and waited as two policemen, both white, got out and slowly made their way over to confront him. His knees were trembling, his hands shaking.

One flashed a bright light into his face, then clicked it off. A nearby streetlamp shone enough for the three to see one another clearly. Officer Swain said, "May we ask where you're going?" He was polite and even smiled.

"Yes sir. I'm a student at Central and I'm just trying to get back to campus."

"Do you have a weapon? Anything in your pockets?"

"No sir. I'm a student."

"We heard that. Please remove your hands from your pockets. Slowly."

Sooley did as he was instructed.

Swain said, "Okay. You're not required to show us any ID, but it might be helpful if you did."

"Sure. My ID is in my pocket. Shall I reach for it?"

"Go ahead."

He slowly reached into a front pocket of his jeans and handed his student ID to Swain, who studied it for a moment and asked, "What kinda name is Sooleymon?"

"African. I'm from South Sudan. I play basketball for Central."

"How tall are you?"

"Six six."

"You're only eighteen?"

"Yes sir."

Swain handed the card back and looked at Gibson, who said, "I'm not sure you're safe in this neighborhood."

The neighborhood was perfectly safe, but for the police who were causing trouble, but Samuel only nodded.

Swain pointed and said, "Central is to the south and you're headed west."

"I'm lost."

They laughed and looked at each other. Swain said, "Okay, we'll make you an offer. Get in the back seat and we'll take you to the campus. It's cold, and you're lost, so we'll just give you a ride, okay?"

Sooley looked at the car and glanced around, uncertain.

Swain sensed his hesitation and said, "You don't have to. You've done nothing wrong and you're not under arrest. It's just a friendly ride. I swear."

Sooley got in the back seat. They rode for a few minutes and

Gibson, the driver, said, "You guys have lost four in a row. What's going on?"

Sooley was gawking at the gadgets up front. A busy computer screen. Radios. Scanners. Of course, he had never been inside a police car. "Rough schedule," he said. "We opened with some tough games, as always."

Swain grunted and said, "Well, you got an easy one tomorrow. Bluefield State. Where the hell is that?"

"I don't know, sir, I'm lost right now. Never heard of them. I'm a redshirt and won't play this year."

Gibson said, "I like Coach Britt. Great guy. Rumor is he might be moving on after this year."

"I don't know. Coaches, they don't talk to us about stuff like that. I guess you guys are Duke fans."

"Not me, can't stand 'em. I pull for the Tar Heels. Swain here is a Wolfpacker."

The car turned and Sooley recognized the street. They were indeed headed to the Central campus. As the front gate came into view, Swain pointed to a parking lot and said, "Pull in there." Gibson did so and stopped the car.

Swain turned around and said, "Just so you won't run the risk of being embarrassed, we'll let you out right here. Okay?"

"Yes sir. Thank you."

"Good luck with the season, Mr. Sooleymon."

"Thank you."

CHAPTER 31

After three weeks on the continent, Ecko was tired and homesick and missed his family. He had scouted a tournament in Cape Town, attended conferences in Accra and Nairobi, and watched a dozen games with coaching friends in Senegal, Cameroon, and Nigeria. He'd logged 8,000 miles between countries and spent Thanksgiving Day stranded in an airport in Accra, the capital of Ghana.

But he had one more stop, one that he could not, in good conscience, blow off, though he desperately wanted to. He landed in Kampala and was met at the airport by an old friend named Nestor Kymm, a coach of the Ugandan national team. Kymm's brother ranked high in the government and knew which strings to pull. Early the next morning they drove to Entebbe International Airport and were directed to the cargo field far away from the main terminal. There they met a smartly dressed officer named Joseph something or other. Ecko could neither pronounce nor spell the man's last name so he simply called him "sir." Joseph seemed to expect this.

They piled into his jeep and circled around two long, wide airstrips lined with taxiways choked with cargo planes, some waiting to take off, others landing. Surrounding the runways were endless rows of huge military tents shielding tons of crates of food. Joseph parked his jeep by an administration building and they hopped out. He glanced at his watch and said, "Your flight leaves in about an hour but nothing runs on time. There's a fifty-fifty chance you can get on it, so don't be disappointed if you don't. We won't know until the last minute. It's all about weight and balance." He waved at the chaos and asked, "Want a quick tour?"

Ecko and Kymm nodded. Sure, why not?

The tents were in a large grid and separated by gravel drives. Cargo trucks and forklifts bustled about as hundreds of workers loaded and unloaded the crates. Joseph stopped and waved an arm. Before them were the tents. Behind them airplane engines roared as they took off while dozens more waited.

Joseph said, "We're feeding a million refugees a day and they're scattered throughout the country in about fifty settlements. Some are easy to get to, some almost impossible. All are overcrowded and taking in more people every day. It's a terrible humanitarian crisis and we're barely hanging on. What you see here is a frantic effort by our government and the United Nations. Most of this food comes from the U.N., but there's also a lot from the NGOs. Right now we're working with about thirty relief organizations from around the world. Some bring their own airplanes. Some of these are from our air force. Others from the U.N. At certain times of the day, this is the busiest airport in the world. For what that's worth."

Ecko asked, "How far away is Rhino Camp?"

"An hour, give or take. There's a Danish group that flies from here to Rhino four times a day and I'm trying to squeeze you on board. If that fails, we'll try another one. As you can see, there are plenty of planes."

It was a stunning assemblage of aircraft, almost all twins and turboprops, short-field workhorses built for narrow and uneven dirt strips. On the ground they zigged and zagged their way from the warehouses to the taxiways where they fell in long lines and waited. On the other runway, a steady stream of the same planes landed every thirty seconds and wheeled onto the nearest taxiway.

Every takeoff and landing created another boiling cloud of dust. The runways were asphalt and could handle the biggest jets, but the connecting roads were dirt and gravel. A mile away, in a much more civilized part of the airport, commercial flights came and went at a leisurely pace.

They watched the show for a few minutes, and Joseph said, "As you might guess, traffic control is a nightmare, ground and air, but we do okay. Haven't had a fender bender in over a month."

"How safe are the flights?" Ecko asked.

Joseph smiled and asked, "Getting a bit nervous, are we?"

"Of course not."

"Well, we can fly only in good weather. These planes are headed to the bush where only a handful of towns have proper runways and traffic control. Most are going to dirt strips with no navigational support. So, what you see here are some of the best pilots in the world. They can fly in all kinds of weather, but often they can't land. So we ground them when it rains."

"Where are the pilots from?"

"Half are from our air force, the other half come from around the world. A lot of U.N. guys, and a surprising number of women. To answer your question, we haven't had a crash in seven months."

Seven months seemed like an awfully short period of time to Ecko, but he firmed up his jaw as if he had no fear. There was no turning back anyway. He'd made a promise to Samuel.

Joseph's radio squawked and he excused himself. Ecko and Kymm retreated to the safety of a warehouse tent, and in the shade watched the incredible, organized chaos before them.

Joseph was back, driving his jeep, and he barked, "Get in. Let's go."

They weaved through the grid and were soon lost in a cluster of tents. When they emerged there were three identical turboprops with workers stuffing boxes inside. On each tail was the name of the nonprofit, something in a foreign language, but under it in small print was "Denmark." Joseph approached one of the pilots, evidently a Dane, and said the magic words. He looked at Ecko and Kymm and waved them over. As they crawled on board and settled into the cramped seats just behind the pilots, Joseph said, "Good luck, lads. I'll see you when you get back, if you make it."

They strapped in and began to sweat in the stifling humidity. A ramp boy closed the door and the pilots began flipping switches. Ecko and Kymm watched them with fascination. As the turboprop began to taxi, the copilot opened his window and a fresh wave of hot air blew in. The line was slow but steady.

Though he was nervous about the flight, Ecko was thrilled with the adventure and was once again pleased with his decision not to tell his wife about this little side trip. He would describe it all when he got home.

From 10,000 feet the Ugandan countryside was beautiful, and Ecko absorbed it all. He was struck by the lack of roads and the remoteness of the villages. And he was once again grateful that his parents had settled in America.

Behind them were three large crates of food, with smaller boxes crammed into every available space. The plane rattled, shook, and vibrated, and this never ceased. Remarkably, he caught himself dozing off.

The descent became interesting when Ecko and Kymm had their first glimpse of the runway. From three thousand feet it appeared to be nothing more than a pig trail hacked out of the middle of a forest. Huts from a nearby village could be seen, but there were no other signs of civilization. On final approach, the copilot turned around and yelled, "Hang on." This was not comforting. The landing was a hard slam dunk that caused Ecko to dig his fingernails into the left knee of his co-passenger. When they could breathe again they managed to laugh. Every successful landing is a good one.

Two cargo trucks were waiting at a small metal building that housed racks of food and water. When the engines died, a crew of teenage boys yanked open the rear doors and began unloading the crates. Within minutes, the trucks were loaded and the plane's engines restarted. The pilots waved goodbye and taxied out.

The truck driver was another Dane. He introduced himself with a big smile and told them to get in the cab. Half of the grounds crew hopped on board and settled among the cargo. Rhino Camp was half an hour away.

Ecko's first look at it caused him to shake his head in disbelief. Tents and shanties stretched for miles and thousands of refugees, most of them his people, South Sudanese, walked the dirt roads, seemingly going nowhere. The truck stopped at a distribution point where other trucks were arriving and unloading. A Ugandan army private was waiting for them and they immediately left on foot. Ecko carried a small gym bag filled with supplies and gifts. For almost an hour they walked through the settlement, passing countless refugees milling about with nothing to do. They passed long lines of women and children waiting patiently for the next meal, and more lines of people outside clinics and makeshift huts where relief workers filled out forms and handed over food, medicines, and secondhand clothing. They passed hundreds of women and teenage girls walking elegantly with pots of water balanced precariously on their heads.

At the Doctors Without Borders hospital, they asked around and found Christine Moran, who led them to a small exam room where Ecko finally said hello to Beatrice and her sons. Chol and James were nattily attired in their spotless school uniforms, though they were skipping classes on this special day.

From the gym bag, Ecko pulled out tee shirts and caps adorned with the NC Central lettering and logos. Eagles everywhere. He handed Beatrice an envelope with a long handwritten letter from Samuel, and a smaller one with cash. For James and Chol, there were colorful Christmas cards signed by the Eagles players and coaches. They talked for an hour about Samuel and his new life on campus, his classes, his friends, his basketball. On his cell phone,

Ecko showed them a video of Samuel and his roommate, Murray Walker, as they sent along their love and Christmas greetings. Another video was of Samuel slamming dunks in practice.

Kymm took dozens of photos with Ecko's cell phone.

Six hours later, the empty Danish cargo plane landed at dark at the Entebbe airport, and Ecko said thanks and goodbye to Kymm. As he waited three hours for his flight to Nairobi, Ecko sent the photos to Samuel.

Roaming the terminal, killing time, he vowed to do whatever he could to rescue the family, though he was well aware of the long odds against it. He called Samuel and they talked for half an hour, expensive minutes on the international plan. He loved the photos and wanted to know everything about his mother and brothers. Ecko walked a fine line between being honest about their living conditions and giving the kid some reason to be hopeful.

· · ·

Down three players due to curfew violations, and including a redshirt freshman, the Eagles rode the bus to the campus of Furman, in upper South Carolina, for a Wednesday night game. Coach Britt played all nine, and nine were not enough. The Eagles lost by 15 to go 3-5.

Mercifully, there were no games for the next week as the schedule broke for exams.

CHAPTER 32

Early Friday morning, December 18, the team once again loaded onto a charter bus for the four-hour ride to Washington, D.C. The mood was light; exams were over, the Christmas break was just around the corner. One more game and they would be off for a few days and all the players, except Samuel, would go home to their families. Inside the Beltway, he replayed his last trip to the capital, back in August when he had spent two days with his South Sudanese teammates as they licked their wounds from the showcase tournament in Orlando.

Those had been painful days for him, the shock still fresh from the news from home. Four months later, his life had changed dramatically, but not a minute passed when he didn't think of his late father and the indescribable fate of his beloved sister. His teammates were excited as their bus inched through central D.C., and, subdued as he was, Samuel tried his best to smile and go along.

The team checked into the Hyatt near Capital One Arena, had a quick lunch, then reboarded the bus for a few hours of sightseeing. At six, they changed into practice gear and drove to the campus of Howard University for a one-hour shootaround. At eight, they walked four blocks to a restaurant and were greeted by Maria Manabol from the embassy of the Republic of South Sudan. She had met Samuel and Coach Britt, along with Ecko, in August at the embassy and confirmed Ayak's death. She had also handled the paperwork to facilitate Samuel's student visa, and since then she had monitored his immigration file. She had called him every other week to make sure he was acclimating to college life. She and her husband, Paul, an American from Pittsburgh, were gracious hosts and welcomed the team to a private dining room where they feasted on prime rib with all the trimmings. After dinner, she spoke briefly about her country and its challenges. She did not mention the plight of the Sooleymon family, though everyone in the room knew their story.

The team was in bed by eleven, with strict instructions to sleep as late as possible Saturday morning. Brunch was at 10:30.

. . .

In spite of its usual role of being the early-season patsy for bigger programs, Howard had lost only two games and had won 10, including a double-overtime upset across town at Maryland. Preseason, the Bison had been lowballed by the experts, who ranked them near the bottom of the Mid-Eastern Athletic Conference. Central was predicted higher, but Vegas thought otherwise and put the Eagles on the board as a four-point underdog.

Two hours before the 3 p.m. tip-off at Burr Gymnasium, Maria and Paul sat in the stands with Samuel and talked about life in general, life on campus, basketball, and, most important, life in the refugee camps. The embassy received many requests from South Sudanese living in the States to find and try to help displaced relatives back home. Maria had been thrilled when Samuel called with the news that Beatrice and his brothers had been located at Rhino Camp in Uganda. That was no small miracle. Getting them out would take a more significant one.

With diplomatic skill, she repeated the warnings Samuel already knew. Immigration was strictly controlled and few from their country made it. And, there were many, many applicants ahead of them. His family had no U.S. sponsor, except for Samuel, and his citizenship was still in doubt.

When it was time to get dressed, he thanked her and Paul, gave them big hugs, and promised to keep in touch. Leaving, he said, "When we come back next season I'll be on the court."

"We can't wait," she said.

. . .

As Lonnie and the coaches feared, the one-week layoff proved disastrous. That, plus the trip to the big city, and the Eagles were completely out of sync. Howard was not. The Bison hit their first five shots and Central couldn't buy a basket. With 12 minutes to go in the second half, and up by 24, Howard began subbing freely, and the guys from the bench proved just as hot as the starters. Lonnie cleared his bench too and everyone played but Samuel. To make matters worse, with 3 minutes to go Harry Greenwood, a backup forward, limped off the court with what he thought was a twisted knee. X-rays would later reveal torn ligaments that would require surgery.

Losing the first conference game by 31 was not exactly the blazing start Coach Britt had in mind. He and the other coaches huddled in the front of the bus, and for four hours sulked and whispered and shook their heads. It was another quiet ride home, another retreat after an embarrassing loss.

In the locker room at The Nest, Coach Britt wished them all a Merry Christmas, sent them home for the holidays, and made them promise to return in a week with a renewed commitment. A new season would begin and he claimed to be optimistic.

CHAPTER 33

On Sunday morning, as the dorms closed, Murray and Samuel stuffed their backpacks and duffels and hauled their dirty laundry to the Walker home ten minutes away. Murray timed their 10:15 arrival perfectly. His parents would be leaving for church and he had no desire to go with them. Sooley said he needed a break too. Secretly, he was baffled by their Protestant worship and often attended Mass alone.

To their pleasant surprise, Miss Ida had decided to cook instead and said she needed the morning off. She welcomed her boys with big hugs and chocolate waffles. As Ernie fried bacon, she showed them around the house and bragged on her Christmas decorations. The colorful tree was the tallest one Samuel had ever seen.

He was delighted at the thought of hanging around the warm house for the next few days, eating huge meals, sleeping at all hours, and, most inviting, spending time with Jordan, who would arrive on Monday night.

"You're still growing," Miss Ida said at one point, as she checked him out from head to toe. "How much do you weigh?"

"Two ten."

She playfully tapped his chest and said, "You look thicker in the shoulders."

Murray said, "He lives in the weight room, Mom. He's gained twenty pounds this semester. Thinks he's playing football."

Samuel laughed and said, "Well, I'm sure not playing basketball."

"That makes two of us," Murray said and managed a laugh, but it was forced. He wasn't playing much and his frustration was growing. Samuel listened to his complaints and tried to encourage him, but losing pollutes an entire locker room and there was some dissension. Privately, Samuel was of the opinion that 10 minutes a game was about what his roommate deserved.

He had gained exactly twenty-two pounds since August. Between the weight room, the long dinners at Miss Ida's table, and a wide-open training table, Samuel was adding pounds and most of it appeared to be muscle. On two occasions, in practice, Coach Britt had quizzed him about off-court workouts. Although he preferred his players lean and flexible, he found it hard to quarrel with the sculpted biceps and thicker legs. Plus, he was only a redshirt, barely eighteen years old, and Lonnie decided to let him pump as much iron as he wanted.

Sooley now stood 78½ inches tall and the added height and weight had not slowed him down. He was easily the fastest and quickest on the team, and his vertical leap was up to an astonishing 46 inches. During the long bus ride back from D.C., one of the assistants, Ron McCoy, had broached the subject of jettisoning the redshirt business and giving the kid some minutes. What was the benefit in waiting? The season could not get much worse. Lonnie listened without much of a protest and promised to discuss it later. With two injured, the roster was down to eleven players. One was a redshirt freshman. One was a walk-on who had trouble scoring in practice.

After a languid brunch, Ernie and the boys cleaned the kitchen, then settled into the den for a long afternoon of NFL playoffs. Watching football with Sooley was painful because he wouldn't shut up. He questioned everything about the game and seemed to absorb none of it.

Miss Ida left them to go shopping.

. . .

At seven Wednesday morning, Samuel eased through the kitchen and waited in the garage for the weekly call from Christine Moran. It came fifteen minutes late, and she explained that their phone system was not working properly and minutes were scarce. Could he please limit the call to ten minutes? He said sure and thanked her as always, then heard the soft voice of his mother. "Merry Christmas, Samuel."

"Merry Christmas to you, Mother. How are you?" He closed his eyes and shook his head and wondered how anyone living in a tent in a refugee camp could possibly think about passing along season's greetings. He could not imagine how hopeless and depressing the holidays must be, and he could not help but think of their last Christmas together as a family.

She said James and Chol were doing well in school and still talking about Coach Ecko Lam's surprise visit the week before. They were proudly wearing their Central caps and tee shirts and were the envy of the neighborhood. The fact that their older brother was in America playing basketball gave them an elevated status. Beatrice promised to say a prayer for Samuel during Christmas Mass, and he promised to remember them too. He couldn't forget them and told his mother he thought of them every minute of the day.

The call was too brief and when it ended, Samuel sat in a lawn chair, in the darkness, and longed for his family.

. . .

Their church was packed for the Christmas Eve service, a remarkable celebration that Samuel enjoyed. The preacher throttled back and gave a shorter sermon. The youth group, in full costume, performed a Nativity skit. The children's choir, in matching burgundy robes, stole the show with their carols. The adult choir rattled the windows with "Go Tell It on the Mountain" and "The Holy Baby."

Jordan explained to Samuel, in a whisper, that the songs had been handed down by generations of African Americans.

. . .

Late the next morning, the family gathered around the tree and exchanged gifts. The pile included clothes for the boys, jeans and casual shirts for school, and perfume and a gold necklace for Jordan. Samuel's big gift was a navy blazer, his first. Jordan gave him a beautiful necktie. He was overwhelmed by their generosity and almost speechless at the number of gifts. He had managed to save a few bucks and had surprises of his own: a bottle of perfume for Miss Ida, a large chef's apron for Ernie, a leather belt for Murray, and for Jordan, a set of small earrings that she immediately put on. They were touched by his thoughtfulness and felt guilty for receiving the gifts, but they did nothing to dampen his spirits.

By the time the gifts were all finally unwrapped they were famished. Jordan put on a CD of Christmas songs as the family moved to the kitchen where every Walker tried to assume command.

CHAPTER 34

The holiday break came to a dreadful end the day after Christmas when the players dragged themselves back to campus for what was expected to be a painful three-hour practice. The coaches were waiting like drill sergeants. Coach Britt's speech began with the unnecessary reminder that they were off to a less than impressive start. Three wins against pushovers, and six losses, two of which should have been avoided. They were better than Campbell, and he took responsibility for that loss. They had a good East Carolina team on the ropes and let them escape. The embarrassing blowout at Howard was inexcusable.

After a fifteen-minute smackdown, he changed his tone and insisted that they put their losses behind them. They had 21 games left, 17 in conference, 9 of those were at home. The games that mattered were ahead of them, and they would waste no more time thinking about their slow start.

The players were with him, but they were also thinking of more pressing matters. On Monday, they would fly to New York City for the rare treat of playing in a holiday tournament against other HBCUs—Historically Black Colleges and Universities. The games would be at Madison Square Garden and most would be televised on one of the ESPN channels. Over a five-day span, Central would play Grambling from Louisiana, Prairie View from Texas, and Fisk from Nashville.

Lonnie talked about the trip, the tournament, and their opponents, all of whom had winning records. In late November, Fisk had manhandled Howard in Washington, on the same court where Central had laid an egg only a week earlier. But enough of the past. His scouting report portrayed the three teams as virtually unbeatable, of near NBA proportions.

It was part pep talk, part fear-mongering, and it left the players unsettled. But they were headed to a big show and were determined to play well. When he blew the whistle they hit the court to stretch and limber up, and then they started running. Their coaches seemed determined to sweat out all the turkey and dressing, pecan pies, fudge brownies, Christmas cakes, and the rest of Grandma's holiday cooking. Fifteen minutes into the wind sprints, the first player vomited.

Driving to the gym, Murray said that he needed to see Robin and would it be okay if Sooley got lost after practice. They needed the privacy of the dorm room. Sooley said sure. He had never said no. Then Murray went on about how nice it would be if she could sleep over. There was a sofa in the commons on their dorm's first floor, and, well, what do you say, roommate? Sooley smiled and shrugged and said whatever.

After the grueling practice, the players slowly undressed, showered, changed, and left. They would be back the following day for more of the same. Sooley doubted if any of them had the energy for sex. But Murray did, evidently. He offered a ride but Sooley said he would walk. Have some fun and see you in the morning. As the managers cleaned up the locker room, Sooley hid in a storage closet. When the lights were off and everyone was gone, he eased back to the court, turned on one light, and began shooting.

After 500 shots, he turned off the light and returned to the locker room. He showered again and for dinner found a sports drink and some granola bars in the team kitchen. He settled into one of the nice cushioned chairs in the cramped room where they watched film and turned on an NBA game. By the second quarter, he was sound asleep.

He awoke to *SportsCenter*, watched some highlights, and realized he was starving. He put on a Central sweatsuit and went in search of food. The student cafeteria was still closed so he left campus. He walked a mile to a soul food café, his favorite, and inhaled two large chicken biscuits. He toyed with the idea of walking another mile to Sacred Heart for Mass but decided against it. The weather was raw and threatening and he would never get accustomed to the cold.

When Coach Britt arrived early in the afternoon, he heard the familiar thumping of a basketball. He looked around a corner of the bleachers and saw what he expected. Samuel Sooleymon firing away, shirt off, covered in sweat. Two things were clear—the kid was growing into quite a physical specimen, and the shots were no longer bouncing off the rim.

.   .   .

Practice began with the game plan for Grambling, their first opponent in New York. The players were excited and energetic, though Murray seemed a step or two slower.

As always, Sooley was relentless in the drills and scrimmage. He was physical to the point of getting hard looks from his teammates. He smiled and yelled and never stopped talking smack.

His excitement, though, waned at times. He would not make the trip to New York.

CHAPTER 35

At nine sharp Monday morning, Coach Britt walked into the locker room and inspected his troops. All were wearing navy blazers, white shirts, khaki pants, and casual shoes, no sneakers. He liked what he saw and tried to insult each one as he examined them. The excitement was palpable and everyone was ready to go. He lined up the four student managers, went through their equipment checklists, and for good measure barked at Coach McCoy because he was not wearing a tie. One was quickly put on.

Sooley sat in a corner in practice garb, watching the show and trying not to appear too deflated. The players spoke to him and got a smile, but they knew he was crushed because he would not make the trip. An appointment with an immigration officer was more important.

When all was ready, they filed out of the gym and into a waiting charter bus where the four coaches' wives were waiting in their Sunday best, all chatting eagerly about the trip. Two of them, and one of the coaches, had never seen the Big Apple. Thirty minutes later, the bus deposited the group at the private terminal at Raleigh-Durham airport. Their nonstop flight was scheduled to land at Teterboro in New Jersey just after 2 p.m.

With the gym deserted, Sooley turned on a couple of lights and began shooting.

That night, Murray called with the news that they had arrived safely, and the two talked half an hour about the trip, the hotel, and the vastness of Manhattan. After the call, Sooley sat in his bed with the lights off and scanned dozens of photos his teammates were posting.

He had never felt so alone.

. . .

At nine the next morning, Miss Ida was waiting on schedule in front of the dorm when Samuel walked out. He was wearing his new clothes—navy blazer, khakis, white shirt, and the lovely tie Jordan had given him for Christmas. He had never worn a tie before and Murray had spent an hour teaching him the proper knot. He had practiced a hundred times.

Miss Ida inspected him and was quite impressed. They got in her car and she drove thirty minutes to the Raleigh field office of the U.S. Citizenship and Immigration Services. Their ten o'clock appointment with a case manager was so important that the date and time could not be moved. Both Miss Ida and Sooley had tried to reschedule so he could make the trip to New York with the team, but they had not been successful. There was an enormous backlog of cases. The USCIS offices were understaffed, and so on. Sooley was desperate to push along his quest for citizenship, and, besides, he wasn't going to play basketball anyway.

They spent an hour sitting on folding chairs in a crowded hallway and watched foreigners come and go. At 11:15, Samuel's name was called and he and Miss Ida were directed to a small corner office where they were greeted by a pleasant young man who apologized for making them wait. They sat with their knees touching his metal desk and chatted about college life at Central. The office had no windows and the thermostat seemed to be stuck on 80.

Reading from a printout, the case manager went through a series of useless questions, most of which Samuel answered with either a "Yes" or a "No." Both answers pleased the man and he made some important entries in the case file. Twenty minutes after entering the office, they quickly left and hustled outside for fresh air. The entire meeting could have easily been handled over the phone or by email in less than ten minutes.

Miss Ida said, "They just wanted to lay eyes on you, that's all."

Samuel preferred not to return to campus—the dorm was deserted and he had little to do—so Miss Ida bought him lunch at a diner and took him to work. She introduced him to some of her staff, then parked him at an old desk and handed him a stack of papers to sort out and file. Samuel happily removed his tie and got busy.

. . .

Late in the afternoon, with Miss Ida tied up in meetings, Samuel left the office and enjoyed a long walk back to campus. The weather was clear and warmer and the stroll lifted his spirits. He was excited because of the immigration meeting and knew that he was on his way to citizenship. When that was attained, he could take the next step toward rescuing his family.

The gym was dark and empty, as was the rest of the campus. He had not seen another person moving around, not even a security guard. There was no traffic; all parking lots were empty. He changed in the locker room and hit the court.

. . .

Central tipped off against Grambling at 8 p.m. and the game was on ESPNU. Though he had become bored with watching the games and not playing, Samuel was nonetheless excited to see his friends on television and playing on such a grand stage. A nice crowd was on hand and the mood was festive.

In his dorm room, Sooley ate a pizza and yelled encouragement. Mitch Rocker, the senior point guard, got off to a strong start and hit his first three shots. Melvin Montgomery and Roy Tice clogged the lane on defense and smothered Grambling's big men. Murray entered the game at the eight-minute mark and immediately got a steal. The score was tied at half-time and Central had played its best 20 minutes of the season. Vegas had the Eagles as 14-point dogs, but someone forgot to inform the players.

As he flipped channels, there was a soft knock on his door. At first he didn't believe it. He thought he was the only person on campus. After the second knock, he opened it and found Robin smiling at him. "Hello, Sooley. Can I come in?"

"Sure," he said, thoroughly confused. She lived in Raleigh, had a car, and seemed to roam at will. She bounced on Murray's bed, her second home, and asked, "Are you watching the game?"

"Of course I am. What are you doing out and about?"

"Just bored. Thought you might need some company."

Like every other coed, she lived on her cell phone. So why hadn't she called first? Could it be that she did not want to be told no? She was wearing tight jeans and a loose sweatshirt. She kicked off her shoes and wanted to chat. She was cute, sexy, vibrant, and seemed to enjoy making him uncomfortable.

The girl got around. She was part of a group of fast women who hung out with the athletes, and Sooley had heard some whispers in the locker room, something to the effect that perhaps she was well known to a few of the other players. And Miss Ida didn't like her at all, a clear omen that she was trouble.

The second half began and they focused on the game, urging on their team, yelling at the bad calls, celebrating the good shots. Grambling went to a 2-3 zone and shut down the middle. Central was not a great outside shooting team, and when Mitch Rocker and Duffy Sunday went cold the game got away from them.

During a time-out, Robin asked Sooley who he was dating.

She knew damned well he was not dating because Murray told her everything.

"Nobody," he admitted.

"That's hard to believe. All the girls I know want to see you naked."

He laughed, nervously. They were distracted for a moment when Murray entered the game at seven minutes to go and Central down by 10. It seemed so wrong to be watching his best friend on television while his girlfriend put the moves on.

Grambling won by 12. As soon as the game was over, Robin turned to him and asked, "Wanna fool around?"

Sooley walked to the door, opened it, and nodded to the hallway. "Not with my best friend's girl. Sorry."

"Come on, Sooley. No one will ever know."

"Please. Get out of here."

CHAPTER 36

Robin texted him throughout the day and hinted that she might return to the dorm. Sooley spent the day in The Nest, alone, taking a thousand shots, watching college and NBA games in the film room. He slept there too, with the door locked.

Prairie View beat Central by eight.

On New Year's Eve, he walked half an hour to the Walker home and had dinner with the family. Afterward, they watched Central lose a well-played game to Fisk, a superior team. Murray played only three minutes in the first half and his parents weren't happy about it. During the second half, Sooley eased away from the tension and went downstairs to the basement to watch the game alone. Jordan followed him, and as they lost interest in the game some serious flirting ensued. At first Sooley was delighted to get so much of her attention, but became rattled when she seemed more aggressive. However, Miss Ida smelled trouble and soon joined them. Sooley was relieved, on the one hand. On the other, he had trouble sleeping on the sofa, his thoughts of nothing but Jordan's fine legs.

. . .

The team arrived home on New Year's Day. The three losses were difficult to stomach, and Coach Britt was not happy. They practiced hard for three straight days, and on January the fifth beat a hapless Division 3 team by 20 points, in front of fewer than two hundred fans. Had their faithful already given up? It seemed so.

And then there were ten. After the game, DeRell Compton, a reserve guard, sent an email to his teammates that read:

> *Hey Guys. I just met with Coach Britt and informed him that I am leaving the team. I'm transferring to Pico Community College in Texas where I'll be eligible to PLAY immediately. I love you and wish you the best. DeRell*

The news was surprising but not shocking. DeRell had been saying too much in the locker room and his dissatisfaction was well known. He would not be missed by the team. His departure left them with eight players, plus Sooley and the walk-on who was seeing almost no action. Harry Greenwood was recovering from knee surgery and Evan Tucker's elbow had not mended well.

Murray was out with Robin and was not back at midnight. Sooley went to sleep and was awakened shortly thereafter when his roommate made a noisy entrance and turned on the lights. He was distraught and said he needed to talk to someone. When Sooley could focus he realized Murray's eyes were red.

"She broke up with me," he said, his voice hoarse and strained.

"What?"

"She ditched me, just like that."

"Did she say why?"

"Of course she said why. We've been at it for the past two hours. Said she'd found somebody else and wanted out. Said all sorts of crazy shit."

Sooley suddenly had a knot in his stomach and was horrified that he might be the "somebody else." "I'm so sorry, Murray. I don't know what to say."

"There's nothing to say so just listen, okay? How can she do this to me? I love this girl and I thought we were on to something great. And, man, was she hot in bed. I mean, one minute we're doing great and the next thing I know she's found another man. I don't believe this." He wiped his eyes and for a long time stared painfully at the floor, completely heartbroken.

Timidly, Sooley asked, "Any idea who the other guy is?"

"No. She was too chicken to tell me."

What a relief. Sooley suspected that the truth was that Robin had slept with several athletes, and he was secretly thrilled that she was out of the picture. His best friend deserved better.

Sooley's phone buzzed quietly. He looked at the screen and was horrified to see a text from Robin: *I still wanna c u naked.*

He put the phone under his pillow and stretched out on his bed. Women!

CHAPTER 37

Conference play began in earnest with a short bus ride to Greensboro for a game against North Carolina A&T, Central's biggest rival. With the students still on break, the small gym was only half full and both teams were sluggish. Midway through the first half, Coach Britt yanked Duffy Sunday, a guard who'd thrown up four bricks, and replaced him with Murray. Still feeling jilted and with something to prove, he promptly stole a pass at the top of the key, sprinted to the rim, and finished with a rousing slam dunk. Sooley had never seen him move so fast and the play inspired the Eagles. The next trip down, he hit a long three and screamed at the bench. The team came to life and went on a 10-0 run that put them up by six at the half. A&T fell apart in the second half, primarily because Murray was all over the court. He played 27 minutes, led the team with 15 points, then led the singing all the way home. Late that night, in the dorm room, he called Ernie and they debriefed for half an hour.

Their home opener was against Coppin State, Monday, January 11. Miss Ida, Jordan, and Ernie arrived early and Sooley visited with them in the stands before the game. They were excited because Murray would be starting. It was amazing how a little playing time could lift the spirits of parents.

Miss Ida said, "He's playing better because he got rid of that girl."

Ernie said, "She was nothing but trouble, but he's playing because he deserves to play."

Sooley offered no opinion on the girl. Robin had stopped texting and had probably moved on to her next victim. When it was time to get dressed, he hugged Jordan and said goodbye for a few months. She would leave the following day for law school.

Murray gave them plenty to cheer about. He and Mitch Rocker controlled the backcourt and kept the pace a little slower, something Coach Britt had planned. Coppin State was small but fast and preferred to run, but struggled from the outside. Murray had three steals and six assists in the first half, and though he didn't score he played 15 minutes. He hit two bombs to start the second half and the Eagles never looked back.

. . .

Four days later, the team left on a chartered flight to Tallahassee to play the Rattlers of Florida A&M. FAMU was a top preseason pick and had beaten Howard at home four days earlier. The Central coaches were hopeful that with two straight wins the team had turned the corner and found some traction. The new lineup, with Murray at guard and Jabari Nix at forward, had looked unbeatable against Coppin State. FAMU was known for its aggressive man-to-man defense, and surprised the Eagles by pressing full-court from the opening tip-off. Murray and Mitch Rocker struggled to break the press and the offense was out of sync. When they managed to cross mid-court, 10 seconds were gone and they couldn't run their plays. FAMU jumped to an early lead and never slowed down.

Flying home, Coach Britt checked the other scores from around the conference and saw what he expected but didn't like. Central was the first MEAC team to lose 10 games. And two of those teams, Howard and FAMU, were even better than the experts had anticipated. At 6-10, with fourteen conference games to go, he had the queasy feeling that his team was in free fall, and he wasn't sure how to save it.

Once home, he shared a late-night pizza with his wife and three kids. He went to bed at eleven, couldn't sleep, finally dozed off, and was awakened at 3:30 Sunday morning by a phone call from a student manager. Four of his players were running high fevers and showing flulike symptoms. Lonnie called the team doctor and arranged for the sick players to go immediately to the student infirmary. He called the other coaches and told them to quarantine for forty-eight hours. It was too late for Jason Grinnell, who had a fever. "That damned airplane was packed," Jason said.

Samuel's forehead was on fire and he shook with the chills as Murray rushed him to the campus-clinic. The flu test was positive. Murray called his mother and she demanded that he bring Samuel home immediately. Murray wasn't sick yet but the bug was racing through campus and she wanted him away from his teammates. She took Samuel to the basement, gave him his meds, turned out the lights, and told him to close his eyes. In her opinion, the best way to fight the flu was with plenty of liquids and hours of sleep. The chills and fevers continued throughout the night, and sleep was impossible.

．　．　．

Down four players and one coach, Central hosted Morgan State the following Monday, and played like the entire team had been stricken with some awful virus. Morgan State was average and their coach was clever. He heard the flu rumors, noticed only six Central players warming up, and quickly changed his game plan to an all-out run-and-gun, up-tempo horse race. It worked, and by half-time the Eagles were dragging.

Sooley followed the game online, but felt so lousy he really didn't care who won. Morgan State by 18. It was his fourth night in the dark basement and he still felt like he'd been run over by a bus. He was tired of the fever, the headaches, the tomato soup. Frankly, he was tired of his nurse, who checked on him every half hour, it seemed. During the day, she called. Ernie called. Murray called. How was anybody supposed to sleep?

Evidently, the strain that hit the campus was particularly virulent. Two of the four players, Roy Tice and Duffy Sunday, recovered enough to make the bus trip to Delaware State. Dmitri Robbins and Sooley did not. Coach Grinnell stayed home too, and it was just as well. Delaware State ran the Eagles out of the gym.

Two days later, the same bus hauled them back home after another bad game, another frustrating effort at South Carolina State. It was their 13th loss, fifth in the conference, and the mood could not have been darker. Coach Britt had stopped yelling.

He had also stopped dreaming of a fine new job at a bigger school. At the moment he was just hoping to keep the one he had.

CHAPTER 38

After a week of quiet mornings, Lonnie unlocked his office door early Saturday and stopped when he heard a bouncing ball. Sooley was back. And it was time for a chat. He watched him for a moment, then pulled him off the court. They sat in the empty stands as the first rays of sunlight peeked through the windows and scattered on the floor.

"The doctor says you're good to go," Lonnie said.

"I'm okay, Coach. It was a long week but I'm over it."

"How much weight did you lose?"

"Ten pounds. Already putting it back on."

"Are you weak?"

"I'm about ninety percent, Coach, and getting stronger every day."

"Do you think you're ready to play?"

"Sure. I mean, you're talking about a real game?"

"Maybe, yes. I hate to burn your redshirt year, Sooley, and I won't do it if you object. But the truth has become rather obvious, hasn't it? We need some help. We need a new lineup. Maybe we need new coaches. I don't know. I'm afraid the players are on the verge of giving up."

"I'm ready, Coach. It sucks being a redshirt. All the practice and none of the games. When do you want me?"

"I'm not sure. We play here tomorrow afternoon. Should be an easy game but nothing is coming easy these days. Rontae's out sick. You get mentally prepared and stay ready, okay?"

"Got it, Coach. Just put me in."

The very thought of getting into a real game, for the first time since August, and his first college game at that, sent Samuel into orbit. He shot baskets with a new determination, and he did so for the rest of the morning. When he left the gym in search of food, a light snow was falling. He took it as a good omen. His first snow the day before his first game.

There was little accumulation, and the streets, though unplowed, remained passable. Still, venturing out on a raw, cold Sunday afternoon to watch two teams with losing records was not appealing to many fans.

Months later, thousands would claim to have been there for his first game, but the number was closer to five hundred.

The opponent was Maryland Eastern Shore. The teams were evenly matched and swapped baskets for the first 10 minutes. Just before the half, Roy Tice picked up his third foul, and a minute later Dmitri Robbins did the same. During the break, Coach McCoy whispered to Sooley to get ready.

At 6:20, Tice was whistled on a terrible call, one so bad that Lonnie lost his cool and drew his second technical of the season. Enter Samuel Sooleymon, with a knot in his stomach so large he at first had trouble breathing. To settle his nerves he sprinted down the court on defense and deliberately ran into his man. The contact felt good. Then he lost him and watched as he hit a wide-open jumper. Coach Britt yelled, "Relax, Sooley."

He tried to relax, tried to keep up with his man on defense, tried to remember the plays on offense, and really didn't want the ball. He was in the lane when their point guard drove hard to the rim and tossed up a floater. Sooley sprang from nowhere and slapped the ball out of bounds. Seconds later, his man shot a jumper from the free throw line, and Sooley slapped it over the press table.

The slapping and blocking was great fun and the Central bench came to life. Sooley's first bucket was a perfect alley-oop from Murray, a play they had toyed with in practice. Eye contact, a quick hand signal from Murray, a sprint to the rim, a highlight reel slam.

Once he was sweating, Sooley realized his nerves had settled, he could play this game. The man guarding him was only 6'4", much too short to bother him. He took a pass from Murray, dribbled to the top of the key, and launched himself high into the air. The jump shot was perfect form, but the ball bounced off the rim.

He finished the first half without scoring again. The Eagles led by eight and the locker room was jazzed. After losing four straight conference games, the team was determined to win.

. . .

The legend of Sooley began with 15 minutes to go in the second half. He entered the game for Dmitri, at strong forward, and set up low. Murray lost the ball, clawed it back, bounced it to Mitch Rocker who had it slapped away. A scramble ensued as players on both teams dived for the ball. It squirted free from the scrum and Sooley scooped it up at mid-court with two seconds on the shot clock. Without hesitation, he sprang high and aimed at the rim. It was not a hopeless effort to beat the buzzer. It was not a Hail Mary. Instead, it was a smooth, confident, perfect jump shot from 42 feet that found nothing but net. The Central bench went nuts. The small crowd screamed. As Sooley backed away, skipping in celebration and smiling, always smiling, he glanced at Coach Britt, who stood frozen, his mouth wide open. He managed to nod, as if to say, "Do it again."

The game was not being televised, but every game was filmed

and "The Shot" was duly recorded. A manager would post it later and it made the rounds.

Melvin Montgomery, the junior center, grabbed a rebound and bounced the ball to Mitch Rocker, who took his time and set up the offense. Sooley shoved his man, peeled off a screen, and popped open deep in a corner. Mitch got the ball to him and he went up, far above his struggling defender, and launched one from 30 feet. Nothing but net.

A minute later, he hit his third straight bomb and Eastern Shore called time to regroup. The short break didn't help. Sooley missed his next one, then faked his man out of his shoes and drove hard for a dunk.

"Get the ball to Sooley!" Lonnie hissed at Mitch as he dribbled by. The play was designed for Sooley to spin off a screen and take a bounce pass and then shoot off the catch. He did and jumped high over their center for an easy shot. With his height and amazing leap, his release was level with the basket and he seemed unstoppable.

Sooley finished the game with 17 points in 14 minutes, plus six rebounds, two blocks, and two steals. The locker room was crazy as his teammates and managers, even the coaches, celebrated their new star, and a new season.

. . .

Early Wednesday morning, Sooley was in the gym, sitting high in the stands and waiting for the call from Christine Moran. He couldn't wait to tell his mother and brothers about the game, but the call never came. He tried calling Christine's cell, but there was no answer, no service. That had happened before and he wasn't worried. His family was safe, and fed, and the boys were in school, so little else mattered. On his phone he scrolled through the collection of photos Ecko had taken at Rhino Camp, and he watched the video of Beatrice and his brothers speaking into the camera and excitedly asking him questions about his new life. He had watched it a hundred times and it always made him laugh and cry.

He turned on the lights and began shooting.

.   .   .

Bethune-Cookman was 12–8 with only two losses in conference. The Vegas oddsmakers had them at 13-point favorites, even on the road, and they took the floor with some swagger. The Nest had 3,500 seats and was almost full. The student section was packed and loud. Sooley didn't start but came off the bench at six minutes and couldn't wait to get the ball. Too eager, he put up a long brick, but followed it with the rebound, which he fired down low to Roy Tice for an easy dunk that tied the score. On the next trip down, he landed a hard elbow in the kidney of his defender, bounced off, took a pass from Murray, and leaped toward the ceiling with a gorgeous shot that caught nothing but net. It was the first three of the game for Central, the first of many.

In practice, and firing away with the confidence of a real gunner, he was now unstoppable from long range. The coaches had decided to turn him loose with a standing green light. The old offense had sputtered badly. Why not build a new one around Sooley?

When he hit his third bomb, Bethune called time. Their best defender was a 6'5" small forward with lightning-quick hands. He dogged Sooley from mid-court on as the rest of the defense waited to collapse on him. Sooley loved a great pass more than a long basket, and he began dishing off to his open teammates. With all five scoring, Central ripped off a 14–0 run and led by 15 at the half.

Sooley reentered the game with 16 minutes to go and quickly hit a 30-footer. He was 5-for-8 from long range. The next time down there were two defenders waiting on him and that made him smile. Everything made him smile. With so much attention, he decided to stay far away from the basket, and smiled as Murray and Mitch Rocker slashed through the lane, often dishing off to Roy Tice for easy baskets. When the defense retreated to protect the lane, Sooley was more than ready to bomb away. Everything worked, and Central routed Bethune by 20, scoring a season high 92 points. Sooley had 24, as did Roy Tice. Sooley also grabbed 11 rebounds, for his first double-double.

Five days later, Central easily beat Norfolk State on the road for its third straight win. Sooley scored 20 and blocked seven shots.

CHAPTER 39

Coach Jason Grinnell's brother, Hubert, had played at Duke and was now an assistant coach. As he did several times each season, Hubert arranged some passes for his brother, who brought a few of his players for a game at Cameron Indoor. On a Sunday afternoon, Jason drove Murray, Sooley, and Harry Greenwood to Duke for a nationally televised game against Louisville. Duke was undefeated at 22-0 and had been number one since long before the season started. Louisville was ranked fourth and had lost only twice.

They arrived early and walked through the tent city, where students who were paying $50,000 a year in tuition camped out for days to get tickets. It was an impressive sight, and Sooley could not help but think of his mother and brothers living in a tent for months now, a tent they were lucky to have but with no idea how long they would have it.

Inside, they toured the Duke Basketball Museum and Athletics Hall of Fame, a plush addition to Cameron. It was filled with trophies of Duke's five national titles and bronze busts of their great All-Americans—Johnny Dawkins, Mike Gminski, Christian Laettner, Grant Hill, Jay Williams, Shane Battier. There were plenty of them. There were highlights on large screens and interactive videos. Hubert welcomed them and showed them around. He led them to the court, named for Coach K, and pointed to dozens of championship banners and retired jerseys hanging from the ceiling. The student section was already packed and the Crazies were roaring, an hour before the game.

Sooley, who had played in the Amway Center in Orlando, was surprised by the coziness of Cameron Indoor. Hubert laughed and told the familiar story of the time when Duke wanted to build a 20,000-seat palace to honor its coach. But K said no. Cameron was good for at least a 10-point advantage against any opponent. Its 9,300 crazed fans could make more noise than any crowd twice its size. Every opposing player would admit privately to some level of intimidation.

Their seats were two rows behind the Duke bench, close enough to almost touch the Blue Devil players. They watched the pregame warm-ups in awe as Cameron rocked with excitement. The four NBA-bound freshmen—Kevin Washington, Tyrell Miller, Akeem Akaman, and Darnell Coe—were all scoring and rebounding in double figures, and the pundits were discussing whether there was room for all of them on the first team All-American. Another favorite argument was which one would go highest in the draft, but there was little doubt they were all first-rounders. Sooley watched them with admiration and no small amount of envy. They were his age, had already attained the status of greatness, and would soon be wealthy stars. Though The Nest was only 2.9 miles away, it was in another world.

The game lived up to its hype. Both teams were loaded with talent and superbly coached, and they played to a draw in the first half. In the second, Duke's deep bench became a factor as its relentless defense wore down the Cardinals. With six minutes to go, the inevitable happened. Duke's long-range bombers got hot. For this game it was Tyrell Miller and Darnell Coe, and they buried Louisville with a barrage of threes. The crowd got even louder and at times Sooley couldn't hear himself think.

He would never forget the experience. He loved the spectacle, the action, the back-and-forth of two great teams, but he was also convinced that he belonged on that court. It was time to step up his game.

And he wasn't alone. Though Hubert had yet to tell his brother, he and another Duke assistant had begun quiet discussions about approaching Sooley with the idea of a transfer. They had heard the rumors, watched some film, and planned to sneak into The Nest for a game. If they became convinced, they would broach the subject with Coach K.

Driving home, with their ears still ringing, Coach Grinnell entertained them with the story of his first and only game at Cameron. He had played for four years at Wofford, and in what was scheduled to be one of those early December cakewalks his team had fought Duke to a tie in regulation, then lost by three in overtime. He had missed a 30-footer at the buzzer, a shot that he should have made and one that would haunt him for the rest of his life.

It was snowing again when they returned to their campus, the other school in Durham.

. . .

Howard rolled into town leading the MEAC with only one loss and playing well. Vegas thought they should win by nine.

Coach Britt mentioned this to his team in the locker room and, of course, reminded them of the egg they had laid in Washington on December 19. An embarrassing loss by 31, and it was time for revenge.

Three straight conference wins, along with the emergence of a freshman star, and the crowds were growing. The Nest was near capacity when the teams took the floor, and the Central students were in a raucous mood. The frigid temperature outside seemed to affect both teams, and neither scored in the first two minutes. At 15:20, and with only four points on the board, Coach Britt called time and put in Sooley and Jabari Nix. When Jabari missed a 10-foot jumper, the rebound went long and Howard broke fast. As its point guard sailed in for an easy layup, Sooley sprang from what seemed like mid-court, slapped the ball hard against the backboard, then grabbed the rebound and rifled a pass to Melvin Montgomery, who was trailing badly. He walked the ball to the rim and slammed it home. A replay would show that Sooley's block was goaltending, but the refs had been too stunned to call it. The Howard coach was livid, wouldn't back down, and finally the refs had no choice but to tee him up. As Mitch Rocker took the penalty shot, the Central students began, loudly, "Sooley! Sooley! Sooley!"

On the inbound, Sooley made eye contact with Murray, who had the ball, and broke for the corner. Murray's pass was perfect, and before any Howard player could react, Sooley was soaring toward the roof from 30 feet with a perfect jumper. He followed it with two more from long range, and the windows in the old gym were rattling.

As a rookie, Sooley was aware of the protocol, and the last thing he wanted was loose talk in the locker room, the kind of tension created by a freshman hotshot who hogged the ball. He passed up a good look and fired a beautiful pass to Roy Tice, who lost it out of bounds. As the clock ticked it became apparent that none of his teammates could buy a basket. Howard was tall and tough inside and gave up nothing. No problem. Sooley backed away, peeled off a screen, and hit his fourth straight from beyond the arc. He missed his next two and began passing. At 3:35, he came out for a breather and watched Howard go up by six. With a minute to go in the half, Roy Tice, a real banger inside, picked up his third foul and Lonnie yanked him. Down by three, and with the ball, Murray killed some clock and set up the last play. His pass was slapped away and rolled to Sooley, who was almost at mid-court. His defender backed away, daring him to shoot, and with eight seconds to go, he did. Wide open, he skied anyway, and lofted a beautiful shot that tied the score.

The crowd roared even louder, and the team hustled to the

locker room with the chant of "Sooley! Sooley Sooley!" in the background.

He had 14 points, four threes, and a dunk. He was the offense, and at that moment his teammates were willing to put the game on his back. So were the coaches. They huddled away from the players and agreed on the strategy: Just get the damned ball to Sooley.

All eyes were on him as he sat on the bench for the first three very long minutes of the second half. When Coach Britt called his name and he walked to the scorer's table, the crowd reacted. So did Howard, but it was impossible to defend a long jump shot cocked high above the head of a 6'7" player who could spring over the backboard. He hit two of them, missed the third, and when he hit his third—and seventh out of nine—Howard called time. Their coach decided that the only way to stop him was to foul, and hard.

Sooley spent most of the second half at the free throw line, calmly making 10-of-12. He finished the game with 39, half the team's total, and the third most in school history. Howard, humbled, limped home with a 12-point loss.

Late that night in their dorm room, Sooley and Murray had a delightful time on social media. The Central faithful were lighting it up. Girls were calling and leaving all manner of messages. Sooley's phone number was out there and the texts poured in by the dozens.

. . .

On Friday, February 12, the Eagles missed classes and rode the bus five hours to Baltimore. At one o'clock the following day, they defeated Coppin State by 18 points. Sooley, still coming off the bench but playing 29 minutes, scored 31 and blocked four shots. They spent two more nights in Baltimore, and on Monday beat Morgan State by 15 in a wild shootout. The Eagles put up 98 points, 36 by Sooley. Back home the following Saturday, they beat South Carolina State by 14 in front of a standing-room-only crowd. The win, their seventh straight, evened their record at 13–13. Though there was now talk of playing in March, they were well aware that their slow start would be hard to overcome.

Coach Britt gave them Sunday off but wanted them to report to the gym anyway. The team doctor had ordered routine physicals. Sooley weighed in at 227 and measured six feet seven and a half, still growing. The team's press guide, printed the previous November, listed him at 6'6", 210 pounds.

The next day Murray showed him how to change his phone number.

CHAPTER 40

The tents were not designed to serve as permanent and began to deteriorate after six months in the elements. The rainy season was over but the water and mud had stained them so badly that the rows of crisp white tents were now a hodgepodge of brown dwellings patched with strips of old clothes and scraps of plastic and sheet metal. Some sagged, others completely collapsed, still others had been moved to other sections of the sprawling camp, many replaced by shanties erected with cardboard and whatever materials could be found. The baking sun further eroded the tents' stitching, seams, and zippers. Patching the holes became a daily chore.

Beatrice purchased three bright blue tarps at the market, one for her, two for her friends on either side, and they draped them over their roofs and tried to secure them with baling wire. The tarps were a luxury and soon attracted unwanted attention.

Each morning they arose early and left to find a line at a food distribution point. After breakfast, she and her friends walked their eight children to school an hour away. Another friend, an elderly gentleman across the alley, kept an eye on their tents. Beatrice paid him with tins of canned meat.

Tensions were mounting in the camp as ethnic rivalries spilled over the border, and as the war back home raged on. The Dinka were blamed by the Huer, Bari, and Azande for causing the current war, the atrocities, the diaspora that forced them into the refugee camps. Insults were common and then the fighting began. Teenagers and old men in gangs attacked each other with sticks and rocks. Ugandan soldiers were sent in to quell the violence, and their presence became part of life at Rhino. With hatreds that went back for decades, the atmosphere was tense, a powder keg waiting for a match.

One morning Beatrice and her friends returned from the walk to school and at first noticed nothing unusual. The coveted blue tarps were in place, but inside the tents everything was gone. Thieves had slashed gaps in the rear of the tents and stolen their food, clothing, blankets, pillows, empty water jugs, the Central tee shirts and souvenirs, everything. Their guard, the old man across the alley, and a Dinka, was missing.

The three women did not panic and said nothing. To do so would be to attract even more unwanted attention, and where would they report the crimes? There were no police, and the Ugandan soldiers were there to stop the fighting, not waste time with petty crime.

They went about the task of figuring out how to patch their tents again. When she was alone, Beatrice sat in hers and had a good cry.

How could someone steal from the poorest souls on earth?

. . .

Central finished the month of February with three more wins—at home against Norfolk State and Delaware State, and on the road at Eastern Shore. They were 12–5 in conference, 16–13 overall, and gearing up for the MEAC tournament, one they had to win to advance to the Big Dance. Sooley was averaging 31 points and eight rebounds a game. He had worked his way into the starting lineup and getting 32 minutes, more than anyone except Mitch

Rocker, who rarely came out. The team had settled nicely into an eight-man rotation with Murray and Rocker in the front court, Sooley and Roy Tice at forward, and Melvin Montgomery at center. Dmitri Robbins, Duffy Sunday, and Jabari Nix came off the bench and were getting plenty of time.

The season's final game was at home against Florida A&M, the regular season champs at 15–2. The game was on a Saturday afternoon, March 5, and three days before, during a practice, the AD interrupted things with the thrilling news that ESPN was coming to The Nest.

The news electrified the campus as 8,000 students scrambled for tickets. The gym's capacity was only 3,500 and a fourth of the seats belonged to season ticket holders. Coach Britt set aside five passes for each player. Sooley gave three to some girls he was hanging out with.

He was featured in a pregame story that tracked the last nine months of his life. There was footage of him hamming it up in Orlando with the boys from South Sudan, and a canned shot of the refugee camp at Rhino Camp South. The reporter talked about the violence back home, the death of his father, the plight of his mother and brothers. There was a request to interview him for the segment, but Coach Britt said no. He didn't want the distraction, and he didn't want any player to get too much attention. Sooley was fine with the decision. Miss Ida had warned him to stay away from reporters, and Coach Britt concurred.

· · ·

On game day, the fans arrived early and choked the aisles. Maintenance had managed to squeeze in temporary bleachers for three hundred more, a move that required approval from City Hall. The mayor of Durham was a Central alum and the AD fixed her up with great seats.

An hour before tip-off, the band roared to life and the students danced under the backboard. The cheerleaders kept the frenzy going. The Eagle Dance Team shimmied and pulsated. The Nest had never been so packed or so loud. When FAMU jogged onto the court to warm up, they were met with a thunderous wave of boos. Seconds later, Mitch Rocker led Central onto the court and the place exploded. After the initial roar, the students immediately began their now customary chant of "Sooley! Sooley! Sooley!"

He smiled, laughed with his teammates, did his layups and dunks, and tried to ignore the racket. He knew he was being watched closely, and he had become accustomed to the attention, but it was difficult to ignore and often an irritating distraction. Life off the court was getting complicated and he didn't much like it. Murray was becoming his advisor, screener, protector, pit bull. Murray was also assuring him that there was no jealousy on the team. Hell, they were thrilled to be in the midst of a 10-game winning streak and to have a sudden star scoring 30 points a game. Fire away, Sooley!

The crowd quieted somewhat for the national anthem, then exploded again when the Eagles' starters were introduced. Television cameras seemed to be everywhere. ESPN banners hung high in the corners.

Coach Britt's dream opening was a long three by Sooley to light up the gym. The play had been practiced at length. Because Sooley could out-jump Melvin Montgomery by at least six inches, as well as every other center in the conference, he was now handling the tip-off. For the fourth game in a row, he tapped it easily back to Murray, who brought the ball up the court. He pointed this way and that, called a play that didn't exist, seemed to be frustrated with something, shook his head, but kept an eye on the clock. At 20 seconds, every Eagle sprinted to a different spot. Sooley spun from the free throw line, darted to the basket, lost his defender to a hard screen by Roy Tice, popped out under the basket with one foot out of bounds, kept moving, peeled off another screen and caught a bounce pass in the corner 30 feet from the basket, with a defender scrambling to catch up. He pulled up high and lofted a perfect jump shot. When it hit the bottom of the net, The Nest exploded.

It would take a few minutes for the FAMU players to adjust to the mayhem, to realize they couldn't hear each other or their coach, to find their groove, to just settle down and play basketball. In the meantime, it was bombs away. The second time down the court Mitch Rocker whipped a pass behind his back and Sooley caught it as he skied from 24 feet. On the other end, FAMU burned almost the entire shot clock before kicking the ball out of bounds. On Central's third possession, Murray missed a short jumper but followed it in, got his rebound, bounced it out to Mitch Rocker, who faked a shot, got his man in the air, then fired a pass to Sooley, who was well-covered. Didn't matter. With his defender hanging on, he sprang high and hit his third straight. A whistle nailed the obvious foul, and Sooley converted for a gorgeous four-pointer. He had the first 10 points of the game, and in less than two minutes.

FAMU missed again and Mitch Rocker walked the ball up. Sooley popped out of the scrum and took a pass standing 35 feet from the basket. He faked a shot, sending two defenders high in the air. He then streaked for the basket and dished off to Roy Tice for an easy dunk.

Down 12–0, FAMU took a time-out.

The Rattlers were not 15–2 by accident, and within five minutes closed the gap to 16–10. After making his first dramatic threes from long range, Sooley cooled off and missed his next two. On a short jumper, he drew a foul from his man, a good defensive player. Sooley decided to work on the third foul, which was called at 8:04. During a TV time-out at 3:56, Central led 39–34, and an old-fashioned shootout was under way. At that pace, both teams would score at least 90.

At the half, Central led 48–41. Sooley had 19 points and was 5-for-9 from behind the arc.

.   .   .

FAMU tied the game at 60. Seconds later, Sooley's man got his fourth foul. His replacement was two inches shorter and a step slower. It was time to make a move. Murray fed him at the top of the key and Sooley drilled an 18-footer. The teams swapped baskets and the lead changed as both defenses began to lag from fatigue. Sooley realized his man was no match and began waving for the ball. He hit two straight threes and suddenly Central was up by 10. The lead vanished when Sooley took a breather at 5:10. Mitch and Murray took turns missing bad shots and Lonnie screamed himself hoarse. They couldn't hear him anyway. He called time with four minutes to go, trailing by two. Sooley reentered the game and his coach gave him the look: "Start shooting and don't miss."

He hit two straight and the students spilled out of the bleachers. He missed one, then hit another, all from far beyond the arc. The Rattlers picked an unfortunate time to go cold and Central was poised to run them out of the gym. When Sooley hit his 11th three-point shot, out of 20, FAMU used its last time-out to stanch the bleeding, but it was too late.

At the buzzer, the students stampeded onto the court in a rowdy celebration. The players were swarmed and hugged and high-fived and thoroughly adored. ESPN was thrilled not only with such an exciting game, but also with the discovery of a true star, one it had introduced to the rest of the country. Sooley scored 47 points, had 11 rebounds, and 10 assists. A triple-double.

An announcer on the sideline tried to interview him, but he was too busy working his way off the court.

.   .   .

He and Murray fled to the Walkers' for a Sunday night pizza. Life in the dorm had become too complicated. Interruptions at all hours. Girls knocking on the door. Indeed, Sooley was finding it difficult to do anything on campus other than hide in the gym. Six weeks earlier he'd hardly been noticed in class. Now he was signing autographs and posing for photos. A ten-minute walk from one class to another took forever as he was pestered. Everyone wanted a photo, something to post, something to brag about. Even reporters were calling. He was ignoring social media altogether.

In the basement game room, they watched North Carolina hand Duke its first and only loss of the season, a double-overtime thriller at Cameron. They watched *SportsCenter* for the recap, and waited and waited for some highlights from the other campus in Durham. It finally came, and it was worth the wait. They had spliced together a video of all 11 three-point shots, and there was Sooley gunning from all over the court as the host narrated the assault. A brief clip showed the cheerleaders and the crowd as "Sooley! Sooley! Sooley!" shook the building.

"A star is born," declared the host. Samuel loved it. Murray was proud of his friend, but he was also beginning to worry.

CHAPTER 41

Samuel moved into the Walkers' basement and Murray settled into his old bedroom upstairs. Early Monday morning, Ida called Coach Britt and unloaded about how the kid was being treated. He couldn't go to class, couldn't stay in his dorm room, couldn't enjoy a meal in the cafeteria, couldn't even walk across campus without drawing a crowd. Lonnie was concerned and promised that Sooley's well-being was his greatest priority.

Before practice, Lonnie met with the seniors, Mitch Rocker, Roy Tice, and Dmitri Robbins, and discussed the problem and ways to handle it. If they took a heavy-handed approach and demanded that the students and fans back off, then their young star might appear arrogant and ungrateful. If they did nothing, Sooley might succumb to all those girls and other distractions.

They decided to ignore it for now and get out of town.

.   .   .

Early Tuesday morning, the bus left campus for the three-hour ride to Norfolk and the MEAC tournament. The players would miss almost a full week of classes, and the coaches pushed them to study on the bus. They opened their laptops and textbooks, put on their headphones, and promptly fell asleep. When they were awake, they listened to music and played video games.

The top eight teams in the conference would square off in the Norfolk Scope, a 10,000-seat arena that had hosted the tournament many times. The winner received an automatic bid to March Madness. Everybody else went home.

The games began at noon Wednesday, and from the first whistle nothing went as predicted. FAMU, the number one seed, was apparently still hungover from its visit to Durham the previous Saturday and came out flat. NC A&T, the eighth seed, shot 70 percent for the game and won by 18. A week earlier, FAMU had been 24–5 and seemed a cinch for the NCAA tournament. Suddenly, they were scrambling to catch an earlier flight back to Tallahassee and wondering what happened to their season.

In the second game, Norfolk State, the seventh seed, easily manhandled Howard, the number two seed, and sent the Bison home in a hurry as well.

Before the third game, Coach Britt yelled at his players and told them that all the underdogs were winning. They might be 11-point favorites against South Carolina State, but season records and Vegas odds meant nothing. His message was well-received. Sooley scored 15 points in the first half, 19 in the second, but he was proudest of his eight assists, five of which went to Murray, who scored 18 points, his career high. Six Eagles hit for double figures and the team shot 64 percent. It was their 12th straight win.

Number 13 followed the next day with a rout of Delaware State.

After the game, the team showered quickly and returned to the stands to watch Norfolk against A&T. They would play the winner on Saturday with the title on the line, with an automatic bid to the Madness.

Because their campus was close by, Norfolk State drew a large, boisterous crowd and The Scope was more than half full at tip-off. The Eagles found an empty section up near the ceiling and snacked on pizza and hot dogs hauled in by the managers. Murray ventured away to find a restroom, and as he was headed back to his seat he was confronted by one of the friendliest faces he had ever seen. Huge smile, perfect teeth, hand thrust out with the greeting, "Hey Murray, I'm Reynard Owen, with Team Savage. Got a minute?"

It was more of an assault and Murray had no choice but to take his hand and shake it. "Team who?"

"Team Savage. We're a sports management company based out of Miami."

Murray managed to free his hand and take a step back. Disengaged, but still very much captive. "What kind of company, you say?"

"Sports management. We represent professional athletes, mainly basketball players."

"Oh, I see. You're an agent."

Reynard shook it off with an even broader smile. "No, I'm not, but my boss is."

Murray took another step back as reality finally hit. "Okay, okay, I got you now. You want to talk about my roommate but you don't want to approach him because that would violate NCAA regs and you don't want to get on the blacklist. Who's your boss, you say?"

"Arnie Savage. Reps a lot of big names."

"Such as?"

Like a magician, Reynard pulled a business card out of the air and said, "Too numerous to mention. Take a look at his website, lots of stars. You think Sooley might want to talk?"

"No, he does not want to talk, not now anyway. Such a conversation is off-limits during the season, you know that. I'm not even sure this conversation is a good idea." Murray started to shove the card back, but decided to keep it for future reference and stuck it in his pocket.

Reynard, who lived this routine daily, had heard it all before and had a dozen routine responses. "Nothing wrong with the two of us having a chat, Murray, now or later. But that kid better get ready for it. He's headed for the draft."

"Don't tell me anything about Sooley," Murray said, suddenly irritated. "I've been with him every day since August and I bang heads with him in practice. I've watched him grow and know him better than anyone."

"He's probably a lottery pick."

"No he's not! What do you know?"

"It's my business."

"Oh really? Did you play in college?"

"Community school near Chicago," Reynard shot back, unfazed.

"Okay, look, I'm not strutting here, but I do play at this level and I know the game. I know Sooley better than anyone, and he ain't ready for the NBA."

Actually, there had been whispers in the locker room. An obscure and less-than-reliable online scouting blog had listed Samuel Sooleymon as a potential new one-and-done after last Sunday's performance against FAMU. But then, what wasn't on the internet? Murray wasn't sure his roommate had even seen it. But there was talk, and that kind of gossip rarely died down, especially when the kid was hitting from almost mid-court.

Reynard was a slick professional and he never stopped smiling. "Okay, okay, let's not argue here. His stock is going up with every game and scouts are taking notice. Arnie Savage is the best in the business. Keep us in mind."

Murray smiled and said, "Sure."

Returning to his seat, Murray debated telling Coach Britt about the encounter, and decided to let it go. If Reynard was right, and a voice told Murray that he was indeed, then the vultures would soon descend.

.   .   .

A month earlier, on January 9, Central had picked up its first conference win on the road in Greensboro against its biggest rival,

North Carolina A&T. It was a 15-point blowout over a seriously outmatched opponent. What no one at Central knew at the time was that six of A&T's players, including three starters, were in the clutches of a nasty bout of food poisoning and almost too weak to get dressed. The coach did not complain, but during a routine phone conversation the following day he mentioned this to Lonnie, an old friend. Once over the bad food, A&T put together a respectable season, finishing 18–12 and 9–9 in conference.

On Thursday night, they defeated Norfolk State in overtime to advance to the finals. On Saturday afternoon, they lined up against Central for the right to advance to the NCAA tournament.

For the sixth straight game, Sooley easily controlled the tip-off, slapping it back to Mitch Rocker. The designed play worked perfectly until the shot bounced off the rim. Sooley missed his first four long attempts and stopped shooting. His defender, Carson, was a 6'6" strong forward who pinched, grabbed, shoved, and never stopped talking trash. He and Sooley tied up on a loose ball and hit the floor, squirming. Two refs dived between them to prevent a brawl, and both players got up ready to fight. The teams were separated and both coaches settled down their players. Sooley, though, had been talked out of his game. He sat the remaining 10 minutes of the first half, sulking, the smile gone. A&T led by eight. He had only two points, a cheap put-back.

Out of sync on both ends, Coach Britt had his work cut out for him at half-time. He barked at Sooley, told him to stop pouting like a ten-year-old, get in the damned game physically and mentally, and so on. Sooley would start the second half down low and try to draw fouls on Carson.

Central's two guards, Murray and Mitch Rocker, slowed down the game and kept the score close. At 14:20, A&T was up by 10 when Carson got his third whistle. Sooley watched with a smile as Carson went to the bench, then hit two free throws.

It was time for the long game. Sooley moved outside, worked

through a screen, took the pass, pulled up from 25 feet and hit his first bomb. His defender, a 6'5" redshirt freshman, appeared glued to the floor. Murray stole the inbound pass and fired a bullet across the court to his roommate, who was in the vicinity of his last launching point. Sooley hit another.

Carson's pit stop was brief. At 12:40, he hustled back into the game and immediately bumped into Sooley, hard. A ref was watching and warned him. Sooley just smiled and relaxed. Roy Tice hit a short bank shot to tie the score. On defense, Sooley backed off Carson, daring him to take a shot. He was not a scorer, but wide open he had no choice. Sooley sprang high, slapped it away, and then laughed in his face. A long rebound kicked out to Mitch who bounced it to Murray in the middle for a three-on-one. Sooley, blitzing from the left, took a short bounce pass and was soaring for a dunk when Carson assaulted him from behind with a fierce body block. Sooley sprawled into the backboard padding and landed hard. Whistles shrilled from all directions as the refs ran in quick to avoid a war. Lonnie was yelling for a technical and both benches were inching onto the floor.

Sooley bounced up with a smile and said he was okay.

The assistant coaches got their players back where they belonged and the situation settled down. A ref got in Carson's face and pointed toward the locker room. It was flagrant, no question about it, and he was out of the game.

Sooley made both free throws. On the inbound, Lonnie called for a play they had perfected. Sooley bounced off two screens, took the ball deep in a corner, alone, and hit his fourth three of the game. Central was up by 5.

The flagrant foul and the near fight ignited the Eagles, and they could feel a run. After winning 13 in a row, and all by double figures, they knew the game and the title belonged to them. They also knew their star had finally found his range. With seven minutes to go, a tight game became a blowout as A&T's defense withered under a barrage of Sooley's long jumpers mixed brilliantly with slashing drives to the basket. He ended up with 28 points, the tournament MVP award, and the Eagles left the court holding a MEAC championship trophy for the second time in their history.

The bus ride home was a riot.

CHAPTER 42

Sunday, usually known as the Sabbath but on March 13 even better known as Selection Sunday, the doors to The Nest opened at 2 p.m. and the students streamed in. For only the second time in Central's history, the team had made it to March Madness and it was a moment to be savored. A celebration was in order. A trophy was coming home, one that would be enshrined in the lobby and admired for decades to come. The crowd was there to celebrate, to say thanks, to admire their heroes, and to find out who their next opponent would be. There were no worries about making it to The Big Dance. Yesterday's win gave the Eagles an automatic bid. Others might be sweating the cut, but not Central.

For smaller schools and less dominant programs, an invitation meant a ticket to join the biggest party in all of American sports. The perennials took the trip for granted, another three or four games added to the end of each season's schedule. For the others, though, it was a rare and cherished moment.

Coach Britt held a team lunch in the locker room. As the players gathered they watched the ESPN and CBS experts ramble on with their bracketologies and predictions. Trying to guess where the committee would place sixty-eight teams was impossible but had never stopped the analysts from trying. In the midst of the avalanche of data, it was mentioned several times that North Carolina Central, with an automatic bid, had the worst record in the field at 20–13. It was also noted that the team had won 14 straight, all going away, and had a star freshman who was averaging 30 a game. These little bits were offered quickly because no one took Central seriously. It was, after all, an HBCU, and those schools had always struggled in the tournament. The MEAC title did little to impress the commentators.

. . .

The NCAA postseason playoffs began in 1939 as a single-elimination tournament with eight teams. It expanded to sixteen teams in 1952 and thirty-two in 1978. As the college game gained popularity, and became more exciting with dunks, three-pointers, and a shot clock, the tournament, nicknamed and then branded as "March Madness," kept growing. In 2000, it doubled in size again with sixty-four teams, half of which received automatic bids by winning their conference titles. The expansion was deemed wide enough, but every year there was controversy as a few teams were left out. In 2011, an attempt to remedy this was put in place with the addition of four play-in games for low-seeded teams. Dubbed the "First Four," these early games were played in Dayton, Ohio.

. . .

Coach Britt, like all coaches, desperately wanted to avoid the First Four. The extra game meant a long road trip and less time for practice. And the play-in teams were routinely routed in the first round.

As he and his assistants ate sandwiches and chips with the players, they listened to the experts. Though no two agreed on much of anything, there seemed to be a general consensus that Central, its automatic bid notwithstanding, was headed for a play-in game. The Eagles' 13 losses bothered everyone but them.

The team enjoyed the atmosphere and soaked in the glory of a fine winning season, especially after such an awful start. One more game, and a slice of March Madness, was icing on the cake.

Lonnie now averaged 21 wins a year for the past five seasons, and though he was focused on his boys, his thoughts of moving on had been revived. He was still reeling from a back-channel call last night from an old acquaintance. An offer from an ACC school to be associate head coach would be arranged, but he had to bring Sooley with him. Lonnie had been so shocked by the call that he had yet to whisper it to his wife. The sport could be treacherous.

The racket from outside was growing as the bleachers and stands shook the floor. The band was at full volume. At 3 p.m., it was time for the team to make their appearance. Mitch Rocker held the MEAC tournament trophy and led the team down the tunnel to the floor and onto a stage under a retracted backboard. The gym exploded with a roar that surprised the players. The court was packed with students pushing toward the stage, like crazed fans at a rock concert. It took a long time to calm them, but when things calmed down the speeches began. The President, a dean, the Director of Athletics.

The scoreboard hung from the ceiling and was positioned high above mid-court. A JumboTron was on the wish list but years away. Four large screens had been mounted, one in each corner of the court, and before Coach Britt took the mike there was a ten-minute highlight reel of the season, with heavy emphasis on the past ten games. The students screamed every time Sooley hit another bomb.

Coach Britt thanked them for their support. He and Mitch handed over the trophy to the AD. Lonnie asked Sooley to step forward and presented him with the plaque as tournament MVP. For at least the fourth time in the past hour, the chant of "Sooley! Sooley! Sooley!" rattled the windows.

When it subsided, Coach Britt motioned toward the mike, but Sooley quickly begged off. The idea of making a speech terrified him.

There was a break in the action as they waited for the Selection. At four, the crowd grew quiet and the players took their seats on the stage. CBS and its A team began by announcing the first four national seeds: Duke, Gonzaga, Villanova, and Kansas. Then the First Four: Cornell would play-in against UMass; DePaul would play-in against Iowa State; BYU would play-in against Creighton.

And Florida would play-in against the Eagles of North Carolina Central, a 16th seed. The crowd roared with delight. The players jumped up with high fives and celebrated for the cameras. The coaches bear-hugged each other as if a quick trip to Dayton, followed by a game with Duke, was just exactly what they had in mind. With a big smile, Lonnie looked at Jason Grinnell and said, "What the hell?"

Jason, smiling, said, "No respect, man, no respect."

Coach Ron McCoy quipped, with a smile, "We're so screwed!"

The celebration eventually died down as the team and its fans watched the rest of the Selection. The coaches managed to keep smiling and feigning excitement, but they felt as though they had been shafted. There was little time for a practice. They knew nothing about Florida, except that they had beaten Kansas in the SEC/Big 12 Challenge, and had beaten Kentucky in Rupp Arena in early January. In an up-and-down season, they had won 22, lost 12, split their conference games, then almost beaten Auburn in the tournament final.

Lonnie left the stage and huddled with the AD. Travel plans had to be expedited. A private air charter would be needed, though it was certainly not in their budget. Other details were vague.

They agreed that they got a raw deal, but they had made it to the Big Dance, barely, and it was important to seize the moment. The assistant coaches were on their phones calling other coaches, scouts, former players, friends, anyone who might know anything about the Florida Gators. When the Selection was over and the crowd filed out, the players returned to the locker room and dressed for practice.

At 9 p.m. the first odds were posted online. Florida was a 26-point favorite.

During the night, an ice storm swept through and paralyzed most of the state. At daybreak, the campus, as well as most of Durham and Raleigh, was without electricity. The airport was closed. The team's charter jet was stranded in Philadelphia. One option was to hop on a rented bus and head to Ohio, but the roads were treacherous for at least the first hundred miles, and no one was really that excited about spending the day on a bus. The gym was cold and dark; practice was out of the question. Coach Britt paced around his house, draped in a blanket, waiting on cell service, waiting on electricity and heat, waiting for the damned ice to melt so he could get his team out of town. He almost cried when he glanced outside and saw snow falling on his patio.

Around 1 p.m., the Raleigh-Durham airport opened with limited service. There was still no electricity in the area and computers weren't online. Some cell service returned around three.

Just after four, the entire metro area blacked out again as power was lost.

At 8 a.m. Tuesday, game day, a charter bus left The Nest with ten players, four coaches, four team managers, the AD, two women on his staff, the sports information director, the director of basketball operations, a trainer, the team doctor, a strength coach, and a volunteer chaplain. For two hours, the driver inched along with the traffic on Interstate 40 until Raleigh was behind them. In Winston-Salem he turned north on I-77 and confronted more ice and slow traffic. Coach Britt, as well as the other three coaches and half the players, tracked their progress with a cell phone app using GPS. Barring any more bad luck, they should reach Dayton at 6 p.m. Tip-off was at eight.

Lonnie was certain that, in the colorful history of March Madness, no team had ever been so ill-prepared. He stayed on his phone, calling friends in the business who might be able to pass along even the slightest insight into the Florida players and coaches. His assistants did the same. The AD, after reporting the team's travel progress to a contact person with the NCAA, and lodging another complaint about getting such a raw deal, called the AD at Florida and discussed the possibility of delaying the game for an hour. The players needed to stretch, unwind, shoot a few, grab something to eat. The Florida AD agreed, but the NCAA said no. There was a contract with CBS.

The Gators had zipped into Dayton by charter jet Monday afternoon and enjoyed a nice practice. They had returned to the court midday Tuesday for a leisurely shootaround.

. . .

The Eagles arrived at the University of Dayton Arena at ten minutes after six. A local television station had been alerted to the story, and the players were filmed getting off the bus, finally. Coach Britt had no comment.

They changed quickly into their maroon road uniforms and took the court. Florida had agreed to keep the gym locked until seven to allow a short, private practice.

In spite of the ice and delays and interminable bus ride, the players were in great spirits and even laughed at their misfortune. Caged for ten long hours, they were eager to stretch, sprint, jump, and burn off some energy. Lonnie would later say that it was the best half hour of practice of the season. Back in the locker room, they feasted on power bars and sports drinks and quietly listened to music with headphones. There were some nervous whispers, a laugh or two.

When it was time for the show, Lonnie huddled them close and said, "Two things, men. There are two things I want you to know. First, the experts believe we are twenty-six-point underdogs.

Twenty-six. That means that they believe we don't belong here. We're not good enough. We've lost too many games. It means that no one respects us. Not those people out there. Not the other team. Not the selection committee. Nobody at the NCAA. Nobody in the press. None of the talking heads on television. We have not one ounce of respect anywhere. So, men, we have to earn it. The second thing is this."

Lonnie held up a sheet of paper. "This is from the *Tampa Bay Times,* the largest newspaper in Florida. Its sportswriters cover the University of Florida. Yesterday, a reporter had a chat with Jerry Biles, Florida's head coach. I know Jerry. He's okay."

With drama, Lonnie studied the sheet of paper. "They were discussing the big game this Friday up in Memphis when Florida will play Duke, the number one national seed, in the first round. Here is what Coach Biles had to say, and I quote: 'We got an easy draw in the first round, not so easy in the second. But we're not afraid of Duke. We beat Kansas and Kentucky and we can play with anyone. Bring 'em on.'"

He lowered it, glared at his players, and repeated, "An easy draw." He wadded it up and tossed it away. "An easy draw, and they're already talking about Duke Thursday night in Memphis. As if this game is already over. As if we don't exist."

No one moved, no one seemed to breathe. Not a sound.

He lowered his voice and said, "I doubt if these jackasses have even bothered to scout us, so we'll shake things up a bit. Sooley, you're not starting. You'll go in around three minutes so stay ready. We'll run Kobe Four so lock in now on the shot."

He tapped his palms together and said, "Men, we don't deserve respect. Yet. Respect is out there on the floor, just waiting for us to go get it."

CHAPTER 43

Florida controlled the tip and Central went into a half-court press, with every player itching to scratch and claw and ready to fight off screens. A bad jumper bounced off the rim and Melvin cleared it to Rocker, who took his time bringing the ball up court. With eight seconds on the shot clock, Murray missed a 20-footer. Florida missed again, as did Central. Both teams were sky-high and still nervous. The ice was broken when Murray mishandled a pass that led to an easy fast break. Florida had two 5'10" senior guards who were quicker and faster than anything Central had seen in the MEAC. The first foul was whistled at 16:38 and Coach Britt yelled for Sooley. Down the court, he posted high and at 15 seconds sprinted toward the goal, fought off a screen, and popped out clear in the far corner. The pass from Mitch was perfect, as was the 30-footer.

Two days of complete rest proved beneficial, and the Eagles were more intense than Lonnie had ever seen them. The ice storm had delivered a gift. They smothered Florida's bigs and the two small guards weren't hitting. When Sooley hit his third straight three from downtown, a whistle blew for the under-16-minute time-out. Central was up 11–6 and Florida seemed off balance. In the huddle, Coach Britt continued to hammer away at their role as heavy underdogs who got no respect from Florida or anyone else. He challenged them to play harder.

Florida made no adjustments and seemed willing to see if Sooley might cool off. He did not. He missed his fourth attempt, hit his fifth from 28 feet, and the next time down pumped a fake, sent his man flying, drove hard to the rim, and dished off to Roy Tice for an easy dunk. The score was 16–8 and Florida took a time-out.

In the 14 games he had played, Sooley was hitting 47 percent of his threes, second in the nation. He had no preferred spot. He hit from deep in the corners, fading away, and from near mid-court. Many games ago, his coaches had realized that, for an offense otherwise lacking in gunners, Central's best game plan was to let the kid fire away at will. Aside from his accuracy, what made his game so lethal was that he often followed his shot and picked off long rebounds that he converted to easy assists down low.

Florida went to their box-and-one and put a 6'5" pickpocket on Sooley. Every time he touched the ball Sooley either took a shot or faked one. The fakes were deadly, as the defender either took the bait or fouled him as he tried to drive. At half-time he had 24 points on six bombs and six free throws. Central led 41–30 but the game did not seem as close as the score. In the locker room, Coach Britt continued his relentless attack on the experts who thought so little of his players. He challenged them to scrap with even more intensity in the second half.

Florida stayed with the box-and-one but put a different defender on Sooley. He was just as ineffective as the previous two. When Sooley hit two short jumpers and stunned the crowd with a behind-the-back alley-oop to Melvin, Florida called another time-out. Their coach stared at the scoreboard in disbelief. 50–34. The Gators were fading and sniping at each other. The sky was falling and there was no way to stop it.

When the lead was 20, with nine minutes to go, Sooley finally saw the chance to make a flashy move, one he had never pulled off in a game. He had tried it in practice several times, with mixed success. The game was not out of reach and Florida had plenty of time for a run, and the last thing he wanted to do was to inspire his opponents with some playground antics. He had an entire repertoire, tricks and odd shots that he learned on the dirt courts of Lotta.

But what the hell? The South Sudanese were known for their daring and risk-taking, and if it worked it would top the *SportsCenter* highlight reel for the First Four games.

He took a pass at the free throw line with his back to the goal. With both hands, he fired the ball over his head, a bullet that had no chance of going through the rim. It wasn't supposed to. He quickly spun around, hooked his man, and caught the ball in the lane as it rebounded hard off the backboard. Melvin recognized the play and got in position. Sooley, still airborne and seemingly weightless, held the ball for a split second then floated a soft pass toward the rim as Melvin sprung behind the confused Florida bigs and slammed it down.

The official scorer, also confused, had no choice but to call it a missed shot, followed by an assist. Sooley didn't care. Lonnie didn't either. It was two more points, and a backbreaker. Florida called another time-out as the Eagles mobbed Sooley and the crowd went wild.

With six minutes to go, Sooley shot from the arc, followed it, missed, and watched a long rebound turn into an easy Gator basket. They pressed full-court and forced Murray to kick one out of bounds. A 10–0 run followed and the Florida bench came to life. At 3:35 and up 66–56, Lonnie called time and settled down his players. He asked Sooley if he needed a break and he said no. He would not take a break in the second half.

The Eagles had not won 14 in a row with a controlled offense, and Lonnie was not about to try something new. With every defender keeping an eye on Sooley, Mitch Rocker hit a wide-open three, and 30 seconds later Murray did the same. Florida pushed the ball hard, pressed hard, and was soon running out of gas. Sooley had plenty left. He hit his ninth three with 1:40 left to put the game out of reach 80–63. Florida took a bad shot and the rebound kicked out to Murray, who gave no thought to burning the clock. He bounced a pass across the court to Sooley, who was wide open at 30 feet and could have either killed time or driven to the basket. He chose neither and pulled up for his 10th three.

His performance fueled the CBS game recap as the country got its first look at the freshman sensation. The blind pass off the backboard dominated the highlights as the commentators shook their heads. He scored 46, seventh on the all-time tournament list, but still far behind the seemingly untouchable record put up by Notre Dame's Austin Carr. In a 1970 game against Ohio, Carr scored 61 points, and that was before the three-point shot. With it, Carr would have scored 75.

Sooley was 10-for-22 from the arc, 8-for-9 from the stripe, with 11 rebounds, 6 assists, 4 steals, and 4 blocks in 35 minutes.

.   .   .

The win was Central's first ever in the tournament, and it did much to melt the remaining ice in Durham. Parties broke out all over campus and in the student apartment complexes nearby. The bars were packed and rowdy, and up and down the streets the chant of "Sooley! Sooley! Sooley!" echoed through the night.

CHAPTER 44

The coaches met promptly at 7:30 for breakfast in the hotel restaurant. They huddled in a booth in a remote corner and sipped coffee as they waited for menus. None of the four could stop smiling. Lonnie put his cell phone in the middle of the table and said, "All phones here, and turned off. Mine hasn't stopped buzzing." The other three phones hit the table.

Jason Grinnell said, "Sooley called me at six this morning, and it was during one of those brief periods when I was actually asleep."

"What did he want?" asked Lonnie.

"Well, today is Wednesday, and he talks to his mother every Wednesday morning at seven."

"He didn't wake you up to tell you that," said Ron McCoy.

"Hang on. He said he had a dream, a bad one that involved a problem with an airplane, said it's a bad omen and he thinks we should take the bus to Memphis. They say the kid is really superstitious."

Lonnie said, "That'll save sixty thousand bucks for the air charter. Our AD will love that."

McCoy said, "The equipment managers can't find his socks after the games. He takes them with him."

Grinnell said, "Yeah. Murray says he washes them himself and hangs them in a window. Said he's been doing it since the first game he played."

"Well, at least they're getting washed."

A waitress stopped by and handed over menus. When she left, Lonnie said, "I like it. Let's take the bus and forget going home. I want to keep Sooley away from the campus, away from everybody. I got fifty emails last night from reporters, other coaches, old friends I haven't talked to in months. Everybody wants a piece of the kid right now."

Jackie Garver said, "According to Murray, the girls are driving him crazy."

"Those were the days," McCoy said with a laugh.

Lonnie said, "Tell the managers to let them sleep. We'll leave around eleven and take our time getting to Memphis."

"By bus?"

"Yes. If Sooley wants to ride the bus, then so be it."

. . .

Duke versus Central. The number one seed versus a number sixteen, a play-in. Never in the tournament's storied history had a number sixteen beaten a number one. Same for fifteen, fourteen, thirteen.

Duke versus Central, the other school in Durham. Duke, with its 5 national championships, its roll call of 32 All-Americans, its 41 tournament appearances, 16 conference championships, its current streak of 22 consecutive weeks at number one, and on and on. Across town, Central's numbers were far less impressive.

Duke, with its tuition now at $50,000 a year, its endowment of $8 billion, its dozens of endowed professorships, its 95 percent graduation rate, its lofty rankings in medicine, law, engineering, the arts and sciences, its billions in research grants, and on and on.

Rich versus poor, private versus public, elites versus upstarts.
The commentators feasted on the story.

And everybody was looking for Sooley.

. . .

FedEx Forum. Home of the Memphis Grizzlies and site of the South Regional. Arkansas is just next door, and its fans poured into the city to watch their beloved Razorbacks easily handle Indiana State in the first game. Feeling even more boisterous for the second round, the fans hung around and eagerly awaited the chance to show their anti-ACC sentiment against Duke. All 18,000 seats were packed, with only a sprinkling of Blue Devil faithful. A thunderous round of booing greeted the number one seed as they took the floor. Seconds later, the crowd flipped immediately and began "Sooley! Sooley! Sooley!" when Central appeared on the court.

For Samuel, the moment was disconcerting. Who wouldn't want to be on the receiving end of such adulation, but he felt as though all eyes were on him. For the past two days he had ignored the cameras and spoken to no one but his coaches and teammates. All of them were watching *SportsCenter* and following the storm on social media. They were determined to shield him from as many distractions as possible.

He smiled and stretched and tried to ignore the crowd. He glanced at the Duke players on the other end and wondered if they were as nervous as he was. They appeared to be immune from the jitters, all calm, relaxed, confident. They were accustomed to being booed and jeered and thrived on creating such noisy resentment on the road. They were far from the madness of Cameron, but they played all their away games in hostile, crowded arenas. It was part of the Duke mystique. The Blue Devils against the world.

Sooley's man was Darnell Coe, a 6'8" small forward scoring 12 a game and considered the best Duke defensive player since Shane Battier. Sooley glanced at Coe a couple of times, then tried to ignore him. Coe, like all the Duke players, seemed to have no interest in the opposing team.

As the lower seed, Central was introduced first and got a rousing welcome, with the "Sooley!" chants drowning out the announcer. Duke's starters were heavily booed but took it in stride. At mid-court they made no effort to acknowledge the Eagles.

Their center, Akeem Akaman, was 6'10". When he stepped forward for the tip-off, he scowled at Sooley, who immediately sprang high and quick and swatted the ball back to Mitch Rocker.

Central's first play was simple. They were where they were for one reason—Sooley and his long game. That's where they would start. That's where they would live or die. He posted high, then sprinted deep into the front court, took a bounce pass from Mitch and dribbled the ball. He was 35 feet from the basket and Coe gave him some room, as if to say, "Go ahead."

Sooley sprung up and took the shot. He didn't follow, but instead backed away and was past mid-court when it landed in the bottom of the net. He skipped back and waved his arms as the crowd erupted.

Duke had no weaknesses. Akaman and Kevin Washington could dominate inside, and Coe, Tyrell Miller, and Toby Frost could burn the nets from anywhere on the court. Central didn't have the bench to survive a physical game with lots of fouls, but no team could afford to give Duke room to run its offense. Coach Britt had decided to play hard and aggressive and hope the refs didn't call a close game.

Frost missed the first shot and Roy Tice cleared the board. Mitch jogged up court with the ball, traded passes with Murray, and at 15 seconds Sooley swept back into the front court, took the ball and launched another shot, this one a bit closer, from 32 feet. Nothing but net. The fans were beyond delirious.

The plan was to start with Sooley bombing away until he missed one. After a bucket by Akaman, Mitch pushed the ball up court in a hurry, and with only 10 seconds gone found Sooley deep in a corner with Coe sticking close. He faked a pass, then sprang from 30 feet. When his third shot found the net, the Forum seemed to shake.

Unrattled, Duke calmly went about its business on offense. Tyrell Miller bounced off a perfect screen and fired a 20-footer that didn't go. Akaman got the rebound, though, and slammed it home.

Coe closed in tight and began grabbing and hacking. Sooley peeled off screen after screen but couldn't shake him. When he got the ball for the fourth time, he faked a shot and sent Coe flying. He streaked for the basket, almost drew a charge, then whipped a perfect behind-the-back pass to Murray in the corner. He missed and Kevin Washington got the rebound.

Toby Frost dribbled the ball up and motioned for his teammates to settle down. At 17:40 Central led 9–4, and the jitters were gone. Frost nailed a three, and Sooley finally missed one. The teams swapped baskets, then swapped turnovers, and at the under-16-minute time-out they were tied at 13. The game was off to a frantic start with both teams seemingly poised to score 100.

Duke's defense, though, found its rhythm and pressured the perimeter. Mitch and Murray tried to work the ball inside but Roy Tice and Melvin Montgomery could not score. Coe stuck to Sooley like glue and denied him the ball. When he finally took a pass he launched another 30-footer, a bad shot that rebounded long and led to a beautiful three-on-one fast break.

Coe was fierce and physical and didn't mind grabbing and hacking. When he hand-checked Sooley hard, a clear foul, and drew no whistle, Lonnie erupted on the sideline and got a hard stare from a ref. He wouldn't shut up or back down. If the refs were allowing his star to get mugged, he was not about to stay quiet. He wanted a technical and finally got one, his third of the season.

As Tyrell Miller took the uncontested free throw, the crowd seemed ready to storm the court.

Duke quickly pulled away, scoring inside and out, and with Sooley bottled up, Central had no answer. Lonnie continued to work the refs and they finally tightened up the game. Coe was whistled for two straight fouls and took a seat. Sooley promptly nailed a 25-footer to cut the lead to 28–20 at 8:03.

It was obvious that the rest of the team would struggle to score. During a Central time-out, Lonnie asked Sooley if he needed a break. No sir, he wasn't coming out. "The game is yours," Lonnie said. "Take it to the basket."

With Coe on the bench, and with Duke protecting the perimeter, he began slashing to the lane. He finished some, dished others, and when Coe reentered at 5:22, the score was 34–30.

The obvious disadvantage of playing a well-coached team with four All-Americans was that someone always had a hot hand. Toby Frost hit two short jumpers and Mitch was called for traveling. Frost then hit a three and Duke was up by 11. Central clawed back, had three impressive stops, then Sooley hit his fifth three-pointer.

At the half, Duke led 46–35 and looked unbeatable. Sooley had 22 points and was 5-for-10 from behind the arc.

The locker room was quiet as the Eagles caught their breath and tried to absorb the enormity of facing more of the same in the second half. Lonnie and the coaches huddled and decided to try and slow down the game. Their man-to-man defense had just given up 46 points and looked helpless. They decided to start with a 2-3 zone, clog up the middle, and hope Duke cooled off from the outside. If that didn't work, and they had serious doubts, it would at least buy some time and save some legs for the finish.

.   .   .

The zone worked well for a few minutes as both teams missed shots and threw the ball away. When Sooley could get his hands on the ball he fired away, but Coe was suffocating him and every shot was fiercely contested. At 17:25 Coe was called for his third foul but didn't leave the game. Sooley was determined to draw the fourth and began driving. He lowered his shoulder and was whistled for his second foul. At the first TV time-out Duke led by 12, 52–40, and Sooley had missed all five shots, long and short.

He broke the drought with a 20-footer. Duke quickly answered. As Mitch walked the ball up the court, Coe grabbed Sooley's jersey, again, and their feet got tangled. Both went down hard, right in front of a ref who angrily pointed at Coe on the floor and whistled him for number four. The Duke bench, always volatile, went nuts and a few tense seconds followed. Coe left the game shaking his head. The announcers ran the replay and there was no doubt he had grabbed Sooley, spun him around, and tripped him up.

Sooley took the inbound pass and in a split second fired from the arc. Nothing but net. Tyrell Miller answered with a three, far away from the zone. Back and forth, the teams traded misses and baskets. Duke went up by 14 and Central cut it to eight, but could get no closer. Lonnie called time at 7:08 for a breather, and Sooley took a seat on the bench for a much deserved break. Duke was up 64–54.

When Sooley reentered at 5:50, Coe did the same, but with four fouls he had to take a step back. Sooley figured as much and launched two bombs. Both missed. With time running down, Lonnie ditched the zone and went to a half-court press and Duke, uncharacteristically, had consecutive turnovers. The Eagles were out of gas but desperate to make a run. This was not the moment to think about fatigue. They fought to within eight, 72–64, and the crowd got back in the game. Duke settled down, worked the clock, and Kevin Washington hit a three. With three minutes left, Duke forced a turnover that led to an easy basket, then blocked a shot that led to another.

In a matter of seconds, it seemed, Duke was up by 15 and Coach Britt called time. The disappointed fans sat down and stared at the scoreboard. The Forum had not been that quiet for hours.

1:58 remained. Duke 79, Central 64.

The next 58 seconds would later be called the most exciting minute in tournament history. Murray inbounded the ball to Mitch who rifled a pass to mid-court where Sooley scooped it up, dribbled twice, and launched a 30-footer that found the net. 1:50. Tyrell Miller grabbed the ball, stepped out of bounds and quickly bounced it inbounds to Toby Frost. However, Miller stepped on the baseline with his pass and a ref saw it and whistled the infraction. Dmitri Robbins inbounded long to Sooley, who was camping near mid-court. He pump-faked Coe, dribbled behind his back, and shot from 27 feet. Net. 1:44. 79–70. Central pressed full-court and Duke worked the ball up. Toby Frost broke free off a screen and was open, until he wasn't. Sooley came flying out of nowhere, blocked the shot, then sprinted two-on-one with Murray dribbling. He bounced it to his roommate, who pulled up from 29 feet and nailed his third in a row. 1:30. 79–73.

Lonnie backed them away and they pressed from half-court. Murray deflected a bounce pass, the ball squirted loose, and four players piled on top of it. In the scrum at least three of them fought over the ball and the ref whistled a jump ball. Possession Central. Sooley fought his way through the lane and managed to crash Coe into a hard screen set by Melvin Montgomery. No foul was called as Coe almost fell to the floor. His man was alone in the corner and Mitch fired a perfect pass. Sooley hit his fourth in a row from 26 feet. 1:10. 79–76. Central went full-court and Murray and Mitch trapped Frost in a corner. His wild pass was picked off at mid-court by Dmitri who, without a thought, led Sooley with a perfect bounce pass. He launched from 28 feet, and when the ball swished the net absolute bedlam rocked the Forum. 79–79 with one minute to go.

Duke, reeling, called time-out and Central's bench smothered their star. Lonnie managed to seat his five and tried to settle them down. But the noise was deafening and he had been hoarse for the entire second half. He switched to a tight man-to-man and told them to expect a long shot. He put Sooley on Toby Frost and told him to foul if necessary.

Frost calmly jogged the ball up the court and Duke set its

offense. Ten seconds, fifteen. Tyrell Miller set a hard ball screen for Frost, then rolled and took a perfect pass. At 41 seconds, Tyrell hit a 24-footer. Duke fell back and picked up Mitch, who passed to Murray. As Sooley fought off Coe and tried to get open, a ref blew a whistle. Coe was called for his fifth foul and Sooley went to the line to shoot two with 18 seconds left. He hit the first. 82–80. Central needed two points, not one, and nobody in the building expected Sooley to put it in the net. As soon as the ref bounced him the ball he fired at the rim and soared after the ball. When it bounced off the front of the rim, he slapped it to Murray, all alone in the corner. His 28-foot dagger was the shot of a lifetime, and Central was up by one. Duke had plenty of clock and used its last time-out.

Unable to sit and barely able to hear anything, the Central players huddled around Coach Britt and yelled at each other to dig in.

Frost hurried the ball up court, swapped quick passes with Tyrell Miller, and neither could find an open man. With five seconds to go, Kevin Washington tried a turn-around jumper from the free throw line but Roy Tice got a hand on it. The ball bounced to Murray, who saw his roommate streaking down the court. He lofted a long pass that Sooley took on one bounce at their own free throw line and hurled himself into the air.

Defying gravity, Sooley soared through the Forum, the ball in his right hand, high above his head, just like Niollo. He finished with a jarring, rim-rattling, windmill dunk that sent quakes all the way to South Sudan.

A mob swarmed the court as the Eagles piled on top of each other at mid-court.

CHAPTER 45

The locker room was remarkably subdued. The players were elated but too stunned and exhausted to celebrate. And they were overwhelmed with emotion. Coach Britt kept the cameras and press out, the door locked and guarded by managers. He quietly went from player to player, hugging each, offering soft words of praise, and he wiped a few tears himself. After fifteen minutes, he addressed his players and told them how much he loved them. His raspy, scratchy voice barely worked and he couldn't think of much to say anyway.

A manager stepped in to say that the tournament officials were waiting. Lonnie asked the three seniors, Mitch Rocker, Roy Tice, and Dmitri Robbins, to follow him. And Sooley too.

The press room was packed. Lonnie took a seat in the middle of the table, with two players on each side, and as soon as he adjusted his mike the questions came in an avalanche. He smiled, held up both hands, and said, "Please, just one at a time." He pointed at a reporter in the front row.

"Coach, did you really believe you could win the game?"

Lonnie laughed and his players smiled. "I don't think I'll answer that question. Let's be honest, no one in this room thought we would win. I think we're all still in shock."

"Coach, was it your game plan to start with Sooley bombing from mid-court?"

Another laugh. "Yes, it was. Our game plan was simple. Just get the ball to Sooley."

Every reporter held a game summary and knew the numbers. Sooley scored 58, tying him with Bill Bradley for second most in a tournament game. He hit 14 threes, had 12 rebounds, 10 assists, 4 steals, 4 blocks. A triple-double.

"Coach, was the crowd a factor?"

"Well, I've never been in a place where I couldn't hear myself think. My ears are still ringing. As you can tell, I can barely talk and at times I had trouble getting through to my players. But, yes, having the crowd on our side was a factor."

"Coach, a question for Sooley." Lonnie shrugged as if to say, "Fire away."

With a big smile, Sooley pulled his mike closer.

"Sooley, you hit fourteen threes, a tournament record. What were you thinking out there?"

Sooley had yet to say a word to any reporter, and the world was waiting. He smiled and shrugged and looked uncomfortable. Finally, "I don't know. I really wasn't thinking." Everyone laughed. "You know, the adrenaline was pumping so hard that you just play, you don't have time to think too much."

"Mitch, what's it like to watch a teammate do what Sooley just did?"

Mitch leaned forward with a grin and said, "No big deal, really. He does it every day in practice. When he gets hot, we just feed him the ball."

"Sooley, you just scored fifty-eight against a great defensive player. What do you think about Darnell Coe?"

"He's tough, one of the best. Very physical, you know. All the Duke players are physical. That's their game. They're a great team."

Mitch leaned in again and added, "The truth is, when he gets the ball nobody can guard him. His shot is too quick and he springs too high. Sometimes in practice we'll put three men on him just for fun. Once he gets up, though, you can't touch his shot."

"Coach, how do you get your team ready for the next game, after a win like this?"

Lonnie replied, "We'll be ready. I can promise you that."

Every reporter, and every fan, knew the story. The death of his father. The missing sister. His mother and brothers living in a refugee settlement. And every reporter wanted to ask something about the past year, but it wasn't the moment for that. Why do anything to dampen the kid's spirits?

. . .

When they were finally dressed, the managers led the team through a side door. They walked eight blocks through downtown Memphis to the Rendezvous, a famous ribs place in an alley. In a private room they began to relax and were soon laughing. Tomorrow they could sleep until noon.

. . .

The upset owned the news. The other seven games on Thursday ended as predicted and there was no room for any other coverage. It was a nonstop barrage of Sooley's greatest hits. His 14 threes, five in the span of 58 seconds to tie the game. His blocked shots. He had his own highlight reel.

. . .

On Friday, he and Murray met Miss Ida and Ernie for a late lunch in the hotel restaurant. And Jordan, who had driven from Nashville for the game. She had planned to stay only for the Duke game, but was as happy as the rest to hang around for the next one. Murray had scored 12, including the golden three that put Central ahead 83–82 with 16 seconds to go. They replayed the game and delighted in the moment. Jordan sat close to Sooley, knees touching knees, under the table of course because Miss Ida missed nothing.

Later in the afternoon, the team had a light, closed practice in an empty Forum. Jason Grinnell went through a scouting report and tried to convince the team that Arkansas was unbeatable. They knew better, and they were still thinking about Duke. Lonnie suspected this and had another sleepless night.

. . .

At 2 p.m. Saturday, the gates opened for the three o'clock game and the Arkansas throng was back. They filled the Forum early and made almost as much noise as they did on Thursday. Their love for Sooley had soured quickly and they were hungry for a win. The school had one national title, back in 1994, and, with Duke out of the way, the Razorbacks had a clear path to the next round.

Sooley picked up where he'd left off, and when he drained his second three, the crowd settled down. The Arkansas defense was jittery and panicked every time he touched the ball. It collapsed on him quickly and left plenty of gaps elsewhere. He began driving and dishing off for easy buckets. At half-time, he had nine assists and 16 points. The second half turned into a horse race as both teams tried to outrun each other. But no one could outrun Sooley. He scored 46 with 13 assists, and Central advanced with a 10-point win.

Off to the Sweet Sixteen.

CHAPTER 46

By Monday morning Lonnie Britt was sick of the word "Cinderella." Every sportscaster and sportswriter used it at least once per sentence. There were no other contenders. Out west, Utah State, a 10th seed, had knocked off UCLA, a number four, in a mild upset, but nothing even remotely close to what happened in Memphis.

Central's President was waiting, his door wide open, his secretary smiling as she offered pastries and coffee. Lonnie had never been so warmly received. As they settled into wide leather chairs, the AD arrived and the door was closed. Congratulations all around. What a weekend!

They covered the logistics of going to Atlanta for the next round. How many tickets would be allotted? How many big donors would be included? Politicians were calling and wanting in. Alumni Relations had never attracted so much attention. And the press! Hundreds of reporters and journalists were angling for stories and access, and while it was important to take advantage of a unique opportunity to market the school, Lonnie was much more concerned with protecting his players. Especially Sooley.

"Where is he?" asked the President.

"He's living in Murray Walker's basement. I think Ida's guarding the door. He's been there for a couple of weeks. The dorm got crazy."

"Is he going to class?"

"Yes, for the most part. But I doubt if many of the players are in class this morning. I'd like to leave for Atlanta tomorrow, after practice, just to get them out of town."

The AD frowned and said, "And miss a whole week of classes?"

Lonnie laughed and said, "Oh, so you think they'll study this week? We play Providence at six on Thursday afternoon, and that's all they're thinking about. This is too big. The kids are overwhelmed. I'd like to practice tomorrow at noon, then hit the road."

The AD looked at the President. Both knew the truth. With three wins already in the tournament the money was pouring in. Start with the NCAA-CBS contract, now worth over $500 million annually, and watch the money trickle down to the conferences and game winners. Central had already earned $600,000 that wasn't expected. And in March Madness, the more you win the more you earn.

Whatever Coach Britt wanted.

Because he felt he had to, the President said, "Okay, fine with me, but please instruct your players to get their assignments and study in their free time."

"Of course," Lonnie replied, because he had to. He would not monitor a single laptop. It was only March. The players had plenty of time to catch up in class and he had no plans to nag his guys during the greatest week of their lives.

The AD said, "We have rooms at a new Marriott downtown. Two players per room."

Lonnie smiled and said, "No thanks. We've already scoped out the hotels and I don't like any of them. I'm hiding my team, okay? There's a hotel in Athens where no one can find us. Two players per room."

The AD frowned and said, "But our team headquarters is the Marriott. That's where all of us, including the fans, will be staying."

"Have fun there. All the more reason to hide the kids. I don't want them getting pestered. Murray told me last night that he's been approached by three runners working for agents. They know he rooms with Sooley and he's reminded them that contact is illegal at this point. But these guys know how to work the system. You see where this is going. The talking heads have projected the kid going high in the draft. The vultures are circling, which will be fine when the season is over. Right now I don't want him distracted."

All three had watched *SportsCenter* and knew the buzz.

The President asked, "You see him in the draft?"

"No. He's too young, too raw, too immature."

But he scored 58 against Duke!

In college basketball, everyone has an agenda. Lonnie was looking for a bigger job and Sooley might help. Sooley would soon be tempted to declare for the draft and explore its options. An agent would whisper wonderful things to him and dangle the cash. Once money was involved, loyalties would begin to shift.

The AD said, "Okay, you want us to reserve the rooms?"

"No, it's already done."

"Will you tell us where the team is staying?"

"Only if you promise not to ask Sooley for a selfie."

The AD laughed and said, "We have a bunch of requests for seats on the plane."

"Save 'em. We're taking the bus."

"The bus? It's a six-hour drive to Atlanta."

"Yep. And Sooley prefers the bus. I'm sure he'll study all the way down there."

"Come on, Coach," the President said. "We can't arrive for the Sweet Sixteen in a bus."

"What do we know about Sweet Sixteen arrivals?"

"Good point."

The AD said, "If Sooley wants a bus, then take the bus."

. . .

Miss Ida had them up and eating breakfast by eight. Ernie lingered for a final word.

They were concerned that their two players had shown no interest in their academic pursuits for at least the past week and would probably want to skip Monday's classes. After Ernie left, Miss Ida made Sooley promise to go to class.

Actually, he wanted to. There were two extremely cute girls in American History. When he walked in five minutes late, the entire class stood and cheered. The professor was a good sport and enjoyed the celebration. Sooley sat behind the girls, in his usual spot, and opened his laptop.

After fifteen minutes, the professor realized that her lecture was not being heard by anyone, especially Sooley, who was online with the girls. The professor walked from behind the lectern and said, "Can I have your attention, please? Thank you. How many of you have younger brothers and sisters at home?"

Almost all of the students raised their hands.

"And how many of you have been asked by your younger siblings to get a photo with Mr. Sooleymon?"

All hands went up.

She smiled and continued: "Thought so. I have a twelve-year-old son, and if I go home without a photo he won't speak to me. Sooley, please forgive me for disrupting your classwork, but, if you will indulge us, I will excuse all absences from last week and this week. Deal?"

The class cheered again and Sooley ambled down to the front.

· · ·

The school wanted some sort of glorious send-off, an old-fashioned pep rally, with speeches, cheerleaders, a band, and students packed in the stands. But Lonnie nixed it. More adulation wouldn't do a damned thing to help win the game against Providence.

He ran them hard Tuesday afternoon, then told them to shower, change, hustle up, and get on the bus.

As they left campus, Roy Tice yelled back: "Say, Sooley, next week when we go to the Final Four can we take a plane? My app says it's thirty-two hours to Phoenix by car. Straight shot on Interstate Forty."

Sooley had his earbuds in and pretended not to hear. His eyes were closed as if in deep meditation. Others began griping about the bus ride, but they were too excited to really care.

Coach Britt got their attention when he ran an edited game film of Providence thrashing a good Butler team in the second round. And he reminded them that, once again, they were on the low end of a six-point spread.

Still, no respect.

CHAPTER 47

The special delivery was loaded into the back of a Ugandan army troop carrier. It was guarded by a couple of soldiers and watched by two army technicians. Coach Kymm rode shotgun with the driver as they left the Entebbe airport in the early morning. He had hoped to fly the shipment on a small cargo plane, like the one he and Ecko Lam had hitchhiked on back in early December, but there wasn't enough room. Food and medicine took priority over everything else, and on this trip he was delivering nothing but entertainment, courtesy of a wealthy Ugandan beer magnate who loved basketball and sponsored Kymm's national teams.

The seven-hour drive on gravel roads actually took nine, and when they rolled into Rhino Camp South it was too late to set up. They had dinner and slept in an army barracks nearby. Early Thursday morning, the technicians scouted locations and found the best spot on a rise not far from the new school. A flat trailer was moved into position, and the technicians and soldiers began unpacking the screens. There were two of them, positioned on opposite ends of the trailer with the generator, transmitter, antenna, and miles of wires and cables between them. Brand-new 150-inch Samsung 8K flat screens, the largest to be found anywhere in that corner of

Africa. Coach Kymm spent the day under a shade tree, watching the project unfold, and occasionally reading a paperback. He tried to call Ecko in Atlanta but there was no cell service.

. . .

Late Wednesday night, after the managers reported that all players were accounted for, Lonnie eased out of his room and went to the hotel bar where Ecko was waiting in a corner. So far, the team's hiding place in an Athens Holiday Inn had not been discovered by the media. Ecko had watched the team practice at the University of Georgia and was staying at the hotel.

They ordered beers and talked about the practice, Providence, a game plan. Lonnie laughed and said, "Actually, when you're a one-man team the game plan is pretty simple."

"What happens when he goes cold?"

"We don't score and they run us out of the gym. I just wish that for one game someone else would get hot and score twenty. Mitch or Murray, maybe even Dmitri from the corner. Take the pressure off Sooley and soften up the defense."

"They're not great shooters."

"Tell me about it. And the more he scores the more the others rely on him. They're turning down good looks to get him the ball."

"I talked to him for a long time this afternoon in his room and he seems to be handling it well. You're smart to keep him away from the media. It's a circus."

"Have you seen the cover of *Sports Illustrated*? Just came out online."

"No. What is it?"

"A photo of the kid soaring through the air, windmill dunking against Duke, elbow about three feet above the rim, with the caption—'Sooleymania.'"

"Clever. I know you're worried about him, but this is really pretty cool. He's in a good spot and he knows it. Nothing has gone to his head. Yet."

"His teammates are smothering him, watching everything closely. A great bunch of kids, Ecko. I love these guys."

"You'll love them even more if they win the next two and take you to the Final Four." They laughed and sipped and looked around. The bar was practically empty.

Lonnie asked, "What's gonna happen to Sooley, Ecko? You talk to more scouts than I do. I'm too focused on the next game and don't have time to think past it."

"Remember Frankie Moka, my summer assistant?"

Lonnie nodded and said, "Sure."

"He's a scout for the Nuggets, says the kid will likely go late in the first round. The upside is obvious, with the added potential of more growth and maturity. The downside is the unknown. Is he a flash in the pan? Red hot for fifteen games, then he's gone? It's happened before. What the scouts want to see is a bad game. No one hits fifty percent from behind the arc, so what happens when he doesn't hit and stinks it up?"

"Please, not now."

"I know. I'm just saying he doesn't have the track record of the other one-and-dones. Those four at Duke were on the radar when they were fifteen years old. The other top prospects have at least two full years in college. Not Sooley. So, that's a concern, but not much. The scouts are as enamored as everyone else."

Lonnie smiled and took a sip. "Have I said thanks for making me offer him a scholarship?"

"You have, and you are welcome. Sometimes we get lucky. You know, it's hard to believe that when I met him a year ago he was six-two, weighed a buck seventy, and had the ugliest jump shot in South Sudan."

"He's a freak, Ecko, plain and simple. We measured him last week. Six-eight now, two-thirty. All he wants to do is shoot baskets and lift weights."

"Girls?"

"I don't get involved but I'm sure he's doing okay."

"Have you talked to him about the draft, and agents and all that?"

"No, not yet. I know the runners are out. It's part of the business. At least three have approached Murray. I've lectured the team in front of Sooley and talked to the seniors when he's not around. They try to protect him, but you know how it works. As soon as the tournament is over, he's fair game and can talk to an agent. Once that starts, he's gone. Nobody can turn down the money."

Ecko agreed. "And he worships Niollo, who turned pro at nineteen after only one year at Syracuse. Of course, Niollo played competitive high school ball here in the States and was even an All-American. Trivia: Who was the only high school prospect ranked ahead of Niollo?"

"LeBron."

"LeBron. And he didn't go to college."

"What does Sooley want?"

"We talked about his family this afternoon. That's all he cares about right now. He's eternally grateful to you and Central and his teammates, but when he's off the court he's thinking about his mother and brothers. I told him that a coaching buddy of mine in Uganda has pulled some strings with the government and they're setting up some big flat screens to watch the game in the refugee camp. Can you imagine? Sooley's mother and brothers watching him play. The kid had tears in his eyes when I told him."

"That's amazing. And you got it done?"

"Sure. It's nothing. You ask what he wants. If money will help get his family over here, then he'll take the money. If earning a degree in four years and becoming a U.S. citizen will make it happen faster, then that's what he wants."

"He'll take the money."

"Probably."

"He trusts you, Ecko. Do you know a good agent?"

"I'd rather not get involved. At that point, Sooley will enter a different world and any advice from me would not be valuable. He's a smart kid and he'll figure it out. Hopefully."

. . .

When Samuel stepped into the mid-court circle for the tip, he took a second to soak in the enormity of Atlanta's State Farm Arena, home of the Hawks. Under one backboard a noisy contingent from Central chanted his name while the rest of the 18,000-plus settled into their seats. As always, he reminded himself of where he came from, and how far he had traveled. A year ago he was playing on dirt courts.

He nodded to the center for Providence, a gangly boy with heavy feet, and slapped the ball back to Mitch Rocker, who took his time and quickly noticed that there were two Friars sticking to their star. The other three were spread across the lane in what appeared to be a zone of some sorts. Mitch drove to the free throw line and kicked out to Dmitri, who missed an easy 20-footer. More misses soon followed, and the double-team on Sooley worked beautifully, as long as no one else could score. Central was off to a dismal start, one that turned ugly when the Friars' leading scorer hit his second three to make the score 12–2. At the first TV time-out, the lead was 20, 26–6, and Sooley had yet to score. The crowd was quiet, but there was a buzzing as if the fans were wondering about all the hype.

With one defender stuck to his back and the other staying between him and the ball, Sooley was having trouble. Out of frustration, he elbowed the taller one and got a whistle, his first foul. They picked him up at mid-court and dogged him every step. Mitch Rocker hit a three, and, after a block by Sooley, Murray hit another one. At 13:05 Sooley managed to take a bounce pass at the free throw line and spring high above his defenders. He was checked hard, got a whistle as the ball went in, and finished off the three-point play. He was on the board and the lead was 15. Roy Tice took a long rebound and fired the outlet pass to Murray who flipped it behind his back to Sooley, who launched a 30-footer that hit and fired up the crowd. Providence slowed down the game and both defenses settled in. Coach Britt chewed relentlessly on the refs, complaining that Sooley was being held and hacked and otherwise mugged. He got a call, then another, and coverage slacked off just enough to spring him. He hit two more threes and Providence called time at 7:40, its lead cut to eight points. Lonnie told Mitch and Murray to start hammering the ball inside and try to take pressure off Sooley. Roy Tice hit two short jumpers and the Friars missed four straight. Sooley missed badly from long range but followed it, got the rebound and fired a perfect pass to Melvin Montgomery for the dunk. At the half, the score was tied at 40. Sooley had 12 points and was 3-for-7 from behind the arc. More important, he was keeping the Friars preoccupied on defense and his teammates were scoring.

. . .

On the other side of the world, Beatrice, James, and Chol stood at the front of a massive throng of refugees and watched the flat screen in disbelief. Before the game started, a Ugandan commander had welcomed the crowd and explained that the game was being brought to them in living color as a courtesy of his government. He talked about the game, a little about the tournament, and introduced, as the guests of honor, the family of young Samuel Sooleymon, the hottest player in America.

Beatrice never stopped crying.

. . .

In the locker room, the Eagles were sky-high. They had clawed back from a disastrous start and had momentum. Lonnie implored them to dig deep and contest every shot. It was only a matter of time before Sooley took control.

He wasted no time. The Friars' first shot bounced off the rim and Dmitri scooped up a long rebound and sprinted with the ball. He found Sooley across court with a bounce pass and before anyone could get near him he shot from 29 feet. Nothing but net. It was the shot the crowd had been waiting for and the fans came to life. After a short bucket on the other end, he fought off his defenders, went up again, and was fouled hard. He made two of three and Central immediately pressed full-court. Murray drew a charge. On the inbound, Sooley sprinted from beneath the basket, took a pass at the top of the key, spun in midair, and hit from 20 feet. Providence scored and Mitch jogged the ball up court. As Sooley peeled off a low screen, one of his defenders grabbed his jersey and a ref saw it. Third foul, time to rest. Inbound, Murray found Sooley deep in a corner for his fifth three-pointer. Providence needed to regroup but the coach decided to wait for the under-16-minute time-out. He should not have. The Friars were being pressed hard and taking bad shots. Mitch Rocker hit a three and Central had its first double-digit lead, 53–42. Its bench was wild and most of the 18,000 fans were cheering for the Eagles.

After the time-out, the Friars settled down and hit two buckets. Sooley missed from 25 feet, followed it, missed the rebound, and Central gave up an easy fast break. Its lead had been cut in half. At 9:20, and up by seven, Sooley squared up from 28 feet and nailed it. He hit another long one, then missed one but drew a foul. With eight minutes to go, he missed a bad one and Lonnie yanked him for a breather. For two minutes he watched Providence score six straight, and when he reentered at 5:50 the score was 63–56 and the game was still in doubt. But his two defenders were dragging and tired of chasing him around the court. He hit his sixth three, then his seventh. When he hit his eighth at 4:45, Providence called time, down 72–58 and out of gas. Central kept pressing and running, and

Sooley, already with 34 points, kept bombing away. When he hit from 30 feet, the crowd began chanting his name and the arena was rocking.

He finished with 40 in a 15-point win. The Eagles were one game away from the Final Four.

CHAPTER 48

The game ended at two in the morning, East African time, and Coach Kymm found a Ugandan sergeant with a sat phone. He called the number of an American cell phone. Sooley was sitting high in the cheap seats of State Farm Arena, with his teammates and coaches, watching Iowa State play Maryland in the second game, when his phone buzzed with a strange number. Seconds later, he was talking to his mother.

.   .   .

There was little time to enjoy being a member of the Elite Eight. On Friday, the team slept late, went through a light workout in an empty Stegeman Coliseum on Georgia's campus, covered the scouting report on Maryland, and watched, off and on, the four games from the other side of the bracket.

On Saturday they slept late again, had brunch at the hotel, and took the bus to the arena in downtown Atlanta. In perfectly matched practice gear, they enjoyed a light shootaround two hours before tip-off. The media was everywhere and they hammed it up for the cameras. With Coach Britt close by, Sooley met with some reporters at courtside and fielded all the usual questions. As he smiled and went through an "aw-shucks" routine, his teammates chanted in the background, "Sooley! Sooley! Sooley!"

One challenge of being the Cinderella team was the nonstop attention, and their coaches relaxed and let them enjoy the moment. Several reporters noted that they were far more laid-back than the Maryland team, who were eight-point favorites.

. . .

Sooley easily won the tip. The Maryland center gave a half-hearted effort because a well-disguised steal worked perfectly and Mitch was stripped of the ball. A quick pass down low led to an easy dunk.

Maryland had seven losses, with five of them in the Big Ten, a powerful conference that had landed six teams in the tournament. Three of them had advanced to the Elite Eight, the most of any league. The Terps were ruthless on defense and had allowed only 61 points a game, second nationally to Virginia. They immediately went into a box-and-one, with four guarding the lane. The fifth, Omar Brazeale, was the Big Ten Defensive Player of the Year, and he picked up Sooley at mid-court and began talking trash. He would soon stop. Sooley circled wide, took a bounce pass from Murray and launched from 30 feet. Brazeale was 6'6", about a foot shorter than necessary, and when the ball left Sooley's hands his defender was far below him. Nothing but net and a taste of what was coming.

Maryland was patient on offense and showed no desire to start running with the Eagles. With four seconds left on the play clock, a shot bounced off the rim. Dmitri Robbins grabbed the rebound and in midair whirled and fired a pass to Mitch, who led Sooley perfectly. He pulled up from 25 feet and drained his second three. Maryland missed again and Murray sprinted the ball up court. Brazeale got caught by a hard screen, his man was wide open, and when Sooley hit his third three in the first 90 seconds the crowd began to chant.

Central hit seven of its first eight shots, and at 14:55, the first

TV time-out, led 18–7. Maryland was too experienced to panic and stayed with its controlled offense. The game slowed considerably as the Terps chipped away. Sooley missed two bombs but drew the first foul on Brazeale. The second came quickly as he banged into Melvin Montgomery on a screen. It was a close call and the Maryland bench was not happy. Brazeale stopped yapping and realized he would spend the rest of the game hopelessly chasing Sooley around the court and fighting off screens. When Sooley hit his fifth three at 7:20, Maryland called time. Central was up 34–24. Sooley had 22 points and was 5-for-8 from behind the arc. The team was shooting 70 percent, a torrid pace that Coach Britt knew would not be sustained. He told the other four to clear the lane so Sooley could take it to the rim.

Maryland patiently worked its offense and hit a three. When Sooley got the ball at mid-court he dribbled twice, head faked, got Brazeale in the air, and rushed into the paint. As the defense collapsed, he rifled a behind-the-back pass to Mitch Rocker who was wide open from 20 feet. He missed and Maryland slowly brought the ball up. Both teams cooled off, trading misses and short baskets. With two minutes to go, Maryland began pressing and forced two turnovers. The Terps finished in a rush and at half-time trailed by only four, 41–37. Sooley had 24 points and was 5-for-10 from long range. More important, Brazeale had three fouls. During the break, Coach Britt drew up two plays designed to draw the fourth foul. At that point, Sooley could go wild.

Maryland missed its first shot of the second half. Mitch set the offense and bounced a pass to Sooley, who was standing in the mid-court circle. He waved his teammates to the right side, as if no one else was on the court but him and Mr. Brazeale. He faked a shot, and when Brazeale didn't take it, he launched from 32 feet and drained it. Maryland killed the clock and hit a short jumper. Sooley set up at the free throw line with Brazeale stuck to him like glue. At 15 seconds, he spun around and took his man through three hard screens as he sprinted to a corner. Brazeale fought through the screens but lost a second. When Sooley went up from 22 feet, Brazeale was airborne and fell into him for his fourth foul. For once, the play worked exactly as Coach Britt had drawn it up on the board. Sooley hit two of three free throws.

With Brazeale on the bench, Maryland put two men on Sooley, and this delighted him. Somebody else had to be open, and Murray, perhaps the weakest shooter on the team, found the hot hand. When he hit two straight threes Central was up by 52–39 and Maryland called time.

Each trip down the floor became another adventure in Sooleymania. The entire defense watched him. When he couldn't get the ball, Mitch worked it low for easy buckets by Melvin Montgomery and Roy Tice. When Sooley got the ball, usually around mid-court, he dazzled his defenders with lightning-fast dribbles and either launched long fade-away jumpers or slashed to the basket where he drew fouls or finished with highlight-reel dunks or dished off to his teammates.

At 6:02, Brazeale reentered the game during a TV time-out. His team was down 16, 68–52, and the crowd was yelling for more.

.   .   .

As loud as it was, the noise inside the State Farm Arena paled in comparison to the constant roar of the masses on the outskirts of Rhino Camp South. Every long shot made by young Samuel sent his people into unrestrained delirium. Beatrice, James, and Chol were treated like royalty and nearly mobbed with each magnificent play.

.   .   .

Up 20, 76–56, Sooley came out for a breather and Maryland put on its inevitable last run. The Terps scored eight straight and Coach Britt called time at 3:35 to settle down his team. Sooley reentered and promptly missed a long one. Maryland did the same. Mitch was called for traveling and Maryland kicked one out of bounds. Both teams took a deep breath and braced for the last two minutes. Mitch called the same triple screen to free Sooley, and when he hit from 28 feet, Maryland was on the ropes again. Roy Tice blocked a shot and the ball landed in Murray's hands. He flung a high, long pass downcourt where Sooley streaked all alone, nonchalantly took in the ball, and stuffed it. Maryland inbounded with a long pass that caught the Eagles off-guard and led to an easy layup. The Terps swarmed the inbound pass but Mitch cleared the press with a long pass of his own to the other end where Sooley was open. He could have killed some clock, or waited to be fouled, or passed across court to avoid a foul, but instead he instinctively went up from 29 feet and drained it.

Coach Britt chose not to back off and the Eagles pressed relentlessly. Maryland barely cleared mid-court in 10 seconds and quickly threw up a brick. Roy Tice grabbed the rebound and was fouled. He made both free throws and the game was over.

. . .

When the bus rolled onto the Central campus late Sunday afternoon, the students were waiting. They lined the streets, cheering wildly, waving signs, throwing confetti. When the bus stopped in front of The Nest, barricades protected the players and coaches as they stepped off and soaked in the moment. Half a dozen news vans were parked haphazardly to one side and there were cameras everywhere. Inside, the place was packed and rocking as 4,000 students and fans filled the stands and covered the floor, all waiting for a glimpse of the school's first Final Four heroes. When Mitch led them through the tunnel and into the mob, the familiar chant of "Sooley! Sooley! Sooley!" shook the old gym.

CHAPTER 49

For the second straight Monday morning Lonnie found himself in the President's office, along with the AD. The President, always a busy man, had canceled all his important meetings. Everything else could wait.

They reveled in their success and replayed the prior weekend's games. They talked about the trip to Phoenix, travel plans, tickets, and so on, delightful details they never dreamed they would have the chance to discuss.

Lonnie surprised them when he said, "Look, I really want to get the team out of town and as soon as possible. The distractions are already overwhelming. I've stopped answering my phone and can't even look at my emails. Everybody wants a piece and Sooley is the main attraction. We've got to protect the kid."

"You want to leave now?" the President asked, feigning disapproval but knowing damned well where this was headed.

"Today. Forget classes this week. Don't think for a minute that these kids will be able to study. Hell, they can't even go to class. We need to go hide somewhere to practice and get away from this craziness."

"You have someplace in mind?" asked the AD.

"Yes. I have a buddy who coaches at Northern Arizona in

Flagstaff, about two hours north of Phoenix. I talked to him last night and he's on board. He'll arrange hotel rooms under his name and give us his gym for the week. We cannot practice here. It's impossible."

The President offered the standard frown and asked, "And miss an entire week of classes?"

"Absolutely. It's imperative. Get the deans on board, talk to their professors, and I'll make sure they keep up online. They'll have plenty of time when we're not in practice. I'll make it work."

All three knew the score. Lonnie's team had just collected another $2 million for the school's athletic programs and he would get whatever he wanted.

The President shrugged as he caved.

The AD said, "I assume you'll want an airplane this time."

Lonnie laughed and said, "Well, Sooley asked about taking a bus and I thought the guys might choke him."

"I'll bet they don't," the President said.

Lonnie said, "No. That won't happen. They are being extremely protective."

"Where is he?"

"In Ida Walker's basement. She's standing guard but she's a bit rattled. Word's out and there were people knocking on her door last night."

The AD said, "Let's get 'em out of here."

The President said, "Agreed. You have the university's full support, in every way."

"Thank you."

The AD said, "And you do prefer to fly?"

"Yes."

．　．　．

When the team boarded the bus Monday afternoon, not a single player knew where they were going. They had been told what to wear and what to pack, and they watched with amusement as the driver followed the signs to the Raleigh-Durham airport. At the general aviation terminal, they got out and were directed to a private charter waiting on the tarmac. They grew more excited as they took their seats. Mitch Rocker finally asked, loudly, "Say, Coach, where we going?"

"To Disney World," Lonnie replied. "Until we get there, I want every one of you to hit the books."

Studying was the last thing on their minds.

After takeoff, the cabin's in-flight navigational system was turned off and all screens went blank. It was obvious, though, that they were headed west. Four hours and two thousand miles later, they began a descent and saw mountains and deserts, rarities in their world, which confirmed the suspicion that they were headed to Arizona. After the plane landed and was taxiing to the terminal, Lonnie addressed the team and laid out the plan for the week. He instructed them to keep their location and practice schedule secret. Nothing on social media.

On Tuesday they practiced early and hard at the Walkup Skydome on the NAU campus, then relaxed and watched an hour's worth of film of Villanova, their Saturday opponent. The Wildcats were the number one seed in the East. The other two teams were Oregon from the West and Kansas from the Midwest. After lunch, they suffered through a one-hour study hall, then boarded a bus and rode an hour to a national park where a giant meteor had landed 50,000 years earlier and changed the landscape. Far from home, the players and most of their coaches had never seen such a rugged and beautiful landscape. They took hundreds of photos, but were strictly forbidden from posting anything on social media. At night, after dinner, they hung out in their rooms and watched and listened as the commentators and talking heads went on and on about the Final Four. The Eagles, and their improbable run to Phoenix, were the main topic.

Their stories and angles varied little. The other school from

Durham taking on established programs. The first Historically Black College to make it so far. The showstopping play of Samuel Sooleymon, a freshman freak averaging 41 points a game, a modern tournament record. A one-man team against far superior talent.

Early Wednesday morning, Sooley talked to his mother and listened with great pride as she described watching him play with tens of thousands of other refugees. He was the pride of South Sudan, or at least of his scattered people.

Wednesday and Thursday followed the same routine. Hard work in the mornings, bus rides in the afternoon. The highlight was a trip to the Grand Canyon.

On Friday, the team rode the bus two hours into Glendale, to the University of Phoenix Stadium, home of the NFL Cardinals. Their coaches had shown them photos of the space-age stadium, indoors and out, and had tried to brace them for the shock of seeing a tiny basketball court in the middle of such a vast venue. But the shock wore off as they went through a light shootaround. Cameras were everywhere and the players thoroughly enjoyed the attention. Afterward, a crew from CBS interviewed the players, with most of the attention directed at Sooley.

Lonnie had been criticized for hiding his team but he didn't care. Once in the glare, they opened up and said all the right things. With his ever-present smile and good nature, Sooley became the darling of the press.

Back at the hotel they watched a movie until eleven, then all lights were out. At ten Saturday morning, they enjoyed a catered brunch in a large conference room while Coach Britt reviewed the game plan and matchups. At noon, they boarded the bus for the return to Glendale. At 2:30 they ambled onto the court and began stretching and warming up. The Villanova players were at the other end, doing the same, and some of the players eventually met in the center and said hello. Coach Jay Wright walked over and introduced himself. The mood was light, even festive, and the Wildcats were an amiable group.

Glasgow Life
Springburn Library

Items that you have checked out

Title: Sooley
ID: C006841390
Due: 04 June 2022

Total items: 1
Account balance: £0.00
21 May 2022
Checked out: 1
Overdue: 0
Hold requests: 0
Ready for collection: 0

Contact: 0141 276 1690 (Option 2)
www.glasgowlife.org.uk/libraries

Sooley chatted with Coach Wright, who introduced him to Darrell Whitley, their All-American forward. With a smile Whitley said, "I got you man."

Sooley replied, "And I got you." It was a dream matchup the pundits had been discussing for a week. Whitley was a junior averaging 20 points and 10 rebounds and was expected to go high in the draft. The Central coaches had watched hours of film and were of the opinion that he occasionally relaxed a bit on defense. Not surprisingly, they planned to go to Sooley.

Back in the locker room, the team changed into its maroon road uniforms and tried to relax. Most of the players wore headphones or earbuds and listened to music.

Sooley checked his phone and was delighted to see a text that read: "Best of luck, Samuel. I am very proud of you. Leave it all out there on the court." It was his third text in two weeks from Niollo. He replied with a quick thanks.

When it was time to play, Lonnie huddled his team around him and told them how much he loved them. Win or lose, they had come together and made history. They were the pride of their school, their families, their state, and all those black colleges and universities that had always struggled to get this far. For the rest of their lives they would not forget what happened out there in the next two hours. The world was watching. Go have some fun.

CHAPTER 50

The Walkers—Ida, Ernie, Jordan, and Brady—sat ten rows behind the bench, in the heart of the Central faithful. Like most of the fans present, they had never watched a basketball game with 75,000 others in such an enormous venue. Ernie didn't like it at all. The court was too far away. Everything was too far away. He could barely hear the band. Ida finally told him to shut up and enjoy the moment.

On the other side of the world, Beatrice and her boys were once again led by smiling soldiers to the front of the pack and given seats of honor. Masses of humanity squeezed closer to the trailer and its two large screens. Even those who could barely see were happy to stand shoulder to shoulder and listen to the American announcers set the stage.

It was late on a Saturday night, with a full moon above. Tomorrow was Sunday, just another day to survive until Monday.

. . .

Being introduced in such a spectacle was intimidating enough. Being introduced as thousands chanted "Sooley! Sooley! Sooley!" was overwhelming, but he managed to appear loose and kept smiling at everything. Central was clearly the crowd's favorite.

The starters met at mid-court and shook hands, in a variety of ways. Villanova's center, Wade Lister, was seven feet tall and could jump. He had controlled every tip of the season and Sooley was no match. When he got pinched in a ball screen, Darrell Whitley calmly drained a 20-footer, and the Wildcats struck first and fast.

Everyone watching the game knew what was coming. Sooley posted low, then busted through the lane with Whitley fighting off screens. Murray bounced a perfect pass that Sooley took on the way up from 30 feet. When the ball swished the net, the crowd, half a second behind because of the distance, exploded. Nova missed from the arc, the rebound went long, and Mitch Rocker took it on a fast break. As the lane closed he whipped a gorgeous pass behind his back and Sooley was in the air again with his second 30-footer.

He looked unstoppable, but, of course, he was not. In the college game, it's rare for a gunner to hit 40 percent from long range. No one has ever hit 50 percent for a season.

After 19 games, Sooley was at 46 percent. For the tournament, he was at 51 percent, a remarkable number that was not sustainable. It was time for a drought, and its timing could not have been worse. He missed his next two attempts and the crowd settled down. Whitley was quick and fearless on defense and slapped one ball out of bounds. When Sooley tried to drive, he lowered his shoulder a bit too much and drew the charge. He missed again from downtown and the offense sputtered. At the first time-out, Nova was up 14–6.

Feeling the pressure, Sooley missed a bad shot from 20 feet and Darrell Whitley hit a quick three on the other end. Murray missed, then Mitch followed with another miss. The Eagles couldn't buy a bucket and their star was ice cold. Behind 22–6, Lonnie called time-out. The crowd was silent. Had the clock finally struck twelve for Cinderella?

For the last eight minutes of the half, Central played some of its worst basketball of the season. Or, perhaps the difference in talent became obvious. Villanova played a tight, team defense and was patient on the other end, rarely taking a low-percentage shot.

With its scorer neutralized, Central began to panic on offense and committed turnover after turnover. With five seconds to go, Sooley finally hit another three to cut the lead to 41–24. He had 11 points for the half but hit only 3 of 10 from behind the arc.

The Eagles' locker room was frustrated, tense, and frightened. Frustration at the sloppy play. Fear that the magical run was finally coming to an end. Was this their destiny? To capture the headlines with a miracle run behind a former redshirt who seemed invincible, only to flame out at the end when the competition became too much? There were appeals from Mitch Rocker and Roy Tice, both seniors. Coach Grinnell gave an inspiring speech. Coach Britt thought a 2-3 zone might work. However, everyone knew the truth. If Sooley wasn't hitting from downtown, they had no chance.

He drew his third foul at 18:40 on a close call that upset Lonnie, who wasn't about to pull him out. He told him to back off and by all means avoid another foul. Sooley immediately hit a three, then another, and the stadium came to life. But Nova was too well-coached and experienced to panic. It ran its offense, double-teamed Sooley when necessary on defense, and extended its lead. At 9:25, the score was 58–39 and a last-minute push by Central looked unlikely. Nova, with a much deeper bench, subbed freely and was wearing down the Eagles on defense. A minute later, Mitch Rocker limped off the court with a high ankle sprain. Nova immediately pressed full-court and Murray struggled to handle it. Sooley helped break the press and was open from 35 feet. It was a bad miss on a shot he should not have attempted and showed how desperate the Eagles were. Through nothing but determination, they stayed within 20 points but could get no closer. At 2:44, and needing a miracle, Sooley got open from 25 feet. If the ball went through the rim, another wild streak might be in the works. Think the Duke game—five threes in 58 seconds. When it rattled out, Nova cleared and walked the ball up court ahead 71–50. Central pressed at midcourt but Nova handled it easily. A dunk put the game out of reach.

. . .

Sooley wasn't much for tears. He had shed buckets of them in the past year, but for real losses, real tragedies. Crying after a basketball game cheapened the tears he had shed for his family.

He and the Eagles hung around the court and congratulated the Wildcats, who were great sportsmen and said all the right things. Sooley did a quick interview courtside with CBS and managed his trademark smile. He blamed himself for the loss and said he had not played well, but it had been a wonderful run for him and his underdog buddies, and they were proud of what they had accomplished. They held their heads high. They had been beaten by a better team.

When they were finally together in the locker room and the doors were shut, Lonnie smiled at his players and said, "Ain't nobody crying in this locker room, you hear me? Just think back to last September when we started practice. Not a single one of us, in our wildest dreams, could imagine we'd be here right now. We accomplished something that's never been done before. You made history, men, and that can never be taken away from you. I love you. Your coaches love you. Let's savor the moment and keep our heads up."

. . .

They managed to sit through the first half of Oregon versus Kansas, but they'd had enough basketball for one day. Their season was over and they really didn't care who played who for the title on Monday night. Mitch, taped up and limping, asked Coach Britt if they could leave. The bus took them to a fancy Phoenix steakhouse where a private room had been reserved. Central's President and his wife were there, along with the AD and some other important people. The coaches' wives joined the party. As Sooley was finding a seat, Ecko Lam walked through the door and hugged him. They sat together at a table with Murray and Dmitri and talked about the game.

Sooley scored 22, almost 20 below his tournament average. There was no doubt that had he been hitting the game would have changed dramatically. He made only 5 of 16 attempts from three-point range. He turned the ball over four times. He had no blocks and only six rebounds. It was a subpar performance on every level and he had no explanation for it. The setting was intimidating at first, but then every other player had the same jitters. They were playing a good team, but they had already beaten several others.

There was no excuse, no explanation. Just a bad night.

Ecko tried to lighten the mood with "You know, it was almost a year ago when I first met you in Juba, at the tryouts. Hard to believe, isn't it?"

Sooley smiled and nodded along.

Ecko looked at Murray and said, "He was only six-two, wasn't too skinny, could jump to the moon but couldn't hit a layup."

Murray said, "Oh, don't worry, Coach. He's told us how great he was back in Africa."

"But he wasn't. He was the last person chosen on our summer team. Did you ever know that, Samuel?"

"No. You never told me."

"I had two assistant coaches at the tryouts and neither of them wanted to pick you. Our last slot almost went to Riak Kuol, that six-ten kid from Upper Nile, remember him?"

"Sure. I was convinced he would make the team."

"Why'd you pick Sooley?" Dmitri asked.

"I don't know. He was pretty rough around the edges, like many of the African kids. Early one morning during the tryouts I found him in the gym shooting all alone. It was hot and he was soaked, but I could tell he loved what he was doing. Just firing away, jogging after the ball, shooting again. He could do it for hours. Plus, I knew his mother is a tall woman and that he would probably grow. I had no idea he'd spike six inches in a year, no one saw that coming. I rolled the dice, glad I did. Then I convinced Lonnie to roll 'em again, and here we are."

"Coach Britt didn't want to sign him?" Dmitri asked.

"Well, you know Coach Britt. He and I go way, way back and we've been close friends for a long time. The story he likes to tell now is that he saw Samuel in Orlando at the tournament and knew immediately that the kid had a lot of potential. Trouble with that story is that there were a hundred other coaches watching and no one saw the talent. No one else made an offer. When Central suddenly had an extra scholarship, I asked Coach Britt to take a chance. To his credit, he did."

. . .

By late Sunday morning, the players were tired of the hotel. They held a team meeting and discussed their plans with their coaches. They could certainly hang around and watch the final game Monday night, then fly back Tuesday morning.

But they wanted to go home.

Part Three

CHAPTER 51

On a beautiful spring day in early April, a Wednesday, Sooley rose early and slipped out of his dorm room to call his mother. Murray, always the deadhead, heard nothing and didn't move.

They had moved back to the dorm for two reasons. First, they had grown tired of living with Miss Ida and Ernie and their bothersome expectations. Second, and far more important, was the fact that the dorm was filled with admiring girls who enjoyed hanging out in their room. The benefits of stardom were quite satisfying. Murray was happy to share in reflected glory.

Beatrice said she and the boys were doing okay with little change in their routines. They were sad that the season had ended so abruptly and worried about Samuel's disappointment, but they were determined to survive until tomorrow. Samuel confessed to his mother that the end of the season was a huge letdown. Suddenly gone was the focus, the daily challenge, the structure of a schedule, the dream of winning and advancing. The weather was turning warm, spring was beautiful, but basketball was behind them.

His mother would be completely unable to understand the decisions facing him: leaving college early, hiring an agent, entering the draft, turning pro, or forgoing it all and returning to Central for another year or two. So he did not burden her with such talk. After fifteen minutes, the pleasant Christine took the phone and said goodbye.

Making as much noise as possible, Sooley showered and dressed and left the lights on, and in doing so did not provoke the slightest twitch from his roommate. He left the dorm early and went for a long walk on campus, one that would not be possible in a couple of hours. He made it to The Nest without being stopped once by a student wanting a photo.

Coach Britt was waiting in his office with Coach Grinnell. Dressed casually, in golf shirts and sweats, they were sipping coffee and appeared to have been talking for a long time.

There were so many postseason rumors roaring through the internet that their lives were unsettled. However, one important decision had to be made soon.

Lonnie said, "You have less than a week to make your decision, Samuel. What are you thinking?"

The NCAA was toying with ways to keep underclassmen in college. One idea was to allow them to hire an agent on a temporary basis, go through a workout and get evaluated by a panel of experts who would rate their chances in the draft, and call it off if things didn't look too promising. They could then stay in school and not lose eligibility. But this was just a proposal. At the moment, if Sooley hired an agent and entered the draft there was no turning back if it proved disappointing. He could probably make a buck playing in Serbia or Israel, but his college playing days would be over.

He loved Central and everything about college life. It was the only home he knew and the thought of leaving was unsettling. However, he was devouring everything he could find online about the draft, player projections, lottery picks, agents, rookie contracts, the millions of dollars waiting out there, and the stars like Kobe and LeBron and Kevin Garnett who turned pro after high school and never bothered with college. He had found a dozen stories about good players who'd stayed in college only to see their careers ruined by injuries.

The question he wanted to ask was: "Okay, Coach, what are *you* thinking?"

The internet was rife with speculations about where his coach was headed, but every blog seemed to agree that Lonnie Britt was leaving Central.

Sooley shrugged and said, "I don't want to leave, Coach, but timing is everything, you know?"

"Have you talked to an agent?"

"Not yet. Their runners are around, bugging me, bugging Murray, but I haven't spoken to an agent yet. You think I should?"

Lonnie nodded, as did Jason Grinnell.

"You need an agent, Samuel," Lonnie said. "But be careful."

Sooley absorbed this with a poker face. He knew damned well that Lonnie himself had an agent and that they were aggressively pursuing openings around the country. His agent was a slick operator from Houston who repped a lot of college basketball coaches. According to the online dirt, and there was a pile of it, Price was trying to manipulate searches at Purdue, Marquette, and several other schools involved in the annual postseason game of musical chairs.

"I'm hesitant to recommend an agent, Samuel," Lonnie said. "There are a lot of them and I don't have much experience. I'm getting calls."

Jason Grinnell laughed and said, "We're all getting calls, Samuel. Every agent in the country, certified or not, is calling and trying to get a foot in the door. I've never had so many friends."

The laughter died and an awkward pause followed. Finally, Sooley asked, "So, what am I supposed to do? Do you think I'm ready for the draft? Or should I stay in school?"

Lonnie smiled and said, "You're every bit as good as the players you faced in the tournament. We believe in you and want you to succeed. Sure, I'd love to coach you for three more years, but that's not going to happen. You can't say no to the money, Samuel."

"What's going to happen to you?"

"I don't know. Lots of rumors. But I'm in no hurry. You, on the other hand, need to make a decision."

"Do you know Arnie Savage?"

"Never met him, but he's rumored to be a decent agent. Why?"

"His runner has been persistent. Showed up in Norfolk, then again in Memphis after we beat Duke. Said hello to Murray and wanted to get together."

"Murray didn't tell me."

"No sir. He didn't tell me either. The contact was unauthorized but, as I've learned, it's really no big deal. Just a runner. I've checked out Savage and he seems to be legit. Has two dozen or so players in the NBA."

Lonnie asked, "You want me to make phone calls?"

"No sir, but thanks. I'm digging for myself, plus Murray's got my back."

Jason said, "You gotta do it, Sooley. You can't say no to the money."

"I know."

.   .   .

Murray sat at the kitchen table with his parents and sipped a soda. No food was present. There was nothing doing on the stove or in the oven, not a whiff of the usual delicious aroma.

Ida was perturbed and had been for some time. She was saying, "He's not even nineteen years old. You gotta be nineteen, right?"

"Sort of. You have to turn nineteen in the calendar year you're drafted."

"That's too young," she said.

"That's the rule, Mom. And what's the big deal anyway? What about baseball and hockey? Every year hundreds of eighteen-year-old kids turn pro right out of high school, been doing it for years, for decades. Al Kaline won the American League batting title when he was twenty years old. Joe Nuxhall pitched his first game for the Reds at the age of fifteen."

"Who?" Ida asked.

"And those old white guys are somehow relevant to Sooley and the NBA?" Ernie asked.

"No, they're not. My point is that eighteen- and nineteen-year-olds go pro all the time now. Duke has three or four of them this year. Kentucky has at least two. Why do you think those guys are more mature than Sooley?"

"He's just a kid," Ida said, again. "I can't believe we're talking about this."

"Get with it, Mom. He needs to sign with an agent and enter the draft."

Ernie was shaking his head. "I don't like it. He needs to finish college and then think about going pro."

Murray said, "I disagree. What if there's a million bucks on the table? And he says no, comes back to Central, then gets hurt? Why take that chance? All Sooley wants is to make some money that will enable him to go get his family. That's what he thinks about. Sure, a college degree would be nice, and he plans to get one sooner or later. But he will not sleep well until his mother and brothers are over here, safe and sound."

Ida said, "He's not going to make a million dollars, is he?"

Murray smiled while shaking his head in frustration. "Mom, I know you don't follow the game online and that's a good thing. But right now most experts and bloggers are picking Sooley to go mid to late first round, probably between the fifteenth and twentieth picks. On something known as the Rookie Scale Contract, that means his first-year guaranteed salary is about two million dollars. Double that for year two."

Ida shook her head in disbelief.

Ernie said, "He can't even drive a car."

"Well, I'm teaching him. In a few months he'll own a Porsche."

"God help us."

. . .

Reynard Owen sat in a booth and watched a cold rain sprinkle the parking lot. The restaurant was on the outskirts of Chapel Hill, twenty-five minutes from Central's campus. On time, the small blue pickup pulled into the lot and parked next to Reynard's sleek black Jaguar. From the passenger's side, Sooley got out, unfolded himself, and looked at the Jaguar. Murray got out and admired it too. One of them said something funny and both laughed as they crossed the parking lot. Inside, Reynard waved them over and they met in a booth, far away from anyone else.

Everything about Reynard was cool. The tailored jacket, designer frames, gold Rolex. He exuded success and wealth beyond his thirty years, but that was expected. Sooley and Murray, a couple of broke college kids, were impressed but they knew they were supposed to be. Reynard was nothing more than a salesman, a runner sent by his boss to break the ice with a potential client.

They talked about the tournament and Reynard asked if they were over the loss to Villanova. No, they were not. They ordered burgers and fries, and when the waitress left Murray said, "Let's get on with the business here, okay? Sooley and I need to get back to the library and study all night."

They were cutting classes right and left. The madness had left them with hangovers and they were still distracted by it. Plus, the Sooley story wasn't going away and now centered on the kid turning pro.

Reynard flashed his perfect smile and said, "Sure. My boss is Arnie Savage, a cool guy about forty-five, played sparingly for Gonzaga decades ago. One of the top agents in the business. I'm sure you've checked him out and could name his NBA lineup."

Both Sooley and Murray nodded. Yes, they could.

"Arnie gets top dollar, but all agents say that. Actually, the money is not a big issue at this stage because it's controlled by the players union. The old guys don't want the young guys to get all the money. I'm sure you're familiar with the Rookie Scale Contract."

Both nodded.

"Depending on where you go in the first round, Arnie will negotiate a four-year deal with the first two guaranteed."

Murray said, "The first round. Are you and Arnie sure he'll go in the first round?"

"Murray, look, if Arnie wasn't convinced, I wouldn't be sitting here right now. He has enough clients already, so he doesn't fool with guys down the draft, okay? Arnie's all about the relationship. He cares deeply about his players and becomes their close friend, their confidant. He'd rather spend time with his players than try to hustle a contract for some kid to play in Europe. You understand?"

They nodded.

"Don't get me wrong. He has clients in Europe, some great players over there, and he works hard to get 'em back over here where, just maybe, they belong. But most of his work is with the NBA."

They kept nodding.

"Other than the friendship and advice, Arnie earns his money with the marketing and endorsements. It's not unusual for one of his clients to make more money off the court than in the games. He's shrewd and understands the real market value of his players."

Sooley said, "And the more we make the more he makes."

"Absolutely. He takes four percent off the top of your playing contract, same as all agents. Right now he has two hundred million in cumulative salaries, so the math gets easy. He's annually ranked in the top ten sports agents. What you don't always see are the deals for endorsements."

Murray was nodding along as if he knew all this. Top five. Twenty-six players in the NBA. Four all-stars.

Sooley's head was spinning. It was exciting enough to see his name tossed around by bloggers playing the draft game. He'd caught himself dreaming of having plenty of money. But, now, sitting across from a man who could connect him to his dreams, he was overwhelmed.

Their platters arrived but all three ignored the food. Reynard was saying, "What Arnie wants is this. Let's go see him. You need to meet Arnie and let him give you the full picture. He can map out the next five years of your life and he can make it happen."

"Where is he?" Murray asked.

"Miami. South Beach. He likes warm weather." He nodded at the window and said, "Sure beats this crap. They're talking rain for the next three days."

"Is that your Jag out there?" Murray asked.

"It is."

"Maryland plates."

"D.C. I cover this part of the country for Arnie."

"How many guys on the force?"

"There are four of us and we travel a lot, especially this time of the year. Watch a lot of games, see a lot of film. Tons of networking."

"You like it?"

"Love it."

Murray was intrigued. A future in the NBA looked doubtful for him. Perhaps he might pursue the agent thing.

Sooley asked, "When does Mr. Savage want to see us?"

"Oh, he'll fly up here. And no one calls him Mr. Savage. He's just Arnie. But it would be much more fun to go down there. He's got a cool place and there's always a party. He'll send a jet and we'll be there in no time."

"A private jet?" Murray asked.

"Sure. He's got a couple."

They were in.

CHAPTER 52

Ecko Lam was in town. He said he just happened to be passing through. The truth was he was needed by two of his friends.

The first was young Samuel. Ecko picked him up at the dorm early on a Friday morning and drove to a diner in downtown Durham. As they took their seats at a table Ecko said, "Good grief, son, are you still growing?"

"Feels like it," Sooley said with a grin. "Haven't been measured lately."

"How much do you weigh?"

"Not enough. Guess who I had a long talk with last night?"

"Niollo?"

Sooley laughed and said, "How'd you know?"

"You told me to guess. I guess I got it right. What did he say?"

"Take the money and run. Said my stock might never be higher. Said there's always the possibility of injuries and so on. He played one year at Syracuse, entered the draft at the age of nineteen and was the seventh overall pick."

They ordered coffee, juice, and eggs. Ecko nodded along. This was old news. He had known Niollo for fifteen years.

Sooley continued, "He said the first year is pretty rough, but it's the same for everyone. It takes a while for your body to adjust to an eighty-two-game schedule, but he thinks I'm mature enough physically to handle it."

"Rumors are he's leaving Miami."

"We didn't talk about that. Figured it was none of my business. I asked about agents and he didn't say much. I got the impression he's not too crazy about his."

"Well, Samuel, I guess that settles it. If Niollo says go pro, then that's what you'll do. Right?"

"What's your opinion?"

"I have a bias in favor of education. I'm very proud of my degree from Kent State because it's the first in my family. If I had things my way, I'd like to see you go to medical school and become a doctor, then go home and build hospitals."

"They would just burn 'em down. That's ten more years of study, Ecko, then I'd make a good living, but not millions."

"So you're dreaming of millions?"

"That's what the game pays now. Crazy money, isn't it?"

"Indeed. I prefer education, Samuel, but let's be honest. I did not have the option of playing in the NBA. My amazing talents were not appreciated. To the surprise of no one, I went undrafted. So, I became a coach."

"And I'm so glad you did. What if we'd never met?"

"That's too awful to think about."

"I know. I read an article about myself last night. These days there are enough of them. Guy writes for ESPN, good writer, and he said that in the history of basketball no player has ever come so far in twelve months. Size, skill, maturity, mileage, all the yardsticks. Along with the tragedies. A year ago I stood six feet two and was playing on dirt courts in the African bush. Now I'm six feet eight and headed for the first round."

"So, you enjoy reading about yourself?" Ecko was amused.

"Sometimes. I like to see what they get wrong. Some guys just make up facts, you know? And Murray scans the internet collecting stories."

"As I say too often, Samuel, savor the moment."

"It wouldn't be wise to turn down the money, would it, Ecko?"

"No. You gotta do it, Samuel. Everybody says you'll go in the first round. I certainly think so. You can't turn down the money."

"I know. The best way to help my family is to make the money and meet important people. That's not going to happen here at Central."

"I'm with you, Samuel."

.   .   .

Lonnie closed and locked his office door. He sat behind his desk and stared at Ecko, who was smiling.

Finally, Lonnie said, "I don't want to leave. I love these kids. I recruited them, made them promises, watched them grow up, had a helluva ride with them last month. How am I supposed to tell them I'm leaving?"

"Every coach has to do it, Lonnie. It's just part of the business. It'll be rough and everybody will have a good cry, then the new guy'll come in and they'll forget about you. That's life."

"I know, I know."

"This is what you've dreamed of and worked for. You've earned it, Lonnie. It's time for a big promotion."

"Have I earned it? Sooley was a once-in-a-lifetime miracle. Take him away, and we were headed for a losing season. I didn't develop the kid. He turned into some sort of freak who got hot and almost conquered the world. The rest of us were just along for the ride."

"You've won twenty games a year for five straight years. In this business, that gets you a promotion and a nice raise."

"A helluva raise. Ten times what I'm making now."

"I rest my case. What about Agnes?"

"You kidding? She wants the money."

"Then take it and stop whining."

"Why can't I take Sooley with me?"

"Because last night he got a call from Niollo, who told him he was old enough to play in the NBA. Said take the money and run. He's running now."

"Good for him." They were quiet for a long time, and somber. Lonnie could not imagine calling a team meeting and saying good-bye. By now his players knew they would lose Sooley. Losing their coach would crush them.

He said, "Truthfully, Agnes is not crazy about moving to Milwaukee. She got enough snow when we were at Northern Iowa. The kids are happy in school here."

"And they'll be happy wherever you go. Don't worry about the snow because the planet is warming, in case you haven't heard. Come on, Lonnie, Marquette is big-time basketball and they're offering you a fortune. You're forty years old and you're going places. How many times have we had this conversation?"

"I know." Lonnie glanced at his watch.

Ecko did the same and said, "I want a nice lunch in some swanky place. It's my turn to get the check but I'm broke and you're wealthy now, so it's on you."

"Okay, okay."

. . .

For at least the third time in a tense standoff, Murray reminded his father that he was twenty years old and capable of making his own decisions, and if he wanted to spend the weekend on South Beach with Samuel and others then he would certainly do so. He was old enough to vote, join the army, buy a car if he could only afford one, and sign other contracts, and, well, there. So be it.

They were in Ernie's cramped office at the downtown food bank. Ernie thought the trip was a bad idea, as did Miss Ida. Both had said no and Murray was chafing under their efforts to supervise. He had chosen to confront his father because Ernie was the softer touch. A "No" from Ida had greater authority.

But it didn't matter. The boys were leaving. Murray said good-bye and slammed the door on the way out. Ernie waited half an hour and called his wife.

They were losing sleep over the prospect of Samuel leaving school and entering the draft. They had practically raised him in the past eight months and had become his family. He was a smart kid but not mature enough to make such important decisions. The money might ruin him. Sharks out there could manipulate him. The temptations would be great. He was just a simple kid who couldn't even drive a car and certainly wasn't ready for fame and fortune.

CHAPTER 53

Right on time, a black SUV stopped in front of the dorm where Murray and Sooley were waiting eagerly. They tossed their gym bags in the back and hopped in. Reynard had said to pack lightly. They would be wearing tee shirts and shorts all weekend. It might be damp and chilly in Durham, but on South Beach it was all blue skies, string bikinis, and sunshine.

It was almost five on Friday afternoon. Sooley looked at his cell phone, frowned, and whispered, "It's your mother. For the third time. I can't ignore her calls."

"Ignore them," Murray said. "I am. They're out of line, Sooley. Forgive them."

"They're just concerned, that's all. I'll call her from the plane."

They arrived at the general aviation terminal and met a pilot in the lounge. He took their bags and escorted them onto the tarmac where a gorgeous private jet was waiting. He waved them up the stairs and said, "Off to Miami, gentlemen."

They bounded up and were met by Reynard, holding a bottle of beer. A pretty flight attendant took their jackets and drink orders. Beers all around. In the rear a comely blonde stood and walked forward with a perfect smile. Reynard said, "This is my girlfriend, Meg.

Meg, Sooley and Murray." She shook their hands as they admired her deep blue eyes.

They settled into enormous leather chairs and absorbed the cabin's rich detail. Meg, whose skirt was tight and short, crossed her legs and Sooley's heart skipped a beat. Murray tried not to look and asked Reynard, "So, what kind of jet do we have here?"

"A Falcon 900."

Murray nodded as if his tastes in private aircraft were quite discriminating. "What's the range?"

"Anywhere, really. We flew to Croatia last year to see a kid, a wasted trip. One stop, I believe. Arnie wants to stop handling players in Europe, though. He has enough here in the States."

The flight attendant appeared with a tray with two iced bottles of beer. Meg asked for a glass of wine. The airplane began to taxi as Murray kept asking about what the jet could and could not do. The flight attendant asked them to strap in for takeoff, then disappeared into the rear.

Fifteen minutes later she reappeared with fresh drinks and asked if anyone was hungry. The thought of eating at 40,000 feet in such luxury was overwhelming, and the boys ordered small pizzas.

Meg proved to be quite the basketball buff and quizzed them on their run to the Final Four. Because of Reynard's line of work, she watched a lot of basketball, college and pro, and knew all the players and coaches and even some of the refs. Reynard estimated that he personally attended at least seventy-five games each season, and Meg was often with him.

Not a bad life, Murray was thinking, and quizzed Reynard about his work. Sooley checked his cell phone, saw that there was coverage, and stepped to the rear to call Miss Ida. She did not answer.

.   .   .

Arnie's sprawling home was on a street near the ocean. It, along with its neighbors, had obviously been designed by cutting-edge architects trying mightily to shock each other. Front doors were taboo. Upper floors landed at odd angles. One was a series of three glass silos attached by what seemed like chrome gangplanks. Another was a grotesque bunker patterned after a peanut shell with no glass at all. After eight months in Durham, Sooley had never seen a house there that even remotely resembled these bizarre structures.

Arnie's was one of the prettier ones, with three levels and plenty of views. The limo stopped in the circular drive and a barefoot butler greeted them. He showed them through the front opening, again no door, and to a vast open space with soaring ceilings and all manner of Calder-like mobiles dangling in the air.

"The party's back there," the butler said, pointing to the rear lawn where a large well-lit pool welcomed the guests.

"We're gonna change," Reynard said, and he and Meg disappeared. In well-worn jeans, sneakers, and tee shirts, Sooley and Murray almost felt overdressed. Everyone wore shorts. Some had shoes. They eased to a corner, found the bar, got another beer, and watched as two girls jumped in the pool. Soft rap barked from hidden speakers. Guests came and went into the house and back.

Someone said loudly, "Hey, it's Sooley!" The stranger walked over with a big smile and even bigger handshake. He introduced himself as Julian somebody and said he and Reynard worked together. Every guest had some connection to the game, and at that moment Samuel Sooleymon was the most famous college player in the country. A crowd soon gathered around him and he chattered away. Someone brought him a fresh beer. Some girls drifted over.

They were attractive and of all shades—black, white, and brown—and all appeared to be no older than twenty. Several strutted around in skimpy swimwear, others in tight shorts with revealing blouses. Murray, as always, began flirting.

A long table was set up in the main room and dinner was served. The guests were other agents who worked with Arnie, a couple of executives with the Heat, some coaches in the area, some friends from the neighborhood. The casual gathering gave the impression that in Arnie's world a party such as this could materialize at a moment's notice.

Where was Arnie? Murray asked Reynard, who said the boss was flying in and should arrive anytime now.

Other guests were arriving. Murray recognized Lynn Korby, a guard for the Heat, who had been injured for the past month. The team was on the road finishing up the season. The playoffs would begin in a week. The sighting of Korby made Sooley wonder if Niollo might show up, but Murray didn't think so.

After dinner, a DJ appeared and cranked up the music. A dance floor emerged from the landscaping beside the pool and was soon crowded with gyrating couples. Behind a row of hedges a smaller party was under way in a large hot tub where half a dozen young ladies skinny-dipped and splashed around while balancing flutes of champagne. Sooley and Murray fell into lawn chairs and watched the show. Murray said, "Sooley, old boy, we're a long way from Durham."

They hung out, danced, drank beers, and otherwise partied until after midnight. With no end in sight, Sooley said he'd had enough. A porter showed them to their bedroom on the second floor, on a wing that resembled a designer dormitory. They retired to matching single beds and fell asleep with the sounds of the party still rocking below.

. . .

Reynard fetched them late the following morning and led them to a deck near the pool. A large canopy shielded the sun and a fan cooled the pleasant air. Arnie Savage was on the phone and jumped to his feet when he saw them. The phone disappeared. He introduced himself, shook hands warmly, and apologized for missing his party the night before. He offered them seats and within seconds a young lady was waiting to take their orders. Omelets, pancakes, ham and eggs, avocado toast, you name it.

Murray looked at Reynard and asked, "What are you having?"

"Poached eggs on avocado toast is always good."

"The best," Arnie said. "I'll take that too."

Murray said, "I like waffles and bacon."

"Me too," Sooley said quickly.

Coffee and juice all around.

Sooley had read so much about Arnie that he felt like he'd known him for years. He was usually rated in the top ten NBA agents, and with his impressive list of clients he was considered one of the most powerful. They were expecting a high-octane salesman, one ready to promise everything. Instead, they were immediately disarmed by Arnie's deliberate cadence and soft voice. He spoke at three-quarter speed and seemed to dwell on each word. He wanted them to talk, and he hung on every word and never blinked.

They talked about their miracle season, the adventures at the Final Four. Of course he had been there. He hadn't missed one in years.

The food arrived and they dug in. Arnie had played in college and still looked game-ready; said he ran ten miles a day and played a lot of tennis. Between bites, he said, "So, Sooley, I guess it's okay to call you that, right? I mean, half the world knows you as 'Sooley' but do you prefer Samuel?"

Murray blurted, "Sooley's fine." Samuel nodded.

"Then Sooley it is. Mind if I ask about the process in selecting an agent? How far along are you?"

"Just getting started," Sooley said. "You're the first. Me and my consultant here thought we would pick out two or three and say hello. Is that the way it's normally done?"

"There's no set way to do things. That'll work just fine."

Murray, now the consultant, said, "So tell us where you see him in the draft?"

"Sure. My team and I have watched you play, live and on a lot of film, and we've talked to scouts at every level. On the plus side, and there are far more positives than negatives, there is the obvious size, speed, quickness, leaping, shooting, everything really. In my opinion you're the perfect age. You're a team player, you smile a lot, and as we all watched, the entire world caught a good case of Sooleymania. You handled it beautifully and every pro team would love to draft you."

"And the downside?" Murray asked, attacking another waffle.

Arnie smiled and sipped his coffee. "Lack of experience. No high school ball. Only one year of college, or half a year really. Virtually every other player that will go in the first two rounds has been well known for years. Those four at Duke played on a national team when they were fifteen and everybody saw them. I don't have to remind you that in the world of sports there are many stories of athletes who came out of nowhere, lit it up for a short time, then faded, never to be seen again. Are you a bolt of lightning, Sooley? Some worry about that. I don't. There is also concern about your last game. You didn't play well against Villanova and some critics couldn't wait to pounce and say you choked under pressure."

Murray said, "He scored fifty-eight against Duke."

"I know. You asked about the downside. There it is. None of it bothers me, Sooley. I'm convinced you have the body, talent, and brains for a long NBA career."

"So where do I fit?"

Without hesitation, Arnie said, "You've seen the projections. Lots of experts out there. We do a mock draft every day in my office and spend hours moving names up and down. There are the four at Duke, two at Kentucky, Nkeke at Oregon, Dokafur at Minnesota, all first years. Then Darrell Whitley at Villanova, Long at San Diego, the big Russian at Gonzaga, and Barber at Kansas. That's twelve, and somewhere around there is when your name gets called."

Arnie rattled these off as if he had every stat memorized and knew what every GM was thinking.

Murray said, "So, twelve at the highest."

"Nine, maybe ten at the highest, fifteen at the lowest. Definitely first round, Sooley. I'll negotiate a four-year contract with two years guaranteed."

"How much?" Sooley asked.

"You know the Rookie Scale, and you know it depends on where you land. But something like ten to fifteen million is realistic."

Sooley couldn't suppress a smile, nor could his consultant. Reynard watched him closely and saw the usual signs of disbelief. Dreaming was unavoidable, but hearing the numbers from a veteran like Arnie was always a shock.

Sooley put down his fork and took a sip of orange juice. His mouth was suddenly dry. His late father had earned about $200 a month as a schoolteacher, and for only eight months out of the year.

Arnie waited, took a bite, then continued, "I'll take my four percent off the top, standard. When the endorsements start coming, and little will happen the first year or so, I'll guide you through them and take ten percent. Again, that's pretty standard. And I guard the money, Sooley. I could write a book about pro athletes who've squandered millions and left the game broke. Not my clients. I have an investment team and we work hard to protect you and your money. My clients do well on the court, off the court, and in the markets."

Murray asked, "So you manage the money?"

"I do. My rookie players get some cash up front to adjust to the lifestyle. You're in the NBA now and certain upgrades are expected. Wardrobe, a sports car, gifts for family and friends, a nice condo. I strongly advise against purchasing real estate until there is a long-term contract and trades look unlikely, though I can't always control the trades. Once you're on your feet and all properly equipped, we decide on how much you need each month. We'll set up an allowance but it's determined by what you want. We never lose sight of the fact that it's your money, not mine. However, if you decide to take all of it, then you can find another agent. Again, Sooley, I protect my clients. If they decide they don't want my protection, then I'm wasting my time."

Sooley had lost his appetite and was nodding along.

Arnie took another bite and gave him plenty of time to ask questions. Hearing none, he continued, "The biggest problem is the entourage. You'll attract all manner of friends, new and old, and everybody will want something. You're lucky to have a friend like Murray."

Sooley laughed and said, "He ain't gettin' nothin'."

They shared a good laugh. Arnie said, "You'll need him. And you'll need his mother."

"My mother?"

"Yes. Ida. I had a long chat with her this morning."

"No! You gotta be kidding. Don't tell me she called you." Murray was shaking his head, humiliated.

"She did."

"I'm so sorry, Arnie. So sorry."

"Sorry for what?"

"She's just butting in. I can't believe this."

"Relax, Murray. We had a good talk. She considers you two to be her boys and she's just being protective."

"I'm sorry."

"Don't be. My mother died when I was ten years old. Be thankful she's there."

Murray and Sooley exchanged confused looks. "What does she want?" Sooley asked.

"Well, she asked to see the agency agreement you and I will sign. Fine with me. I'm an open book, Sooley. There are no secrets, no hidden language. She's a lawyer and it's a good thing for her to take a look. Any objections?"

Sooley raised both hands, palms up, and said, "Look, whatever Miss Ida wants is fine with me. I can't say no to her."

Murray said, "She's tough. She'll probably want to cut your four percent."

Arnie laughed and said, "That's not gonna happen. I'm sure Miss Ida and I can find plenty of common ground. I've been negotiating with GMs and owners and shoe companies for almost twenty years."

Murray said, "And I've been negotiating with her for twenty years. Guess who usually wins."

"Well, she did say she wants you two home in one piece. And I promised."

Sooley asked, "Can we stay till tomorrow?"

"Sure. Got an idea. I have a sixty-foot boat, nice little rig. Let's take it out this morning and catch some fish."

"Awesome."

CHAPTER 54

Late Monday night, the Central players received emails from Coach Britt calling for a team meeting. By then it was no surprise he was leaving. Speculation had been rampant. Two websites did little more than track coaching changes in major college sports, and since the end of the season there had been the usual deluge of gossip about who was getting fired and who was moving up. At least ten major schools were getting new coaches.

They gathered in the locker room at 4 p.m., and the mood was somber. The seniors—Mitch Rocker, Roy Tice, and Dmitri Robbins—were invited, though they had played their last game. They had been recruited by Coach Britt and he wanted to say goodbye. And Sooley was there too, though everyone knew he wouldn't be back.

As always, in those dreadful farewells, there was a sense of betrayal. The returning players had committed four years of their lives to the coach and his program. Suddenly, his program wasn't good enough for them. He was moving on to bigger things and more money. On the one hand, they were happy for a coach they loved and wanted to succeed at the highest level. On the other hand, they simply wanted him to stay. As a team they had just accomplished the unthinkable and the future looked bright.

Lonnie made it as brief as possible. He said he had agreed to a four-year contract at Marquette and would be leaving town soon. He apologized for his departure, for leaving behind the guys he'd recruited, guys he loved, but such is the nature of the game. Everybody moves on; nothing remains the same.

He surprised them with the news that Jason Grinnell would be named as his successor. The players were visibly relieved to hear this. Not a word had leaked and there had been nothing online. Jason was popular with the players and had helped recruit most of them.

As his voice began to break, Lonnie thanked them for the great times they'd had together, and said he would always remember them. Then he wiped his eyes, smiled at them, and left the room in tears.

Jason Grinnell stood and took over the meeting.

.   .   .

Two days later, Sooley signed a contract with Arnie Savage and entered the NBA draft. Central promptly issued a statement. No one was surprised.

The contract had been combed through by Ida Walker, who wanted a few changes. Arnie's lawyer had emailed it to her, and when she printed it and first held it she felt like she needed to wash her hands. But the more she wrestled with it the more comfortable she became. It was as straightforward as Arnie had promised. His lawyer was easy to work with. Hey, they were all on the same team and pursuing the same goals.

Sooley was slowly beginning to resent her attempts at surveillance and control. For Murray, her involvement was beyond irksome. Though he doubted he would ever have the courage to do so, he was toying with the idea of taking a gap year and working as Sooley's assistant. His friend needed him now and his life was only going to get more complicated. And Murray was seduced by the money, the private jets, the girls, the reflected glory, the sheer excitement of living through an NBA season.

Dream on, he kept telling himself.

. . .

Classes finally ended on May 2 and Sooley barely made it to the finish line. How was a guy supposed to study when he wasn't returning in the fall? How was a guy supposed to stay motivated and think about three more years of college followed by an eternity in grad school when he was about to make millions playing his favorite game? It was simply not possible. Nor could he be bothered studying for final exams.

The break came in the library one night when he was supposed to be preparing for a biology final but was really just killing time and staying away from his dorm room. Murray had it for a couple of hours. Reynard texted and asked how things were going. Sooley stepped outside into the cool night and called him. When Sooley said he was studying for finals, Reynard actually began laughing and couldn't stop. Sooley indeed felt rather foolish.

"Got an idea," Reynard said. "Instead of worrying about final exams, why don't you ride down with me to Arnie's place for a few days? He's got a couple of NBA assistants in town and he thinks it would be a great benefit for you to work out with them and talk about the Combine. I'll pick you up tomorrow."

Without hesitating, Sooley said yes.

He slept late the following morning and waited for Murray to leave. He crammed as much clothing, toiletries, and other assets as possible into a large gym bag and a backpack. When the black SUV rolled to a stop in front of the dorm, Sooley tossed his bags in the hatch and hopped in the back seat.

Leaving campus, it hit him hard that he would probably never come back, and that saddened him almost to the point of tears. He had arrived in August, a broken kid still reeling from the horrors at home, uncertain who in his family was still alive, if anyone. His father's death had been confirmed but the rest of them were missing. Coach Britt had offered a sympathy scholarship, one that had paid off nicely.

He thought of Beatrice and how disappointed she would be to see him leaving school, but he couldn't worry about that now. She might understand one day.

He waited until he was at South Beach before he texted Murray: *"In South Beach at Arnie's for a few days. Please don't tell your mother. All good."*

To which Murray replied: *"Douchebag!! What about final exams?"*

"What about them?"

"I'm telling Mom."

.   .   .

Arnie's impressive spread did not include his own basketball gym, so he borrowed one from a private school around the corner. Late in the afternoon, on the drive to the gym, Reynard explained that Arnie was in Philadelphia meeting with Darrell Whitley of Villanova. If he signed him, the company would have two first-rounders, every agent's dream.

Van and Herman were shooting baskets and waiting for them. Introductions were made and they seemed delighted to meet Sooley. Van was once an assistant with the Mavericks and Herman once scouted for the Magic. They were somewhere in Arnie's orbit but their positions were not clear. Van took training seriously, and Arnie had asked him to guide Sooley through half an hour of stretching and slow movements, and to emphasize that the routine was now a part of his daily life. Once he was properly loosened, they began shooting drills. After days off, it felt great to bounce a ball again and take some shots.

During a break, they talked about the Combine. Van thought it was a good idea. Herman had reservations. Arnie had not yet decided whether Sooley should participate. About half of his clients did so, and he was known to be less than impressed with the event.

Each year the top sixty to seventy draft hopefuls were invited to the NBA Draft Combine, a three-day, media-heavy beauty pageant. The players were measured in every way possible: height with shoes and without, weight, body fat, agility, wingspan, speed, hand size, and vertical leaps—both standing and running. There were shooting contests, light scrimmages, lots of interviews and preening for the press.

Sooley was eager to go and strut his stuff. Herman said it wasn't a good idea. His stock had never been higher. Why run the risk of a bad workout?

The practices continued each day, once in the morning and again late in the afternoon when the gym was available. The cast of coaches and players changed almost daily, as Arnie's pals came and went. Some lived in the area but most were passing through, always on business related to basketball.

The longer Sooley stayed at Arnie's sumptuous pad, the longer he wanted to stay. His finals were over, as if they mattered. School was out and Murray, his consultant, was hard at work hauling and stacking boxes for the food bank at $8.00 an hour.

He ordered a late breakfast and ate by the pool with whoever happened to stay in the house the night before. He met an incredible collection of coaches, scouts, former players, other agents, reps from shoe companies, and quite a few folks whose jobs were not well defined. Reynard whispered that most were hangers-on, guys looking for a cushy job in someone's entourage.

Arnie was rarely at home. He was on a jet almost every day and relied on his staff to manage the house and the ever-changing lineup of guests.

Sooley really had no place to go. He leaned on Reynard to make sure he was not overstaying his welcome. To which Reynard laughed and said, "Come on, Sooley. You're a first-rounder. Primos can stay forever."

He talked to Murray every day and Miss Ida occasionally. He called his mother every Wednesday morning but had not mustered the courage to tell her about his change in plans. He slept late most mornings, took long walks on the beach, spent at least an hour pumping iron, and worked out with various coaches twice a day. When Arnie popped in for a quick stay-over they talked about the draft and the projections. Sooley, quite naturally, was keen to know where he might land, and thus where he would be living in the years to come. There were thirty teams from coast to coast, and some cities had more appeal than others. Not that it really mattered. The money would be glorious wherever he landed, but it was one thing to be a star for the Celtics or Lakers and something else to play for Sacramento. Like all players, he was dreaming of a lucrative contract with a storied franchise, one in a huge television market.

Arnie talked to general managers and scouts all day long and was still of the opinion that Sooley would go in the middle of the first round. Brooklyn, Denver, and Houston looked likely, but things could change in an instant as the draft neared. Each year brought a bewildering flurry of trades that sent players packing from one team to another.

In early May, Arnie decided that the Combine was not a good idea after all. The scouts had seen enough of Sooley. Indeed, no college player that spring had generated more interest and more footage than him. His speed, quickness, leaping, shooting, were all well-documented, and the Combine would only be more of the same. A bad workout, or one that did not meet lofty expectations, could only harm his stock. Sooley was disappointed but trusted his agent implicitly.

Then Arnie was gone again, off chasing another deal. Sooley begged Murray to hop down for a weekend of parties and girls, but his parents had him handcuffed to his job at the food bank.

Sooley met a girl. Her name was Valerie but she went by Val or Vallie, either one would work. She was one of the girls who hung around the pool in a skimpy bikini and enjoyed showing off her

well-toned legs and abs. She said she had played basketball at South
Florida until a knee injury ruined her career, and she was quick
to show him the scar on her leg, the only blemish on an otherwise
perfect body. They spent the first night together in Sooley's room
and had a late breakfast by the pool. The second night they went to
her small apartment around the corner and rarely came up for air.
She said she was twenty-four, sold real estate, and worked her own
hours. By day three, Sooley was thoroughly smitten. Day four was a
Wednesday, and he slept late and forgot to call his mother.

If Reynard had been around instead of on a plane, he would
have warned Sooley that the girl was probably trouble. Arnie's uni-
verse attracted many young ladies who certainly livened up the parties, but many of them were stalking the money and the big life.
Arnie knew better than to get involved. He viewed his home as the
entryway for his clients, a transition from the shelter of a campus to
the glitzy world of big-dollar entertainment. Once they became pro-
fessionals they would face more temptations than any college freshman could possibly imagine. He felt obliged to help them get ready.

As lenient as he was, Arnie tried to watch everything. His laid-
back staff monitored their guests, took notes, and reported to him.
Sex, booze, and pot were to be expected and there was plenty of
it, but if the harder stuff was being passed around and consumed
Arnie wanted to know about it. He had banned several dealers and
bad actors. Same for gambling. If a player of his had a weakness for
the spreads and tables, he did not hesitate to get involved.

Arnie was informed that Sooley had a girl and she appeared to
be a stalker. He gave the word to watch them as closely as possible.

CHAPTER 55

The draft was held on June 8 at the Barclays Center in Brooklyn. Sooley invited Murray to the party and he eagerly said yes. Sooley also invited Murray's parents but they declined. They didn't want to spend the money and still disapproved of him leaving college. Sooley only made matters worse when he offered to pay their travel expenses to New York and back. They found the offer insulting, but held their comments. They would never, under any circumstances, spend money earned by young Samuel, nor would they humiliate him by rebuking his genuine effort to include them. As Ida said, "He just doesn't know any better." They politely declined, citing work obligations.

Vallie didn't make the trip either, though not from a lack of trying. Arnie made it clear that, while the trip was planned as a celebration, there would be important business at hand and he did not want his prized client distracted. He did not want the woman near Sooley when they discussed contract negotiations. Sooley whispered to Reynard that, frankly, he was relieved and needed a break from the girl. At Reynard's invitation, they detoured their jet to the Raleigh-Durham airport and picked up Murray, a guy who both Reynard and Arnie felt was a good influence on Sooley.

Arnie and company arrived a day earlier and set up camp on

the top floor of the Latitude Hotel, a swanky five-star place three blocks from Barclays. In the penthouse suite, a buffet and bar was set up for anyone who wandered in. Along with Sooley, Arnie had signed Darrell Whitley from Villanova, a projected top ten pick, and Davonte Lyon from Auburn, another nineteen-year-old who turned some heads at the Combine. With three potential first-rounders, Arnie was the agent of the moment, and his headquarters became a hive of activity as team officials, scouts, reporters, players, coaches, and women came and went or just hung around to soak up the action.

Darrell Whitley arrived with a big smile and a bear hug for Sooley. They had last seen each other in Phoenix, in Central's last game. Darrell introduced his two brothers and two friends. Sooley had only Murray in his entourage. How many would be enough? He would need to ask Reynard. Davonte Lyon appeared, said hello, and introduced three of his own men. Sooley really began to feel inadequate. The guys were in a fabulous mood and hung out for hours. Arnie had them booked for a fine dinner but afterward they were on their own. Darrell said he knew the city and they could hit the clubs.

.   .   .

The draft was televised live on ESPN and livestreamed on The Vertical. In Durham, Ernie closed the door of his cramped office and watched it on a small TV. Ida went to her conference room at Legal Aid and watched it with her staff on a much larger screen. At South Beach, Vallie went to a sports bar with some girlfriends and started drinking an hour before the draft. At Arnie's home in South Beach, everyone—staff and guests—gathered in the small cinema in the basement and waited for the fun. Lonnie Britt watched from a hotel room in Des Moines where he was chasing a star recruit. Ecko was at home in Cincinnati and sitting in the den with his fifteen-year-old son. Former teammates, both from the South Sudan summer team and NC Central Eagles, tuned in to watch with anticipation and great pride as their beloved friend became a millionaire.

Sooley and Darrell had invitations to the Green Room, a staging area in front of the draft podium where they, along with their agents, families, and a few friends, waited for their magic call. The Green Room allowed the draft to move along nicely as the top picks, after hugging those who loved them, bounded up the steps and onto the stage where they held their new team's jersey and posed with Commissioner Adam Silver. The invitations were carefully handled because of the possible embarrassment of a top player waiting and waiting and then finding himself relegated to the second round. This had happened, and to avoid it only the top twenty or so were invited.

The chosen gathered and slapped hands and ribbed each other, all trying to appear calm and cool and not the least bit nervous or concerned with what team would call their names, make them rich, and launch their spectacular careers. Sooley sat between Arnie and Murray, who seemed even more jittery than his friend. Imagine just being in the same space with twenty guys his age all of whom were about to start signing big contracts, and some of whom would even become all-stars, even legends.

The first pick went to the Timberwolves and Adam Silver announced the name of Tyrell Miller of Duke. The Green Room exploded with applause as everyone congratulated the top pick. Tyrell posed with the Commissioner and smiled for the cameras.

The next four picks went exactly as projected. After the fifth, Arnie, who was watching it all without notes and with a pleasant cockiness, said to Darrell, "You're next, big guy."

Cleveland chose Darrell, and as he took the stage Arnie whispered to Sooley, "They'll trade him tomorrow. To Indiana."

Sooley had no idea how to respond. The draft, with its lottery picks and especially with its deal-making and trading, was at times incomprehensible. Each selection sent dominoes falling in different directions. When Phoenix took Antonio Long from San Diego

State, Arnie whispered to Sooley, "You're going to Detroit but they'll trade you to Washington."

"Now?"

"No, number nine! How does Washington sound?"

"Where do I sign?" Sooley instantly liked the idea of Washington because it was a city he'd actually seen. Except for the March trips to Dayton, Memphis, and Phoenix, he had never left the East Coast. Durham was not far away. The Walkers would be practically next door. He'd seen the campus at Howard, the South Sudanese embassy, some of the monuments. Yes, Washington would work just fine.

When his name was called as the ninth pick, he stepped onto the stage, and some fans in the crowd began chanting, "Sooley! Sooley! Sooley!"

· · ·

As his players partied in the big city, Arnie worked well into the night on the trades that sent Darrell Whitley to the Indiana Pacers and Sooley to the Washington Wizards. At seven the following morning, he had breakfast with Washington's GM and ironed out the contract, a four-year deal worth $14 million, with half guaranteed.

· · ·

Flying home, Sooley decided he needed a break from South Beach. He got off the plane with Murray at Raleigh-Durham and said goodbye, and thanks, to Arnie and Reynard. From the sleek Falcon they walked through the private terminal to the parking lot, and to Murray's little blue pickup truck that was so old the odometer had stuck at 220,000 miles. The automated parking meter demanded $18 on a credit card, and Sooley happily paid.

Driving away, he asked, "Did you hear the part about the loan?"

"Not all of it. Arnie advances some money?"

"Yeah. I told Reynard I didn't have a car and he said no problem. Arnie will loan me a hundred thousand now and I'll pay him back in a month when the first check comes in."

"Is that legal?"

"Reynard says it is. Says some agents loan players money long before the draft and that's not exactly legal."

"Yeah, that kid from Arizona State got caught a few years back, didn't he? The NBA decertified the agent and he filed suit. It was a big scandal."

"Well, Reynard says it's okay now because I'm out of school and officially a pro. How do you like that?"

"Sounds okay. I guess we're going car shopping, as soon as you pass the driver's test."

"Oh that. Look, Murray, here's the deal. I need some help. I need to buy a car and find a place to live in D.C., right? I need to do a lot of things and they're all pretty intimidating. I want you to help me out, at least for the rest of the summer."

"You trying to hire me?"

"That's it. Reynard offered to help but he's a busy dude. And I trust you, Murray. What do you say?"

"How much?"

"Eight dollars an hour." Both roared with laughter that went on and on, and when it died down they rode in silence for a while. The thrill, and disbelief, and giddiness of the past two days began to soak in.

Murray finally said, "You'll have to convince Miss Ida. She won't like it."

"I'll bet she likes it a lot more now, with fourteen mil on the way. Plus, I can talk her into it. She thinks I'm special."

"You are special, Sooley."

"Still Samuel to you."

"Whatever."

More silence followed, then Murray asked, "So what kind of car are you thinking?"

"A Ford Explorer, that SUV."

Murray laughed and said, "No, no, Samuel. You don't sign for this kind of money and drive a Ford."

"I've made up my mind. Coach Grinnell has one and he let me drive it."

"Coach Grinnell is married with three kids. You're in the NBA, Samuel, and you can't drive a Ford. You need some fancy sports car, like a Porsche."

"I'm not ready for that. Plus, they cost too much. I saw a Porsche online for over a hundred thousand."

"So?"

"So, I picked out a Ford Explorer for only forty thousand."

"Wow. You have so much to learn."

They stopped at a Wendy's for burgers and fries, then drove to the Legal Aid office where Sooley got a hero's welcome. Miss Ida had tears in her eyes as she hugged him and showed him off.

When they were alone in her office, she got down to business. She was pleased to hear of the trade and that he would be living so close. She explained, with little room for questions or disagreement, that she would prepare a simple will that would leave everything in trust for his mother and brothers.

"I never thought about that," Sooley admitted.

"There are a lot of things you haven't thought about, but I have. Health insurance, your visa. Other stuff. When do you expect to sign the contract and get the money?"

"In about a month."

"Okay. The amended contract you signed with Mr. Savage requires that ten percent of the money comes into your bank account. He keeps the rest for allowances and investments. You understand this?"

"Yes ma'am."

"So, you'll need to add the name of someone else to your account in case the money needs to be accessed. This person can't touch it unless something happens to you."

"Why are you worried about something bad happening to me?"

"Because I'm a lawyer and you're my client. It's my job to worry about everything."

"Come on, Mom," Murray protested.

"Just do as I say, okay."

"Arnie's loaning me a hundred thousand until the big money comes in."

"I assume that's legal."

"It is."

Murray said, "He needs to buy a car. Wants a Ford Explorer."

"That's up to you."

Sooley said, "I'd like to send some money to my mother."

"We'll talk about that. I'm not sure it's safe. She's already been robbed once."

"But I want to help her."

"I understand, Samuel. So do I. We'll figure it out."

"Can I sponsor her now and get them out?"

"Let's talk about that later. I'm due in court in half an hour. We'll talk tonight. What would you like for dinner?"

"A bottle of champagne."

"You'll get ice tea. Something to eat?"

"Yes, that baked lemon chicken you do, with the mushrooms and sauce."

She smiled and said, "Whatever you want, Samuel."

CHAPTER 56

The excitement of shopping for a new vehicle was crushed when Sooley flunked the driver's test. He did okay on the road, though still mortified in eight lanes of traffic, but he missed too many on the written. He was embarrassed and admitted to Murray that he had found studying difficult. He had been distracted and did not take the exam seriously.

Miss Ida was amused by it and admitted to Ernie that the humiliation was probably a healthy blow to his expanding ego. The two agreed to allow Murray to work for Sooley for the remainder of the summer and run interference. He did need help on so many fronts. He was entering an exciting new world, but one with many potential pitfalls. And truthfully, there was no way to tell Murray that stacking tons of food in a warehouse was more important than helping a friend. It was an opportunity so unique that they put up only token resistance.

The day after the exam, Murray borrowed the family sedan and took off to D.C. with Sooley. They found a room at a downtown hotel and began scouting out swanky condos and apartment buildings. Sooley wanted something large with plenty of bedrooms for his mother and brothers, but Murray talked him down. He should start small and move up when necessary. The prices for all of them, large and small, were outrageous. Sooley was overwhelmed with the process but excited at having such a nice space all to himself. Murray convinced him to put down a $5,000 deposit for a new, unfurnished two-bedroom apartment in CityCenter, not far from Capital One Arena. The lease was for twelve months.

They stopped by the Wizards' headquarters and met the front office, all of whom were thrilled to meet their new star. They had lunch with the GM in a fancy restaurant. Sooley took a call from the owner, a private equity swinger who had bought the team four years earlier for $900 million, according to online business magazines. The owner was eager to meet him and wanted lunch when he was back in the country. He welcomed him aboard and promised a great future together.

.   .   .

The Rauncheroo Reggae and Rap Music Festival was held in June every year at the Acropolis Resort on Paradise Island in the Bahamas. In addition to attracting tens of thousands of wild fans from around the world, it had become known for getting the biggest acts in hip-hop and island music. It was also a favorite of celebrities, the place to be seen and often touched by adoring fans. Murray had heard of it, Sooley had not, but the night before the draft Darrell Whitley and his gang were talking about the party while they hung out in a Brooklyn nightclub. It was a three-day blowout, with lots of girls, many from Europe. As soon as they returned from Brooklyn, Murray mentioned it to Sooley and the two checked it out on social media. They drooled over the thousands of photos and it became abundantly clear that the festival was not to be missed. It was favored by plenty of actors and pro athletes, some big NBA names wanting to blow off steam after the season, and some football players taking a break before their training camps. And the lineup of singers and musicians included virtually every name they could think of. Sooley mentioned it to Vallie, who, not surprisingly, was all in. He talked to Whitley and the two of them devised a plan. They would invite Reynard and lean on him to get a jet. Two first-round draft picks could not be expected to arrive on commercial flights.

The day after they returned from the house-hunting trip to D.C., Sooley mentioned over dinner that he needed to see Arnie in South Beach and discuss some endorsement proposals. Murray should go too. They did not mention the festival to Ida and Ernie because they did not want the drama. Sooley was growing weary of their nosiness and Murray was itching to return to Arnie's place in Miami.

The following day they flew down on Delta and arrived at the mansion in a lowly cab. Reynard was excited about the trip and had secured tickets and accommodations, along with an airplane. Arnie, who was divorced, had attended the festival two years earlier and said he might join them later. Whitley arrived with Jared, one of his brothers, and Reggie, his "manager."

Murray liked that title and from then on introduced himself as Sooley's manager.

They slept late the next morning, then loaded into two limos for the ride to the airport where a sleek Gulfstream 6 was waiting. Their party consisted of Sooley, Murray, Darrell, Jared, Reggie, Reynard and his girl Meg, and Vallie. For good measure, Sooley had invited two of Vallie's friends, Tiff and Susan, a couple of attractive former athletes who hung around Arnie's pool. A total of ten on a jet that could seat fifteen. The flight attendants were pouring champagne before they buckled in. More bottles were opened and consumed during the fifty-five-minute flight to Nassau. There, a string of colorful limos waited to collect the rich and famous who were arriving by the dozens.

They checked in at the Acropolis and found their rooms. Sooley's grand suite had two bedrooms, one for him and Vallie, the other for Murray, Tiff, and Susan. The sleeping arrangements were not exact but no one seemed to care. There were at least three sofas in the suite. They had a long lunch at a massive buffet near one of the pools and enjoyed people-watching. The concerts started around two, no schedule was strictly adhered to, and a mob gathered around the open-air stage. Loud rap echoed throughout the resort, which had a thousand rooms, no fewer than eight pools, water slides, hot tubs, saunas, three casinos, and restaurants and bars everywhere. Fans poured in, few of them over the age of thirty, and various languages could be heard. Sooley was often recognized and proudly posed for photos.

It was unbridled hedonism with seemingly no rules.

Murray liked cards, especially blackjack, and late in the afternoon, when they finally lost the girls, he and Sooley slipped into a casino for a few hands. It was much quieter at the tables and they appreciated the retreat from the music. Sooley spotted Alan Barnett of the Knicks playing all alone at a high-end table. He was rumored to be one of the biggest gamblers in the NBA and a hellraiser to boot. Rudy Suarez, the all-pro quarterback for the Vikings, stopped by and said a quick hello to Barnett. How cool was that? Sooley couldn't wait to start playing and winning and meeting other famous athletes like himself.

He lost $500 in his first hour and took a break. It would take a long time for him to adjust to burning cash. Murray, though, was winning big and didn't want to leave his table. Sooley went to a bar, got a beer, and watched the action on the floor.

After dark, the festival crowd swelled to capacity as 30,000 rowdy fans packed around the stage. There was no seating, just a crush of humanity, with each person holding a drink and bouncing to the relentless, pulsating beat. The night's headliner, Dock Ripp and his bad boys from Philly, were scheduled for eight. They went on at ten and the music got even louder, the crowd even rowdier. Sooley was in the thick of it, dancing with Vallie, making out, groping, and taking an occasional break at a bar.

When the music stopped at 2 a.m. the crowd relaxed and hit the bars. Sooley and Vallie were drenched and exhausted. They went to his suite, showered, and fell asleep. There was no sign of Murray.

They slept until noon and had brunch and champagne by a pool, in a secluded part of the resort. Murray found them and was quick to report that he was up $4,000 at blackjack. Sooley observed that maybe it was time to cash in his chips, but he had bigger plans. He ate with them as they watched the people. After he left, they changed and jumped in the water for a lazy afternoon by the pool. Darrell, Jared, and Reggie found them, as did Tiff and Susan. The men could not help but gawk at the endless parade of string bikinis.

The second night was similar to the first, with one notorious act after another. During a break, Sooley bumped into Darrell, who informed him that he had met Wazy Starr, a TV actress, and she and some friends were planning a late-night party in their suite. Sooley and Vallie were tired of the music and the crush of people, and eventually made their way to the party on the eighteenth floor. The suite was twice the size of Sooley's and was packed with people he did not know. Murray was not in the crowd. Jared Whitley rescued them and introduced them to Wazy, who was stoned out of her mind. A thick fog of marijuana smoke hung just above their heads and everyone seemed to be hitting a joint. Vallie took one, gave it to Sooley, and he took a hit. At a dining table some Hollywood types were laughing over lines of coke. A waiter appeared with a large tray of plastic cups filled with some sort of rum punch. Vallie grabbed two, gave one to Sooley, and they drifted to another group. Someone recognized him and he smiled for a camera. He was lightheaded but thoroughly enjoying himself. A tall blonde asked for another photo and Sooley happily held her close. Vallie eased away, looking for another drink. The blonde said her name was Jackie and she worked in "film." She tugged his hand and led him to another room where the music was louder. Sooley looked around, wanting to find Vallie, but she was nowhere in sight. Jackie clung tight and at the first chance kissed him on the lips, then asked him where he was sleeping that night. In his room, he said. She asked for the number and he laughed it away. She grabbed two rum punches off a tray and handed one to him. She reached into a pocket and pulled out some small pills.

"Ever try these?" she asked.

"What are they?"

"Mollies, and they're wonderful. A couple of these and you can go all night long." She took one, swallowed it, and washed it down with the drink. If she could do it, so could he.

Sooley knew that Molly was another name for Ecstasy, a drug he had only heard about. But for a little pot here and there, after the season, he had no experience with any drugs.

She handed him three more and said, "Save these for later. I'll come find you."

He took them and quickly stuffed them in a pocket. Jackie said, "I see trouble."

Sooley turned around and saw Vallie at the door, talking to another girl.

Jackie said, "Let's hook up later, okay?"

"Sure," he said, eager to get away from her. He found Vallie, who did not seem irritated, and they decided to leave the party. They returned to the concert where everyone was dancing. Sooley began to feel sharper, happier, quicker on his feet, and his vision, blurred by alcohol and pot, was suddenly sharper. Vallie was all over him and at one point asked, "Who was that girl?"

"Don't know, babe, never saw her before."

Sooley danced like crazy and felt like he could take the stage and belt out a few numbers of his own. He had never felt so exhilarated, so invincible. When Vallie left to fetch drinks, he followed behind her, and quickly swallowed another Molly.

When the music ended, they made their way to the suite, where Murray had another party in the works. Tiff and Susan were dancing by themselves while four guys Sooley had never seen before watched and egged them on. Sooley suddenly felt dizzy, lethargic, and lead-footed. Though he had been sweating for hours, he noticed that his forehead was extremely warm. Not to be outdone, Vallie stripped out of her tight tee shirt and began dancing with her friends. Murray started dancing with them as another group arrived with bottles of champagne. The party was too much fun to miss, so Sooley eased into the bathroom and swallowed another Molly.

CHAPTER 57

Murray awoke to screams. Vallie was standing in his door, hysterical. "He's not moving! He's not moving! Do something, Murray!"

He found a pair of gym shorts, pulled them on, and almost fell over. His head was splitting and his vision was blurred, but suddenly none of that mattered. He raced to the other bedroom where Vallie stood gawking at Sooley on the bed, partially covered by a sheet.

He was wearing gym shorts and nothing else, and he was as stiff as a board. Murray jumped on the bed and shook him vigorously while he pleaded with him to wake up. Tiff and Susan watched in horror as Murray tried everything to revive him. Finally, he stopped and backed away, and the four of them gawked at the lifeless figure.

"What did you give him?" Murray yelled at Vallie.

"Nothing, absolutely nothing. He was drinking and there was a little pot, but nothing. I swear, Murray, I gave him nothing and I didn't see him take anything."

He called the front desk and pleaded for a doctor and an ambulance. He called Reynard's cell but there was no answer. "Get dressed," he barked at the girls, and he pulled a sheet over his friend. He sat on the edge of the bed and started sobbing.

Two medics rushed in, followed by a man in a dark suit, security. As Vallie, Tiff, and Susan sat on the sofa and wiped their faces, and with Murray hovering, they checked him with a stethoscope and grimly shook their heads. A second man in a suit, the house detective, arrived and surveyed the situation. He began asking questions. None of them had given the deceased any drugs, they swore. The detective did not believe them. Murray assured him that his friend was not a drug user. Sure they had been drinking, and too much, and they had smoked pot, but nothing more serious. He did not believe them.

When Reynard finally arrived, he almost fainted when he realized what was happening.

The detective saw a pair of shorts in a chair and asked who owned them. Vallie said Sooley had worn them the night before. He went through the pockets and found a single pill. One look, and he said, "Ecstasy. Where did he get it?"

The four, and Reynard, were clueless. And no one believed them.

. . .

They wrestled his body onto a stretcher, one built for average people but not long enough for a man who stood six feet eight. They covered him with sheets and tucked them tight, but his bare feet dangled off the end.

"Don't leave this room," the detective growled as he followed the stretcher.

When they were gone, Reynard looked at Murray and said, "We have to make some calls. I'll call Arnie. You call your mother. We have a PR guy who'll prepare something. It's gonna be awful."

"It already is," Vallie said, sniffing.

Murray's thoughts were an incomprehensible mash of fear, blame, disbelief, dread, loss, and excuses. The only thing that was clear was that he could not imagine calling Miss Ida. He finally stood, wiped his cheeks again, walked to the other bedroom, with his phone, and closed the door.

Ida left her office in tears and drove home where Ernie was wait-ing. They were almost too stunned to speak, so they sat in their dark den with ESPN on mute, waiting for the news to break. At 12:02, a bulletin interrupted *SportsCenter,* and there was the smiling face of Samuel Sooleymon, his death in the Bahamas now confirmed. Age eighteen, dead from a possible overdose.

The news spread fast and their phones began buzzing.

Ecko Lam was in Juba, scouting talent for his summer Under 18 team and getting it ready for the showcase, when his wife called with the news. He went to a locker room and closed the door. Later, he sat his players down and told them that Sooley, their new national hero, was dead.

Lonnie Britt was in his car on a Milwaukee freeway when he took the call from Jason Grinnell. He barely managed to pull onto the shoulder where he sat for a long time and tried to collect his thoughts.

On campus, a group of students gathered in front of The Nest and sat on the front steps crying. It was a Sunday in June and the gym was locked. Other students drove by and joined them. Two more showed up with the first bouquet of flowers and a poster with Sooley's smiling face in the middle of it. Handwritten above in bold letters were the words: "So Long Sooley. Love Always." The crowd grew and before long a news van from a Durham station stopped with a crew sniffing for a story, but the students refused to say any-thing on camera.

After being released by the police, Reynard got his group together and most of them left Nassau as soon as possible. He and Murray stayed behind to do whatever one does with a dead body. On the flight home, the Gulfstream was as somber as a morgue.

Arnie passed them somewhere over the Atlantic. He and his lawyer had quickly chartered a smaller Lear and were sprinting to Nassau. Reynard was forbidden from leaving the hotel and couldn't meet them at the airport. They took a cab to the resort and were briefed by the police, who were still investigating. They had recorded statements from all those around the deceased and were still looking for an unknown woman, an American, tall and blond, who was seen briefly with Sooley last night. The body was at the morgue and awaiting a decision about an autopsy, which could take up to two weeks. However, in some cases the autopsy could be expedited. There was little chance the police would release the body to be sent home for an autopsy, but that decision would be made by the Governor.

Arnie's lawyer hired the largest law firm in Nassau, one with plenty of connections. He wasn't worried about criminal prosecution. Indeed, so far the only possible crime was possession of illegal substances by the deceased himself. Arnie, though, had learned years ago that it was always safer to lawyer up.

Jackie heard the news as it roared through the resort. She whispered to her best friend that it was time to head back to the States.

The death was certainly sad and shocking, but the festival was in its last day and the party must go on. The music began at two.

. . .

After the initial numbness, Ecko began to attach one thought to another, and he was worried about Beatrice. It was unlikely she would hear the news. How could she? Where would it come from? But Sooley had become such a famous person throughout his country, and with four million South Sudanese refugees scattered in camps and settlements there was a chance that the news could make it all the way to Rhino Camp South.

He called Christine Moran's cell but there was no service. He waited an hour and tried again. No service. Being a Sunday, maybe things were slower. She answered the third time and Ecko reintroduced himself. They had met briefly in early December when he visited the camp. She said that she remembered him, then listened as he broke the awful news. Then, he asked the mother of all favors: Would she find Beatrice and tell her Sooley was dead?

Christine was horrified at the thought and quickly declined. Ecko pleaded with her and tried to explain that there was no one else to do it. He was in Juba coaching a team and he couldn't leave. Who else in the world could even get to Rhino?

Christine said she would consider it but needed some time. She rang off and immediately called the Doctors Without Borders office in New York. Of course, it was closed on Sundays. She called a DWB friend in Paris, at home, and asked him to verify the story. She said her coverage was not good and gave him a sat phone number to call back in one hour. He did so and verified the death.

By then Christine realized that she had no choice. She had seen more death than most war veterans, and she had seen it so many different ways, and she thought she was hardened enough to handle anything. But not this. She had come to know and admire Beatrice. Telling her that her oldest son was dead was unthinkable.

She huddled with two nurse friends and they decided it would be best to do it in the hospital, in a private area where Beatrice and the boys could grieve. There would be sedatives available.

Christine thought about taking one. She sent an errand boy to fetch the family.

.   .   .

By late Sunday, several hundred students were at The Nest, hugging, crying, supporting each other. Dozens of bouquets covered the front steps, and posters honoring their hero lined the sidewalk. Candles were passed out, to be lit after dark.

Ida called the Mayor and asked for two patrol cars to be parked in front of their house. There had been some traffic, a few knocks on the door, and they were in no mood to deal with reporters or anyone else. The television had been turned off. Jordan was flying in from Houston where she was spending the summer clerking for a law firm. Brady was headed home from Boston.

And Murray was at the resort waiting for the authorities. It wasn't clear who would make the next few decisions, but "the Governor" had been mentioned a couple of times by the police.

As they killed time, Murray, Arnie, and Reynard agreed to stick together and not point fingers. Sooley had wanted to attend the festival. He wanted to celebrate and have some serious fun. It was his idea to join forces with Whitley and ask for the jet; his idea to invite the girls; his idea to stop by the last party. At some point the night before, he got some Mollies and took them. No one forced him to. That, for Murray, was still hard to believe. Sooley was not a drug user, Murray said over and over. They had lived together for almost a year and Murray knew him inside and out. The guy did not use drugs! He was proud of his body, his stamina, his talent, and he was determined to become a star.

Murray went along with the plan to deflect blame while not beating up on Sooley, but he knew what was waiting for him at home. He knew that his parents would always feel that he had led Sooley astray. He did not look forward to facing them alone.

Murray called them every other hour. He called the funeral home in Durham. He found a funeral home director in Nassau and hired him. He called the airline to arrange the transfer of the body—$4,000 to ship it out, $2,000 to receive it at home. Arnie was covering all expenses. Murray worked the phones with a purpose and he made calls out of boredom.

Arnie was impressed.

Late Sunday night, the police called to say the autopsy would take place in an expedited manner, at nine o'clock in the morning, in Nassau. In the opinion of the chief detective, the autopsy was not that significant. The cause of death was obvious. He no longer believed foul play was involved, though his investigation would proceed until terminated.

He said, "Looks like the young man had too much fun."

CHAPTER 58

On Monday afternoon, Arnie and Reynard jetted back to Miami. They offered Murray a ride but he politely said no. He needed to take his friend home.

On Tuesday morning, he left Nassau on a Delta flight, his seat by the window. Somewhere below him in cargo, there was another passenger, his beloved friend, in a coffin. Sooley loved to tell the stories of his trip from Juba to Orlando the summer before, how it was the first flight for every kid on the team, how they had been so excited they couldn't sleep the night before, how the trip took thirty hours and by the time it was over they were no longer infatuated with air travel.

That was his first flight. This was his last.

Murray began wiping his eyes before takeoff, and he put his sunglasses back on and wept.

Regardless of how tough he acted in front of Arnie, he was blaming himself and he knew he always would. And so would others. And there was nothing he could do to convince himself or anyone else that he had not failed Sooley.

He bit his lip to keep from sobbing, and he had never ached, physically and emotionally, so much in his life.

. . .

On Wednesday, Ida and Ernie made the decision to hold the memorial service at The Nest. Central's President lobbied for this and finally convinced Ida that the school, and especially its students, wanted to pay their respects in a grand way.

Ernie wanted a private ceremony at Sacred Heart Church with a quick burial afterward. At first Ida seemed to lean that way, but Murray agreed with the President because he knew the students wanted to take part in the farewell. Murray was functioning well and taking care of the details. Ida was not.

He posted a statement online announcing the service would be held at 3 p.m. Saturday afternoon at the gym, open to all. A private funeral Mass would be held the following day at the church.

Then he dealt with the press. Would it have access? Could the service be televised? Who would be speaking? Would there be music, and by whom? Murray battled away and had several conversations with Campus Security.

. . . . .

The autopsy report contained no surprises. The illegal drug MDMA, an acronym for its chemical name 3,4-methylenedioxy-methamphetamine, and commonly known as Ecstasy or Molly or any one of a dozen other street names, was present in the body. The one pill found in Sooley's shorts was a tablet containing 120 milligrams of MDMA. At least two and perhaps three were taken in the five hours before death. The lab that made that tablet also added caffeine, ephedrine, and cocaine. His blood alcohol level was .20. The deceased was quite intoxicated. Marijuana was also present in the blood. His body temperature increased to a dangerous level and resulted in total kidney failure, the cause of death.

Arnie's lawyers in Nassau succeeded in preventing the autopsy report from being released.

. . .

The backboards were raised. The court was covered by rows of perfectly matched folding chairs, all filled. The gym was packed—the floor, the movable bleachers, the permanent seats, the aisles. The mourners sat still and somberly as a ladies' choir sang a soft funeral hymn. When they finished, there was a noise in the rear and a door opened. A priest in a white robe appeared and the casket was behind him. All 4,000 stood and turned to watch the procession. Eight Eagles walked beside the casket, each with one hand on it. Behind, two by two were the rest of the team, then the coaches, led by Lonnie Britt, who held his wife's hand. Behind the coaches was the family—all of the Walkers, Ida and Ernie first, Murray and Jordan, then Brady.

The procession moved slowly down the center aisle as a string quartet played "Amazing Grace." They parked Sooley at the foot of a makeshift stage and below a pulpit borrowed from a church. The priest motioned for all to sit and by the time the crowd settled in, women were sobbing. Another mournful hymn from the choir only rattled the emotions even more.

Murray, out of frustration, had finally banned all cameras, except for ESPN. They had agreed to broadcast it live and share footage with other outlets. When Lonnie Britt walked to the podium he knew he was facing a wide audience.

He began with "Sooley. Sooley. By the time you said his name, and saw that smile, you knew that you loved him." With the composure, cadence, and preparation of a seasoned preacher, he talked about the kid from South Sudan. No one fought to hold back tears, including his coach.

After another hymn, Murray stepped forward to struggle through a eulogy he still could not believe he was being called upon to give. He choked up, battled on, got a few laughs, and finally quit when he was overcome. He returned to his seat beside Ida, who patted his knee and whispered, "Nice job. I love you."

On big screens, they ran a collage of Sooley bantering with reporters, of him soaring through the air with unforgettable dunks, of him bombing away from mid-court. He never missed, and the crowd managed to cheer and cry at the same time.

CHAPTER 59

Two days after the burial, and with the Walkers still sleepwalking through the aftermath, Murray finally forced himself down to the basement to go through Sooley's things. His laptop and cell phone were on the ping-pong table, untouched. Murray didn't have the heart to try and access them, and he didn't know the passcodes anyway. He didn't want to know what secrets, if any, they held. He did know that Sooley had been spending more time on social media. After the first-round upset of Duke, back on March 17, Sooley's fame spread like crazy and he was the talk of the sports world. His Facebook followers went from 20,000 to 400,000 in a matter of days. He posted more photos, chatted with his fans, and shared insights into the tournament. As Central advanced and became the epicenter of March Madness, his numbers skyrocketed. By the time the team traveled to Phoenix for the Final Four, and Sooleymania was raging, over five million fans liked his page. They followed the draft closely and he played to his audience. His shocking death left everyone clamoring for more and the number doubled.

Murray looked at his page almost daily, but the brokenhearted messages from his fans were often too much to read. Emotions were simply too raw. He would swear off, leave the page, but return the next day for a quick look.

He went through Sooley's backpack and rifled through a pile of notebooks and sports magazines. In a daily planner that had been rarely used, Murray found some notes that were intriguing. Stapled to one page was a business card for a company called Aegis Partners and an "Advisor" named Gary Gaston. He opened his own laptop and a quick search revealed little about the outfit. It was based in Bethesda and advertised itself as a player in the vague field of "international security." On the back of the business card, Gaston had evidently scribbled his cell phone number. Murray called it and a voice curtly announced, "Gaston."

Murray explained who he was and what he was doing and was surprised when Gaston said, "Oh, I knew Sooley pretty well. Even met him once, just a few days ago when you guys were in D.C. looking for an apartment."

Murray was surprised and said, "I didn't know that."

"You were taking a nap and I went to your hotel. The Hyatt. Met Sooley in the bar and we hit it off."

"Mind if I ask why you were talking to Sooley?"

"Well, first, I'm very sorry about what has happened. It's quite a shock and I'm sure you guys are reeling right now."

"We are. I was Sooley's closest friend and I never heard him mention you or your company."

"We're very private, that's our business. We do a lot of work in Africa, complicated stuff I can't go into, but from time to time we're hired to extricate people and bring them here."

"Extricate?"

"That's it. Sooley was convinced he was about to make some money, I guess he was right about that, and he wanted to hire us to get his family out of the refugee camp in Uganda."

"And how do you do that?"

"Look, I prefer to avoid the phone as much as possible. Same for email and texts. Everything leaves a trail."

"Okay. I noticed that your firm's website doesn't say much about your firm."

"We don't advertise, okay? Sooley found us through a nonprofit that works with refugees."

"He knew them all, didn't he?"

"I guess he did."

"So, you can't tell me anything?"

"Sure I can, but not over the phone. If you want a cup of coffee, I'm happy to explain things."

"When can we meet?"

Gaston put him on hold for a moment, then said, "Day after tomorrow work for you?"

"Sure. When and where?"

"I don't know. Look, I'd like to help. I really liked the kid, watched the draft and all, love college basketball, and I was excited about doing the job. I have some time. Let's meet halfway and have lunch."

"When and where?"

"Looks like Charlottesville is three hours for you, about the same for me. My wife is from the area, so let's meet there. Day after tomorrow."

Over dinner, Murray briefed his parents, who, given his recent history of unexpected trips, were skeptical. But he had little else to do, now that his job as a manager was over, and he was not to be denied.

He drove three hours to Charlottesville and met Gaston at an outdoor café on the downtown pedestrian mall. To his pleasant surprise, Gaston was African American, about fifty, and instead of the black suit Murray expected, he wore a gray designer jogging suit with state-of-the-art Adidas sneakers. The air was hot but their table was in the shade. They ordered ice tea and salads, and Gaston began talking.

He was a graduate of the Naval Academy and had spent a career in military intelligence before joining Aegis a few years earlier. Without much background about what the company did or did not do, he said he knew Africa quite well, had traveled throughout the continent, and had many contacts.

Murray went through a windy narrative of how he met Sooley and the delightful year they had just been through. Gaston seemed to know many of the details, especially about the season. He said, "The contract was reported to be worth fourteen million. Don't suppose Sooley got his hands on any of the money, did he?"

"No. He had not even seen the contract. His agent said it would take about a month after the draft. That's all history now."

"Too bad."

"Everything about it is tragic. You used the word 'extricate.' Can we talk about that?"

"Sure. We were putting together a plan and Sooley was excited about it."

"How was it going to work?"

The salads arrived and they began eating. Gaston said, "First, we were to arrange paperwork for his mother and brothers. Ugandan passports, visas, applications for entry into the U.S., basic stuff. We'd make arrangements with certain people in the Ugandan government to sort of look the other way. Not surprisingly, they're not at all hesitant to get rid of some refugees. They're trying to feed a million and the number keeps growing. We'd facilitate their removal from the camp, take them to Kampala, give them nicer clothes and new identities, and put them on a plane bound for the U.S."

"Easy enough."

"Easy enough if there's plenty of money. The most expensive part is the air transportation. Commercial flights won't work because there are no nonstop flights between Kampala and here. You have to stop and change planes. Stops mean more nosy people in customs asking for paperwork. We had a failure last year that has turned into a mess."

Murray took a bite and waited for more. "Care to talk about that?"

"Briefly. We had a project involving a Somalian family living in a refugee settlement in Kenya. Their relatives here scraped together some money and we decided to try it. It was a mistake. The family could not afford a private jet. No one can, unless, of course, someone in the family happens to sign a big NBA contract. Anyway, we got the family out of the camp, got them on a commercial flight from Nairobi to London. British immigration can be tough and they stopped them at Heathrow. Their phony paperwork was discovered, all hell broke loose. The family is now stuck somewhere in the U.K., in custody, and will probably be sent back to Somalia, where they will not be safe. Needless to say, that was our last project involving commercial air travel."

"How does the private jet work?"

"Well, it's a seven-thousand-mile trip that takes between thirteen and fifteen hours, depending on wind, weather, stuff like that. There is only one jet with that range. A Gulfstream G650."

"I've been on a Gulfstream, thanks to Sooley, of course."

"Most Gulfstreams don't have the range. It has to be a G650."

"How much does the flight cost?"

"Three fifty."

"Three hundred and fifty thousand dollars?"

"Yep. Roughly thirty hours in the air, terminal to terminal, at ten thousand bucks an hour. Plus four pilots, expenses, profit, it adds up quickly. The entire trip takes four to five days, if everything goes smoothly. And few charter companies want to go to Africa."

"Would the charter company know the real story?"

"No. Our documents are really good, that other story notwithstanding. Their pilots would have copies of the passports and ID cards, but once Sooley's family was cleared by Uganda customs, then they'd have been home free. Until they arrived here."

"What would happen here?"

"Well, Murray, that's where Miss Ida would step in."

Murray almost laughed. He shook his head in disbelief and asked, "How do you know my mother?"

"Sooley thought of everything. He knew that she could handle U.S. Immigration. When the plane landed in Raleigh, the family would surrender to Immigration, same as hundreds do each day at the borders. They'd be detained and taken into custody. She would immediately seek asylum, get an expedited hearing, and get them released and placed in a nice house pending their trial, which could take months."

Murray was still shaking his head. "What would happen to the charter company? I mean, surely they would get in trouble."

"Probably, but we were counting on a small fine. Again, we were hoping Miss Ida could deal with Immigration. Since the amount of the fine is unknown, it was the one figure we weren't sure of."

"So how much was the entire operation?"

"Half a mil. As I said, virtually no one can afford it. We're talking about refugees and their families, folks who have nothing."

"That's a lot of money."

"It is. It takes some cash to grease the skids in Uganda. There are other expenses and my time is valuable. I have to make the trip to guarantee everything works well."

"Might I ask if your company has pulled off any of these extractions?"

"Two, but I can't go into details. Let's just say they involved wealthy Syrian families here who wanted their people out of the camps."

"So, this is not your primary line of work."

"Oh no. We deal mainly with hostages and kidnappings. We rescue people and get them out. Unfortunately, kidnapping is big business in the developing world and we have some expertise."

Murray shoved his salad away and said, "It sounds as if this extricating business requires a fair amount of criminal activity."

Gaston smiled and took a sip of ice tea. "Depends on how you define it. If you want a laugh, go online and search 'fake passports.' You'll see a hundred sites brazenly advertising the preparation and sale of fake passports. That's a crime. We buy them all the time, so, yes, in one sense we're breaking the law. But there's little harm and almost no enforcement. And, I'm sure that somewhere in Uganda there's a law on the books that prohibits the bribing of customs officials. Or maybe there's not. At any rate, it's a way of life in the Third World. It's simply how business is done. Sooley understood this and was willing to take his chances. His hands wouldn't get dirty. He would pay our fee and we would take care of the rest."

Murray marveled at the extent of Sooley's planning, and without a word to his roommate. "I can't believe he didn't tell me about this."

"It was happening pretty fast. He made contact with me about two weeks before the draft, when it looked like he would indeed go in the first round. The money was almost within his grasp. He would have told you eventually because he needed Miss Ida."

"I guess so. He was a smart guy."

"Very smart, and very determined. We were excited about helping Sooley because, obviously, he had the money. Or at least the prospect of it."

"That's what he dreamed about. Getting his mother and brothers over here."

"I'm sorry we can't help, Murray. Those poor folks will spend years in that camp, won't they?"

"Probably so. And Sooley can't help them."

"I assume his mother has heard the news."

"Yes. Some aid workers in the camp told her."

"That poor woman."

"She'll never know how close she came."

"Mind if I ask what happened in the Bahamas?"

Murray shrugged and said, "He had a bad night. Got some pills from a girl. Sooley wasn't a user, not even close. He didn't smoke pot until the season was over, and then he didn't like it. He'd have a few beers, nothing more. It's so sad. He was a great guy."

"He was. I'm very sorry."

"Thanks. And thanks for your time."

Gaston paid for lunch. They shook hands and promised to keep in touch.

CHAPTER 60

Murray took as much time as possible driving back to Durham. He was in an even worse funk and the thought of spending another night with his parents in a gloomy household was not appealing. Over dinner, he described his trip to Charlottesville and the lunch with Gary Gaston. They were amazed at Sooley's plans to extricate his family, big plans that had not been shared with them.

July Fourth came and went with no hint of a celebration around the Walker home. Jordan was there for a few days but not even she could lift their spirits. On July 6, Murray drove to Charlotte where the first round of the international showcase was being held. Ecko would be there with his latest installment of young South Sudanese talent. Central's new head coach, Jason Grinnell, would be there, along with Lonnie Britt, no doubt watching Ecko's players more closely and hoping to discover another star.

He found them at the Spectrum Center, home of the Hornets, and they invited him to the coaches' suite to hang out with their friends. There was a lot of talk about Central's miracle run to the Final Four, and Murray enjoyed the attention.

That night, over a long dinner with the three coaches, they tried hard to talk about anything but Sooley. It didn't work. All four men were deeply wounded and still stunned by the loss. Each took turns telling stories of how friends and strangers had reached out to them and offered to help. Sooley had thrilled the basketball world and touched many people, many of whom were still eager for some connection to the kid and his remarkable story. Jason Grinnell said that the Central program had received over $50,000 in small gifts from fans everywhere. Ecko's program had also received many small gifts to support players in South Sudan.

He said, "Sooley still has millions of followers on social media. I check it all the time and some of the comments almost make me cry."

Jason said, "I tried to look too, but it's overwhelming."

Ecko said, "Here's an idea, Murray. You should try to capitalize on Sooley's popularity. Why don't you consider starting a foundation in his name with the proceeds going to something like humanitarian relief for our people?"

Lonnie added, "Great idea. I'll bet you could raise a fortune."

Jason said, "And how about a few bucks for dear old Central?"

Murray said, "How do you start a foundation?"

Ecko said, "It's easy. Everybody's got a foundation. The one I work for has some lawyers who'll guide you through it. All you need is a mission statement, a cool website, and somebody to run it. It doesn't have to be fancy. Post the link on Sooley's social media and I'll bet you'll get an amazing response."

"Don't you need IRS approval?" Lonnie asked.

"Sure, but you can get started as that is pending," Ecko replied. "I've heard the lawyers talk about it. I'll bet your mother knows the ropes. Her Legal Aid is a nonprofit, right?"

"Oh yeah. You never hear them talk about profits. What's the mission?"

Lonnie said, "It could be three-fold. First, humanitarian relief for refugees. Second, to support youth basketball in South Sudan. Third, to raise money for scholarships in Sooley's name at Central."

Ecko said, "The three of us can serve on your board, along with anyone else you want. We'll see how much money comes in and decide how to give it away."

Jason smiled and whistled and said, "This could be huge."

.   .   .

For the first time in memory, Murray arose early the next morning and hustled back to Durham. He bought sandwiches and took them to Ida's office for a working lunch. Typically, she was skeptical of any idea or scheme that tried to profit off Sooley's name. He objected to the word "profit," and she apologized saying she had used the word carelessly. Of course, there were no thoughts about making money. She had not seen him so engaged and excited since he and Sooley had returned from the draft in New York. She suggested that they discuss it with Ernie over dinner and sleep on it. That was all the approval Murray needed.

Borrowing from the funds that Sooley had borrowed from Arnie, a loan that so far had not been mentioned by the agent, Murray spent $4,000 on a website design, $2,500 on legal advice, and $2,000 on a nineteen-year-old kid who ran his own company specializing in online marketing. He opened a bank account, rented a post office box, and read with discomfort the proposed bylaws and IRS regs sent over by the lawyer.

On July 19, one month to the day after that horrible Sunday morning at the Acropolis, The Sooley Fund was launched. The website featured a beautiful color sketch taken from Murray's favorite photo of his friend. There was Sooley, with the ball held high over his head, and a wicked smile on his face, soaring high above the rim for another rattling dunk. There were photos of the refugee settlements, the starving children, of healthier teenagers playing basketball on dirt courts, and a tribute to the great Central team that had so captivated the sports world. The website and social media pages were linked to each other in every way possible.

By midnight of launch day, over 50,000 viewers had visited the site and 11,000 had sent money, a total of $148,000. Murray forced himself to close his laptop and he tried to sleep. By noon the next day, the money was at $305,000 and the deluge was on. The Fund was going viral.

Sooley's popularity was astonishing. His tragic death only heightened the public's desire to help in some small way. The comments and condolences were overwhelming and poured in with the money.

After seventy-two hours, more than 100,000 people had paid by credit card, with the average gift at about $8. After four days, the Fund topped $1 million and Murray was giving interviews.

He sent a long memo to his board—Ecko, Lonnie, Jason, and Ida—and described in detail Sooley's desire to extricate his family and his plans for doing so.

With the board's approval, he called Gary Gaston.

CHAPTER 61

Three weeks later, Gaston arrived at the Walker home for a preflight briefing. He brought with him an African American woman named Silvia, who he described as one of his associates. She specialized in "extrication logistics," something as vague as Gaston could possibly make it sound, but the Walkers were not about to ask for any clarification.

A week earlier, Gaston had explained to Murray that a woman would be a nice addition to the team because Beatrice and the boys might feel more comfortable around her. They were likely to be thoroughly rattled if not traumatized, and women handled those situations better. There was some loose talk about Ida making the trip, though she was not keen to go. That talk got nixed when Gaston explained that he and Murray, along with whatever woman they took, would run the slight risk of being arrested upon their entry into the U.S. The charge could be aiding and abetting an illegal entry. Gaston was prepared to risk such a minor charge. Murray was undaunted. Ida preferred not to be arrested and flatly said no. She needed to stay behind and organize the legal team and deal with Immigration. Gaston said that with two prior extrications, both involving Syrians, the planes landed in Bangor, Maine, where Immigration was not known to be as aggressive as, say, Miami. The families surrendered to the authorities, were detained, and Immigration never pursued anyone for aiding and abetting.

Over dinner at Ida's table, Gaston walked them through each step of the extrication and answered all their questions. He showed them the forged passports for the Sooleymons. Using photos that Ecko had taken with them in December, the forger had done what appeared to be a masterful job of producing Ugandan passports. Since Sooleymon was a familiar name throughout East Africa, and Beatrice, James, and Chol were not uncommon, their new passports used their real names. Murray had been able to obtain their birthdates from Ecko.

Gaston expanded on the story he had told Murray about the failed extrication a year earlier at Heathrow. The paperwork had been fine, but the Immigration official became suspicious when the mother flubbed her fictitious birth date.

Ernie wanted to know what could go wrong. Several things that they knew of and several that no one had ever heard of. The biggest fear was the airplane. The Gulfstream 650 had a range of 7,500 miles and Entebbe was 7,300 miles from the airport at Raleigh-Durham. Flying west, they would certainly face headwinds, and if they were strong enough the jet might be forced to make a pit stop. Landing anywhere but the U.S. was risky. However, the pilots would monitor the weather closely and would know what they were facing before they took off. Plan B would be to land in the Canary Islands, a favorite fueling stop for international flights and a place known for customs agents who could be convinced to look the other way. Gaston had contacts there.

There was always the chance that trouble might erupt at Rhino Camp South and prevent a quiet exit by Beatrice and the boys. There were other risks, but on the whole Gaston and Silvia were confident.

After they said good night and left for their hotel, Murray went to his room and finished packing. As he did almost every hour, he checked in with the Fund, now at over $3 million and counting. He had been forced to hurriedly hire a part-time secretary to deal with the details and make sure the donors, all 265,000 of them, were properly thanked. Their systems were upgraded; more powerful software was added. Murray was chasing his tail and in need of full-time help, and the last thing he needed was a trip to Uganda.

But he wasn't about to miss the adventure.

. . .

Before they were buckled in, the copilot welcomed them aboard and briefed them on the flight. Thanks to a tailwind, their estimated flight time was only thirteen hours. Thirteen sounded only slightly better than fourteen or fifteen. Just minutes before their scheduled 11 a.m. departure, the flight attendant took their drink orders and handed them lunch menus.

The jet seemed plated with gold. The leather recliners were soft and deep. The carpet was thick, plush. A mahogany dining table sat midway aft, and beyond it were two sofas that folded into beds, complete with silk sheets. Screens were everywhere and there was an endless selection of movies and channels.

It would be Murray's third trip on a private jet, and something told him it would probably be his last. Classes started in two weeks and it was back to the grind. Then basketball, without Sooley and without Coach Britt, and a season that looked less than promising.

Murray found a chair in the rear, kicked off his shoes, buckled himself in, and vowed to enjoy the trip.

. . .

The two soldiers were Ugandan Defence Forces, the usual troops seen around the camp. They wore the standard green fatigues, shiny black boots, smart black berets, and, as always, had Kallies strapped over their shoulders. They found Beatrice behind her tent tending to her small plot of vegetables. They were friendly and polite and asked her to step away for a private word.

They informed her that she had been selected to move to a newer section of Rhino Camp South, to a nicer home. Keep it quiet. She had heard the rumors of new housing to replace their rotting tents, but those rumors had been around for months. The refugees spent half their time sifting through rumors, or creating more of them.

They returned to her tent where a third soldier was waiting with two army duffel bags. Beatrice balked and said she wasn't sure she wanted to leave. Her close friends lived on each side of her and she wouldn't go without them. The soldiers smiled and said her friends would make the move tomorrow. Within minutes, she had packed everything she owned—clothing, blankets, pillows, tins of food, some notebooks from school, and two plastic jugs for hauling water. The soldiers carried the duffels as they left the area. Beatrice looked back at her tent, her home for the past year, and wondered if she would ever see it again. An army jeep was waiting. The soldiers helped Beatrice into the front passenger's seat and tossed her bags into the back where another soldier was sitting. The jeep weaved slowly through the settlement and came to its edge, near the school. Standing in front under the shade of a tree was a teacher with James and Chol.

Beatrice asked the driver, "Why are we getting the boys?"

"We have a surprise. You'll like it."

The boys squeezed into the back seat of the jeep and waved to their teacher. They had never been in a jeep before. In fact, they could barely remember their last ride in a motorized vehicle, the old pickup owned by their uncle in Lotta.

Their rides would only continue to be upgraded.

As they left Rhino, Beatrice was concerned. Again, she asked the driver, "Where are we going?"

"To Kampala, then to America." She was stunned and speechless. They rode for almost an hour over a busy, wide gravel road, dodging supply trucks and troop carriers. At the airport, a small Ugandan air force cargo plane was waiting as another one landed and taxied to the warehouse.

In the rear seat, the soldier asked the boys, "Ever been up in an airplane before?"

They shook their heads no and watched wide-eyed as the jeep stopped next to the cargo plane. Beatrice had never considered air travel, and thus had no opinions about whether or not it was for her. However, at the moment she was stricken with fear and didn't want to leave the jeep. The soldiers gently coaxed her out with promises of safe travel, and a visit to the big city before leaving for America. Once inside they strapped her in, the boys too, and wished them well. The two engines sputtered to life and the old plane shook itself. Two cool pilots in aviator shades turned around, smiled at them, and gave them thumbs-up. Beatrice was too stiff to move, but the boys were grinning from ear to ear.

.   .   .

Murray, Gaston, and Silvia were lounging under a wide umbrella by the pool, sipping drinks with no alcohol, and waiting, for the second day in a row. In the bush, the best-laid plans often go awry, and the delay was being blamed on some confusion regarding cargo planes. It didn't matter and it wasn't a big deal. Delays were always expected. There were worse ordeals than hanging around Kampala Serena, a five-star hotel in the middle of the commercial district.

Gaston's phone rang and he got to his feet. He said, "One hour. Great." He put the phone away and nodded at Murray and Silvia. They went to their rooms, changed, and returned to the lobby where they waited. The family arrived in a white van with no military markings, proof that Immigration had now taken over. The driver was an officious-looking man in a suit. He slid open the side door and helped Beatrice to the pavement. The boys followed and all three stood frozen, unsure of what to say or do, or where to go. The Serena hotel was a vast and beautiful building, and they had just driven through the chaos and congestion of a big city, their first ever.

Gaston stepped forward and said, "We represent your American family. We're here to take you home."

Murray smiled at the boys and said, "I'm Murray. I lived with your brother and he was my best friend." They immediately recognized him from the videos Samuel had sent. They awkwardly shook his hand.

As they entered the lobby, the always courteous doormen smiled and then exchanged looks. Three well-dressed Americans and three bewildered and somewhat ragged refugees from the bush.

It came as no surprise that the boys wanted lunch. They had never eaten in a restaurant before, neither had Beatrice, and once their bags were checked in, they followed Gaston to a corner table where they could talk. And talk they did. As Beatrice realized that they were indeed headed to America, she had many questions. The boys asked Murray what they should eat and he ordered cheeseburgers and sodas. And, of course, they wanted to talk about Samuel.

For people who had slept last night on the floor of a tent, and every night for the past year, and who spent hours each day waiting in endless lines for food, and who had lost half their family and all hope in the future, and who had no idea why they had been plucked from the camp, the moment was simply overwhelming. Beatrice cried a lot, and then she laughed, and ate, and tried her best to understand Murray as he tried his best to explain how a nonprofit worked in the U.S. He finally gave up and said, "Let's just say that Samuel is responsible for this."

After a long lunch, they escorted the family to their large room with two beds. Murray showed them how to work the shower and toilet. From the balcony, he pointed below to the beautiful pool and told the boys he would take them swimming as soon as they changed.

Gaston called the front desk and organized a van to take them shopping, and he and Silvia left with Beatrice to buy new clothes. It was imperative that the family, now full-fledged Ugandans, looked the part of well-documented immigrants headed for America. If a customs agent somewhere checked their luggage, he would find some nice new clothes and nothing out of the ordinary. And new clothes were certainly needed. Staying clean in the camps was impossible, and the dirt and grime had become part of the fabrics.

In the pool, Murray marveled at how skinny James and Chol were. They were already tall for their ages, eleven and thirteen, and he could almost count their ribs. He had never seen kids so thin in America. As they frolicked in the water he watched closely for the slightest hint or sign that they shared the same marvelous DNA as their brother. They could not swim so they stayed in the shallow end, and as he listened to them chatter and play he remembered many wonderful stories Sooley had told about his little brothers. He said James looked just like him, and he was right. He said Chol would be the best basketball player in the family. They would soon see about that.

Water became the topic. Water in the pool. Water in the tub. But especially water from the tap that ran nonstop and they could drink all they wanted. The boys took shower after shower, and Murray didn't have the heart to tell them that in Durham there would be a monthly water bill. When they were bored with the shower, they returned to the pool.

Murray recalled that the team managers had been amazed at how little water Sooley consumed.

After another fine meal at dinner, they met in Gaston's room to walk through tomorrow's schedule. So far, each leg had gone as planned. Gaston often smiled at how far a little cash could go in the developing world. Cash under the table certainly worked back home as well, it just took more of it.

CHAPTER 62

Ida believed the optimum time to land at Raleigh-Durham International was around two or three in the afternoon. Though she had been negotiating with Immigration and Customs Enforcement and thought they had an understanding, she knew from experience that things could go wrong. She might need an hour or so to run to Immigration Court, where a judge was on standby.

. . .

They left the hotel in the same van at 4 a.m. and drove an hour to the airport at Entebbe. Gaston thanked the driver and tipped him heavily. He'd been tipping a lot in Kampala. A woman with the same sense of authority as Ida Walker met them at the general aviation terminal and led them inside. The word "Customs" was embroidered above the pocket of her shirt and she seemed to own the place. It was deserted and there was little traffic in this corner of the sprawling airport. She collected all six passports, pointed to a pot of coffee in a corner, and disappeared. On the tarmac, their beautiful jet was glistening in the lights as the pilots went through the preflight routines.

James and Chol wore matching khaki shorts, white golf shirts, and white socks and sneakers. Beatrice had found a bright yellow gomesi, the floor-length traditional dress of Ugandan women. She would have preferred something from her own country, but for the moment she was pretending to be Ugandan. At any rate, the three looked adorable and gave every indication of being a prosperous family headed to a new adventure in the United States.

Without asking for their ID cards, the customs official brought the passports back stamped and ready to go. Two men in uniforms scanned the bags and put them on a cart to be pushed to the jet. Clearing customs took less than fifteen minutes. On board, Murray introduced the family to the flight attendant, a person he now knew well. She situated them in a club area with four large chairs and asked what they wanted to drink. Of course, the boys were hungry and they were soon talking about breakfast.

James, the clown and a spitting image of Samuel, said to Murray that this plane was a bit nicer than the Ugandan cargo twin they had used the day before. Murray showed the boys around, stepping around the feet of the adults, and promised that they could watch as many movies as they wanted over the next fifteen hours.

. . .

At 2 p.m. Eastern Time, Ida and her team gathered in the lobby of the private terminal at Raleigh-Durham International. She had two lawyers from her office with her, and she asked Tyler Guy, Sooley's pro bono immigration lawyer, to join them as well. Ida had been working with the International Rescue Committee, and Ms. Keyser was on hand. She had met Samuel the previous September.

Four ICE officers arrived and things were immediately tense. Ida managed to lighten the mood with some banter, but the ICE boys were not easy to mollify. They had a job to do: to arrest and detain people caught entering the country illegally.

When the Gulfstream landed at 2:10, it was directed to a place on the tarmac fifty yards from the terminal. By the time its engines were cut off, three ICE SUVs were waiting, all with as many flashing blue lights on as possible.

On board, Silvia sat with Beatrice and the boys and tried to reassure them. She said, "I know we've been through this before, but there's no way around what's about to happen. You will be arrested and taken away, but you won't be locked up for long. Whatever you do, smile and be polite to the agents. They're just doing their jobs."

Now that reality had hit home, Murray had a knot in his stomach. Why go to all the trouble of sneaking in refugees if they're just going to be arrested? But, he knew his mother was in charge.

Gaston collected the fake passports and ID cards from the family, and said, "Just keep smiling. Everything is going to be fine."

Ten minutes passed, then fifteen. Ida and her team watched nervously from inside the terminal. Finally, the jet's door opened and ICE agents walked up the steps. Ten more minutes passed. Ida had been promised that she would be allowed to speak to the family before they were taken away. Finally, Murray appeared, and was followed down the steps by Silvia, then James, Chol, Beatrice, Gary Gaston, then the ICE agents. The three were not handcuffed and were led into the terminal where Ida stepped forward and said, "Welcome, Beatrice. I'm Samuel's American mother and I'm delighted to meet his real one." They embraced, and kissed on both cheeks, and Ida was struck by how tall Beatrice was.

Murray introduced James and Chol and for a few awkward moments they chatted and welcomed them to American soil.

As promised, the ICE agents then, rather gently, handcuffed all three and led them away. They were driven to a federal detention facility near Raleigh where Beatrice was placed in a cell on the female floor. James and Chol were placed together in a juvenile wing.

They knew a brief stint in jail was unavoidable, but it was still unsettling to be behind bars. James and Chol laughed at the fact that the night before they were hanging out in the luxurious Serena hotel, while the night before that they had gone to sleep in their tent at Rhino Camp South.

Compared to the tent, the cheap bunk beds in one corner of their cell didn't look so bad.

. . .

U.S. law requires that any person who enters the country illegally and requests political asylum be detained by ICE for as short a time as possible before being brought before an Immigration judge.

At ten the following morning, Ida and her team were waiting in the courtroom of the Honorable Stanley Furlow, a former intern at Legal Aid and a Central law school graduate. Beatrice and the boys were brought in, all smiling, all wearing what they had worn on the plane. They spent a few minutes talking to their lawyers and getting oriented. Judge Furlow called their case and proceeded to separately ask all three the same basic questions. There were no real issues to contest, not at that point anyway. In a trial several months down the road, the government could argue that the three did not meet the requirements for asylum, but that was another fight for another day.

Some paperwork was passed around and the lawyers whispered to their clients. After about an hour, Judge Furlow ordered the family released to the custody of their sponsors, Ernie and Ida Walker, and a date for their trial would be set later.

A small caravan left downtown Durham and ten minutes later turned onto a street near Central's campus. The house was one of three in a triplex. It was new and had been built by an affordable housing coalition in partnership with the city. Murray had kicked in some money from the Sooley Fund. The home's exterior walls were a bright yellow and almost matched Beatrice's gomesi.

A crowd was already there. The IRC had rounded up a dozen South Sudanese refugees in the area and invited them to the open house. Most of Ida's staff was there, along with Ernie. Coach Grinnell and his wife had stopped by.

When Beatrice and the boys walked up the sidewalk, the

crowd clapped and yelled, "Welcome to your new home." When they stepped inside and saw the furniture, the pretty pictures on the wall, the rugs, and a table covered with food, they were overcome.

. . .

Late in the afternoon, long after the guests were gone, Ida asked Beatrice if she wanted to visit the cemetery. She replied that she was ready for it. The families took two cars and drove ten minutes to Rustling Meadows Memorial Park, a modern-style cemetery without vaults and tombstones. All the graves were identical and were laid out in large perfect half-moons that covered a long rolling meadow.

They parked by the chapel and walked along perfectly land-scaped trails until they drew close. Ida stopped and pointed to a newer grave with red dirt and fresh flowers. Murray took James and Chol by the hand and led them closer. A new granite plaque read: "Samuel Sooleymon, Born August 11, 1997. Died June 19, 2016."

Both boys started to cry and wiped their cheeks. Murray backed away and watched as they each leaned on their mother.

It was a heartbreaking scene, and neither Murray nor Ida nor anyone else could begin to imagine their pain.

. . .

Two days later, after work, Murray stopped by the house and collected James and Chol. He had told them to wear their new sneakers. He drove them to the campus and parked outside The Nest, in Coach Grinnell's reserved space. He proudly showed them his own key, opened the side door, and led them through the underground hallway until they emerged onto the court. They tried to absorb the place, with its shiny wood floors, its thousands of maroon seats, its banners hanging from the ceiling. In one corner there was a huge photo of Sooley in action.

Murray said, "This is where he played."

They roamed around the floor, from one end to the other, trying to connect with the history left behind by their big brother, but they were too overwhelmed. Murray found a rack of balls and tossed out a couple. Chol was thirteen and already pushing six feet. He bounced a ball twice, pulled up, and fired away from 20 feet.

Nothing but net.

CHAPTER 63

On a spectacular autumn day in early November, a small crowd gathered, by invitation only, in front of the McDougald—McLendon Arena, also known as The Nest and the home of the Eagles. Under an oak, and with a gentle breeze scattering leaves, they sat in folding chairs and waited for the unveiling. Next to a small podium was the reason they were there. Under a maroon-and-gray drape, there was obviously a work of art or piece of sculpture.

The guests included all members of the current Eagles team, along with their coaches and managers. A dozen or so staff from the AD's office. Another ten from the President's. Some student leaders. The Walker and Sooleymon families and some of their close friends. About a hundred in all. A larger celebration had been discussed, but the brevity of the event dictated a smaller crowd.

There was only one short speech. The President took the podium and began, "Thank you for coming. This will not take long, but it will be something you will remember for a long time. We gather to honor the greatest hero in our school's history, and to unveil a bronze image of him that will last forever. Sooley arrived on this campus a year ago, an unknown student-athlete who could not go home. This university gave him a scholarship and took him in. We had no idea what was coming. We freely gave to him and could not envision what he would give in return. He took us places we've never been, and, frankly, never thought we would go. He played the game with an enthusiasm that was contagious, and he played it with a talent that grew with each game and reached heroic levels. We will never forget Sooley, his big smile, his boyish excitement, his exuberant love of the game, and his intense loyalty to his teammates. We will never forget what he did for this university.

"Back in August, his roommate and best friend, Murray Walker, approached me with the idea of memorializing Sooley with something permanent here on campus. We met with our art department and the ideas began. What you're about to see is a bronze image of the great Sooley in action. It was commissioned by one of our own, Ronnie Kelso of Wilmington. I'll ask Sooley's mother to come forward and do the honors. Ms. Beatrice Sooleymon."

Across the street, a group of students stopped to watch. Others joined them.

Beatrice stood in the first row and took three steps. The President handed her a small cord, which she pulled gently, and the draping fell to the ground. Everyone clapped politely as Beatrice admired the likeness.

It was Sooley, soaring through the air, the ball cocked high, and ready for a dunk. At its base was a plaque that read: "Sooley. In 2016, Sooley played 20 games and became the most popular player in college basketball. He led the Eagles to the Final Four. And then he was gone, but he will always live in the hearts of those who saw him play."

From across the street, the students began chanting, quietly and respectfully: "Sooley! Sooley! Sooley!"

Author's Note

When I was thirteen years old I sat mesmerized in the stands one night watching Pistol Pete Maravich score 40 points against the Ole Miss Rebels. He was amazing—cocky, unstoppable, and, obviously, immensely talented. His performance altered my life because from that moment on I was determined to become a star just like him. I couldn't decide on an appropriate nickname, but I was certain the fans would settle on one. I shot buckets for hours, made the high school team, and dreamed of college recruiters lined up in the driveway.

They never found our house. Around the age of sixteen, I realized that, as with baseball and football, my prodigious ability to dream was no match for my glaring lack of talent.

So, like most ex-jocks, I finally called it quits and became an avid sports fan. Later in life, I decided that since I couldn't play the games I might as well write about them. Thus, *Bleachers, Playing for Pizza, Calico Joe*. And now *Sooley*.

Special thanks to those who could play the game and eagerly passed along advice: Barry Parkhill, Tony Bennett, Evan Nolte, and Levelle Moton. Thanks also to Bryan Kersey, Jack Gernert, John Montgomery, Alan Swanson, Neal Kassell, Talmage Boston, and Kyle Serba at UNC Central.

John Grisham
February 8, 2021

HE IS THE ULTIMATE AUTHORITY AND THE ULTIMATE KILLER

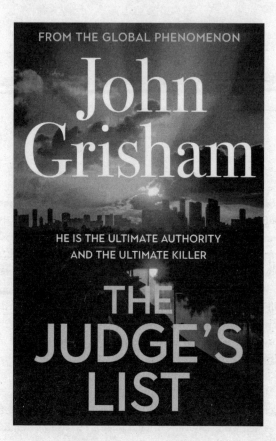

THE PHENOMENAL NEW NOVEL FROM INTERNATIONAL BESTSELLER

John Grisham